French Fling

A Foreign Affair

French Fling

A Foreign Affair

A Novel by

Nancy L. Milby

A Word with You Press®
Editors and Advocates of Fine Stories in the Digital Age
Moscow, Idaho

Nancy L. Milby © 2016

www.awordwithyoupress.com

Milby, Nancy
French Fling

ISBN-13: 9780982909416
ISBN-10: 0982909411

French Fling is published by:
A Word with You Press®
310 East A Street, Suite B, Moscow, Idaho 83843

For information, please direct emails to:
info@awordwithyoupress.com or visit our website:
www.awordwithyoupress.com

Book cover design by Teri Rider from a photograph by Nancy Milby

First Edition, November 2016Printed in the United States of America

10 9 8 7 6 5 4 3 2 1   16 17 18 19 20 21 22 23 24 25

A Word with You Press®
Editors and Advocates of Fine Stories in the Digital Age
Moscow, Idaho

Prologue

Philadelphia, Pennsylvania, somewhere on the waterfront

Wet, cold, and scared, the kid called Bean huddled in the trash shed. Wedged between two bins, his position was protected from the rain and security lights, yet he had a direct line of sight to the old warehouse door. He was as safe as he could be, given the circumstances, but the stench of rotting garbage made him want to retch. Or maybe that was the panic that threatened to swamp him. For the twentieth time in two minutes, he checked the display on his phone.

Gooseflesh rose on his skin, and his heart dipped to his belly when a dark sedan crept into view. A moment later, another arrived from the opposite direction. Both sets of headlights were off, but Bean could make out the silhouettes inside. Two men each, exactly what he'd been told to expect.

Careful not to lean against the bin that concealed him, he braced himself for balance. Raising one gloved hand to frame the scene through the screen of his phone, he yanked off the other glove with his teeth and tapped the screen with a bare finger to start the recording.

In choreographed synchronicity, the men exited their vehicles. The passengers clutched large metal cases, the drivers carried guns. Meeting in the middle between the two cars, there were terse nods but no shaking of hands.

Words were exchanged, then the cases. One driver was recognizable due to his massive girth, but they both stared each other down while the others examined the contents of the cases. Both sides apparently satisfied, the men all turned back to their cars.

Two never made it. In a move so fast, Bean never saw it coming, the driver of the sedan that had been the first to arrive, the fat one, raised his silenced gun and put a bullet between the eyes of the other driver. That driver's companion, who had already slid into the passenger seat, scrambled for his own weapon but wasn't quick enough. A single bullet pierced the windshield and found its mark in the man's forehead.

Bean flinched at the sound of the glass being punctured and jostled the phone. He steadied it in time to capture the image of the first passenger calmly walking over to retrieve the metal case from the dead man's grasp. In a blink, the first car was pulling away, nothing but the flash of brake lights visible as it retreated down the row of warehouses.

For five long minutes, Bean held perfectly still, eyes glued to the grisly scene, before slipping from his hiding place. Keeping to the shadows, the hood of his black parka pulled low over his face, he ducked back through the hole in the chain-link fence that was supposed to keep people like him out, sprinted across the road, and then weaved his way through the deserted, rain-soaked streets.

If the promises of crooks were to be believed, the recording on his phone would buy his mother freedom from the life that was destroying them both.

Vinnie Salentino watched the early-morning news from the breakfast nook of his Delancey Street townhouse as a wide-eyed reporter broke the story. The words *Execution-style double murder at the waterfront* blazed across the bottom of the screen, though the salient part of the story, according to the reporter, was not *where* the men were found—in the back lot of a warehouse rumored to have connections to organized crime—but *who* they were: both victims were veteran members of the Philadelphia Police Department. Vice Squad. Police Chief William Forrester was unavailable for comment, but that didn't prevent the newsman from making wild speculations as to what the cops had been up to. *Big-city corruption at its finest,* Vinnie thought, shaking his head in disgust.

The newspaper beside his plate made no mention of the killing—the bodies had been discovered after the morning edition had gone to print—but he looked forward to weeks of amusing reading as the investigation played out. The looming shit storm would paralyze the PPD for a while, and cause other problems as well. Fingering the flash drive that held evidence the killer would kill again for, should he ever learn of its existence, Vinnie considered how best he could use it.

Family loyalty, along with a healthy dose of self-interest, kept him from turning it over to the police. Though admittedly, the loyalty angle was a stretch. His not-so-little half brother was becoming more than just a large nuisance. Arrogance, rather than intelligence, was dominating his actions, as demonstrated by Claudio's rather indiscrete message last night.

Vinnie knew of other events, too, courtesy of a very well-placed mole in his younger brother's inner circle. A man who had been loyal to their father, whom Claudio mistakenly thought was loyal to him, too. The man who had alerted Vinnie to last night's plan.

The dirtbag cops deserved what they got, as far as Vinnie was concerned, but it was shit like that that made trouble for the legitimate businesses. And Vinnie was all about growing the legitimate side of things.

Claudio's stunt was a shot across the bow—a blatant challenge to Vinnie's street authority—and guaranteed to stir up more trouble than cops spinning out of control. The move was shortsighted in more ways than one, even for the power play it was intended to be. If Claudio thought taking out two dirty cops on Vinnie's property would spill over to Vinnie, he'd miscalculated. The character trait that had brought Claudio the most street respect had just turned into his greatest weakness. Because Vinnie's little brother always did his own dirty work.

Insurance, he decided. There was no reason to throw Claudio under the bus just yet, although Vinnie would have to make a show of paying a visit. Unlike his half brother, Vinnie was a relatively patient man, and he understood, in ways Claudio never would, that the last thing the city needed was a violent, power-hungry mobster. Especially when so much progress had been made without one, or rather, with only the *illusion* of one. Keeping the flash drive secret was critical, and he knew just the man for the job. Reaching for his phone, he made the call.

One

Nîmes, in the south of France, one year later

The canvases were covered with thick, bold color, yet the images conveyed sorrow, as if the artist had been unable to open his heart to the joy of what his eye perceived. Lorilee Sheridan stood in front of a landscape—a tilled field in late autumn—and felt cold despite the warmth of the afternoon sun captured in the image. *Emptiness.* The thought washed over her, and she sighed. The next piece, a tall, narrow canvas, showed a single cypress tree standing against the purple-pink hues of a dawning sky. The colors were rich, yet the painting screamed *loneliness.* Another variation on the theme of despair that permeated this stunning, disturbing show.

From across the room, Laurent Dubois watched her study the paintings. She was singular in that she *was* studying the artwork; most in attendance gave the pieces no more than a cursory glance. Unaccountably, he found himself wishing that he could read her thoughts. The artist—his late brother-in-law—had made these last pieces in the months before his death. Ironically, they were some of his best work.

Previously Jacques's paintings had been all about the joy of life. This collection seemed to mock that idea. Not that Laurent could blame him. Robbed of the happily-ever-after that he and Laurent's baby sister had dreamed of, Jacques could have incorporated even more anger into his work. He glanced around, spotting Julia among a group of her friends, thankful once again for the close-knit group that had rallied around her, providing support, shoulders to cry on, and funding for this show. But even among her friends, she looked dazed—a guise she'd worn since Laurent's arrival three months ago, after Jacques had passed quietly in the night.

His eyes drew back to the woman across the room. An artist herself, perhaps? She certainly dressed the part. The flowing skirt and long-sleeved tunic belted low on her hips complimented her willowy frame, with several scarves draped artfully around her neck. The soft beige and muted blues of her attire stood out among the other patrons—another reason he'd noticed her—all of whom were pierced, tattooed, and dressed in black.

Himself included.

The object of his scrutiny had soft-looking wavy hair of variegated gold, caught up in a loose twist at the base of her neck. A few tendrils fell to frame her face, and Laurent decided that the Bohemian look fit her.

At that precise moment, she turned, as if she'd felt the weight of his gaze, and he found himself staring into the palest blue eyes he'd ever seen. Other than those he saw each morning in the mirror.

Lori felt like she was being watched. When she turned to look, her vision crashed into that of a stunning man who stood against the far wall. He didn't look away when she caught him staring, but rather held her gaze. The light was wrong, at this distance, for her to see the exact color of his eyes, but the intensity of them practically bowled her over. *Huh. Wow.*

It had been quite some time since she'd experienced such a physical reaction to anyone. Or *from* anyone. She let herself look at him for a moment, long enough to appreciate his tall, impressive physique, swathed in *de rigueur* black. The chiseled features of his face were hard, his dark hair just shy of military short. The glow of gallery lighting highlighted silver streaks in what length there was. And the tribal tattoo that boldly hugged the left side of his neck—*Yikes! How far down his body does it go?* Realizing she was now the one staring, she nodded and turned back to the painting in front of her. *Did it suddenly just get warmer in here?* Unconsciously loosening the scarves knotted around her neck, she fanned herself with the brochure.

Laurent continued to watch her, smiling inwardly. *Felt that too, did you?* He certainly had. And what a surprise that was. Since his last rotation in Djibouti he'd been unable to muster enthusiasm for any woman. He'd even turned away his go-to girl when he arrived back at his home base in Chaumont a few months ago. An occurrence that surprised him as much as it angered her. Just as well, because her reaction had gone beyond the bounds of their arrangement. So what was it about this one, who was likely older than he, that made his all-but-dormant male parts suddenly take an interest?

A passing waiter with a tray of drinks swerved toward Lori and offered a glass of Champagne. Doing her best not to guzzle it, she resisted the urge to look back toward the wall where that man had been standing. And she was almost successful, but when she finally let herself peek, he was no longer there. *Figures.*

"*Que pensez-vous de l'exposition?*"

The question made her jump, and she sloshed the contents of her glass. *My God, that voice!* Without looking, she knew who the deep baritone belonged to. Clearing her throat, Lori called up the French needed to answer the question.

"*Tristesse, caché parmi les couleurs de la joie.*" *Sadness, hidden among the colors of joy.*

In the ensuing silence, she turned to him, only to find the man staring at her with an unreadable expression. The hard planes of his face were more acute at close range, and his scrutiny unnerved her.

Heat rose up her neck, and she glared at him. "If you're not prepared to accept the answer, don't ask the question." The words came out in English, irritation for the need to defend her point of view coloring her tone. Or perhaps it was self-defense to his intensity.

"On the contrary, *madame.* Your observation is astute. You are American?" Laurent couldn't recall enjoying any American accent nearly as much as hers. It made him want to converse with her in French, a language she was clearly adept in, even though his knee-jerk reaction to her accusation had been to respond in English.

"*Oui,*" she said with a smirk. "*Et vous être français, bien sûr.*"

He cracked a brief smile. "*Bien sûr.*"

3

Lori allowed a shadow of a smile to cross her own features, feeling like she'd held her own in a verbal sparring match with someone used to winning. And that's when she let herself take a clear look at his eyes. *Whoa.* Pale-blue irises like hers, only his were sharp, icy. *They'd be creepy if they weren't so beautiful,* she thought, turning back to the piece she was studying. It was another landscape, large and bright. Sunlight glinted off an ice-encrusted creek—the effect was rather like his eyes—but its water was too swift to freeze completely as it tumbled down the slope between two snow-covered fields. The artist had captured the movement of the water so that it virtually danced on the canvas.

"This is what I mean," she said after a moment, confident he was still listening. "The sky is bright, the scene pleasing, and the colors vivid, yet the overall effect is stark. To me, this whispers of desolation."

Laurent watched her closely, keeping his hands in his pockets to prevent himself from reaching out to touch her. She'd nailed Jacques to the brushstroke.

A gallery employee sidled herself between them to apply a small red dot to the title card. The young woman made a show of it, wiggling her tightly clad *derriere* in the process, then turned around to pout prettily at Laurent. "*Désolé, monsieur,* but this one has just sold."

Lori rolled her eyes and stepped over to the next canvas.

"Are you here by yourself?" That seductive voice was impossible to ignore. Apparently the hot little body in black spandex and plump red lips hadn't been much of a distraction.

"Yes, I am."

"Where is your husband?"

"My—" Lori threw him a scowl. *Really?*

Then he held up his left hand and wiggled the fingers. His were bare.

Ah. She lifted her left hand, the stunning diamond solitaire hard to miss on her ring finger. With pursed lips she tried to come up with an answer that might make sense. "Gone."

He frowned. "I'm sorry."

"Don't be," she said, realizing he mistook her meaning. "He's not dead, just gone from my life."

His reaction to that statement was the lifting of one eyebrow.

"He decided it was time to trade in for a younger model." *Huh?* Why she just blurted out to this stranger the most humiliating experience in her life, she had no idea. Gathering bravado, she added, "I liked the diamond, so I kept it. Notice, no wedding band." Her hand rose higher to prove her words.

"Then he's an ass and doesn't deserve you. Move the diamond to the other hand."

"Thanks, but you don't know anything about me." Leaning in, she lowered her voice to a stage whisper. "I could be the witchy wife from hell."

His lips twitched. "You could be. But I'd guess, hmm … probably not."

She felt her skin heat up again. *What is it with this guy?* Just then someone jostled her elbow. Looking around, she saw that in the space of their short conversation, the gallery had filled up. Any chance of getting close to the paintings at this point was slim.

"Listen," Lori said, amusement in her voice. "It was nice talking to you, but I think I'll take off. This sort of crush isn't my thing."

Another person bumped her from behind, pushing her into Laurent. He steadied her with both hands on her shoulders, but when he should have let go, he didn't.

"Have dinner with me." The words were out before he could stop them.

Her eyes narrowed. "I don't even know your name."

"Laurent Dubois." A ghost of a smile. "Don't worry, I don't bite. Unless you ask me nicely."

She laughed awkwardly. "As pick-up lines go, that's not terribly original. Or enticing."

The smile faded, and he dropped his hands. "It's not a pick-up line. As it turns out, I share your aversion to crowds, and I'm hungry. Have you dined?"

"No." As she looked up at him, chancing a glance at that tattoo before meeting his extraordinary eyes, she admitted to herself that she didn't want their encounter to end just yet.

"Then join me. There's a decent restaurant around the corner. I can meet you there if you don't trust me to walk with you." Now there was amusement in those eyes.

It made her smile, and she nodded. *Why the hell not?* "I'll risk the walk with you."

The amusement in his eyes intensified. "*Bon.* I'll meet you out front—I need to tell my sister I'm leaving."

Before she could ask—his sister?—he'd disappeared into the crowd.

As she made her way through the press of people, Lori allowed herself an inward smile. When was the last time she'd had dinner with an interesting man? At least, she assumed he'd be interesting, in a dangerous sort of way ... there was something about him that put her in mind of leashed power. That, and the fact that her shoulders still tingled from his touch. *What's that all about?* She had no idea but decided to just go with it. And dear God, that tattoo! *New beginnings, new experiences* ... that was her new motto.

She'd been back in France for only a few days, and she was already shedding her stuffy old self. It felt good. Actually, at this moment, it felt great.

Outside, the April night was chilly, too cold for outdoor dining, and she vaguely wondered which restaurant he was thinking of. Across the street the Maison Carré stood out against the dark sky, its ancient white stones aglow from well-placed spotlights. Beyond the monument dozens of tables teemed with people, serviced by the row of cafés on the far side of the square. Hugging herself, she regretted not bringing a sweater, but the exhibit had been just a short walk from her hotel and the evening had started off warm. Was this crazy? What was she doing, accepting an invitation to dine with a man she didn't know?

Laurent appeared behind her as if out of thin air, and she jumped when he touched her shoulder. "*Désolé*, I didn't mean to startle you."

Lori laughed to cover her shiver. "I didn't hear you." *Too late to back out now.*

"You're cold. Come, we're going this way." He took her elbow and steered her away from the square. Noticing the quick glance over her shoulder, he shook his head. "The place I'm thinking of is just on the corner up here."

"Oh! The one inside that big gate? I passed it on the walk here—my hotel is on the same street."

"That's it. Have you eaten there?"

"Not yet."

He let go of her elbow and offered her his right arm.

"Such a gentleman." She laughed, taking the appendage in the customary manner.

With a tilt of his head, he gave her a teasing look. "No one has accused me of that in some long while. My *maman,* God rest her soul, would be amused."

Theirs was a cozy table beside a fireplace filled with an artful flower arrangement instead of andirons, the soft light revealing the sparse but elegant details of the restaurant's interior.

"This is so perfect; I almost think you prearranged it."

"Just lucky." Laurent looked at her intently, ignoring the menu that had been placed in front of him, that ghost of a smile playing on his face. His pale eyes seemed to darken a fraction. "Your name, *madame?* Or will you have me dine with a stranger this evening?"

"A stranger with a name. Lorilee Sheridan. Lee," she clarified on impulse, holding out her hand. "Late of Philadelphia, recently retired." To the rest of the world she was Lori, but Lee was her secret favorite nickname, used only by her father—much to the dismay of her mother. No one else even knew of it … but this was a new beginning, and it somehow felt right. What better way to shed her conservative Lori persona than to become, if only for one night, a mysterious woman called Lee?

He took her hand then leaned forward and brushed his lips across her knuckles, sending a shiver down her spine that had nothing to do with being cold.

"What a coincidence. So am I."

The waiter broke up the intimacy with the delivery of aperitifs, spent a few moments describing the specials, then left them alone again to peruse the choices.

"Your sister works at the gallery?" Lori closed the menu and leaned back, reaching for her glass of *crémant* as she asked the question.

"No. The exhibit was for her. The artist, Jacques Breton, was her husband."

"Oh. I'm so sorry." She set her glass down and regarded him solemnly. "I understand he died recently. It's why I came to the gallery when I learned of the show. His work is popular in Philadelphia. I've seen it, but I confess I was surprised to find these pieces so ... depressing. Wasn't he fairly young?"

"Too young," Laurent said with genuine sadness. "My sister—half sister— is eighteen years younger than me. They'd been married only a year and had just started a family when he was diagnosed with cancer."

"That's so sad."

He simply nodded in agreement as the waiter returned for their order.

"Your analysis of his work was perceptive," Laurent said when they were alone again. "Jacques's sadness virtually drips from those canvases. There was much love between them. As hard as it is for her to part with his last works, I think even she recognizes that the emotion in them would continue to haunt her."

"What will she do?"

"For now, she has her hands full with Sebastien, my energetic and precocious three-year-old nephew. I'm staying with her for now, helping out where I can. She has a popular café in Uzès that she took over from her mother some time ago. It's how they met. Jacques was in town for a show at one of the galleries there."

"Staying busy is probably what will pull her through her grief. I'm sure she appreciates your being there, too. Were you close? As siblings, I mean?"

"As close as possible, given my circumstances. But, Lee"—he leaned forward, her name a silky whisper—"why do you ask about my sister when you really want to ask about my tattoo?"

The words were spoken so casually, his voice so sexy with that yummy French accent, that Lori almost missed their meaning. When it registered, her hand froze on its way to her wineglass, her mouth dropping open. Heat crept up her face as those water-blue eyes held hers, challenging her to deny it.

And why should she? He was right, damn it, but she hadn't thought she'd been so obvious. The wineglass found its way into her outstretched hand, and she took a sip. More like a gulp.

She let her gaze slide to that sinuous dark swirl that caressed his neck. Until now she'd taken only quick peeks, thinking it rude to stare. But he'd just given her permission to ogle it, hadn't he? As her eyes traced the sensual curves, he tilted his chin so she could get a better view, watching her all the while. His blatant challenge hit its mark, and she smiled. Two could play at this game.

"I don't want to ask about it so much as I want to touch it."

One masculine brow arched in response. "Do you, now?"

She nodded, swallowing to soothe her suddenly dry throat. Bringing her hand to her own neck, she traced a pattern there that followed the lines of the design then dipped lower, to her collarbone. "I've been wondering, since I first saw you, how far down it goes. What the whole design looks like."

"How far do you think it goes?" He was not as unaffected as he pretended to be, not by a long shot, especially as she caressed her own neck so sensually. He'd thought to tease her, enjoying her blushes, but the boldly honest answer was far more to his liking. There was a passionate core to this woman, and he had a sudden, burning desire to explore it.

With a slow shake of her head, she all but whispered, "I'm trying not to think about it at all."

Two

With that confession the tone of the evening changed, and dinner passed in a playful haze of increasingly heated innuendos. They fed each other forkfuls of delicious morsels, drank from the same wineglass, and shared a spoon for the decadent dessert. But the conversation throughout was not frivolous, revolving around favorite books, places in the world where one or the other had either been or wanted to see, world politics.

As much as he enjoyed the repartee, Laurent found himself waving off coffee in favor of the check. The invitation to dinner hadn't been made with seduction in mind, merely an enjoyable social interlude, but he found himself more aroused than he'd been in recent memory. It was a relief after months of apathy, yet his attraction to this woman was more than simply sexual. She fascinated him. Intelligent, witty, and generous, she was more desirable to him than the brigade of tight-bodied twentysomethings that scrabbled after him in Chaumont.

The walk to her hotel was short—too short. Instead of heading into the foyer, Laurent guided her beyond the circle of light spilling from the glass doors of the entrance. Leashing his instinct to pull her hard against him, he cradled her face in both of his hands and leaned down to press his lips against hers. She kissed him back without hesitation, settling her hands on his hips, and when she opened her lips a tiny bit, it was all the invitation he needed. His tongue stroked inside as he slid one hand around her nape and the other down her back, anchoring her to him. They stood there in the shadows, for many minutes, making out like teenagers.

By the time he broke the kiss, they were both out of breath. Lips pressed against her temple, pulse hammering, he cradled her head against his shoulder. "If you don't want me to come up with you, tell me now."

Her muffled laugh against his shirt made him smile.

"Kiss me witless and then expect me to think straight? Guerrilla tactics."

"Witless?" He came in for another round.

Lori brought her arms up and curled her fingers together at the back of his neck, pressing herself against the length of his body, feeling his heat as he slanted his head to deepen the kiss. She was on fire, the smoldering embers of their verbal foreplay at the restaurant igniting into flames with his kisses. Completely out of character but unwilling to waste time analyzing it, she wanted nothing so much as she wanted to drag him up to her room.

It had been a long, long time since she'd been sexually attracted to a man, including her ex-husband. That romance had fizzled out years ago, though she'd remained faithful. And with the cold surprise of being dumped after twenty years of marriage, the notion of looking for someone new had been too daunting to contemplate. Now, out of the blue, she was going up in flames for this enigmatic man, and by some miracle, he wanted her, too.

Is this insane? She knew nothing about him. *Do people even do this anymore? Jump into the sack with someone they just met? Do psycho killers hang out at gallery openings and notify their sisters when they're leaving?*

Maybe she was the most naïve person to step off the plane in a foreign country, but her gut told her this would be okay. Then she stopped thinking about all the reasons she *shouldn't* invite him in, and started anticipating her very immediate future. Perhaps the strength and stamina she'd gained from all those years of yoga would finally pay off.

Coming up for air again, Laurent rested his forehead against hers. Pale blue met pale blue in the dim light. That icy edge in his eyes was gone, replaced by blue fire. Her skin tingled with anticipation. Tracing one finger along the sinuous design inked on his skin, she flashed a mischievous little grin.

"I want to know."

He settled a light kiss on the corner of her lips. "You'll have to undress me."

Oh, God. "I can do that." *New experiences indeed.*

"I look forward to it." He took her hand and led her inside.

———————————— ✦ ————————————

Philadelphia

"Vinnie needs that file, Marty."

God damn it. Martin Malone would have fired his brainless assistant for letting Joseph "Uncle Joe" Carlucci into his office while he'd been out, if not for the painful fact that he'd just finished paying off the bills from their wedding. An insanely expensive party that had taken place six months ago. For the hundredth time, he asked himself why he'd married her. Why he'd left Lori.

Okay, so the sparks had long been missing from the relationship with his former wife of two decades, but it was a comfortable coexistence. They'd genuinely liked each other. She was smart, organized and witty, interested in the world, and didn't live and die by reality TV. And she was attractive enough—more than enough. She'd had a serious career, too—a job that was as good as his, if not better. And did he mention smart? He, on the other hand, had been a moron. Classic example of the little head doing the thinking. If only he could roll the clock back in time …

"Uncle Joe," Martin said, combing his fingers through his hair to regroup. "Even if you refuse to use email, I'm pretty sure you mastered the telephone a couple years ago." Martin turned his back on the old man who'd made himself comfortable on the couch and took off his coat. As he settled it over the back of his chair, he scanned the papers strewn across the surface of the desk. *Fortunately, nothing to worry about,* Martin assured himself—he didn't put it past his uninvited guest to snoop.

Uncle Joe, who was no more Martin's uncle than he was his aunt, regarded him with rheumy eyes. "I've been asking you for this file for two weeks now, Marty. Vinnie is running out of patience." He was also running out of time, and Martin understood this better than Joe did. And why the hell was Joe even here, when Martin had had a similar conversation with Vinnie a couple of days ago?

Vinnie, meaning Vincenzio Giancarlo Salentino, widely considered to be the top mob boss in the City of Brotherly Love. Firstborn son and successor to Roberto Salentino, whose ample backside was currently parked in a federal penitentiary halfway across the state, doing three consecutive life sentences. Only Martin, and a small handful of others, knew Vinnie's real agenda. Uncle Joe was not one of those people.

"The file is safe, Joe." But a niggle of unease wormed into his gut. Had something happened in the last two days that Martin was unaware of? Rather than ask that question, he repeated the words he'd said to the boss. "It must have somehow got left behind when I moved out of the old townhouse, and now Lori is traveling. I have no idea when she'll be back, but I did call her when you first asked about it. She said she packed up the office and put it all in storage." So she could rent the place out. "If anything of mine was in there, it's in the storage unit now."

He cleared his throat, hoping like hell that file—not a paper file, but a flash drive—was with the rest of Lori's stuff. He'd been careful going through his things when he'd left, especially the files for *this* client. The flash drive had been taped to the inside of one of those folders, but he hadn't specifically looked for it when he'd packed up. Forgotten all about it, in truth. He and Lori had maintained separate file cabinets in the large home office they'd shared, thus it made no sense that the thing would have landed with her stuff, but he'd asked about it anyway.

"Unfortunately, I don't have a key to the storage unit. But I already told Vinnie, I've been through the house and there's not so much as a utility bill. Lori is very thorough, very organized. He doesn't need to worry."

Uncle Joe stood, all lanky six-foot-two of him, any avuncular semblance disappearing in the dangerous glare he leveled at the boss's lawyer. "Marty. I'm not asking you. I'm telling you. Vinnie wants that file, and he wants it now. I don't give a shit where your ex-wife is vacationing. Get the key to that storage locker, and get that file. Are we clear?"

Across town, in the back room of an old Italian family restaurant, another meeting was taking place. Claudio Salentino, a man who resembled a market-ready hog in both countenance and girth, smacked his pudgy hand on the table, causing the plates to jump. His audience made a show of jumping, too. When Claudio was angry, he pounded his fist on the table, unless there was no convenient table, in which case he relieved his urge on someone's face. And if he was really angry, he pulled out his .45.

"It's almost time. My *dear brother*"—the words came out on a sneer—"is weak, distracted by his fancy businesses and his *charity* projects." Claudio's porcine jowls jiggled with disgust. "He's not paying attention, and that will be his downfall. Nothing can stop us now. We *will*"—emphasis pounded on the table—"have our turn. And when we do, we will *own* this city."

Nîmes

The room was dark. In lieu of switching on a light, Lori moved to the window and yanked open the drapes. The street lamps below provided enough muted light to see without revealing *too* much. Regardless of how well she kept herself in shape, she'd celebrated her fiftieth birthday more than a few years ago. No sense in giving the guy a reason to change his mind.

Before she could turn around, he was there, pressing up against her back, unwinding the scarves from around her neck and kissing a trail of fire across her nape. On an exhale, she leaned into him, steadying herself on the armchair positioned in front of the window. The scarves dropped to the floor.

Then he was pulling the pins from her hair, all the while caressing her sensitive skin with his lips. Once her hair was free of its twist, he gathered it up and combed his fingers through the silky strands.

"So soft," he whispered against her skin. "Everywhere, you are so soft."

She couldn't stop the nervous bubble of laughter that erupted from her throat. "Not something an old lady like me wants to hear."

Another hand snaked around her waist, fingers splayed wide across her flat belly, pulling her back against him. "You know that's not what I meant."

Those fingers caressed her, sliding down to where her belt lay across her hips. When he started to work the buckle, she laid a hand on his.

"I thought I was going to undress you."

"We'll get there." The words were spoken against her neck where he continued to press soft kisses, his other hand gently fisting her hair to keep it out of the way.

She slipped open the buckle herself, letting the belt fall to join her scarves on the floor. He stroked up her body, slowly, fingers caressing as they moved, and she leaned her head back against his shoulder, reveling in the warmth of his touch. A hand slid across her breast, pausing only briefly to gently shape the small mound, his thumb scraping minutely across the beaded tip before stroking up her throat. Tilting her chin toward him, he claimed another kiss.

Sensation jolted through her at that brief, intimate contact, and she yearned for another, firmer touch. Meeting his tongue stroke for stroke, she reached behind to anchor one hand on his hip while gripping the chair with the other. Slowly, he turned her, and as he did, he took hold of the hem of her tunic and drew it off. Her arms went up automatically when he broke the kiss. The garment was whisked over her head in a smooth motion and tossed aside. And now she stood before him in the shadows, naked to the waist but for a lacy bra.

Shyness overtook her, and she closed her eyes. Then she risked a peek, only to find him watching her.

"*Tu es belle.* You have no reason to be shy." His eyes followed his hands as they spanned her waist and moved up, over her ribs, coming to rest on her breasts. A sharp intake of her breath pushed them against his palms, and he smiled. Calloused thumbs stroked across the hard points through the sheer fabric until she moaned.

On a hitched breath, she reached out to hold on to him, her hands landing on the bunched muscles of his biceps. Dear lord, he was like rock beneath his shirt. She couldn't wait to get a look. Then she remembered the tattoo.

As much as she enjoyed the tingles of pleasure from his touch, she figured—hoped—there'd be more of that later. For now ... Grasping him tightly, she spun them both around and pushed, planting his backside in the armchair. His playful smile as he landed on the thick cushion told her she got him there only because he'd let her, but that didn't matter. Before she could overthink it, she hiked up her skirt and straddled him, her booted feet hanging off the pad on either side of his knees.

"Let me take these off," he said, sliding a hand beneath the fabric of her skirt to find the zipper of her left boot. His fingers brushed against her bare thigh as he tugged the footwear off, and a zing of heat went straight to her belly. After repeating the procedure for its mate, he sat back, idly caressing her calves. Who knew calves could be such an erogenous zone?

"That's better." A sensuous, masculine smile. "Your turn."

While he had been removing her boots, she'd watched the play of muscles in his shoulders. Now, she reached out and traced the dark lines that were visible above his shirt collar, following the circular pattern with her fingertips.

"It's so beautiful. What does it mean?" Stroking the swirls of black, she used her other hand to slip his buttons free. Reaching the last one, trying not to get distracted by the hard pattern of muscles that she could feel through the silk, she pulled the fabric from his slacks. Such was the intensity of her concentration as she used both hands to slowly spread the placket that she failed to notice he hadn't answered her.

Laurent stilled as she opened his shirt. Plenty of women had appreciated his physique, but none had stared wide-eyed with unguarded fascination as Lee did now. He'd never cared one way or another what anyone else thought—the ink meant something to him, and that was all that mattered—but now he found himself hoping that she liked what was revealed.

His chest was a sculpted masterpiece, flawlessly bare but for that incredible tattoo. It was a work of art, the most beautiful design she'd ever seen, suited to his body like he'd been born with it. Boldly masculine, it started with an enticing swirl that cupped the left side of his neck then followed the contours of his shoulder to spill down one side of his ripped torso in a flowing pattern of sinuous curves, ending in another graceful swirl at the base of his ribcage. Her fingertips traced down the edge, and his muscles twitched under the featherlight touch. She glanced up at his face, and their eyes locked for a moment before she dragged her gaze back to her fingers as they followed the swirling pattern inked into his skin.

"Beautiful" was all she could say.

"It's a Celtic design." The words were low and gravelly. "It stands for loyalty, courage, and … humanity."

Her eyes snapped back to his. "Humanity?"

Now was not the time to go into it—the ink had been a solidarity of sorts with his team in the darkest parts of Africa—but he needed to give her something. He nodded slowly. "Every time I see myself in a mirror, it reminds me that I'm human."

"You're a soldier."

No surprise that she understood without needing an explanation, but it was an incredible turn-on. His body hardened even more. "I was. Not anymore."

"Good," she said then leaned in and used her tongue to trace a line of ink on his upper chest.

Holy shit. Laurent felt the momentary wet heat—then when she pulled back and blew cool air on his skin, he felt the goose flesh rise. His nipple beaded, and she rewarded him with a sensual smile.

"Hmm." Then she let her tongue play upon that small bit of flesh. She bestowed soft, almost tentative laps across his skin before her hands rose to push the shirt off his shoulders. When it was gone, she settled in to explore. As she learned him with her mouth and hands, roaming the expanse of his chest and shaping the contours with seductive strokes, he did likewise.

She felt the lacy scrap of her bra fall away before her small breasts were cupped in his palms. For a mature woman, her skin was smooth, her muscles firm and toned, and her breasts were surprisingly perky. A late-in-life benefit of not having the more ample endowments that she had so envied on her friends, she laughed to herself. But he seemed to be enjoying them. He pinched the rosy tips as her teeth scraped against his flesh, and she sucked in her breath, shivering at the sensation.

But then she turned shy again, leaning back to look at him through her eyelashes. Running her hands down his torso, she traced the rectangular bumps of his abdomen and let her fingers slide under the waistband of his trousers. That's when she noticed his rather prominent arousal. She looked up at him in surprise, hardly crediting that *she* had done this to him. It had been so long since she'd been with a man that she could barely remember the mechanics, and here was this incredibly virile *younger* man, getting hard for her.

"Don't look so surprised, *chérie*. You've turned out to be quite the seductress."

Her reaction was not what he expected.

"Oh, God." She brought her hands to her face as if she had something to be ashamed of, elbows covering her breasts.

Incroyable, he thought as he gently pulled her hands from her face and laced his fingers through hers. "*Chérie,* you are magnificent. So sexy, you're driving me insane." He rocked his hips up in emphasis. "This can't be faked."

One brow lifted, and that sensual, albeit shy, smile returned. "It's been awhile for me. I might have forgotten that detail." Then she gasped as he gathered her in close, cupped his hands beneath her bottom, and stood. With an easy, fluid motion, like she weighed nothing at all.

"The chair is nice, but I think we need more room." Taking the two steps to the bed, he leaned over and set her down. Before she could protest, he was kneeling in front of her, tugging on the elastic waist of her skirt and stripping it off. Her panties matched the bra he'd already shed from her: sheer, lacy, and barely there. "Now that is a picture," he whispered before taking her lips in a searing kiss.

Lori was combusting into flames. This man was unreal, larger than life, sexier than anything she'd ever seen or imagined. His lips devoured hers, his hands stroked her skin with a touch that seared her flesh. Somewhere she'd fallen down a rabbit hole and landed in a steamy romance novel. Definitely an alternate universe. Why question it? Because, no matter what happened tomorrow, incredible sex—of the sort she'd never experienced—was on the agenda tonight.

Three

With a stealth that had saved his life more than once, Laurent extracted himself from the bedsheets and found his clothes. Dressed in a trice, he let his eyes linger for just a moment on the lovely, slumbering form of Lorilee Sheridan. What an unexpected evening it had been. An ache bloomed in his chest, in the vicinity of his heart, and he pressed his fist over it. It wasn't supposed to be like this. Tenderness was not part of his DNA. Before he did something stupid, like strip down and climb back into bed with her, he forced his feet toward the door. Silent as a mirage, he slipped from the room.

The cold of predawn slapped his face like a splash of water but did nothing to loosen the knot of emotion threatening his air supply as he walked the short distance to where he'd parked his Ducati. Unlocking the helmet, he slapped it onto his head and started the bike with a roar. Within seconds he was speeding through the deserted streets of Nîmes in a futile attempt to outrun a desire he was in no position to deal with.

Lori woke, disoriented and momentarily blinded by the sun streaming in through the open drapes. Sitting up, she squinted into the light and looked around. Awareness surfaced through her sleep-dazed brain as she recognized her hotel room in Nîmes. Why were the sheets such a mess? Wait, she was naked. *Oh.*

Images of the night came roaring back, and she closed her eyes for a moment. Had it even been real, or did she have too much to drink followed by a really hot dream? She retrieved the pillows that were scattered across the foot of the bed, plumped them up against the headboard, and leaned back, surveying the room.

The pile of clothes on the floor in front of the chair looked familiar—the tunic and scarves she'd worn last night. Then she caught sight of one boot peeking out from beneath the ottoman. She leaned over the edge of the bed. Yep, there was her skirt. Sadly, hers were the only clothes in evidence. But the ache between her legs and the small marks on her breasts—love bites, she guessed, having never had them before—was all the proof she needed. She really *had* had sex with a stranger. And *hoo-boy*, what a stranger.

Disappointment that she'd awaken alone started to crowd in on her, but she pushed it away. There'd been no promises, after all, nothing beyond a night of mind-blowing pleasure. And he'd certainly delivered on that. She shivered just thinking about it. Criminy, and who exactly had *she* been! Someone she barely recognized. But damn if it hadn't been amazing, *freeing*, to spend one incredible, memorable night with a beautiful, sexy man. The playful, sensual banter at the restaurant, followed by more of the physical variety here in her room. And, she reminded herself, he enjoyed it as much as she did. In his own words, some things couldn't be faked.

She ran her hands over her belly and up to her breasts, cupping their diminutive size like he had, brushing her thumbs across the tips. They immediately stood to attention, and the erotic jolt went straight to her core. It was like he'd awakened something in her, something that had been there all along but hadn't found its way to the surface. He made her feel alive. And she liked it. Too bad he'd disappeared.

Pragmatic as always, Lori vowed to herself that she would have no regrets about the night. Even the part about not seeing him again. *What's meant to be is what will be, and there's a reason for everything*—part of her new outlook on life. If, by some crazy coincidence, she happened to run into him again—*and* if they connected again like they had last night—then she'd embrace it. Otherwise, she would keep the memory of him dear and use it as a reminder that she was her own woman, independent. Who just happened to finally discover what mind-blowing sex was all about at the age of fifty-five.

The jangle-ring of her cell phone made her heart jump. Had he somehow managed to get her number? Scrambling off the bed to find her purse, she tried to put a stranglehold on her hopes. *No regrets*. But when she fished out the phone and looked at the caller ID, she almost threw the thing at the wall. *Damn it!* Definitely not Laurent. It was stupid to even think he might call, and now she was disappointed all over again. Tossing it back in her purse, she let the call go to voicemail.

Philadelphia

"Marty, she's not answering her phone." The sentence was punctuated by a loud pop of gum.

"Keep trying." Martin set down the document he was reading, closed his eyes and pinched the bridge of his nose, pushing his reading glasses up to his forehead.

"But, *Maaarr-ty* ..." The breathy whine finally made him snap.

"God damn it, Teresa, just do what I ask for once without complaining, would ya?"

The pout on his wife's puffy red lips turned to an ugly sneer. "Asshole. If you don't want me to complain, don't ask me to call your ex in the middle of the fucking night. I'm through with this bullshit. You can call her yourself. I don't even know what the stupid file looks like anyway, 'cause I ain't never seen the damn thing!"

"Haven't," he corrected automatically as she spun on her fluffy kitten-heeled slippers and stalked from the room, leaving a drift of perfume in her wake. The door slammed, and a framed painting on the nearest wall shifted.

Why, why, why *did I marry her?* Martin was learning the hard way that big pillowy breasts came with a very high price. But this latest tantrum was probably his fault; he should have kept Teresa out of it. A glance at the clock on the mantle showed that it was almost one in the morning, putting it close to 7:00 a.m. in France. Lori was always an early riser. Why the hell wasn't she picking up? Sighing, he reached for his phone, scrolled through his contacts, and tapped the CALL icon.

It rang and rang. "Come on, Lori, answer your damn phone."

21

She didn't, so he had to settle for leaving a message. *I need that flash drive, damn it.* He'd turned his file boxes inside out looking for the thing. A niggling whisper of doubt surfaced but poofed away like a popped bubble as quickly as it arose. Tired and distracted, Martin let it go. *It has to be with Lori's stuff.* There was just no other answer.

And he had to get to it. One way or another, he had to get to it.

———◆◆———

Nimes

Four missed calls, four voicemails. And this was retirement. After that first call that she ignored, she'd pulled on sweats and gone out for a long walk. Without the phone.

"What the hell do they want?" She asked to the empty room when she saw who the calls were from. The first one she deleted without listening to it. The triple-D airhead who answered to Mrs. Malone these days had nothing to say that Lori wanted to hear. The calls from Martin, however … as tempting as it was to ignore those, too, three calls within an hour, and in the middle of the night for him, no less, probably meant it was something important. She tapped the screen for voicemail.

"*Lori, hey, it's Martin. Sorry to bother you, but I need your help with something. Call me as soon as you can. Hope you're enjoying your trip. Talk to ya soon.*"

"My trip," she muttered. "What an idiot. Try *my new life.*"

"*Hey, Lori, me again. Listen, babe, I really gotta talk to ya. Call me.*"

Babe? Jesus Christ. That bimbo has really sent him over the edge. The third one just pissed her off.

"*Lori, God damn it. Call me!*" A pause, then in a calmer voice, "*Please. It's urgent.*"

"Well, since you asked so nicely … *geez.*" She'd been out for almost two hours, enjoying the old section of the city in the crisp spring air, and it was now three in the morning in Philadelphia. No way was she going to call him at that hour.

Instead, she dialed a different number.

Annie Shaw Macallister ran inside the house to catch her ringing phone. Scooping it up off the kitchen table, she looked at the display and whooped in joy, then swiped her thumb across the screen.

"Hey, girlfriend! I thought you'd never call!"

Lori laughed. "You sound out of breath. What are you doing?"

Friends since college, Annie and Lori had worked at the same international accounting firm for many years, until Annie had chucked it all and moved to France to marry Kaden Macallister. More than twenty years had slipped by since then, and Annie was still doing the happily-ever-after routine. Lori had been working in Paris at the time, and it was on a fateful trip to visit her friend that Annie and Kaden had met. Lori had returned to Philadelphia and continued her career with the firm, but the two had remained close friends. Over the years, they'd had plenty of visits together, and now it looked like they might finally be living in the same time zone.

"I'm planting tomatoes, but I sprinted into the house when I heard my phone. Where are you? Are you here? You must be here, it's the middle of the night in Philly."

"I'm here. Actually I flew in a few days ago, but I wanted to get acclimated before imposing myself and all my baggage on you."

"Aw, come on, don't be ridiculous. You know we've got plenty of room. Where are you?"

"Nîmes."

"Oh! So close! Awesome. When can you come out?"

"How does today sound?"

Annie whooped again and pirouetted on the tile floor. And realized she had an audience. Grinning at the two men standing in the doorway, she told them the news. "Lori's in Nîmes! She'll be here today!" Then to the phone, "Sorry, Kaden and Henri just caught me doing the happy dance."

Warmth spread into Lori's heart. Annie was her best friend and the sister of her heart, and Annie's family treated her like one of their own. She'd definitely made the right decision in coming back to France, even if the logistics were a little challenging. "I can't wait to see you! This last year's been crazy, and I'm *so* looking forward to putting it all behind me. I've got a few things I need to do here, but I should be there by the middle of the afternoon."

Philadelphia

Bean stood in the alley behind his mother's flower shop, his thin body pressed against rough siding whose paint had peeled away long ago, listening through the open window as the fragile hope he'd allowed to build inside him crumbled to the dirt.

"Don't think I don't know who owns this joint." The south Philly accent sounded like any other in this part of town, but for the raspy menace that it carried.

"I ain't never said otherwise," his mother replied. "So what? He owns a lot a' these businesses down here. Someone's gotta run 'em."

"You can't be makin' dick here, Angie."

Bean heard a scraping sound, like maybe a stool being moved. "I got a roof over my head and my boy's in school. We eat." There was a pause. "It's enough."

"Come on, Angie. You can feed that crap to your kid, but don't bullshit me. Look at this dump. You wanna come back."

"No." The word was barely whispered, and Bean had to strain to hear the rest. "I can't. I'm clean now. Don't push me."

The man snorted. "Look at you. Wearing rags. No makeup. Hair's a mess. And when's the last time you had a little fun?" This last was said on a leer, and Bean clenched his fists.

Silence stretched. Bean could picture his mother, bony arms wrapped around herself, head down, rocking back and forth. *Don't do it, Ma.*

"See, what I don't get is, why?" The menace in that voice sent a prickle of fear up Bean's spine.

"I told you why! My kid don't need no hooker junkie for a ma. He helped me get clean. I owe him."

"Not that why, Angelina."

Oh, shit. Bean's mother didn't know what he'd done, only that it was something for Vinnie Salentino. Bean hadn't even said *that* much, but, duh, the flower shop—the whole block—was his, a fact that was common knowledge on the street. But she'd taken what was offered, made it through the detox program, and taught herself flowers with the dedication of a woman who understood she'd been given a second chance. She was pretty good at it, too, and in the ten months since she'd taken over the shop, business was enough to sustain them. Though she wore secondhand clothing and her face still bore the evidence of a once-hard-core meth addict, Bean thought she was ... not happy, precisely, but content. But Bean had seen enough, even in his short life, to know that anything could happen to shatter the fragile peace. He'd been waiting for it, while praying it would never come. And now ...

"I don't know."

"Bullshit." The voice roughened, took on a cruel edge. "What are you doing for him?"

"Nothing. Nothing but this flower shop."

Ding-ding-linga-ding!

Bean closed his eyes, relief washing over him at the sound that signaled a customer coming into the shop.

"This ain't over, Angie."

Ducking behind the dumpster when he heard heavy footsteps coming toward the back door, Bean shrunk back into the smallest ball he could make himself as the screen slammed open against the wall, bounced, then sprung back. It wasn't until the sound of footsteps became barely audible that he risked taking a peek. *Him!*

Rasteau, France

Lori passed between the stone pillars marking the entrance to Domaine de la Terre des Roches—so called because of the large stones that covered the surrounding vineyards—just as a flash of lightning from the black clouds overhead announced the start of a downpour. Driving around to the back of the house as thunder rumbled, she pulled up beside a beat-up old truck and sprinted for the kitchen door. Annie yanked it open then engulfed her friend in a tight bear hug.

"You made it!"

"Just in time. Cripes, I hate driving in this stuff." They both looked out into the yard where the rain pounded down, already forming puddles in the gravel driveway. Another huge bolt of lightning flashed on the hill above the house, followed immediately by a resounding clap of thunder. Both women jumped.

"*Shit!* Get in here." Annie pulled her friend from the path of the door and swung it shut. Then they looked at each other and broke out in laughter. Which is how Kaden found them a moment later.

"Causing trouble already, I see." He grinned, gave Lori the standard French kisses, then held her at arm's length. "Welcome to Rasteau. Annie's been like a kid waiting for Christmas." He looked at her appraisingly. "You look stunning, *chérie.*"

Annie laughed at Lori's startled expression. "He's right. You really do."

Lori blushed. "Thank you." Then she grinned at Kaden. "You do, too, but that's nothing new."

Lightning flashed again, accompanied by another loud crack of thunder. The lights blinked a few times but stayed on.

Kaden cursed. "Excuse me, ladies. I need to unplug the router before we lose the wifi again. Henri!" he yelled as he disappeared down the hall.

"Got it, Papa!" came an answering shout from somewhere within.

"I'll get the Champagne," Annie said, intent on celebrating her friend's arrival.

"Sounds great. I'll grab the glasses." Lori looked around, trying to remember the layout of the kitchen. Annie pointed to a cabinet on the other side of the room as she opened the refrigerator door.

The rain pelting down outside suddenly became even more intense, the volume of the deluge drowning out all other sound.

"Crap," Annie said, leaning over the sink to look out the window, frosty bottle of Champagne in hand. Her newly planted garden was already a muddy puddle, the fragile shoots, less than half a day old, now floating from their moorings in a swirl of reddish brown water. "There go my tomatoes."

A thick bolt of lightning landed right outside the window as an enormous clap of thunder split the afternoon apart. Annie jumped back with a yelp, losing her grip on the slippery bottle. It fell to the floor and exploded on impact, sending pieces of glass and frothy liquid everywhere. "*Shit!* Ow, *fuck!*" She started to step back, then stopped herself. "*Damn it!* Kaden! Help!"

Across the kitchen Lori had her hands full with glass flutes and was momentarily frozen as Annie stood in the middle of the mess. Her feet were covered only in socks, and those socks were now soaking up the spilled Champagne. At least one shard of glass had sliced through the thin material of her leggings where a streak of red was visible.

"Oh my God, don't move!" Lori looked around desperately. "Where's a mop and a broom?"

More lightning flashed with another clap of thunder, this time accompanied by a loud *bang pop* that caused both women to flinch and plunged the house into a murky darkness. It was only midafternoon, but the storm blocked out the sun so effectively that it might well have been night. "God damn it. *Kaden!*"

"I'm here, love." He appeared in the doorway, voice calm, followed closely by Henri. In three steps he was at her side, his boots crunching over glass to get there. He plucked up his wife and carried her across the mess, depositing her in a chair at the kitchen table. "Are you hurt?" Kneeling in front of her, he stripped off her sodden socks and examined her feet. "Did you step on any glass?"

Annie was trembling. "No, I … shit." She ran her fingers over the gash in her leggings, her fingers coming away red. "I think I only have this cut." She looked up at him. "I dropped the bottle."

Assured that she was not badly injured, Kaden let himself smile. "I gathered." He kissed her nose. "You know you're supposed to leave the Champagne bottle opening to me."

It was an old joke between them, and Annie wrinkled her nose playfully. "I intended to—I was just getting it ready." Then she looked over his shoulder. "Be careful, you guys." Lori had started collecting the big chunks of glass while Henri dragged out the mop.

"We've got it, Mom," Henri said then grinned at Lori. "You certainly know how to make an entrance."

"Not funny." But she laughed anyway.

Four

The mess on the kitchen floor was a memory, Annie's shin had been cleaned up, and a second bottle of Champagne had been retrieved and opened, which Kaden now poured around. "Nothing like a little excitement," he said then held up his glass. "Now then, Lori, welcome to France."

Annie held hers up. "And here's to retirement."

"Cheers," Henri added.

"Thanks, you guys. It's great to be here, crazy storm notwithstanding." She clinked her own glass against theirs and took a sip. "*Ahhh*. Wow, that's good." She looked at Annie and couldn't help smiling at her old friend. "I'm *really* glad to be here."

Then she eyed Henri, who was grinning at her over the rim of his glass. He'd filled out significantly in the three years since she'd seen him last. He was as tall as his father, topping out a couple of inches above six feet, and had the same broad shoulders, dark hair, and smoldering good looks. Only his eyes were different; they were dark brown like Annie's rather than Kaden's hazel green. She wondered how many hearts he'd already broken. "Don't tell me you're old enough to drink that."

He rolled his eyes. "I'm twenty-three, Aunt Lori." She wasn't his aunt, but he'd always called her that.

Lori slapped her hand over her forehead and closed her eyes in mock despair. "Dang it. That means I must be getting older, too."

The rain had begun to let up, the nasty thunder cell having wreaked its havoc in their neighborhood and moved on. Annie looked at Kaden and grimaced. "I'm pretty sure my garden is toast. I saw the tomato plugs floating away right before I dropped the bottle."

Kaden and Henri exchanged a glance, one that Annie read with sudden awareness.

"Oh, crap," she said, putting a voice to their concern. "The vines."

Unlike their neighbors, the Macallisters were not financially dependent on their vineyards and winery operation, but a ruined crop for them meant the entire neighborhood could suffer the same fate.

"We're a good month from flowering," Henri said with the cautious optimism of a farmer. "But that was a pretty intense storm." After another silent communication with his father, he stood. "I'll check the breakers here and in the barn, then go out and have a look."

Kaden stood as well. "I'll go with you." He leaned over to kiss Annie's forehead then tugged on one of her curls. "Careful with that Champagne bottle, *chérie*." Then he winked at Lori, grabbed a jacket from a hook on the wall, and followed his son out the back door.

Annie shook her head and reached for the bottle, refilling Lori's glass then her own. "Come on," she said, standing. "Let's move the party into the other room. Kaden got a fire going about an hour ago." At that moment the lights flicked back on.

"Aw, I kind of liked it in the dark." Lori trailed her friend into the large, comfortable main parlor and took a seat in a big cushiony chair. She'd always liked this room, especially with a fire burning in the huge stone hearth. There was just something so appealing about these old stone farmhouses. She couldn't wait to get settled into her own.

"So what's your plan?" Annie tossed another log on the coals, poked it around a bit as it caught, then sat on the couch across from her friend and curled her feet up beneath her. "Did that place work out for you?"

"It did, but I can't get into it until the first. Think you can put up with me for a week?"

Annie snorted. "I don't know, let me think about it." She sipped her Champagne. "Where is it?"

"Ménerbes."

"Oh. Well, that's not too far." Annie had hoped it would be closer, but with the highway, Ménerbes was only about forty minutes away. "Tell me what it's like."

As the old friends chatted the afternoon away, catching up, making plans, and enjoying the Champagne and a warm fire on the wet spring day, Lori's cell phone rang and rang. But since she'd left her purse in the car when she dashed for the house hours earlier, it continued to go unanswered.

It was therefore a surprise when, later that evening, Henri called Lori to the landline in Kaden's office.

"Who could possibly be calling me here?"

"It's Martin." Not *Uncle* Martin—Henri had never called him that—and now his eyes held an apology.

Christ. Lori took the portable phone with a mumbled thanks and a small amount of guilt before carrying it off to a quiet corner. With the storm, the broken bottle, and catching up with Annie, the small detail of Martin's increasingly desperate calls had slipped her mind.

"Why aren't you answering your phone?"

The barked question evaporated that momentary twinge of remorse. "Not the best way to start a conversation if you're calling for something other than to wish me well," Lori replied with cool civility.

Martin knew the tone well, having lived with her for so long. "Sorry, babe, it's just that I've got a very stressful situation and I've been trying to get hold of you since last night."

"I'm sorry, too, *babe,* but before it was a decent hour to call you back, I was caught in the lightning storm from hell and had to abandon my car before it was practically washed away. My cell phone wasn't a priority." It was close enough to the truth, anyway. "What is it that's so urgent?"

"I gotta get into your storage locker."

"What? Why on earth—"

"It's important, Lori. I wouldn't ask otherwise. Remember that client file I mentioned a couple of weeks ago? I've run a fine-tooth comb through all the boxes I took from our office, and it's not there. And I *know* it was there, before." Before he'd dumped her and shacked up with the large-breasted airhead. "The only thing that makes sense is that it somehow got mixed up with your stuff."

This again? "That's impossible, Martin. I already told you, I went through every one of my files as I packed them. File by file, piece of paper by piece of paper, because I didn't want to waste storage space on anything that wasn't important enough to keep. If your file had been in with my stuff, I would have seen it." And possibly chucked it, but he didn't need to know that. In any event, she honestly didn't remember seeing it.

"Lori, give a guy a break here. It's not a paper file, okay? It's a flash drive. It could have easily fallen into one of your boxes. I need to be sure."

"Fallen into one of my boxes after you packed up yours? That's far-fetched, Martin. Even for you."

It was, but he was desperate. "That doesn't mean it's impossible."

With a great huffing sigh, Lori tried reason. "What, exactly, do you expect me to do? It's a Public Storage unit, Martin." The lie fell easily from her tongue. "With a padlock, for which there is one key." At least one. "That key is in my possession, and I'm in France. I have no intention of jumping on a plane back to Philadelphia just because you've lost some file. I can guarantee you, it's not in my locker."

"Then overnight it to me."

"No!" There was more in her locker than sensitive files. She could probably trust Martin in there—it wasn't like he didn't know her things—but she couldn't trust him to keep Mrs. Silicone Malone from poking around in her most private possessions. The temptation for the dingbat would be too great, and Martin had already proven his inability to deny the woman anything.

"Lori, God damn it. I'm trying to be reasonable. I could just cut the fucking lock."

That made her laugh. "Really, Martin? Do you have any idea where it is? How many Public Storage locations are there in the greater Philadelphia area? And they have on-site security for a reason," she pointed out. "To keep jerks like you from pilfering through people's things. Goodbye, Martin. Good luck finding your file, but it's not in my locker."

Ending the call, she hung her head, closed her eyes, and took several deep, calming breaths. *God damn it.* She hadn't seen any flash drives, but she allowed that it might, could have possibly, dropped out of something into the bottom of a box. If Martin wasn't being such an ass about it, she'd be tempted to let him use the duplicate key, the one she'd left with her friend who owned the storage unit complex where she'd rented the locker. But she absolutely did not want him, or, God forbid, his infantile wife, touching her personal things.

And her files were confidential in any case. Client files, personal copies of position papers, and other critical documents that, if the firm was ever sued over something she'd worked on, she'd have her own documentation for defense. Not that she expected to ever need any of it, but one could never be too careful in this day and age of unchecked litigation. She'd seen it happen, which is why she'd been so careful to keep duplicates in her possession. She couldn't allow anyone—especially not potentially opposing counsel like Martin—access to them.

Philadelphia

In his twenty-fourth-floor corner office in a downtown high-rise, Martin stared at the rain sluicing down the outside of his window and cursed. The bitch of it was, he believed her. Lori was nothing if not thorough, exacting, and extremely organized. If she said the flash drive wasn't mixed up in her files, then it wasn't. But where did that leave him? Screwed, that's where.

After the fact and way too late, Martin had come to the realization that he did, in fact, love his ex-wife. Courtesy of the recent months of living with the not-so-bright bulb that he'd hastily, stupidly, married, Martin had finally recognized his mistake. So what he was contemplating didn't make him feel like a terrific person. But then, he hadn't been terribly pleased with himself for some time now. And he had no choice ... no choice but to use Lori as a short-term distraction while he tried to find that God damned wedge of plastic and microcircuits. She was buried in the south of France somewhere—exactly where, he had no idea. And didn't that give him the perfect excuse? He could use her absence without endangering her because no one knew where she was.

In the back of his mind something niggled, but he was too tired and way too distracted to focus on whatever it was.

Rasteau

"What did he want?" Annie wanted to respect her friend's privacy, but when Henri told her who had called, she was waiting to pounce. And judging from the expression on Lori's face, the conversation had not been a pleasant one.

Martin was an ass in Annie's opinion, though she'd stopped voicing it after Lori married him. The man was unmistakably popular among the cream of Philadelphia society, but Annie had never managed to warm up to him. Despite the polished veneer, he could be pushy and impatient, although to be fair, that described half the population of his hometown. He was the third or fourth generation to reign over the law firm that bore his family name, and Annie had always wondered who his clients were. She also suspected that Lori had never actually been in love with him. Lori might have *loved* him, in her way, but she hadn't ever been *in love* with him. They'd met soon after Lori's return to America and seemed to *rub on well enough together,* as Kaden put it. Compatible, both professionals at the top of their game, but they'd always maintained fairly separate lives despite sharing a roof. As unexpected as their breakup may have been to Lori, Annie hadn't been terribly surprised. If it didn't mean that Lori was now facing the back half of her sixth decade alone, Annie would have applauded the split. She was protective of her friend, though, and didn't trust Martin to keep himself from doing something stupid.

"What? Oh, nothing. Well, he thinks I have one of his client files in the boxes I stored when I packed up all my personal stuff. He's wrong, but he's tenacious." Lori shrugged and made a valiant attempt at a smile.

Annie was pretty sure there was more to it, but she let it drop.

Five

Lacoste, France, two weeks later

Etienne Matisse was pouring a glass of wine for his wife when his cell phone buzzed. A surprise, because most anyone who might call him was, at that very moment, within the large tent that stretched across the yard between his house and the orchard beyond. He handed the glass to Sabine then pulled the phone from his pocket, frowning when he saw the name on the screen.

"Matisse," he said into the device as he stepped out of the tent.

"*Bonjour, Matisse. C'est Laurent Dubois.*"

"*Dubois. Bonjour.*" Matisse had not seen or spoken to Laurent for more than two and a half years, not since the elite ops colonel had assisted in breaking up the human trafficking ring that Matisse's stepbrother had operated from the property next door. It was that episode that led to Matisse meeting, and ultimately becoming housemates, with Louise Marcel. The woman whose wedding reception he was hosting that very moment. "This is unexpected."

"I need a favor." Direct as ever. The special ops team had made it possible for that takedown to happen with a minimum of casualties, and although Matisse had taken a bullet to the chest, courtesy of his stepbrother, Laurent knew that his old friend would do whatever he could to help him out now. The fact that more than two years had passed did not diminish their connection.

Matisse looked back at the tent, where the band was beginning to tune up, and resigned himself to missing a few minutes of the celebration. "If I can help, you know I will."

"I need you to find someone. A woman." After a few beats of silence, "It's personal."

"I see. How urgent is it? I'm in the middle of hosting a wedding reception."

A whistle came through the phone. "Do you mean you've actually married that sweet little American?"

"In fact, you'll be surprised to learn that I did marry a very sweet lady just a few months ago, but not the one you're thinking of. But the party today is for her—Louise and Alex were married this morning."

"Ah, of course. And the baby girl?"

"Ellie is two and a half now, and running rampant among the guests as we speak. So you'll forgive me if I don't have a whole lot of time here—"

"Got it. Listen, it's urgent, but only because I fucked up. I met the lady a couple of weeks ago and I … *merde,* I let her get away without … well, all I have is a name. I tried the hotel where she was staying, but they won't help. She is American, but she was planning on staying in France for a while. Somewhere in the south." Laurent hoped he didn't sound as desperate as he felt. "I need you to track her down for me so I can … Christ, I don't know. I just need to talk to her." He let out a huffing breath. "This sounds pathetic."

If he'd heard this story six months ago, Etienne would have been unable to resist a sarcastic comment. Now, after having reconnected with the woman who held his own heart … a smile evident in his voice, he let his friend off the hook. "*Je comprends.* I'll do what I can. What's her name?"

"Sheridan. Lorilee Sheridan."

Stunned, Matisse turned to look at the knot of people standing around the bride. "Say again?"

"Lorilee Sheridan … S-H-E-R-I-D-A-N, I think."

But Matisse was barely listening. Rather, he was watching Annie Macallister chat with her old friend, the one who'd recently arrived from Philadelphia. Who had just taken a rental house in a nearby village. "She's here."

"Yeah, here in France. Probably somewhere in Provence."

"No, I mean she's *here.* Standing not twenty meters from me."

"What?" Laurent thought he couldn't have heard correctly. "How the hell can that be? You have no idea who she is."

Matisse chuckled at the colossal coincidence, but it had to be the same person. "Tall, slender, attractive, probably in her fifties"—this he suspected due to her connection with Annie—"but looks younger, with blond hair that reaches about halfway down her back?"

"Pale-blue eyes."

"That's her. Remember Macallister? The tech investor who got us the surveillance equipment? His wife is American, and you somehow managed to meet her best friend. She's recently retired and planning to relocate permanently to the south of France. They're all here at the reception."

Laurent could barely process it. "Tell me you're not just yanking my chain."

"God's honest truth. Where are you?"

"Uzès."

"Then get your pathetic self over here. The party just got started. I'll tell Lou we have a surprise guest coming. She'll be delighted to see you."

Matisse slid the phone back into his pocket and rejoined his wife. Sabine took one look at him and recognized amusement in those dark eyes. She let him capture her hand as she stood on tiptoes to plant a kiss on his jaw. Shifting back half a step, she arched a shapely brow in question.

"It appears there will be one more guest. A surprise, but by no means unwelcome. He won't arrive for another hour or more."

"Who?"

"An old friend." His smile gave nothing away as he leaned down to kiss her cheek. "Prepare to be entertained."

With that cryptic statement hanging in the wind, he relieved her of her empty wineglass and headed to the bar.

The party was in full swing when Laurent stepped inside the tent, the band banging out a lively tune that had most everyone bopping around on the dance floor. Scanning the crowd, he easily spotted Matisse, but when he caught sight of the woman with whom his friend was dancing, his eyebrows rose in surprise. Statuesque and stunningly beautiful, even from a distance. Matisse glanced his direction then leaned down to say something to the woman, who looked his way and smiled. Hand in hand, they moved away from the cavorting crowd and came toward him.

"Dubois," Matisse said, holding out his hand. "Glad you could make it."

"*Merci pour l'invitation.*" Laurent took the proffered hand in a quick shake, but he was looking at Sabine. "If this is your new bride, you are a very lucky man, my friend."

"The luckiest," Matisse agreed and made the introduction, explaining to Sabine their connection but not the reason for his appearance. When the song ended, Etienne motioned to the other end of the tent. "Come, let's let Louise in on the surprise."

About half the crowd moved off the floor as the band launched into a slower song. A sweep of honey-blond hair caught Laurent's eye, and an uncomfortable sensation bloomed in his chest when he saw the man she'd been dancing with. Tall, good-looking, older than her but not too old, he was laughing with her as they walked toward the tables, his left hand resting at the small of her back in easy intimacy. *What did you expect?* He pulled his gaze away, tamped down his emotions, and searched for Louise. First thing's first.

Louise and Alex were indeed surprised and delighted to see the colonel, who insisted on kissing the bride. Lou made a show of fanning herself afterward. "Whew, being the bride has definite advantages," she said then laughed at Alex's scowl. "But what brings you down here? Are you working nearby?"

"Actually, I'm retired," he said, slanting a glance at Matisse. "It's a recent development. I'm in Uzès for the time being, with my sister."

"*Maman!*" The happy shout cut off whatever reply Louise might have made, relieving Laurent of the need to change the subject. She bent down to scoop up the little girl who barreled toward them in a pink cloud of flouncing crinoline.

"Hey, sweetheart! Are you having fun?" Louise kissed the little button nose.

Blond curls bounced as Ellie nodded her head emphatically. "I dance!"

"I saw you out there. You were awesome!" She smiled at Laurent as she hugged her adopted daughter. "Beautiful, isn't she?"

Laurent could only return the smile and nod, his throat going suddenly thick. The little girl was indeed beautiful, and so very, very lucky; her life could have turned out far different—would have, in fact, had they not found her when they did. And she was very much loved, by the looks on the faces of the adults around her. When he found his voice, his words were sincere. "I'm glad it worked out for you. For all of you."

While that reunion was taking place at the front of the tent, Lori Sheridan, seated at a table near the back, could only stare at the people clustered around the bride and groom. Or rather, at one person in particular. Because there could be no doubt as to the identity of the sharply handsome man who had suddenly appeared to offer *félicitations* to the happy couple. And by the look of it, he was no stranger to them. Even if he hadn't been standing so she could see his tattoo, she would have recognized the wide shoulders and sexy military haircut growing out of its regulation length.

It shouldn't have surprised her to see him there—after all, she knew next to nothing about him, including who his friends were. She also had no idea what to do, now that he was there. An unwelcome emotion rolled through her chest, one she recognized as hurt. Damn it, that was *not* what she wanted to feel, but the truth was, hard as she'd tried to view their encounter in a realistic context, she'd not been entirely successful. In the past two weeks, she'd been unable to stop thinking about him. She'd even made a few attempts at sketching the design of his tattoo, wondering if she was brave enough to get some ink herself. Maybe a smaller, more feminine version of his. How crazy was that?

Louise set Ellie back on her feet, and the little girl scampered off to her next distraction, taking a trajectory that pointed straight to Lori. The adults all watched her go, indulgent looks on their faces. Then Laurent's gaze lifted, and he looked right at her. And he did not look surprised. In fact, he looked determined. *Yikes.* Holding her with his eyes, he said something to the others and started walking toward her.

Feeling like a deer caught in headlights, needing to flee but unable to move, Lori sat perfectly still as he came closer. He was gorgeously masculine—all leashed power beneath his dress slacks and dark button-down shirt—and intensely focused. On her. Just as he reached her, the music shifted to a soft Jean-Jacques Goldman song, "Doux," and he smiled. That seductive smile she remembered oh so well. Lori could only blink.

"*Danser avec moi?*" His smoky baritone was equally seductive as he held out his hand.

She forgot whatever it was she was going to say. She almost forgot her name. Good thing she didn't need her wits to breathe. Acting on its own, Lori's hand rose from her lap and landed in his grasp. His fingers closed gently around hers, a victorious glint flashing in those pale-blue eyes, and he reeled her in. Literally. Her body followed her hand, and before she could credit how it happened, she was in his arms, following his lead across the dance floor.

The French lyrics filtered into the small part of her brain that was actually working. Something about a big bad wolf. How appropriate.

"You look beautiful." Holding her close, holding her gaze, Laurent felt his body unclench a fraction. The blush his words caused had his blood rushing south. Or maybe it was her proximity. It felt too good, having her back in his arms. *This is bad in so many ways,* none of which he could remember at present.

"How are you here?" She let the hand that was resting on his shoulder slide to the side of his neck, tentatively tracing the curved edge of that tattoo. Confirming that it was real. That he was real.

"I could ask the same of you."

She felt a small smile flirt at her lips. "I asked first."

"I've missed you," he said instead of answering the question.

Her smile slipped. "Deflection."

"Busted." Spinning her gracefully around the floor, his hold on her confident, the words to the song filled the space between them as he held her eyes with his.

Mais je serai doux, comme un bisou voyou dans le cou,
Attentionné, tiède, à vos genoux,
Des caresses et des mots à vos goûts, dans la flemme absolue, n'importe où,
Mais doux.

Oh, God. There was no resisting this man. Not when she knew he could categorically give her those things. Had given her those things. All except the *absolute laziness.* Because he'd left. And didn't that thought just splash cold water over her head?

"Forgive me for pointing out the obvious, but if you wanted to see me again, you could have stuck around long enough to get my number."

As direct hits went, it was good, and he closed his eyes momentarily, hearing the hurt in her words.

"I deserved that." They moved in rhythm while he struggled to find the right words. And failed. "I was … you were … ah, hell." He stopped midturn, raised his hand, and tilted her chin up. How to explain that he'd run not from her, but from himself?

"I'm sorry, Lee. I … panicked."

She arched a brow, broadcasting how ridiculous that statement sounded coming from him. The song ended and she drew back, giving herself a little distance. "There were no promises. On either side."

"I know that, but it doesn't excuse my behavior. You deserved better."

On a shrug, she looked around, focusing on anything but his face. She agreed with him, but it wasn't like she'd been totally surprised. Theirs was nothing more than a random hookup, after all. Not something she'd ever done before, but the truth of it was, she had enjoyed it—enjoyed him—immensely.

"I got over it." Mostly. "But you still haven't answered my question."

The band was taking a break, leaving them standing alone on the empty dance floor. "I've known Etienne Matisse for many years. He was assigned to my unit during his military service. Would you join me for a drink?"

And just that easily, he disarmed her. Not that she had been locked and loaded, precisely, but his appearance at the party had rattled her. His apology sounded sincere and there was no denying the chemistry between them— it was just as potent as it had been two weeks ago. In truth, she was more interested in exploring the coincidence of their overlapping circle of friends than staying hurt. He was here now, and evidently determined to keep her company.

But she wasn't going to be a pushover again. "On one condition."

He waited, his expression suggesting he expected to hear something he wouldn't like. Too bad. Her request was reasonable.

"Don't leave without saying goodbye." Her eyes flashed a hint of vulnerability before she narrowed them at him, daring him to deny her this small courtesy.

His admiration for her ratcheted up a notch, and he struggled to keep his hands at his sides. "You have my word."

She studied him as if assessing the trustworthiness of what was offered. Because he was studying her, too, he saw the moment her internal debate concluded in his favor. He relaxed another fraction but continued to wait.

"Then I would like to have that drink." She took the elbow he winged, smiling when he winked at her, and they made their way to the bar. "You know Louise and Alex, too, I take it?"

He nodded. "Are you familiar with how they came to have the little girl?"

Lori had heard the story not long after it had all gone down. "My friend Annie told me. Her husband is Alex's cousin."

"Ah, that's right. Matisse told me you are Annie's friend. I'd like to meet them both."

They arrived at the bar, and the couple in front of them turned as one to regard them with undisguised interest. Lori laughed. "Well then, you're in luck. Annie, Kaden, this is Laurent Dubois. Laurent, meet my dear friends, Kaden and Annie Macallister."

Macallister being the man that had been dancing earlier with her. Of course. A little more of the tension unraveled. Laurent shook both of their hands.

"It's a pleasure to meet you, *monsieur-dame*," he said, not yet out of the military habit. "I led the team that came down here a couple of years ago to help, er, liberate Louise's niece and the rest of the women."

"Oh!" Annie said, her eyes lingering for an instant on his tattoo before spearing her friend with a knowing look that nonetheless asked a thousand questions. "God, that whole thing was so awful."

"Disgraceful," Laurent agreed, not missing her reaction to him, then turned to Kaden. "We appreciated the equipment you were able to provide for that operation. I'm recently retired from active duty, but I understand we have you to thank for much of the, er, more sensitive equipment we used in special ops."

Kaden acknowledged the compliment with a nod. As an investor—a very successful, well-connected investor—he had, over the years, led the funding of many incubator companies that focused on security-related technology for both commercial and military applications, from firewall protection to surveillance equipment and more. Militaries around the globe benefited greatly from those developments. "I was glad to do it. And we very much appreciated your help on that particular mission. It was personal all around. To think what might have happened to Ellie …"

"A sentiment my entire team shared." Laurent stepped forward and snagged two glasses of wine, handing them to Annie and Lori, then reached for two more, giving one to Kaden.

"So you've kept in touch with them?" The question came from Lori.

Laurent cleared his throat and rubbed the back of his neck in what even he recognized as a nervous gesture. "Well, no, not exactly." He looked at Lori then at the other couple. "When I called Matisse earlier today and he said he was hosting a wedding reception, I assumed he was finally marrying Louise."

"What?" Lori's eyes flew to Annie, who had started to laugh.

"He set me straight," Laurent admitted.

"I may not have told you that part," Annie said, eyes sparkling. "When they all first met, Alex was crazy about her, but he wasn't sure Lou didn't prefer Etienne. Then Etienne invited her to become his roommate when she decided to adopt Ellie. Alex got over his jealously when he realized Etienne and Louise were truly just friends, almost like siblings, and eventually he moved in with them, too. At the time, none of us knew that Etienne's heart already belonged to someone else." Annie smiled at the romantic notion as her gaze found the stunning couple across the tent.

"It surprised us all when he finally acted on it," she continued. "Especially when it turned out that Sabine was just as much in love with him as he was with her. Why they waited so long to sort it out is beyond me, but now they all live here together. It's an unusual habitation arrangement, but it works for them. And Ellie gets the benefit of what amounts to two sets of parents."

Laurent hadn't known any of that; he only remembered the easy affection he'd witnessed between Louise and Matisse, but now that he thought about it, he did recall Alex hovering around Louise, too. Having quit the area as soon as his mission was over, shipping out shortly thereafter to Djibouti, it never occurred to him to wonder how those relationships had developed. But today he'd seen the way his old friend regarded his new wife, and he recognized soul-deep contentment when he saw it. It was what his little sister had found, before—

"So you just happened to call today and learned of the wedding?" Annie's question popped him back to the present. "That's so nice of you to come. I bet Louise and Alex were happy to see you."

Kaden studied Laurent, surprised that his normally perceptive wife hadn't asked the question that was first and foremost in his own mind—how had these two met? Because he'd seen Laurent zero in on Lori earlier, had watched their interaction, both before and after they moved to the dance floor. It was clear the two were not meeting for the first time tonight. He took a guess at why the man had called Matisse. "Etienne is a convenient friend to have, when you need to find someone."

Six

Laurent did not choke on his wine, but it was a near thing. He did, however, discreetly clear his throat. Meanwhile, Annie was regarding him with a knowing look, Lori was draining her glass, *not* looking at him, and Kaden was smirking.

"I'm beginning to understand how you've been so successful," Laurent said dryly.

"It's a talent," Kaden returned, amusement in his eyes. "So, when did you two meet?"

"Kaden." Annie tugged on his arm. "You're embarrassing my friend."

"She's my friend, too, love." Kaden winked at Lori then looked at his wife. "Yet somehow, I think you know the answer to my question."

The conversation had taken a sharp turn toward awkward, and Lori needed to escape. "I'm getting more wine." She'd all but guzzled the last glass. Annie knew the highlights—maybe not *all* the highlights—of her night in Nîmes with Laurent. They were best friends, after all, and Lori had come clean with it the afternoon of the lightning storm, but not in her wildest imagination had she foreseen this bizarre meeting.

"Girlfriends," Annie said with a grin in response to her husband's observation, holding up two crossed fingers as a symbol of closeness and solidarity.

"And here I am, feeling so left out." Kaden planted a kiss on his wife's forehead then looked pointedly at Laurent, playful expression disappearing.

"We met in Nîmes a couple of weeks ago," he answered, not bothering to disguise his irritation at the nosy question. "What are you, her guardian? I'm pretty sure she's of age."

Unfazed, Kaden shrugged. "Never can be too careful. But if Matisse vouches for you …" He glanced over his shoulder at Lori, who studiously ignored them. "Forgive me for being protective of the people who are important to me. What'd you do, lose her number?"

"Kaden, stop it." Annie smacked his arm, doing a bad job of trying to suppress a grin.

———————————

Philadelphia

Bean waited for the blond lady with the big tits to swing her car out of the driveway before climbing off his scooter and carefully removing the wrapped bouquet of flowers from the box lashed to the back. Checking down the block to make sure she was gone, he scampered across the street, not to the front door but around back to the kitchen, and rapped on the doorframe.

It was Saturday afternoon, and Bean knew the weekend routine at this house. Could set his watch by it, if he wore one. The lawyer played golf in the morning—usually in a foursome that included Vinnie Salentino—then as soon as he arrived back home, the missus took off. Where she went, Bean didn't know or care, as long as she stayed gone long enough for him to make his report. And when she came home, there was always a nice bouquet of flowers waiting for her. At least, he assumed the flowers were for the wife. Not that it mattered. The trip from his mother's flower shop near downtown to the lawyer's Chestnut Hill house took close to an hour on his moped, but the man always paid him well, so Bean didn't mind. Especially when lunch was included.

Martin Malone knew the routine, too. He was standing at the kitchen counter with sandwich fixings spread out around him, slathering mustard on a piece of freshly toasted rye that would crown the pile of his favorite deli pastrami, when the rap on his kitchen door sounded. Setting the bread in position, he wiped his hands on the towel draped over his shoulder and walked over to open the door.

"Hullo, Mr. Malone." Bean did his best to enunciate the words correctly, rather than let his south Philly accent carry the day. It was something Mr. Malone had gently corrected him for during the initial weeks of their association, and once Bean had realized the man was trying to help him not belittle him, he'd stopped being resentful and demonstrated his appreciation by trying to improve.

"Good afternoon, Benjamin."

Bean hid his wince behind the flowers. He didn't love his given name, even if its use by this man was meant as a gesture of respect. Barely anyone used it—certainly not his mother—and it made him feel like an imposter. Like he was trying to be something he wasn't; trying to reach for something that he didn't deserve.

"Let me just fix up the flowers, sir." Bean waited for Martin to nod and wave to the cupboard that contained the vases before moving through the room to attend to the bouquet, pretending not to notice the two enormous pastrami sandwiches under construction on the counter.

"The Jackal came back last night." This admission was spoken through a mouthful of pastrami, and the gentle scowl he received for the gaffe made Bean blush. "'Scuse me," he managed, then chewed with focused intent before swallowing. He took a sip of the iced tea Mr. Malone had served him along with the sandwich then wiped his mouth with his napkin, as he'd been taught.

"What did your mother do?" Martin knew Angelina Stripling was still clean, but he also understood that the temptation to retreat back into her old life hovered at the edges of her current "respectable" existence. If it weren't for her son …

"She didn't let him in." Bean almost took another bite but caught himself, put the sandwich down, and looked beseechingly at his benefactor. "She wanted to, was afraid not to, but I wouldn't let her." He puffed out his chest like he'd saved her from certain doom. And he probably had. "I hugged her so hard she couldn't go to the door. Jackal pounded and cursed and threatened, and Ma cried, but I kept her from opening the door. The bastard finally left—sorry, sir, but that's what he is. He threw out a bunch of threats before he disappeared." Bean finally gave in and picked up his sandwich.

Martin watched him chew, the boy's eyes carefully diverted. *Such a brave kid,* he thought, feeling a twinge of regret that he was, himself, childless. Martin had mixed feelings about Vinnie, but in this, Martin wholeheartedly agreed. He only wished Vinnie would make his efforts more public. Because what very few people knew, and probably no one else would ever believe, is that Vinnie Salentino cared about the underprivileged kids of Philadelphia. The deal he'd made a year ago with Benjamin Stripling—Bean to pretty much everyone who knew him—was one that allowed young Ben to have as close to a normal life as possible. It depended on the kid's integrity, and the cooperation of the mother, of course, but Angelina had been willing to try. And she had done. And now that scumbag Claudio, through one of his fuckhead minions, was trying to drag her back into the gutter. Martin didn't blame Ben for being terrified.

Martin waited until Bean's scooter had cleared his neighborhood before calling in what he'd learned. Such a blatant move on Vinnie's turf was a show of disrespect that even Martin, who made a point not to pay attention to such things, recognized. And this new information was just one more reason why he had to find that God damned flash drive.

"Marty, I'm glad you called. Nice game today, by the way."

Of course Vinnie would say that—he'd played to the lowest score and thus had collected a tidy sum of cash from the others in the group.

"You played well." The truth, and Martin didn't mind admitting it. "But, Vinnie, we've got a problem."

In the back corner booth of his second cousin's restaurant on South 9th Street, Vinnie Salentino held the phone to his ear and frowned into his pasta as his lawyer repeated what he'd learned. *Damn it!* It was a cheap shot, and the last thing he needed. Trouble on his street, where most everyone had a past—and lived on the razor's edge of being recaptured by it—would discredit Vinnie, and worse, distract him. Which Claudio knew, the fucking bastard. Preying on a weak woman was just his style, too.

Vinnie dropped his fork into the unfinished bowl and pulled the napkin from his shirt collar. Clearing his throat, he wiped his mouth and nodded to his cousin that he was finished. Ever patient, his lawyer waited on the line for him to speak.

"Then it's just as well, what I have to tell you."

Martin didn't like the tone of his client's voice. "Tell me what?"

"Uncle Joe has a guy who's been tracking your ex-wife's credit cards. She's in some small town in the south of France. He's on his way there now."

A bolt of panic speared Martin, and he had to suck in a breath. "What? What do you mean he's on his way there?" Had Joe found her? "What's he gonna do? She doesn't have the file, Vinnie."

"Calm down, Marty, and pull your shit together. I need that file, like *yesterday*. This shit with Angelina just proves it, and you weren't making any progress. She's ignoring you, and I'm outta time."

"Vinnie." Forcing calm into his voice when he wanted to scream, Martin repeated his question. "What is he planning to do?"

A pause. "Well, first he's gotta actually *find* her, which may be easier said than done."

Martin let out the breath he was holding. So Joe didn't know exactly where she was. "Listen, if she knows someone's coming after her, she'll work with me. I'll make sure of it."

"You better. Joe hates airplanes, and he won't be in a good mood when he finds her. And he *will* find her, eventually. He's good like that. He won't hurt her, but if you don't want him scaring the shit outta her, get her to come back and open up that storage locker."

Oh, God. Martin stared at the phone in his hand for long minutes after the call ended, a cold sweat breaking out across his body.

He'd miscalculated. Badly. And now he'd endangered the one person he truly cared about in the world.

Joe was apparently more resourceful than Martin had given him credit for, and fucking hell, the bastard was on his way there now. It wouldn't take him long to find her—Vinnie was right about that. He had a couple of days, a week at most, to talk some sense into her. Because if Joe found her first ... Shit. There was no telling what sort of threats Joe might use to get her on a plane. Vinnie claimed Joe wouldn't hurt her, but there was no question the old thug would do his best to scare the crap out of her.

Ask any citizen of Philadelphia and they would say that Vinnie Salentino was a criminal, his businesses nothing but fronts. Laundering operations for the money coming in from drug-running and prostitution. And that had been true, back when Roberto Salentino had been head of the family. But things were different now, a condition Martin had worked hard for—had been well paid to achieve. In the years since Roberto's incarceration, Vinnie had corralled the old criminal elements while quietly and systematically cleaning up the streets of his old neighborhood. And he'd hired Martin's firm to help overhaul the businesses. But he wasn't stupid. Vinnie let people believe what they would, and that mob-boss reputation served him well.

It was the main reason Claudio had stayed in the background. Claudio, who made no bones about running his own drugs and prostitutes, not to mention killing dirty cops. Who was now making a move, believing his big brother had weakened.

And the one piece of ironclad evidence that could get that fat bastard off the streets for good had gone missing.

The could-have-dones and should-have-dones were irrelevant now. Vinnie had made a bad decision, in Martin's opinion, one that was coming back to bite them hard. He'd blown the perfect opportunity to get his little brother off the street for good, thinking he'd use the evidence to control him while keeping him out of jail. But Claudio was so out of control that Martin doubted any threat would stop him. Only a lead plug to the heart would do that.

He had to warn her. She was so damned stubborn, but he owed it to her, owed her a chance to get herself back to Philly on her own terms before "Uncle" Joe Carlucci—a loose cannon if there ever was one—got carried away.

But Lori wasn't cooperating, at least not with Martin. Once again, his calls went to voicemail. What the hell was wrong with her? She used to take that phone with her everywhere—it practically never left her hand. Now, it seemed, she chucked it in her purse and left it wherever, like she couldn't care less if she missed calls. It was such a foreign concept that Martin couldn't fathom it.

Ménerbes, France

Lori turned onto the narrow road that led to her new home, then turned again between the tall hedgerows onto the driveway of the property. For the entire ten-minute drive from Lacoste, she'd second- and third-guessed her decision to invite Laurent home with her. And for the twentieth time, she checked her rearview mirror to confirm he was still following.

The downshifting gears of his motorcycle cut through the night, and Lori felt a flash of guilt for the neighbors. In truth, it wasn't *that* late, and the house was relatively isolated, but to her ears, even inside her car, the guttural roar of the Ducati's powerful engine sounded overly loud. Or was that just the pounding of her own heartbeat?

Rows of trellised grapevines planted inside the hedges limited visibility, and the night was black, but the outdoor lights were on at the house, illuminating it in the distance. The lane made a sharp right around the vineyard, the tall hedge on her left blocked the view of the fields beyond. *Wow,* she thought as she looked around the dark yard enclosed on all sides. *This place really is isolated.* Her eyes landed on a chaise lounge beside the pool that was just barely visible in the shadows. A silly grin stole over her features as a sudden vision filled her head. *We could have screaming sex outside under the stars and no one would hear us.* Blushing at thoughts she'd never *once* considered while married, she made the final turn and parked beneath the wide plane tree in front of the house.

The motorcycle came to a stop alongside when her cell phone rang. Frowning, she fished it out of her purse and checked the display. Martin. *No, thank you.* She shut off the power and tossed it back into her purse.

"It's a little rustic," Lori said as she climbed out of her car. "And it's too big for me, but I have nieces and nephews who might come to visit—" The

51

words babbling out of her mouth came to an abrupt halt when she caught the look on his face. *Whoa.*

"I look forward to seeing it all. Later." Without breaking eye contact, he looped his helmet over a handlebar and reached for her.

The heat that had been simmering since that first dance hours ago suddenly flamed up. She welcomed it, and him, leaning into his hard frame as he conquered her with a kiss that was as hot as it was gentle. And just like in Nîmes, she could muster no defense against this man.

Laurent felt her surrender, and it made his blood surge. They stood in the cool night air for long minutes, kissing, tasting, relearning. The throb in his groin matched the pounding of his heart. This woman just did something to him, made him feel something that was both frightening and amazing.

"Come," she whispered and threaded her fingers with his to lead him through the kitchen door.

The house was an odd split-level design with lots of archways designed for people far shorter than either of them. With a grin and a warning to watch his head, she drew him up a narrow flight of steps and through a low archway into a high-ceilinged space that served as the main lounge. The bedroom she'd claimed for herself was the largest, up another short set of steps from the lounge.

Pausing in the dark for another kiss, Lori basked in the sensation of being in this man's arms again. There had been no question in her mind when they left the party that Laurent would be sharing her bed tonight. Whether he was still there in the morning …

She kicked that thought out of her head and, drawing him up those last few stairs, focused on what was right in front of her.

Large and airy, the room featured long windows that allowed the light from the courtyard below to filter up through the sheer curtains. The night was still and quiet as they undressed each other, communicating with touch rather than words. In a déjà-vu moment, he untwined her scarf, letting the soft fabric caress her neck. Then he felt for the zipper at the back of her dress. As he drew it down, slowly, erotically, over her spine, his other hand slid down alongside of it while she slipped the buttons of his shirt free. Reaching his belt, she tugged the fabric from his pants and spread it open, taking a moment to admire what she revealed before going back to work on his buckle. When she started in on the fastener of his slacks, her dress fell forward off her shoulders. He freed her arms from the sleeves one by one then let the garment pool at her feet. Lifting both of her hands in his, he spread his arms wide and stepped back.

"*Belle,*" he whispered, letting his gaze roam down her body, clad in nothing but a matched set of sheer lingerie, the same pale-blue as her eyes, and a sexy pair of heels.

He drew her out of the circle of her dress then reached down to retrieve it, draping it over a chair before encircling her waist to bring her in close. The next kiss was not gentle. His hands roamed the smooth contours of her back, and hers slid up his chest, pushing the shirt off his shoulders and caressing his neck. The shirt sailed through the air a moment later in the direction of the chair, but his hands were back on her in an instant.

"Lee." The word came out on a warm breath next to her ear, and she shivered as his lips whispered along her jaw and up to her temple. Then he cradled her face in his hands and took another deep, soul-ripping kiss. *Jesus,* but the man was going to burn her alive.

A moment or an eternity later—Lori wouldn't have been able to say—they lay spent, sated and languorous, her head resting on the hard flesh of his biceps. As the air in the room cooled their heated skin, he pulled her close, settling her bum against the cradle of his hips, her back to his chest, and drew up the comforter that had been kicked away earlier. One hand held firm against her belly while his lips wandered along the back of her neck. Tracing her fingers over his, she asked the question that had been rolling through her mind all evening.

"Did you really call Etienne Matisse to find me?"

Another light kiss, a soft brush of his lips against the downy tendrils at her nape, and his hand began to roam, stroking her skin with the pads of his fingers. Just when she decided he wasn't going to answer her, he did.

"*Oui, ma chérie, j'ai fait.*"

Were the French words spoken with the hope she wouldn't understand, or was the desire to find her after he'd fled so embedded in his romantic French heart that it was the only language in which the answer made sense?

Either way, the admission set her heart aglow, even as the practical side of her tried to make sense of it. "How would he even do that?" She had a vague idea that Matisse was involved in law enforcement, but had nothing beyond that.

"It's a secret. I could tell you, but then I'd have to lick you to death."

She gasped as he ran his warm tongue across the skin he'd been kissing, then shivered when he blew cool air over it.

"It might be worth it," she managed before he rolled her beneath him and set himself to the task of distracting her from questions he wasn't prepared to answer.

Seven

The rumble of a tractor engine somewhere nearby pulled Lori from her sleep. She barely felt the usual morning chill of the room for the human furnace that snored softly beside her. *He's still here,* her brain registered before she opened her eyes to confirm it. Curled on her side facing him, not exactly snuggled up but legs touching, she lifted herself to her elbow and gazed down at him.

The raw power of him was banked, his wide chest rose and fell in steady breaths, and that hard jaw—softened not one bit in slumber—looked devilishly good with a salt-and-pepper sprinkling of whiskers. That's when she realized he'd been clean shaven both times she'd been with him, and the impressive growth over just one night meant that he likely had to shave more than once a day to keep it that way. Military habit, she guessed, since the style of the day leaned toward casual scruff.

Sprawled on his back, one arm flung above his head and the other resting low on his waist, his position afforded her an unencumbered view of his magnificent tattoo. Her eyes traced the swirling pattern as her fingers itched to do. Unwilling to wake him, she forced her fingers into a fist to keep them from wandering of their own accord. The sheet rested low on his hips, and she faced another challenge to keeping her hands to herself, plainly visible beneath the thin cloth. *Wow. Is that normal?*

Laurent felt her eyes on him. He couldn't hear her breathing, but he felt her proximity, which could only mean she was awake. And watching him. The heaviness in his groin intensified. Morning wood was an inconvenience, primarily because he made a habit of *not* waking up with the women he bedded—but now he welcomed it. Stretching like a cat, he pushed the arm that was above his head to the headboard and lifted his hips before he opened his eyes to spear her with a heated look that said he knew she'd been ogling him.

"Busted," she said with a shy grin, echoing his word from the wedding, a pink tinge coloring her cheeks. But then she took advantage and let her fingers wander where they would, tracing the curves of ink on the side of his ribs before heading down to explore beneath the sheet.

It was another hour before their craving for coffee got them moving. Lori watched with wide-eyed appreciation as the sexy man who'd shared her bed strolled naked across the room and into the bathroom, shamelessly displaying what was, without a doubt, the finest male tush she'd ever seen. *Whew!* And the tattoo, while it didn't roll down his back like it did in the front, caressed the smooth bulk of his shoulder with sensuous dark swirls, making her want to explore it some more. Even after what had just gone on between the sheets, she felt a blush creep into her cheeks.

Not bold enough to prance around naked herself, she snagged her kimono robe from the hook inside the massive antique wardrobe and headed for the downstairs loo. The sound of water in the shower behind her meant she had at least a few minutes to make herself presentable. She tried not to think about the perky sweet-young-things he was probably used to waking up beside. Then she got a look at herself in the mirror.

Holy shit! Her cheeks were the color of a rosy peach, and her lips were a puffy cherry red. Not as in smacked-in-the-mouth red. More like kissed-to-within-an-inch-of-her-life red. God, even to her, it was sexy. She touched them lightly. No wonder Botox was so popular. Her bed-tousled hair gave her a soft look she'd never be able to achieve on purpose, and her eyes had a dreamy edge to them. Great sex had a lot to recommend for itself.

A quick splash of water on her face followed by a fast swish-swish over her teeth using one of the new toothbrushes intended for future guests, she finished up quickly. Wanting to get the coffee started so Laurent would have a homey welcome when he came down, she hustled into the kitchen, only to skid to a stop.

Dressed in the dark slacks and button-down from the night before, damp hair combed back and face clean shaven, Laurent was pushing the plunger down on her coffee press. He glanced up at her and gave her a slow, sexy smile.

"How …" Lori blinked. "I just left you a minute ago in the shower. How did you …" She waved her hand at his showered, *shaved,* dressed person. He even had his boots on.

He crossed the distance and kissed her enticing lips. "More like five minutes ago. You look delicious, *chérie.* Coffee?"

Delicious? Holy God. Brain, kick in now, please. "But … you already boiled the water. Doesn't it take at least a few minutes to do that?" *Oh, yeah. Very intelligent.*

"It's a military secret." He winked and went back to the coffee press, pouring the brew into mugs. "I could tell you, but …"

The wink did it, along with the thoroughly domestic scene unfolding in front of her and the rich aroma of freshly brewed coffee. She walked over and wrapped her arms around his waist from behind, laying her cheek against his muscled back. "Then you'd have to what, lick me to death?"

"Eat you up, more like." He pivoted then propped a hip against the counter and she was suddenly in his arms instead of the other way around. Taking her lips again in a heated kiss, he groaned.

"I'm all for full disclosure." *Is that breathy voice really mine?*

"*Hmm, je considère que ce. Après du café.*" *I'll consider it. After coffee.*

Their eyes held. Pale blue on pale blue. She saw that now-familiar heat flare in his and wondered what hers looked like. Like she was panting for him, no doubt, because it was the truth. In an attempt to regain what little equilibrium she still possessed, she stood up on her toes and planted a smooch on his lips, then peeled herself out of his arms.

"Do you take milk?" She opened the door to the fridge and stuck her face in, allowing the cool air to wash over her cheeks while pretending to search for the carton. The way he spiked her heat was like having hot flashes all over again.

"No, just sugar if you have it." Then he surprised her. "In the field, coffee was the one thing we could always count on having. Someone was always brewing a pot. But the only milk came from the scrub goats, and even when it was fresh, I didn't care for it. I got used to drinking it black."

It was the first time he'd offered anything about his military life. When they'd talked at the restaurant that first night, beyond the basics he had kept the conversation focused on her. She turned, milk carton in hand, and regarded him. "Will you tell me something about your time there?"

His gaze dropped to the steaming mug in his hand as he slowly brought it to his lips. He sipped, paused, then sipped again. She watched, standing in the open door of the refrigerator, unsure if he'd shut her out or let her in.

"There's not much to tell," he said at last, not meeting her eyes. "Not much that I *can* tell because most of what I did was classified."

That, in itself, was something of an admission. She waited.

He looked at her then, a sad sort of smile tugging on his beautiful lips. "I don't know how much you follow French politics, but as a country, we've had peacekeeping forces in Africa for decades. Mostly in the French-speaking countries."

"I do have some idea of that. I remember there was some big struggle years ago when I was living in Paris and the city became flooded with refugees." She shut the fridge door with her hip and slid a sugar bowl toward him before pouring milk into her coffee. Propping herself against the counter in imitation of his stance, she nodded at him to continue.

"Many were from Somalia, but also Djibouti." A spoonful of sugar landed in his cup and he stirred, watching the liquid swirl around. "It's a very small country that borders Somalia to the north, strategically situated at the mouth of the Red Sea, which is to say, one of the busiest shipping lanes in the world. Civil war broke out there in the early nineties, but people had begun fleeing before that. Paris was the obvious choice for most, if they could get there, because of the language and the hope of jobs."

"Yes, I remember it now." Because of its location and what was at stake, it had been brutal. "You were there?"

"In and out." On covert missions aimed at stopping the war, but nothing they did, no matter how bold, had been able to stop that train wreck. "The war lasted for ten years." He took another sip of his coffee.

"And more recently?" That war had ended at the turn of the century, fifteen years ago.

Laurent glanced out the window and had a sudden urge for open space. The sun had risen above the tall hedges on the eastern edge of the property, and the enormous stone table outside was awash in the morning rays. "Let's take our coffee outside."

Without waiting for an answer, he unlatched the door and stepped out into the cool air. It felt good and carried the fresh, clean scent of spring. A reminder that he was no longer in Africa.

"It's nice out here." He turned back—she hadn't moved—and tilted his head in encouragement before taking a few more steps into the yard.

His boots crunched on the gravel then paused. She heard a shuffling sound then more crunching, and then he reappeared in the doorway. He looked at her and arched an eyebrow, extending a hand.

"Laurent …" She padded over to the threshold as if drawn by a magnet, torn between taking his outstretched hand and staying in the metaphorical safety of her kitchen. Plus, she was barefoot.

"Hang on to your cup." That was her only warning before she was scooped up against his chest and carried to a cushioned chair at the stone table where he'd set his own cup. He spun another chair around to face her, brushed off the cushion, and plopped down into it. Then he reached for her feet and brought them to his lap. His hands were warm—heck, his whole body radiated heat—and she wasn't too ashamed to bury her toes between his thighs.

"Better," he said and reached for his coffee.

They were silent for a while, sipping coffee, letting the morning sun warm their faces. Birds twittered and flitted through the hedgerows, but otherwise the morning was peacefully quiet, the early tractor having apparently finished its chores for the day. Mug cradled between her hands for warmth, toes buried in a place that made her hot just thinking about it, she watched him over the rim. And then he surprised her again.

"Sometimes walls get claustrophobic. Probably from so much time out in the open bush. It was more scrub desert, really. Blistering hot during the day and not much cooler at night. The winters were the best."

"What happened there recently?" She repeated her earlier question, hoping she might begin to understand the shadows that lurked behind those intense, haunted eyes.

He set his empty mug on the table and cupped her feet in his big, warm hands. Those hands stroked her ankles almost absently, as if his mind had retreated to some past event that he was seeing inside his head.

"In the last decade, piracy has been … a serious problem. Despite its location and the money that comes in from port fees and all that, Djibouti is a poor country, with small villages and a struggling population." Not unlike the majority of Africa. "The pirates, they're mostly Somalis, but there are plenty of desperate men on the continent. Outside of the main city, no one is safe from their brutality." He'd seen enough of it to know firsthand.

He wasn't looking at her, but past her, lost again in old images running through his head. "There's been so much useless bloodshed."

Lori wasn't sure he was even aware that he'd spoken the words aloud. "Humanity," she said softly.

"*Eh?*" Laurent jerked to attention as if she'd poked him with a hot branding iron.

"Your tattoo. You said it was there to remind you that you are human."

His eyes, those beautiful eyes that could hold such fire, turned to ice for an instant. So cold she actually shivered, and her reaction seemed to snap him out of whatever place he'd found himself.

But the chill remained. Abruptly he set her feet aside and stood. "I have nightmares. They're ugly, and you don't want to be around me when they come."

"Everyone has nightmares, Laurent. They are not your sole prerogative." Her voice held understanding, and what sounded like a gentle scold. "Some are worse than others, but they're all relative. No one, not even you, has cornered the market on imagining things that go bump in the night."

It was a morning for surprises, it seemed, for at that silly euphemism, he laughed. The ice melted from his eyes, and the fire returned. He leaned down, caressed her cheek, then kissed her on the tip of her nose.

"*Tu es sans pareil.*" He plucked her empty cup from her hands, picked up his own, and disappeared into the house.

Apt, Luberon Valley, France

Uncle Joe arrived in France in the same frame of mind as many tourists; that is to say he was disoriented, tired, and cranky. And spoke not a word of the native language. In short, he did no credit to his country and went a long way toward reinforcing—to anyone who had the bad fortune to deal with him—the stereotypical image of an Ugly American.

His flight landed in Marseille on time. Predictably, the Hertz desk was a trial, as was navigating his way out of the airport and onto the correct highway. The roads were relatively empty, it being only nine o'clock on Sunday morning, but it still took him longer than he'd anticipated to reach his destination. When he finally arrived, even more tired and cranky, he learned that he was too early to check in. In his present mood, if his handgun had been in his coat pocket instead of secreted inside his luggage, he would have pulled it out and shot the poor *mec* at hotel reception desk for delivering that news.

Sensing the volcano of an Angry American about to blow, the clerk took self-serving initiative and begged him to wait just a moment. With a few quick taps on his keyboard, he upgraded the room and handed over a key. His reward was a grunt, but then, he'd managed to save himself from whatever blast had been about to come his way.

Up two flights of stairs, Joe opened the door to his room, dropped his bag onto the queen-sized bed and went straight to the minibar. Finding no American whiskey but several tiny bottles of Cognac, he grabbed two, cracked the seal on the first one, and chugged it. Hissing in his breath at the burn, he repeated the process. Then he flopped back on the bed, closed his eyes, and slept.

Ménerbes

The morning turned glorious, as one comes to expect in Provence: warm sun in a brilliant blue sky with the occasional puffy cloud floating overhead, and the short walk up to the village *boulangerie* was pleasant. Lori rolled her eyes at women's reactions when they got a look at Laurent, then laughed to herself when she realized hers had been no different. It wasn't just the young ones, either; she caught a couple of hunched-over grannies in their faded flower-print dresses, thick rolled stockings, and sensible shoes ogling him while pretending to look at the apple tarts. Her amusement fled when the curvy thirtysomething behind the counter asked if he was free that evening.

"Merci, mais j'ai été pris." Thanks, but I'm taken.

Lori smiled at his declaration while wondering at his choice of words, thinking perhaps her scattered wits had caused her to mishear. Wits that were scattered even more when he followed up with a fast, hot kiss as if to emphasize his statement. And he didn't give the woman a second glance once he dropped the proper coins on the counter.

"I may need to find another *boulangerie*," she said as they exited the shop hand in hand. "I have a feeling there might be burnt croissants in my future at this one."

They ate *pain au chocolat* as they walked back down the hill, or more precisely, Lori nibbled on hers while Laurent wolfed down two pastries in as many minutes and then cast greedy eyes at hers. She smiled as she tore off a chunk and handed it to him.

"So, *chérie,* if I hadn't interrupted your evening and imposed my person on you last night, what would be on your agenda today?"

"You mean besides making another attempt to sketch a replica of your tattoo?"

That surprised him. *"Oui,* besides that." Tilting his head, he regarded her thoughtfully. "You have done that, *vraiment?"*

"Crazy, right? I just …" She shrugged. "I couldn't get it out of my head, so I thought maybe sketching it would make it stop haunting me."

"Perhaps I will model for you. So you can get it just right."

Her brows rose. "Be careful what you offer up there, big guy." The idea of him stretched out, half-naked while she tried to capture the design on paper … *Whew!*

They crossed the road at the bottom of the village, a two-lane with ditches for shoulders, and she was glad they were forced to walk single file along the edge of the smaller road that led to her house. Her cheeks were flaming from the image in her head.

"Actually I was planning on venturing into Coustellet. It turns out that little nothing of a crossroads you passed on the way here has a big Sunday market. My kitchen is well equipped, and I'm enjoying the freedom to cook again. Although cooking for one is a bit anticlimactic." *And didn't that sound a little pathetic?*

"I need to get back to Uzès."

Ouch. Bubble, meet needle, and *pop* went her good mood.

"I texted my sister last night so she wouldn't worry," he continued, unaware of the stink bomb he'd just dropped. "But Sebastien has become used to me being there." The tone of his voice suggested he wasn't exactly pleased with that truth.

Lori guessed that the little boy was not the only one who had come to rely on him. *None of my business!*

"Of course. I don't want to keep you from your family."

The flatness of her normally warm voice made him frown. They'd reached the entrance to her property, and she stepped across the metal plate that spanned the ditch before picking up her pace with the intention of putting some distance between them. But she didn't get far because Laurent reached out and snagged her hand, drawing her to a halt. That she didn't wrench her hand from his was … a good sign.

"You aren't." With his free hand, he traced rough knuckles across her cheek then used them to tilt her chin up until her eyes met his. There was hurt lurking in those pale-blue orbs, despite her effort to hide it. Rewinding their conversation in his head, he realized what he'd said and how it must have sounded out of context. *Merde.*

"There is no place I would rather be at this moment than right here, with you."

Their eyes held for a moment before she looked away. "That's sweet of you to say—"

"I'm not sweet, *chérie*. I'm honest." The fingers beneath her chin now cupped her face, and he ran the pad of his thumb across her cheek. "And I'm telling you the truth when I say that I want to spend more time with you."

She studied him, searched his eyes for that truth.

He held still, held his breath even, not understanding why this was so important to him. Just that it was. A chill ran up his spine as his mind processed that perhaps this wasn't such a good idea. For either of them.

His natural instinct was to stay detached, like the loner he'd always been. It had been that instinct that had him running from her two weeks ago, despite the draw, the inexplicable emotional tug to stay with her. And he'd spent those two weeks wishing he'd stayed. Wishing that he could explore whatever it was about her that drew him. Now that he'd found her again, he wasn't going to hightail off like a coward. There would be no third chance, of that he was certain. So he let her see the emotion no matter how vulnerable it made him feel.

"I'd like that, too." She squeezed his hand then tugged, and they resumed the walk around the vineyard to the house.

"I need to—"

"But you need to—"

They spoke at the same time, and she smiled, nodding for him to go first.

"I need to spend some time with Sebastien and make sure Julia will be okay on her own for a few days, but then I want to come back here. Back to you." He cast around like this was new for him, which in fact, it was. He didn't do dates or, God forbid, relationships. He did hookups. But this woman was so much more than that. "I haven't actually seen much of this area. How about playing tourist with me for a few days?"

Pleased and surprised in equal measures, she grinned at him. "I was going to say that you need to go home and spend whatever time you need there, but then I was going to ask you to come back to me." She leaned in and kissed him. "I would love to play tourist with you. But I have a condition."

"Another one?" The playful flash in his eyes warmed her.

"Well, maybe more than just one. But what I was going to say was … this might sound silly, but I'd like to come back here and cook dinner at night." She looked around the enclosed property, taking in the vineyard, pool, dilapidated tennis court, and rustic stones walls of her wacky farmhouse. The sun was high enough in the sky now that the huge plane tree was doing its job, the beautiful stone table with its cushioned chairs looking inviting beneath the shade of those broad branches. "I really do love to cook, and this is too nice—too private—not to enjoy."

"Sounds like another condition I can live with. Let's start tonight."

Eight

Uzès, France

"Sebastien missed you this morning."

Julia's declaration, made in lieu of a greeting when her brother walked into her house around noon, was a partial truth. Because while her son had, indeed, asked after his uncle, *she'd* been the one who missed his presence.

Her growing dependence on Laurent in the months since her widowhood wasn't something she was proud of, but neither could she shake her need. He'd been her idol since she was a little girl, and though his career had taken him far away for months—sometimes years—at a time, her adoration of her big, strong brother had never faltered. Even when she'd fallen in love and married Jacques, Laurent continued to be her emotional anchor.

And he understood all of that, including the subtext of her statement.

"*Désolé, petite.* Is there something you need me to do?" Shrugging off his jacket, he glanced around the room.

Little boy detritus—the perpetrator nowhere in evidence—littered the rug in front of the television. Mail was strewn on a low table beside the couch, along with an open newspaper. A dirty plate holding crumbs and a smear of jam had been left there, too.

A lifetime of military discipline and sharing small living quarters with large men had ingrained a habitual tidiness, but Laurent stifled the urge to clean up the mess. Instead, and before she could answer his first question, he asked, "Is there more coffee?"

Julia had not risen from the dining table in the corner, where more papers were scattered around the laptop that was open in front of her. At his second question, she glanced down at the mug cupped in her hand as if perplexed as to how it had gotten there. The movement put her face into a beam of sunlight that highlighted her fatigue. "It's not fresh," she said then looked back up at him.

Her listlessness, coupled with her opening salvo and the disarray of the room set, off an alarm in his head. "*Chére,* has something happened?" He was beside her in three strides, bending down on one knee and tipping her chin so she had to look at him.

A heart-wrenching sadness poured from those pretty brown eyes, along with a fresh batch of tears.

"Aw, honey." Laurent gathered her in his arms, and she clung to him, an internal dam bursting as her small frame was racked with sobs. He held her, gently stroking her back, letting her pour it all out. When she pulled back to wipe her nose on her sleeve, he gave her space but kept his hands on her shoulders.

"What happened?" Then he cocked his head, realizing his nephew had not yet appeared as he normally did when Laurent arrived. "Where's Sebastien?"

Julia reached for a box of tissues and blew her nose before taking a deep breath and meeting his gaze. "He's with Adele." The neighbor whose interest in the boy had blossomed with Laurent's arrival in Uzès.

"This came in yesterday's mail." She picked up a piece of paper and handed it to him.

It was a check. From the gallery, Laurent realized, that had hosted Jacque's show in Nîmes. His eyes widened at the amount, which was astronomical. Far more than he ever considered the paintings would sell for, not that he had any real idea of their value. Then he frowned.

"But, *chére,* why are you upset? This is wonderful." It meant she wouldn't need to worry about money for the foreseeable future. Or ever, if she handled it properly.

More tears leaked from his sister's red-rimmed eyes, her misery clear. "I didn't sell those pieces to b-benefit from his death!" It was a wail that held the heart-wrenching pain of a wounded animal.

Huh? "Of course you didn't, but sweetheart, you had to know that their value would be higher now." Now that her husband was dead.

"It just … it feels so … wrong." Head hanging down, she blew her nose again.

"Julia, look at me." Still kneeling beside her chair, he waited for her to lift her eyes to his.

"Jacques would have wanted this—he'd be so damn happy that he could give you this last thing." Laurent couldn't do much to help his sister get beyond her grief, but he could, at least, say *that* with total confidence. Jacques had done well with his art, and his pieces had commanded high prices in recent years, but like many young couples who assumed they had all the time in the world, they'd not yet begun saving for the future when he'd been diagnosed. And after, between the new baby and Jacques's medical bills, they'd never had the opportunity.

It took some coaxing, and a fresh pot of coffee, but Laurent was eventually able to get her to see reason. Guilt for surviving, despair for the same, or some combination—whatever it was, Laurent hated the pain he saw in his baby sister's face.

Not for the first time, he wondered whether love was worth it. Having never had any attachments beyond immediate pleasure, he couldn't imagine it was. Although a certain American had recently made him think that perhaps he didn't have the right of it.

Impatient as he was to get back to Ménerbes, he called on years of honed discipline to do what he needed to do at the expense of what he wanted to do. His sister needed him. Even if it was just his silent presence. She'd been doing well, had seemed buoyed by the response of collectors and followers at the show. Despite what it represented, that check had set her back, and in her fragile state of mind, he was afraid to leave her alone. Biting back a frustrated curse, he sent a text to Lori.

Coustellet, Luberon Valley

The ping from her phone had Lori fishing it out of her shoulder bag to read the text message.

Julia had a setback. Need to stay close. Be back ASAP tomorrow. Forgive me?

Disappointment flooded her senses, but she forced it away. *Stupid!* She had no business harboring any expectations when it came to the sexy soldier, despite what he said, or how much she wanted to. But she focused on the plea for forgiveness. Did that mean he cared about her opinion?

Of course. I'll miss you. Hope all is okay.

His reply was instantaneous. *It will be. Miss you already. À demain.*

Well that was something, at least. On a sigh, she tossed her phone back into her purse and reconsidered her dinner options for the evening.

All those years ago in Paris, Lori had fallen in love with the outdoor markets that were so much a part of French culture. She hadn't lied to Laurent—Coustellet was not much more than a crossroads, but its Sunday *marché* was robust, drawing mostly locals with plenty of quality vendors across the spectrum. The town also held the distinct advantage of being home to the finest butcher shop in the valley.

In anticipation of sharing a few nights of meals with Laurent, she took pleasure in looking at everything displayed among the stalls and playing menu ideas through her head. Most of what was offered came from local farms, as fresh and seasonal as it could get. It was still too early for cherries or other stone fruit, but the melons were just coming in, and there were plenty of tomatoes, lettuce, and other great looking produce. When she finally stepped into the crowded *boucherie* and took a number, her market bag was full of goodies.

A breeze had kicked up by the time Lori reached home, the cerulean sky of the morning giving way to heavy gray clouds. She put away groceries then prepared what had become her typical lunch: leafy greens with ripe tomatoes and a splash of mustard vinaigrette, today augmented by a small slice of the pâté she'd purchased at the butcher shop and a hunk of fresh baguette. Determined to remain upbeat about Laurent and keep whatever was building between them in perspective—he was a very welcome distraction, but a fling with a sexy Frenchman was not her *raison d'être*—she forced herself to focus on why she *was* in France.

Lunch plate and cup of tea in hand, she settled herself at the sturdy desk beside the ground-level fireplace. She momentarily considered building a fire—a romantic notion—but rejected the idea as too much bother (as well as a little *too* romantic), though she did fetch a sweater to ward off the increasing chill. Booting up her laptop, she opened a French language program. Over the years she'd managed to retain some skill with the language, but now that she was back for … however long she could stay … she intended to improve. Since the start of her lease, she'd stuck to her goal of spending an hour each day on it, determined to re-master the language. The self-inflicted lessons were a necessary augmentation to the actual experience of living there once again.

A splash of rain against the window grabbed her attention from the computer. Looking out through the water-streaked glass, she cursed her lack of foresight, spying the outdoor cushions that were already drenched. Then she thought of Laurent riding that demon motorcycle through the squall and was almost glad that his sister had had a meltdown.

The room was dark now, though it was only three o'clock, and she realized she'd been at her desk for more than two hours. *No wonder my ears hurt,* she thought as she pulled off the headphones and rubbed away the ache.

Still seated at the desk, she switched from the French program over to her email account. Other than a not-so-subtle inquiry from Annie about how the weekend was going, there was nothing much else of interest. Certainly nothing to take her mind off Laurent. They'd kissed *au revoir* just that morning, for crying out loud, yet she missed him.

He'd begun to open up to her, and instinct told her that hadn't been easy for him. Anyone who spent as much time in a war zone as he had would not want to burden others with their experience. *Nightmares.* He'd confessed to nightmares. As a warning? Did he think she'd kick him to the curb the first time he cried out in the night? Or worse, think he was weak?

Hell no. She wasn't some crystal vase that would shatter at the first tremor.

With a flip of her hand, she closed the laptop. Moving through the house, turning on lights to push back the gloom created by the weather, she ended up in the kitchen. And stopped. *Damn him!* She'd not been lonely for one second until he'd showed up at the wedding. They'd shared another amazing, wonderful night, and now she was pining for him.

———————◆◆———————

Uzès

Laurent's hope of making a polite retreat after fetching his nephew from the babysitter evaporated with the calculating look she directed his way. Adele had apparently chosen this moment to step up her game from suggestive flirtation to blatant pursuit.

"Laurent"—she pouted prettily—"are you sure I cannot persuade you to come back?" He could swear that even the ever-present Chihuahua held in the crook of her arm looked at him in expectation. Adele raised a hand to touch his chest, but he caught her wrist, a warning in his gaze. He really didn't want to have this conversation in front of Sebastien.

"Non, mais merci pour la proposition."

Her pout turned into a sour pinch of painted lips at the same time she assumed a provocative pose, hands on her cocked hips with shoulders back to expose her cleavage to maximum advantage. The dog whimpered. "I think perhaps you don't like women."

So much for subtle. Hoping she wouldn't punish Julia for it, he returned the insult. "I adore women. I'm just not interested in you. *Bonsoir.*"

Before she could say something even more inappropriate, he turned to the small boy who'd been standing quietly beside him, clutching a wooden fire truck to his little chest. "Come on, *mon petit bonhomme.* Let's go home."

"Fine. Tell your sister I'm not available for babysitting this week. Maybe not next week, either."

Damn her. He stopped and turned back, making no effort to disguise his disgust. "I will tell my sister that it's time to upgrade her child-care arrangements. It troubles me, the thought of what an innocent boy might be exposed to while in your care."

Not waiting for a response, he scooped up his nephew, fire truck and all, and walked the short distance back to his sister's house. The door slammed behind him at the same time fat raindrops began to land on them.

"*Désolé, petite,*" he said to his sister after Sebastien had raced up to his room. It was becoming an uncomfortable refrain today. "Adele said she wouldn't be available this week."

"Damn. Did she say why?"

The look he gave her was all the answer she needed. Julia was not blind to her neighbor's motives. "Oh." Despite the bad news, she looked amused. "Finally cornered you, did she?"

"*Oui.* And taking my rejection out on you just proves what kind of person she is. You're better off finding someone permanent. Someone you can depend on."

Julia's shoulders slumped, her body seeming to deflate just a little, and Laurent knew he needed to get it all out there. "*Chére,* there's something else. I wish the timing was different, but—"

"You're leaving again."

"I never meant to stay this long."

"I know."

Laurent felt like a bastard for the bleakness those two words conveyed. His sister rarely asked him for anything—wouldn't do so now—and that made it that much harder to abandon her.

"I'm sorry I've been so selfish," Julia said, hugging herself. "It's just been so good to have you here. I knew it wasn't going to last."

"You have not been selfish at all. Don't even think it. And I'm not going far—I won't break that promise." Jacques's passing had been the final impetus for Laurent to resign his commission—something he'd been considering since that last tour in Africa. At the time, he'd vowed to his sister that he'd stay close. *Close,* not in her pocket. He had no intention of replacing Jacques as a father figure for Sebastien. He would continue to grow his relationship with his precocious nephew, but the more he hovered over them, the longer it would take them all to move on.

"When?"

"Tomorrow."

"So soon?"

"Something came up, and I need to, ah, explore an opportunity." He wouldn't lie to his sister, but neither was he prepared to mention Lori. Not only was it too new, Julia would take it wrong. Better to let her believe it was a job opportunity he was investigating.

"It will take me out of town for a few days. Maybe a week."

"Oh." Curiosity, mixed with a dose of concern. "Can you tell me what it is?" She was used to not knowing where he was or what he was doing, but she always worried.

"Not quite yet, not until it's a sure thing. And it's nothing dangerous, I promise." At least not physically. His emotional well-being, however ... "I need to leave some gear here, if that's okay. But either way, whether the, ah, situation pans out or not, it's time for me to find my own place. Somewhere nearby."

She looked like she might cry again but was valiantly holding off the tears.

"Julia," he said softly. "You know it's time."

A nod, followed by a watery smile. Before any more could be said, Sebastien came charging back into the room.

———————◦◦———————

Ménerbes

Culinary inspiration eluded Lori regardless of how long she stared into the fridge. Much longer and she'd be refrigerating the entire room. Thick wool socks covered her feet, and she wore a bulky sweater. She loved her ancient farmhouse, but it was frickin' chilly, making her crave something warm and cozy for dinner. Unfortunately, the rain limited her options to indoor cooking. The ringing of her phone distracted her from the menu dilemma. She shut the door as she reached for it then made a face when she saw who was calling.

Martin. *Why can't the man just leave me alone?*

She hesitated then tapped the DECLINE icon. There was not one thing he could possibly have to say that she wanted to hear. He was probably calling to whine about that stupid flash drive. Why he thought it was with her stuff, she didn't understand, but she knew it wasn't. And the last thing she had any intention of doing was leaving her new home. Not now.

The beep that indicated a new voicemail made her sigh, but she didn't listen to it. The only concession she made was to not delete it out of hand. She pushed aside a niggle of doubt that threatened to insinuate itself into her peace of mind. The message would still be there tomorrow, when the broad light of day might make her feel more charitable toward her cheating ex. Placing the phone back on the counter, she opened the refrigerator door again.

Philadelphia

Despite the fact that it was Sunday, Martin was in his downtown office, not his home office, because it was a location in which he was far less likely to be harassed. Or harangued.

"Lori, it's Martin again. Would you please give me a call? I know you hate me right now, and frankly I don't blame you, but it's fucking urgent that I talk to you. This situation here has gotten completely out of control. Please."

The minute he ended the call, his phone rang and he jumped. *Maybe she just couldn't reach her phone in time to pick up!* But no, it wasn't Lori. *Damn it!*

He punched the TALK button. "Vinnie."

"I got a *courtesy* call from the city manager just now," his client said with no preamble.

"Today?" On a Sunday? *Shit.*

"Yeah, just now qualifies as *today.* Seems there's some concerns about what's been going on at that warehouse in the redevelopment district. First the cop killings last year—now I hear there's been some drug busts there."

"What the fuck?"

"My sentiment exactly. First I heard of it. If it's true."

"And?" Martin had a sick feeling.

"At the City Council meeting this week, my application for redevelopment is going to be kicked back for *further review.*"

A polite way for the city officials to give Vinnie the bird. Because as far as Martin knew, and he was well-informed, not one viable application had been denied. The city was all about waterfront redevelopment and was practically paying property owners to come to the table. Of course, anyone who made that sort of investment was all but guaranteed to make a profit, but it still took effort, capital, and risk.

"Fuck."

"Yeah, you could say that."

"Do you think Claudio is doing this on purpose?"

"Marty, for fuck's sake. *Of course that fat bastard is doing this on purpose!* He's thumbing his nose at me and spreading his sick disease all over the city. I won't be surprised if the fucking mayor ends up dead at this point, to be found floating off my fucking dock."

Vinnie paused, and Martin heard a deep inhale and exhale. "I gotta find that thing, Marty."

"I know, Vinnie. I'm trying."

Uzès

It was early, predawn, but Laurent had given up on finding sleep. Worries for his sister tangled with a burning desire to get back to his smart, sexy American. The fact that his yearning went beyond simple lust should have stopped him in his tracks. He had no business foisting his damaged psyche on any woman, much less a decent one. But this time the well-practiced refrain was ineffective, overridden by a deeper need.

With an efficiency born from a lifetime of military discipline, he packed a duffle and tidied his room, squaring away his meager possessions on a high shelf in the closet out of the reach of curious little boys. Downstairs he found Julia, illuminated by the soft glow of a reading lamp, curled up in the recliner with an enormous marmalade cat in her lap.

"I'm glad you're up, *petite.*" He set the duffle on the bottom step and crossed the room to her, kneeling down to eye level. "I didn't want to wake you, but I didn't want to leave without saying goodbye."

"I couldn't sleep, and I had a feeling you'd be off early." Julia gave her brother a sad smile, reaching out to smooth a lock of hair off his forehead. "Your hair is getting so long."

Laurent ran his hand across the thick fur of the cat, liking the feel of his sister's caress, reminding him of another's touch. "I'm not sure what to do with it."

"I like it. It makes you look more …" She cocked her head. "More approachable."

He laughed. "I'm not sure that's a good thing." Then he leaned in and kissed her forehead. "I'll call you when I can. Tell Sebastien to be a good boy for me, and I'll bring him something when I return." It was an old promise, one he'd been making to her for as long as he could remember. When he hadn't been able to tell her where he was going, or how long he'd be away, it was his way of reassuring her that he'd be back. Now, he made the promise for Sebastien, but they both knew it was for her.

"Be safe," she whispered, but he was already gone.

———————— ❈ ————————

Ménerbes

The guttural roar of a downshifting motorcycle engine yanked Lori out of an ugly dream—one that involved Martin, a storage room full of boxes, and a sneering thug holding a gun against her temple. *What the hell?* Her heart was racing and sweat drenching her body beneath the down duvet, her unbound hair clinging to her clammy neck. The sound of the motor slowed, and her brain narrowed in focus. *Laurent.* The engine's growl increased, and she could picture the bike coming through the tall hedgerows. Kicking off the stifling covers, she leaped out of bed.

Not stopping to question the anticipation that surged through her blood, she bolted for the bathroom. Splashing cold water on her face and taking only half a minute to swish a toothbrush across her teeth, she scolded herself to calm down. The last thing she wanted was to appear needy—a needy *older woman,* curse the saints—but she craved him, had missed him in the hours since she'd seen him last, and she had no intention of playing coy about her pleasure in having him back.

Dawn's colors had only just begun to streak the sky when Laurent turned the Ducati down the narrow lane that led to Lori's house. He drove as slow as possible, doing his best to keep the engine noise down for the sake of her neighbors, but it was a beast of a machine, and even idling, it was loud. Pulling through the narrow opening in the hedgerows that marked her driveway, he knew he was arriving way too early and figured to just wait in the chilly morning rather than wake her up. Regardless of how much he wanted to.

He cut the engine and let the bike coast to a stop beside her car, then kicked out the stand and swung his leg over the seat. The helmet he left hanging on the handlebars; the duffle he untied and carried across the gravel to the table. He'd just set it down when the latch on the kitchen door clicked.

The sight of her standing there, barefoot and wrapped in nothing but a filmy silk robe, hair sleep tousled and hiding a yawn behind her hand, made the chill that had settled over him from the long ride disappear. They stared at each other for a moment in the soft light of the breaking day. Then she smiled and held out her hand.

Nine

Apt

Monday morning in the medium-sized town of Apt mimicked the start of the workweek in any other city across the globe, but with a charming French twist. A steady stream of traffic lumbered down the main boulevards while clusters of school kids in uniforms made their way through the square. Amidst adults scurrying to their jobs, octogenarians stood in doorways surveying the activity or leaned against the counters at the local bars with the morning's first beer. Shopkeepers swept their front stoops in anticipation of the day's custom. Everyone seemed to have a jaunty scarf wrapped around their neck, though the morning was mild.

Wholly uncharmed, Joe clomped down the sidewalk not bothering to make eye contact with those he passed. In this, he fit in. His pleasure at finding a Starbucks in the center of town turned sour after his first scalding sip of the thick brew. *Fucking frogs. Can't even make a decent cup of coffee.* Though the pastry was unexpectedly moist and delicious.

After passing out in his room the day before, he'd awakened to a dark sky outside his hotel window. Dismayed at how long he'd been out, he showered, put on fresh clothes, and left the room, intent on getting the lay of the land and finding something to eat.

His hotel was not convenient to the city center, necessitating a trip by car to that destination. Parking was easy because, unfortunately for him, the town was all but dead on a Sunday night. It was also wet. Eaves dripped and water ran in the gutters from a recent squall. A few restaurants on the fringes were open, but the commercial district was rolled up tight.

It had not occurred to Joe when he volunteered for this trip that he would need to communicate with people who spoke a language other than his own. Rather than humbling him, the situation made him angry. And hungry. He stood for a few minutes outside one of the few open restaurants, trying to make sense of the menu, before throwing up his hands in disgust and returning to his car. Thinking he could pick something up at the grocery store that the Sheridan woman had frequented twice in the last week, he drove to that location at the edge of town with the help of GPS, only to find it closed up tight as well. Apparently the French hadn't heard of 24/7 shopping.

In the end he returned to his room hungry and the furthest thing from tired. Raiding the minibar again for a meal of snacks, he downed the rest of the liquor and tried to find sleep. Another unsuccessful endeavor so close on the heels of his afternoon slumber.

Now, eyes gritty, to-go cup in hand, he settled on a bench in the town's central square. The French road system, he'd discovered on his drive from the airport, was peppered with infernal roundabouts. The square in which he now sat—a circle, in truth—was surrounded by a large one that appeared to serve as the town's main ingress and egress. Pulling out his notebook, he mapped the locations where Malone's ex-wife had used her credit card as he periodically watched the passing traffic. Both, he discovered, had a pattern.

———— ▸◂ ————

Ménerbes

Coffee at the stone table under the plane tree was a lovely habit, particularly when the weather was so fine after a stormy night. The outdoor cushions—soaked from being left out in the rain—were spread across the now sun-drenched gravel to dry. Two dry chairs had been retrieved from the shed attached to the side of the house and unfurled in the dappled sunlight beneath the tree.

Despite the bucolic surroundings, no specific responsibilities, and the promise of a lazy day with a far-too-scrumptious man, Lori felt ... off balance.

Like she was having an out-of-body experience, looking down on herself rather than out from her own eyes. That dream had rattled her more than she wanted to admit.

"Where are you, *chérie?*" Laurent gazed at her over the rim of his cup.

She lifted one quizzical brow. "I'm here enjoying the morning. Where are you?"

"Been here all along, but I should warn you—I spent more years than I care to admit observing people who made it a point to conceal their emotions. You left me, just now, for some distant place."

"Perhaps my wits are still wandering after your enthusiastic greeting."

That comment was greeted with a wolfish, all-too-satisfied male grin. "My pleasure to oblige."

Laurent wasn't fooled by the deflection, but neither did he pursue the point. Something was nudging into their time together, and he would, eventually, get it out of her. But not now. Now, this morning, while proving he could be as thoughtfully organized as any local, he would begin his campaign to learn everything there was to know about the enchanting woman in the blue silk robe sharing coffee with him.

———————◆◆———————

Apt

Contrary to Martin Malone's assumption, Joe knew his way around computers and the internet. His smart phone was the latest version, to which he'd added an international data and call package. Tossing the unfinished coffee into a trash bin, he climbed back into his rental. With GPS as his guide, he merged into the morning traffic and reconnoitered each place where Lori Sheridan had made charges in the last week.

Through that electronic record, his contact had tracked her from Philadelphia International Airport to Charles de Gaulle to Nîmes, where she spent a few days that ended with the settling of a hotel bill. There followed a five-day blank spot when she'd not used her cards. Then last week she'd reemerged in the immediate area of the Luberon Valley—or so he surmised, as her credit card usage had been limited to this area, including several trips to the supermarket in Apt and what turned out to be a butcher shop on the main road. There were also restaurant meals in villages between those two locations, ATM withdrawals, and payments made at various shops in those same towns. A charge for gas, too, at a station on the main road through Apt. But nothing to indicate where she was staying.

It was tempting to request an update on any charges over the weekend, but Joe had already called in a marker, one that squared an old debt. The cost of the additional information was more than Joe was willing to bear. If it was merely a question of cash, he wouldn't have hesitated, but this particular source dealt in a far more dangerous currency—favors—and was someone that one did not willingly become indebted to. Joe would just have to make do with what he had.

Monday and Wednesday had been grocery days for his target. According to Marty, his ex-wife was an accountant and an organizational neat freak. Joe was counting on this translating into some sort of predictable pattern. Otherwise he might as well be chasing a shadow.

His investigative circuit brought him back to the supermarket by mid-morning. Parking in a space with an unencumbered view of the store's entrance, he settled in to wait. A printed photo courtesy of her former employer's website was propped against the dashboard where it was in his line of sight. He'd memorized her features, but the added visual never hurt.

With one eye on the people going in and out and another on the list of her spending, he considered the obvious pattern that emerged. Restaurants, specialty shops, grocery stores. Lots of money spent at the grocery, suggesting she wasn't at a hotel. Reading up on Provence on the flight over, he'd learned that outdoor markets were popular. When he entered *outdoor markets in Provence* in his browser, several sites popped up. Selecting one, he surveyed the list, looked at the dates on the restaurant receipts, and smiled. Ms. Sheridan apparently enjoyed hitting the local markets. Her lunchtime restaurant charges in each town coincided with the day of each town's market. *Score one for the internet.*

As luck would have it, there looked to be a promising Monday-morning market in a largish town at the mouth of the valley. It was time to see what these markets were all about—and perhaps catch a disobedient American unawares.

It was a good idea but far more difficult than Joe had imagined. First there was the problem of parking. To call the traffic chaotic would have been a gross understatement. The French parked wherever they wanted and weren't shy about partially blocking the roadway, which made the snarl of vehicles that much worse. Finally wedging his car behind a delivery truck, he followed the stream of pedestrians and discovered one reason why parking was such a problem. The tents and canopies of the market were set up in what appeared to be the town's main municipal lot. *Fucking frogs.*

And the place was jam-packed. His height was an advantage as he worked his way to the center of the crowd, dodging hunched-over grannies pulling wheeled canvas bags and young mothers pushing strollers. For two hours he stood, his back to a fountain, surrounded by the swirling humanity of market goers, until the crowd thinned and the vendors began to pack up their wares. *Well, hell.* Considering the possibility that he'd missed her in the crush, he strolled along a street that held a long row of restaurants, their colorful awning-covered patios teeming with life. The French, he realized, took the experience of eating to a whole new level. There was not a Burger King or McDonald's in sight. Which was problematic in the extreme because Joe was hungry.

———◆◆———

Fontaine de Vaucluse

Thirteen kilometers across the valley, Laurent held out a chair for his lady on the edge of a tree-covered patio that overlooked the crystal clear, frolicking headwaters of the Sorgue River. Its impressive wellspring lay tucked into the base of a cliff at the end of the canyon they'd just hiked. Though *hike* was a bit of a stretch.

The path to the spring was wide and mostly paved, the asphalt giving way only in the last fifty meters to a packed-dirt track that a determined wheelchair-bound visitor could navigate. The gaping hole that was the mouth of the spring was quite a sight—an enormous natural well—but it was the crystalline water gushing from an underground aquifer to give life to the river that was most impressive.

It was as if the rocks themselves gave birth to it. Beyond the well-like cave, there was a dry cascade of boulders, then suddenly, a river. Not some little trickle but a full-blown flow that surged from the rocks and tumbled down the boulders as it picked up speed. By the time it had gone two hundred meters, it was strong enough to turn an old moss-encrusted waterwheel that powered a fifteenth-century paper mill. A mill that still operated today, turning out beautiful hand-hewn paper for sale to visitors. Fontaine de Vaucluse was a tourist destination to be sure, and Laurent had playfully purchased a logo coffee mug for Lori at one of the kitschy souvenir shops that lined the paved portion of the path.

Their destination had been Laurent's idea, the tiny village a place he'd always wanted to see. Less than twenty minutes by car from her house, it seemed a perfect place to start their adventures. And it was lovely.

Over delicious crêpes and a carafe of local wine, Laurent explained the reason for his interest.

"That spring," he said after their plates had been delivered, "is the largest in France, and something like the fifth most powerful in all the world. The well marks the entrance to an elaborate underground network of water that spreads for hundreds of kilometers."

"Do people actually dive down into it?" Lori shuddered at the claustrophobic thought.

"An old schoolmate of mine used to talk about it. He joined the navy with hopes of being part of the team to explore it, but it's proved to be too dangerous even for the military. Jacques Cousteau nearly died down there back in the forties. After a few others made aborted attempts to explore it, the government pulled the plug. The most extensive exploration has been made by robots, and even some of those didn't survive."

"Then how can they know the extent of the cave system?"

"Robots have been able to penetrate fairly far, and other underground sonar-like systems have helped. The entirety of it is still a bit of a guess."

"Wow. I had no idea." Lori took a sip of wine and regarded him over her glass. "Have you ever been tempted to cave dive?"

An emphatic shake of his head made his feelings about it clear while he chewed the bite he'd just forked into his mouth. "*Non*. I've done *spéléologie* ... what is the English word for crawling through caves?"

"Spelunking?"

"*Oui, c'est ça.* I've done spelunking as part of training, and in Africa we had some interesting cave experiences. But I prefer to keep broad sky above my head, *merci beaucoup.*"

He was so direct, his rough charm so appealing, hinting at such interesting experiences. And then there was the tattoo. Lori knew she was in more trouble than ever.

Their evening was as relaxed as the day had been, cooking together with easy intimacy in her old-fashioned farmhouse kitchen. With the twilight had come a cold wind precluding any thought of outdoor dining. Instead they sat on stools at the ancient butcher block in the middle of the roomy kitchen.

In the way of new lovers, they shared snippets of their lives, snatches of history, passions, hopes, and regrets that had shaped who they'd become. Laurent knew that Lori had been a partner in some big accounting firm, but he was now treated to anecdotal glimpses of just what sort of high-powered career she'd had. She didn't describe it that way—was fairly casual about it, in fact—but he read between the lines and drew his own conclusion. He'd never met a woman who had wielded that sort of power ... never thought he wanted to. And to learn that Annie Macallister had done the same thing, reached those pinnacles in business before chucking it all for Kaden ... well, it was eye-opening to say the least. No wonder Macallister, with his own background and track record, had fallen so hard for his wife.

Laurent considered his own life choices and knew that others in his position might feel intimidated around these people, but he didn't. In truth it was

Lori's perceptive intelligence that he had found so captivating from the start, and his respect and regard only grew as he learned more about her. He was not ashamed of his military career, nor was he uneducated: a degree in political science—emphasis in international conflict resolution—had been part of his training at Saint-Cyr. And his rank of colonel was well earned; he was a seasoned combat leader and a skilled negotiator-slash-interrogator, having led strategic missions into dangerous territories, acquired high-value targets and provided pertinent intelligence to his government. But for the first time in his life, he was interested in a woman who was quite possibly smarter than he was. It was an intoxicating turn-on.

The moment the dishes were washed and the kitchen put to rights, Laurent was done with keeping his hands to himself. He wanted to make Lori forget whatever it was that troubled her and prove to her that he would not leave her alone. For despite the casual comfort she displayed in his presence, he knew there was something lurking nearby that frightened her. He prayed it was not *him* that she feared. The intensity that was so much a part of him, despite his efforts to keep it tamped down, was more than most women could easily handle.

Not to mention the nightmares. Just because they hadn't come yet while he shared her bed didn't mean they wouldn't.

That night he loved her with a tender sweetness, determined to go slow, to worship her in a way that she would be unable to resist. In a way that would bind her to him. But when her arousal heated up and her naturally shy reserve melted, he made no attempt to stifle the wild passion that erupted between them.

By morning the weather was an issue, last night's chilly breeze having whipped into the dreaded mistral that invaded all of Provence with a powerfully cold wind. Though the sky was clear, temperatures had dropped precipitously. The inhospitable weather rendered their original plan for the day—a boat tour of the fjords off the coast of Cassis—sheer folly.

Lori studied the man in her kitchen while she waited for the hot water to soak up the grounds in her coffee press. He sat with his back was to the window and his long legs stretched beneath the table, reading some French news daily on his tablet computer. Morning sunlight glinted off his silver-tinged dark hair, a thick mop that was getting longer by the day. The hardness of his life had left its marks, but he was so solid, so beautiful in a very male way, it took an effort not to turn into a drooling puddle of mush.

Corralling her inner teenager, she concentrated on pressing the plunger down in a slow and steady motion. "How about wine tasting in the Rhône Valley today?" In truth, she missed her best friend, and the crappy weather gave them a good excuse to stop in at the Rasteau estate.

"Don't your friends live out that way?" Laurent looked up from his screen and winked.

She laughed. "Coincidentally, they do. Are you up for a visit? We could all have lunch together." She poured coffee for him and walked it over, wrapping her arms around his broad shoulders after setting it in front of him. And just because she could, she leaned in and whispered a kiss on that sensuous, swirling tattoo on his neck. "And despite the hard time that Kaden gave you at the wedding, I think you would enjoy each other's company."

"Perhaps because of it." He stroked her hair and turned his head to capture her lips. "Anyone who is as protective of you as he is cannot be all bad."

Ten

Gordes, Luberon Valley

Joe was not happy. And the freezing-ass wind wasn't helping his mood. He'd driven all over the valley Monday and got nothing but indigestion from what passed for KFC in France. Now he sat in a packed restaurant watching market vendors brave the weather as they fought to keep their wares from blowing away.

This was an altogether different experience from yesterday, with large gaps between the tables suggesting many of the vendors had stayed home. Those who made the effort were rewarded with a miserable showing of shoppers who spent more time huddled against the gusts than eyeing the goods on display. Fair weather clearly played a role in the success of market day.

The small table Joe had claimed fronted a window closed tight against the howling wind, affording him a good view of the entire square. The room had become increasingly stuffy as more people gave up on the wind and crowded in until the sour scent of unwashed bodies and stale cigarettes threatened to overwhelm him. With an effort he got the serving girl's attention and managed to communicate that he wanted another coffee. It was bitter and strong, but with enough sugar it was drinkable.

It was probably a waste of time, but this was where Martin's ex-wife had been the week prior, at this very café, so here he was and here he would stay. Although if his quarry had any brains at all, she'd be curled up in front of a roaring fire with a good book rather than out fighting this godforsaken wind. Joe would not have minded doing the same thing.

Domaine de la Terre des Roches, Rasteau

There was nothing like a mistral to clear the air in Provence. Every single particle of dust was blown out to sea, leaving the atmosphere polished so clean, it seemed as if the landscape itself was magnified. If one could stand the stiff buffeting, one was rewarded with extraordinary views from high places. The upper ridge that demarcated the northern edge of the Macallisters' Rasteau property counted as such, where Lori and her friends now stood admiring the expansive valley that lay stretched before them.

"The vines love the wind. And when it comes after a good rain, it's the most effective and efficient deterrent to rot there is." Kaden had to raise his voice to carry over the whistle of said wind as it sang through the pine trees at the upper edge of the home vineyard. "We farmers learn to appreciate it." To call himself a farmer wasn't a stretch but neither was it an accurate description of the man Lori's best friend had married.

"While the rest of us humble souls learn to tolerate it," Annie grumbled in a good-natured tone. Her curly hair had always had a mind of its own, and now the ends cavorted around her head where they stuck out from underneath her knit cap. Dressed in jeans, boots, and a warm fleece with a scarf that engulfed her neck up to her chin, she still budged up against Kaden for warmth. "The first time I was here, it was just like this. About this time of year, too. It was kind of fun, but it can wear on you."

"My sister dreads it because most of her tables are outside." Laurent made this comment without turning. His eyes were trained on the horizon to the southwest, as if he could see those now-empty tables.

Lori shared a glance with her friend. Did Laurent assume she'd mentioned his sister to them? She had, of course, in the way that close friends share confidences, but now she felt like it may have been an invasion of his privacy. Yet he brought it up as if it was common knowledge. She gave Annie a don't-ask-me look.

He turned then to Annie, as if realizing his words were out of context. "My sister owns a café in Uzès, where I've been staying since I mustered out. Do you know the town?"

"We go there occasionally, for the flower market. Where is her place?"

"On the upper end of the loop, there's a fountain on the square. She's just next to the Tourist Office there. It's called Le Jardin."

"Oh! We do know it! Do you remember?" She peered up at Kaden from her position under his arm. "That cute café with the great coffee and interesting wine list? It's got big planters full of flowers all around the tables."

Julia had made an effort on that wine list. Rather than buying the cheap stuff that was available everywhere, she searched out quality product from *vignerons* in the surrounding area. That these savvy people had noticed it gave Laurent an unexpected surge of pride. "That's it. She serves a selection of sweet and savory tarts along with coffee drinks and tea, and as you noticed, very good wine."

"We love that place. Her tarts are really good."

"They are." Laurent smiled. "Julia makes them herself."

"Wow. You must be so proud of her."

"I am. It's hard for her right now, but ... I think the routine helps." The wind blew the words away.

When he declined to say more, Lori changed the subject. "How much of what we see here is yours, Kaden?"

Relieved by the shift of topic, Laurent attended with interest as the boundaries of the estate were pointed out, along with its idiosyncrasies. It was beautifully situated, and Laurent felt a stirring of envy for the strong connection these people had to their land, conveyed in Kaden's passionate tone of voice more than his actual words.

"I can only imagine what it must be like to work these fields year in and year out, to be part of the cycle of life." In Africa he'd seen the locals toil in their scraggly fields, and sometimes he and his men had helped out, but this seemed different. Less duty, more passion. "How did it come to be in your family?"

The cold wind was taking its toll, and there were no complaints when Kaden gestured to the path that led to the house. As they made their way back down through the vineyard, he told the story of his uncle Henri, who had purchased the neglected hectares and dilapidated house for his new bride some fifty years ago, their struggles to improve it, and a very short version of how he himself came to live there.

"Another pair of strong hands in the vineyard never goes amiss," Kaden said. "Let me know if you ever get the urge to participate." He was only half-joking; there was always plenty of work for the willing, and he hadn't missed the note of envy in the other man's sentiments.

Rather than return to the house, he led them around the back and farther down the track to the cellar. The old barn had been greatly expanded since Uncle Henri's passing ten years ago. In addition, a broad cave had been dug into the hillside behind the original barn that still housed a line of tall stainless steel tanks and old oak *foudres*. Rows of barrels stretched toward the back of the underground extension, along with long racks of bottles that held vintages going back to the original Henri's very first foray into making his own wine. Connecting the working cellar and the cave, a stone annex had been fashioned as a tasting room. Natural light from a wide skylight spilled onto a tall plank table that served as a bar. Hand-hewn stone sinks were set into the two corners adjacent to the cave entrance. Kaden flipped a switch, and the sinks turned into fountains that served as spittoons. Separated from the cave entrance by a glass wall and an iron gate, the room was as attractive as it was functional.

The current Henri joined them to conduct the tasting, and Laurent could see the pride in the young man's demeanor—and his father's—as he walked them through the current vintages.

"How about something from Uncle's time, Papa? We haven't tasted the '89 in a while." Henri's enthusiasm was charming.

"Let's do a vertical," Kaden suggested. "Pull the '89, '98, and '07. Also something from the '70s, just to compare." When his son had disappeared into the cave with a metal basket to gather the bottles, Kaden asked Laurent if he was familiar with these older vintages.

"No," the colonel admitted. "I've spent more time in Africa than France in the last twenty years. My opportunities to appreciate our wines have been limited."

"Well then, you should enjoy this."

In fact, they all enjoyed it. The older vintages showed well, having evolved into more complex, earthy versions of the youngest vintage.

"The common factor across these vintages is the structure," Kaden explained. "A wine needs a quantity of natural acidity to age well and tannins to keep it balanced."

"And of course, good expression of fruit," Henri added. He swirled the dark-garnet liquid in his glass and took a sip, then slurped it around in his mouth before spitting it out into one of the sink fountains. "Some have more staying power. This 2007 isn't even close to its highest potential, Papa. It's still an infant."

Kaden laughed and agreed. Father and son tasted, discussed, and dissected each vintage in the vertical, while Annie tossed in her opinion now and then. Laurent and Lori simply enjoyed the wine and the animated discussion that was beyond their level of knowledge.

"This seems like an awful waste of good wine," Lori said, surveying the line of open bottles, each with only a small amount of liquid missing.

"Not at all," Annie said as Henri began resealing the bottles and returning them to the wire basket. "We'll take them with us."

"Bruno will match these vintages from his own cellar," Kaden added, speaking of the owner of the restaurant where they had a lunch reservation waiting. "It's always nice to see how Rasteau holds up against the big boys."

It wasn't until late afternoon that Lori and Laurent returned to the Luberon Valley, having thoroughly enjoyed Bruno's generous hospitality. The meal was highlighted by the vintage comparisons of little Rasteau, recently bestowed of its *cru* status to the more famous wines of the original *cru* village in the area, Châteauneuf du Pape. Amidst much tasting, debate, and good-natured razzing, the restaurateur finally admitted that the "upstart village" might be on to something.

For Laurent, the comfortable camaraderie had been equally important. Kaden and Annie were connected to the world in ways that Laurent could barely comprehend, a fact Laurent knew only because Lori had clued him in, but he would never have guessed the extent of their wealth even after spending most of the day with them. They were, first and foremost, warm and generous people who loved sharing their passion with their friends. Laurent was very glad that his new lover had such fiercely loyal friends. He had the disconcerting notion that she would need them.

"I was thinking we could stop at the *boucherie* for something to cook tonight, but honestly, I'm stuffed." Lori emphasized her condition by cradling her full belly while Laurent drove.

"Fine with me, *chérie*. There's still some pâté and charcuterie left from last night if we change our minds later."

"Oomph, not going to happen. For me, at least."

Laurent smiled at her expression as they drove past the butcher shop. Neither paid the least bit attention to the cars that lined the short commercial strip of the town, thus neither saw the man sitting in the driver's seat of a gray Renault parked directly in front of the butcher's door.

Joe had been sitting in his car for more than an hour and was beginning to attract some attention. He started the car, intending to make a quick U-turn and park across the street, but as he checked his side mirror, the signal in the intersection behind him changed and the traffic moved forward, forcing him to wait. Watching in the mirror as vehicles rolled by, he spotted a smallish Renault like his own, only red. He was randomly thinking it might be another rental when he caught sight of the woman sitting in the passenger seat.

It was her! The car was past him in a blink, so surprised he was to have seen her that he failed to see who was driving, and the truck that followed immediately behind them obscured his view. *Red Renault, a model like mine.* He cursed his luck as the traffic continued by in a steady stream. When there was finally an opening, he darted out, intent on passing whatever cars he could to come up behind them.

Alas, it was not to be. The late-afternoon traffic was too heavy, and there was no opportunity to pass. And worse yet, that truck, the one that had been behind his quarry that he could still see up ahead, stopped the whole line of vehicles to make a left turn, an event that took many precious minutes due to oncoming traffic.

By the time the truck made its turn and traffic rolled again, the road ahead was clear. Joe pounded his hand against the steering wheel in frustration. He had been so close! At least seeing her confirmed that she was somewhere nearby. But the fact that she'd not been alone could be problematic. Who had been driving the car?

———————◆————————

Wednesday morning dawned clear, cold, and windy, the mistral having lost none of its strength or enthusiasm. Lori woke to the tingling whisper of calloused fingertips stroking down her spine beneath the blankets. For a moment she simply savored the sensation. Curled on her side against the sensual heat of the man who shared her bed, she stretched into the touch while letting her own fingers trace across his smooth, hard chest.

As soon as Laurent realized she was awake, his strokes became bolder. While the wind wreaked havoc with the leaves in the trees outside the bedroom window, he set up a sultry, seductive pattern that soon spawned more than a little havoc of his own and had her purring with pleasure.

That morning, cocooned together beneath warm blankets, the sweetly accommodating gentleman of the previous few nights disappeared, and Laurent gave her a taste of his true nature. His explicit, erotic demands had her trembling with arousal until she was begging for relief, even as he prolonged her pleasurable agony with diabolical teasing. As he suspected would happen when he finally unleashed his inner sexual beast, she did not back away but rather gave every bit as good as she got.

Was it possible to be rendered unconscious from pleasure? Apparently it was, Lori decided in the fraction of her brain that was functioning, because she was pretty sure she'd passed out. *La petite mort,* indeed. Laurent's prone body was a heavy weight on her, but he'd shifted to the side so he wasn't totally squashing her. The wind howled outside, the branches of the trees thrashing and cavorting against the side of the house, but inside her bedroom was toasty warm and calm. Well, except for the pounding of her heart. Laurent stirred, snuggled his face against the nape of her neck and mumbled something unintelligible, then tugged her with him as he rolled over onto his side.

She wrapped her arms around the forearm that held her securely. They lay spooned together, warm, content, and exhausted. It didn't take long for them to drift off back to sleep.

The wind howled past his window when Joe awoke. Damn it! More wind meant the local market, wherever it was this morning, was probably out of the question. He consulted his list, and his map, and concluded that there was only one market in the valley that morning, at a smallish town quite close to his location.

Fortified with a cup of coffee, he drove to the little town and staked out a sheltered spot at a café to watch. The market was pathetically small, whether due to the wind or the town's lack of consequence, Joe didn't know. He held his table through three espressos and two croissants before giving up. Just past noon he decided to give the supermarket another try.

"I haven't slept till noon since … well, I don't believe that I ever have." Lori sounded more astonished than concerned, which was a relief, since Laurent was not concerned in the least.

"I've not either, but then, I can't remember having so much nothing to be responsible for." He leaned over and kissed her, and when he pulled back, a few strands of her hair caught in his whiskers. He carefully disentangled himself and ran a palm across his unshaven face.

"Sorry," he said with an unapologetic grin. "I hope I didn't give you whisker burn in sensitive places." Then he reached for her. "Maybe I'd better have a look to make sure everything is okay down there."

"Laurent!" Lori laughed and swatted his hand away. "If you touch me again, we'll never get out of bed today." She jumped up and made a dash for the bathroom.

His grin grew as he watched her bare backside, though she didn't see it. "I don't see that as a problem," he called after her as the door swung shut.

Showered, shaved, and dressed, Laurent surveyed the contents of the refrigerator. "Perhaps we should have stopped at the butcher yesterday. There's not much in here to inspire."

Lori peeked over his shoulder. "I can make us an omelet, but you're right. We'll need something for tonight. Unless you want to go out?"

He reached behind him and snagged her hand, then stood and shut the fridge door. "You take quite a risk, *chérie*, offering to make an omelet for a Frenchman. Don't you know that is the most basic of sustenance for us? I may never forgive you if you don't get it right."

She laughed. "Since I make the best omelet on the planet, I think I'm up to the challenge."

"*C'est vrai?*" Laurent's eyebrows rose high, evidence of his disbelief.

"*Mais, oui. Asseyez et prête à être impressionné.*" *Sit down and prepare to be impressed.*

"*D'accord, mon amour.* If your omelet is *exceptionnelle,* I will reciprocate and cook for you tonight. If it is merely *satisfaisant,* I'll take you out."

"Hmm, I hope you can cook." Then she shooed him out of her way and commenced to concoct the lightest, fluffiest, most sublimely delicious omelet he had ever tasted.

He actually groaned after taking his first bite. "This is too good. *Très exceptionnelle.* You play very dirty, *chérie.* You didn't cheat? You must have."

"Darn it, you got me. My secret three-star chef just slunk out the back door. By the way, I adore lamb. And duck."

"Are you sure you don't want me to come with you?" They'd finished what essentially amounted to lunch, given the time of day. In addition to whatever it was that Laurent had planned for their evening meal, Lori gave him a grocery list of other basics. He hadn't been exaggerating about the lack of food in her fridge.

"Positive, *chérie.* I need to contemplate how best I can please your palate, which may take me some time, and I imagine you could use some time without my humble self underfoot."

That was a true statement. As much as Lori adored being with him, she needed to do a few things, like a good, hard yoga session and another French lesson that she was too shy to do with him around.

"You're hardly underfoot." She grinned. "More like under the sheets."

He advanced on her then, his all-too-familiar hungry look gleaming in his eyes, and she held up her hands in surrender. "Okay, okay! You win. *À bientôt.*" She kissed him then watched as he drove her little car out through the hedgerows.

Laurent parked, locked the car, and strode over to the Plexiglas shed that housed the shopping carts. Years in the field had honed his senses, and he knew instantly that he was being watched. He inserted a coin into the slot to release a cart then wheeled it to the entrance of the store. Taking his time, he pretended to check for his wallet while letting his gaze wander.

There. An old man, in a gray Renault rental much like Lori's.

A fleeting thought—*He doesn't look French*—skidded across his mind as he studied his unsuspecting watcher. Perhaps it was just a coincidence and the *mec* was simply bored while waiting for his wife. Laurent wheeled the cart through the entrance and channeled all the domestic vibes he could muster, focusing on his business at hand.

Yet the old man in the gray Renault was still in the same spot when Laurent emerged from the store a good forty-five minutes later. And he watched Laurent with as much attention as he had earlier. *Huh. Whatever.*

Groceries stowed in the back, Laurent wheeled the cart back to the shed, retrieved his euro, and drove out of the lot, promptly forgetting about the old man. The quality of meat available at the supermarket had been good, but Laurent needed great for the meal he planned to cook for his lady that evening. Although he had not yet personally been to the *boucherie* in Coustellet, he trusted her opinion on it. Especially after that *omelet exceptionelle*. And besides, when it came to food in France, the independent operators were always better than the chains.

Midweek afternoon traffic on the N900 being what it was, it took about twenty minutes to drive the distance. As Laurent turned left across the oncoming lane into the butcher's parking lot, he happened to glance at the line of cars behind him. Five cars back, he could swear he saw the gray Renault driven by that same old man. The opportunity for this to be a coincidence was deteriorating. Had he left someone hanging on his last assignment?

His business with the *boucher* took another twenty minutes because there were others ahead of him, and he used the time to peruse the wine cellar. Having learned a thing or two from Kaden Macallister the day before, he made a few selections and hoped for the best.

When it was his turn at the counter, he spoke his request and watched the proprietor fabricate, assemble, and wrap his order. A glance out the front window confirmed the man in the gray car was there, waiting. For him? He'd soon find out.

The Luberon Valley was a patchwork of small- to medium-sized farms, vineyards, and orchards interspersed among the picturesque hilltop villages and the occasional clumping of modern homes. As Laurent drove the main road toward home—funny that he thought of Lori's rented house in that way when he'd had nothing close to resembling the idea since he'd left his childhood home—he confirmed he was again being followed.

So be it. He pulled out his phone, scrolled through his contacts to Etienne Matisse, considered, but then dropped it on the passenger seat. He could deal with this himself.

He decided against calling Lori, too. She didn't know how long he'd planned to be out, and the last thing he wanted was to worry her, or God forbid, bring his own problems to her doorstep.

Eleven

Joe followed the red Renault from about five cars back, hoping he wasn't wasting his time again. He hadn't caught the plate number of the car Marty's ex-wife had been in, but then again, he hadn't noticed any other cars of the same make and model in that bright-red color. When his target exited the main road and drove up toward the village of Lacoste, Joe followed, slowing as the car ahead slowed, indicated with the left blinker, then turned into a driveway. It looked like a private residence so he continued on, making a U-turn at the first opportunity and backtracking.

The road was lined with deep ditches on both sides, but just before the driveway, there was an access road into the fields that surrounded the property. He parked there on the verge and got out.

Laurent hadn't gone to Matisse's property but the one adjacent, one that he was also familiar with. Having no idea if the place was occupied, or what had become of it after the takedown he'd assisted with a couple of years ago, he simply took advantage of the circular driveway.

The man following him wasn't even subtle, pulling into the weeds beside the driveway. Watching through gaps in the hedgerow, Laurent gave him just enough time to exit the car and take a few steps away before he pulled out of the driveway and continued on the way he'd been heading. He glared at his pursuer to ensure the man understood he'd been made before glancing at the license plate of the gray Renault, committing it to memory.

Long before the old *mec* could scramble back into his car and take up the chase, Laurent was gone.

The country roads connecting the charming hilltop villages of the Luberon Valley were a crisscrossed maze but intuitive enough if one had an understanding of the lay of the land. As a longtime soldier and strategist, knowing the local geography was as basic to Laurent as breathing. Ensuring he wasn't followed, he circled back to where he'd initially led his pursuer, but this time stopped at the adjacent property that was accessed by a long drive-way from an opposing road.

Halfway to the house, he stopped, pulled out his phone, and hit the CALL button.

"Matisse."

"Sorry to bother you again, *mon frère,* but I might have another small problem that I could use your help with. Do you have a minute?"

"Where are you?"

"In your driveway."

"Convenient, and good timing. Ellie just went down for a nap."

This time Joe parked his backside at a table just inside the doors of the supermarket instead of standing watch from his car. The in-store coffee shop was something of an afternoon hangout for the older crowd and Joe fit in, though the French newspaper in front of him was a mere prop. As he sipped his sugar-laced coffee, he rewound in his head his pursuit of the red Renault and how it had ended. There was military somewhere in that guy's back-ground, Joe guessed, or some sort of similar training. Either that or Joe wasn't as good as he thought, because his target not only made him, but turned it around on him. At least he now had a license plate number of a car that may or may not lead him to the Sheridan woman. Then again, he could be com-pletely off base, which was why he was back at the grocery store.

Thirty minutes after driving away from the gray Renault, Laurent parked beneath Lori's plane tree. He'd spent less than ten minutes with Matisse, the big man being disinclined to chitchat, but then had driven around the maze of back roads between Lacoste and Ménerbes to ensure he hadn't picked up another tail.

"You must have had quite the excursion." Lori held the door for him after pressing a kiss to the cheek he offered her, his arms full of grocery sacks. "Did you leave anything for the next guy?"

"I take my challenges seriously." Setting the bags on the counter, he turned and caught her hand, reeling her in as much with his wicked smile as with the gentle tug. She was wearing yoga pants and a wide-necked, loose-woven sweater over a snug tank, feet covered in a pair of what he was coming to realize were her favorite socks. Her hair was pulled into a haphazard ponytail on top of her head.

"You look comfortable." The words were spoken against the soft skin of her neck, just below her ear, as he wrapped both arms around her waist. "Were you productive?"

"Very."

He continued nuzzling her neck. "I guess I missed yoga then. Too bad." This sentiment was expressed as one large hand ventured down to caress the skin-hugging fabric that covered her *derriere*.

"Actually you didn't," she said on a shiver. "I got absorbed in my French lesson and was just about to pull out my mat when you drove up." She leaned back and grinned. "Care to join me?"

He kissed her nose and regarded her playful expression, running his hands up and down her toned arms. "I admit the thought of watching your lithe body contort into all those positions is appealing. I won't even begin to attempt it, but I do have my own stretching and strengthening routine that I've sadly neglected."

"Been distracted, have you?"

"Very." He winked then let her go and turned to the grocery sacks. "If we push back the furniture in the lounge, we could do our forms together."

Lori watched him move around the kitchen as he unloaded and stowed the purchases, a gleam in her eyes. "Okay, but I have a request."

One dark eyebrow cocked in question as he unzipped his leather jacket. "Not a condition?"

She shook her head but met his gaze. "It's optional. But I *request* that you do your routine shirtless."

Market day in Ménerbes was typically a smaller affair than what could be found in the more popular villages in the area, but since the mistral had raged for the last two days, the market was busier than usual. And Ménerbes did host a very respectable market, with a full complement of vendors offering the usual local produce, olives, spices, cheese, meat, fish, and quintessential Provençal souvenirs.

Lori stopped to admire a display of baby *aubergines,* their dark skins glossy and smooth in sharp contrast to their prickly green stems. "Look at these little beauties. How about ratatouille tonight?" She glanced down the table and saw young variegated squash and early tomatoes. "We could grill the *merguez* you picked up yesterday to serve with it."

A few days ago she would have been reluctant to wander a *marché* with Laurent, much less discuss meal options with him. But the previous night had changed her mind. The experience had been as sensuous as it was delicious.

He'd brought home lamb shoulder, an inelegant, frankly peasant choice that had surprised her. After making fast work of chopping and sautéing the *mirepoix*—a classic start to stocks and stews consisting of onions, carrots, celery, garlic, and herbs—he seared the meat and set it to braise amidst the vegetables in a bath of *demi-glace* and red wine. It simmered for several hours into a mouthwatering, succulent stew.

While the food chemistry did its thing in the kitchen, they worked through their respective exercise routines in the main parlor. The routines were followed by a very fast shower, a heated romp in Lori's big bed, and another far more relaxing shower.

And the lamb stew, when they eventually got to it, was perfect. Served with steam-sautéed fingerling potatoes laced with garlic, parsley, salt, and pepper, the meal was humble yet pure. Just like her man.

"You don't mind lamb two nights in a row?" Laurent could eat lamb every day and it wouldn't be too much, but he knew that many people had a less enthusiastic palate for the strong-flavored meat.

"I love lamb. And you obviously do, too, or you wouldn't have bought the *merguez.*"

"I was thinking of adding it to the stew, but in the end it didn't need it." He also preferred the spicy lamb sausage grilled plain with a good loaf of bread and sweet butter to sop up the juices, but her suggestion of adding ratatouille was very appealing. They could do both, in fact.

Just then he felt a tingling at the base of his neck. "Pick out your *aubergine*. I think the tomatoes at that last table looked better than these." Backtracking into the crowd, he used the excuse of dodging a baby carriage to look around. Nothing. But he knew better. Someone was out there, and he could guess who. *Damn it.* There was no way the *mec* could have missed who he was with, which meant he could possibly be endangering her.

Laurent had considered telling Lori about his encounter, but with no idea of who the guy was or what he wanted, he would have only caused her unnecessary angst. And selfishly, he had been loath to spoil the evening. It had been so comfortable. Intimate, relaxed, and very enjoyable.

There'd been plenty of space for them both in the main lounge once the coffee table was moved aside. To the soft strains of Tibetan reed pipes, Lori had worked her way through an impressive hour of yoga while he'd done three successive forms of taekwondo that first limbered, then centered, then challenged each muscle in his body. By the time he finished, sweat was beading on his skin and Lori was sitting on her mat in a calm, meditative position watching him, her own skin glowing from her exertions. The open appreciation in her eyes, combined with the endorphins flowing through his body from the long-needed workout, stoked his arousal, and they barely made it into the shower before succumbing to their mutual desire.

With one eye alternating between Lori and the flow of people around her, Laurent selected and paid for the tomatoes. He scanned the edges of the crowd for the tall man with a badly done comb-over but saw nothing. Moving back to Lori, he reached her just as she turned from the table with her purchases.

"Let's get a baguette." She slung the market bag over a shoulder and reached for his hand. "I'll do my best to protect your virtue from the temptress at *la boulangerie*. Laurent? What's wrong?"

His eyes had turned to ice, the earlier warmth in his features evaporated. He wasn't even looking at her, but over her shoulder. At her words he blinked, his predatory look easing. Those eyes, however, remained hard.

"Nothing, *chérie*." He squeezed her hand. "I thought I saw something." Then he leaned in and kissed her lips. "Forget it. Let's get the baguette."

Unconvinced, she nevertheless remained silent, keeping hold of his hand as she wove her way through the crowd and up the street to the bakery. There was a line inside, not unusual for market day. As she took her place at the end, just inside the door, Laurent eased the bag off her shoulder. Opening it, he added the sack of tomatoes he was carrying but didn't hand it back.

"I'll wait for you outside." At her questioning look he smiled—a smile that did not reach his eyes—and kissed her cheek. "I need to make a call."

Perplexed, she watched him go. *What the hell just happened?*

The last few days had been the most enjoyable, enchanting days that Lori could ever remember experiencing. Laurent Dubois, former badass soldier, was as affectionate and playful during the day as he was passionate at night. She felt like a giddy schoolgirl with her first crush. But within the space of a few heartbeats, his entire demeanor had changed. One minute he was the warm and charming man she'd come to know, and the next ... The next, he was distant and closed up. Like a soldier on a mission.

"Find anything?" Laurent growled the question the moment Matisse answered his phone. Good thing Etienne was not the sort to expect small talk.

"*Oui*. In fact I was just about to call you. The car is rented to a Joseph Carlucci of Philadelphia. He arrived in Marseille on Sunday and has the car reserved for a week."

Laurent frowned. "Philadelphia?" Not what he expected to hear.

"There's more." With Matisse, there usually was. Laurent waited. "Carlucci is associated with one Vincenzio Salentino, son of Roberto Salentino, a convicted mob boss currently serving three consecutive life sentences in a US federal penitentiary. The son is considered the head of the family now, but according to my sources, all is not roses in the family. There's a younger half brother who is causing trouble."

The fact that Etienne Matisse had dug up this much information so quickly was not surprising. The content of it, however ... a feeling of unease roiled up in Laurent's gut. Having some mercenary on his own tail was one thing, but this ...

"I am afraid, *mon ami,* that his purpose here very likely has nothing to do with you." Matisse's words echoed his own thoughts. "It turns out that Lori Sheridan's ex-husband, name of Martin Malone, is a board member and counsel of record for a collection of companies that are owned by this Salentino."

"Fuck." Exactly how Matisse had learned that, Laurent had no idea, but he did not doubt the integrity of the information.

There was a moment of silence, and if Laurent didn't know him well, that pause might have been interpreted as the end of his report. "I took the liberty of calling Annie Macallister. Annie said that Malone has been pestering Lori about some missing file. She apparently told him to sod off. Annie didn't know any more details, but you know how I feel about coincidences."

Laurent felt the same way, which is to say he didn't believe in them.

"You might want to ask her about it," Matisse suggested.

At that moment, the object of their discussion exited the *boulangerie,* baguette in hand, along with something else in a white paper sack. *"Merci beaucoup.* I'll be in touch."

"You do that. And don't forget that cross-border crime is well within my jurisdiction. That includes a *threat* of a crime, *mon frère.* Don't go off half-cocked without me."

"Roger that." Laurent ended the call and tried to arrange his features into something other than the fierce warrior that had obliterated the polite façade he'd become accustomed to wearing. *Bloody fucking hell.* Clearly without success, given the way Lori was looking at him.

"Laurent, you're scaring me." Lori stopped a few feet away from him, eyeing him like he might pounce on her at any moment. "What's going on?"

He wished he knew, but one thing he was certain about. "We need to leave." He held out his hand, but at her hesitation, he softened minutely. *"Chérie,* I need you to trust me."

"Will you tell me what's wrong?"

"Yes."

The calculating look she gave him made him want to howl in frustration at the same time his chest swelled with pride at her tenacity, followed by relief when she took his hand. Rather than head down the street that would lead them to the bottom of the village and home, he drew her up a narrow cobble-stone lane lined with private residences, toward the church that commanded the town's highest point.

The market's buzz and *joie de vivre* fell behind them as they walked up the deserted street. Laurent made sure no one was behind them before guiding her over to a low stone wall bordering the churchyard where he had a clear view of the lane they'd just traveled.

"Laurent—"

"*Désolé, chérie.*" He set the canvas bag at his feet, wrapped his arms around her, and did not mince words. "Someone followed me yesterday. Once I got a good look at him and his license plate, I shook him off my tail. I assumed he was after me, but now, after learning who he is, I have reason to believe it is you he is after. I don't know what he wants ..."

His voice trailed off as he saw her reaction. Her concern and surprise at his opening statement was understandable, but at *I have reason to believe it is you he is after* she looked not fearful as he was braced for, but furious, those pale-blue eyes flashing with ire.

"God damn it!" She pushed away and propped her fists on her hips, look-ing at him with exasperation.

He cocked his head, confused.

"Let me guess—sixty, dark hair going gray at the edges, cut conserva-tively?" Her anger ramped up with every word. "I didn't think he'd actually come all the way over here to—"

"No."

"Huh?" That single word took the wind out of her sails. "No—what?"

Laurent looked at her very carefully. "That's not him. You are describing your ex-husband?"

It was a guess, but she nodded, her brows drawn together in consternation.

"The man who followed me is older, balding, and his name is not Martin Malone."

She snorted at that. "Oh, of course. He couldn't be bothered to come himself, the selfish bastard. Sent one of his—" His words finally penetrated. "Wait. How do you know his name? Did you actually talk to him?"

"I did not. But Matisse tracked the license plate of the car he was driving and learned some very interesting things." Laurent regarded her carefully, trying to make sense of why she wasn't frightened that some goon was likely looking for her. "When is the last time you spoke to your ex-husband? Is it true that he thinks you have some file of his?"

Stunned, Lori just stared at him for a moment. "How did you know that?" Her mind flashed back to the call that she'd let go to voicemail a few days ago. A message she'd still not listened to.

"Matisse spoke with Annie. But *chérie,* there's something going on here. How much do you know about your ex-husband's clients?"

"Not much at all. I always made it a point not to. But ..." Her mind tracked back over the last couple of weeks. Martin's pleas for her to return, to let them search her locker for that file, the calls she'd ignored.

"He thinks one of his client files got mixed up with mine, and they're desperate to find it. I don't know why, but ... it's more than a stretch to think it somehow ended up in my stuff. I've told him that, but he's been so persistent that I've stopped taking his calls. The last one ..."

She paused, locked eyes with him. Then she dug into her purse for her phone, the ringer turned to mute. *Oops.* She'd not just missed one call, she'd missed a bunch of them, and texts too. And not just from Martin; Annie had called this morning and she'd missed that, too.

"Shit." Lori scrolled through the list of messages, selected the first one, and turned it on speakerphone.

Lori, it's Martin again. Would you please give me a call? I know you hate me right now and frankly I don't blame you, but it's fucking urgent that I talk to you. This situation here has gone completely out of control. Please.

"When was that?"

"Sunday. Here's another one."

Lori, God damn it. Why the fuck can't you call me back? The missing file has turned everyone here ballistic, and you could be in danger if you don't get back here. Would you just call me?

"From when?"

She looked at the phone. "Monday." When she looked back at him, all the fear he *hadn't* seen before was in her eyes now. "What do you think he meant, that I could be in danger? Danger from what?"

"From *whom* is the more appropriate question, I think. Let's hear the rest of them."

All equally vague but increasingly desperate. The last message was from Annie, direct and to the point.

What the hell is going on with Martin? Etienne called asking about him. Call me.

"Crap." Lori gave him a guilty look. "I turned off the ringer after that first call from Martin. I guess I forgot to turn it back on." And had been mightily distracted since.

"I'm afraid ignoring him may no longer be an option," Laurent said then relayed what he'd learned from Etienne Matisse.

Joe lost sight of the couple in the crush of the market, just after he'd recognized that look on the big man's face. Somehow the guy had sensed him, and Joe had managed to duck behind the fish truck before he could be made again. When he looked back, the two were nowhere in sight.

Rather than risk exposure by shouldering through the crowd to search for them, he retreated to the lower reaches of town where cars were parked. Typical of the French, vehicles were wedged in every which way along the road that led to the heart of the village. He traversed the entire stretch of pavement, but the red Renault was not there. Was it possible that *this* was the village she was staying in and they had walked rather than driven to the market? In that case, the car would be parked at or near the place. If he could find the car, he'd find her.

He headed back the way he'd come, keeping to the fringes of the market. The village was situated on a ridge, its commercial section located in the dip of a saddle with homes climbing the rises on either side. The lace-like ironwork of the church steeple could be seen rising above everything on the top of the west knoll. The road wound up one side of the hill, where the market was located, traversed the centerline of the saddle, then exited out of the village down the other side. Following it while watching carefully for his quarry, he passed antique shops, a bakery, and a number of restaurants before finding the other side of town, where many more cars were parked along the lower road. Still no red Renault. That left the residential sections up above. With a curse, Joe walked back up the hill.

"*Vinnie Salentino?*" The name came out on a squeak. *Shit.* "But he ... he's ..." Lori felt suddenly weak in the knees.

"He's the head of a family linked closely with organized crime, according to Matisse."

"Yeah." She crossed her arms over her chest in a defensive posture. "I mean, yeah, I know who he is, but I had no idea of Martin's association with him, honestly I didn't. If I had ..." If she had, she would have hightailed it out of Philly a long time ago. But not before gutting her rotten, cheating husband. Ex-husband.

It almost broke Laurent's heart to see his brave woman look so vulnerable. It also pissed him off. That bastard of an ex had no right to get her involved in this.

"It's up to you, of course." Barely keeping the anger from his voice, Laurent paced a few steps away, then turned. "But I think you should call him and let him know we've spotted his man. Whatever his purpose here, whether it's to scare you or harm you, or somehow try to drag you onto an airplane, he could cause more trouble than it's worth to them."

She shot him a confused look. "What does that mean? How can I—"

"You *do* know that both Matisse and his wife are special agents for INTERPOL?"

As in, the international police? No, she hadn't. "So?"

"So, *chérie,* they can make things happen. Make certain people very uncomfortable."

"But ... why would they?" They hardly knew her, for Christ's sake. And they were currently babysitting a little girl while her adoptive parents enjoyed their honeymoon. The last thing Lori wanted to do was impose on people that she barely knew.

"Because there is an American here in their backyard who is acting suspiciously, with the possible intent to harm to one of their new neighbors."

Lori just stared at him. "You don't know that—"

"I don't have to, not the way he's been moving. I'm not about to take chances where your safety is concerned."

"Laurent, I can't ask you *or* them to—"

"You aren't. It's already done." Before Lori could protest, he crowded her and gently touched his fingers to her lips. "No protests. This is my country, and I am a soldier. Matisse is one, too, in his own way. We protect what we hold dear. And Lori-love, we have the law on our side." Then he kissed her soundly, quite effectively cutting off her ability to protest.

In the end, she capitulated. Partly because Laurent was as immovable on the subject as the rock wall they were leaning against, and partly because she'd known, in the small corner of her mind where she'd tried to shove Martin and his problem, that she'd get dragged into it somehow. It was a relief to have some help even as she felt guilty about it.

"I'll call Martin, but it's still too early there. Let's go home." She needed to call Annie, too, and said so. With this stupid situation heading the direction it was, and Etienne and Sabine involved, her friend would be hurt if she didn't get to toss her two cents into the ring.

"*Bonne idée.* Are you up for having them all for dinner? It will be easier to make a plan that way, with everyone together, and you'll have only to tell the story once." He squeezed her hand. "Once more. I can go get more *merguez*."

"And more wine, too," she said with a resigned sigh. She would certainly be needing it even if no one else did. "I still can't believe this is happening."

They left the churchyard by way of a well-used trail that traversed the forested slope, bypassing the town to end up on the village road below the market. From there, they continued past the parked cars to the bottom, crossed the main road that circled the base of the hill, and made their way to the small lane that would take them to Lori's farmhouse.

At the top of the village where they'd stood not ten minutes prior, Joe lifted himself to standing on top of the low stone wall that surrounded the churchyard. Surveying the countryside below, he identified plenty of properties that lay within walking distance of the village, farms mostly, and he was resigned to investigate them all. No red Renault had been parked in the residential sections of the village, but he knew in his bones that it had to be at one of these country places. He stood there taking in the view—studying the landscape not in appreciation but with a calculating eye—when something flashed below.

It was just a car on the lower road, the sun hitting the windshield at the perfect angle to flash like a mirror. But after the car passed, Joe saw something else moving down there. Two people, a dark-haired man with a shopping bag hanging off one shoulder and a blond woman with a baguette in her hand, walking single file along the road leading away from the village. *Bingo!*

He lost sight of them as they moved beneath a large tree. Watching the section of road beyond the tree, he waited for them to emerge, but they never did. Stopped in the shade to catch their breath? Unlikely, he thought, studying the terrain in the immediate vicinity. There. Off to the left. Though it was obscured by a row of trees and bushes, he could see now that there had to be another, smaller road. Leading, most likely, to the collection of farm properties spread out beyond. Joe held his position for another fifteen minutes, but the couple did not appear beyond the tree. They went somewhere, however. Of that, Joe was certain.

Twelve

After spending nearly half her life with Martin's indifferent version of emotional support, it was astonishing for Lori to find herself amidst people who seemed to truly care about her predicament. Or back among them, more like, since she and Annie had always had each other's backs. But despite their close friendship, they'd not resided in the same time zone in nearly three decades. It had been a long, long time since they'd lived cheek to jowl, all but in each other's pockets as college roommates, but Lori had always cherished those years.

Now, at what seemed like the drop of a hat, a crowd of supporters, including her dearest old friend, was gathering to sort out what the hell was going on. In typical French style, it would take place over a meal. Good thing they'd overbought on vegetables.

In deference to Etienne and Sabine, who had charge of little Ellie, it would be an early supper.

"Give me time to arrange for a babysitter," Matisse said when Laurent called him back, "and we'll be there as soon as Ellie is settled."

For the first two years of Ellie's young life, Louise had relied on Etienne, at his own insistence, for child care while she worked a part-time job at the local college. As he had been retired then, it made sense for everyone, and during that time Etienne developed a special relationship with the little mite. But since the harrowing episode last winter when Sabine had become embroiled in a dangerous situation up north and Etienne had come out of retirement to assist, coordinating child care had become a bit more challenging. It became clear to all the residents of La Ferme du Vieux Pont that occasional backup was required. Especially given his reinstatement with INTERPOL, albeit in a reduced capacity. Now was one of those times. Matisse could have brought Ellie along, but like most children her age, she tended to demand the floor when she wasn't asleep. And this was not a social call.

"I won't be long." Laurent shrugged into his leather jacket and grabbed his phone from the charger on the counter. It was such a domestic thing—his charger plugged into the socket next to hers—and the intimacy of it seized her with a sudden urge to not let him leave.

"But, you don't need to go. I can—"

Touching his fingers to her lips, he ended the protest. "I need to take the Ducati out for a blow, while the weather is good." Then he replaced his fingers with his lips and kissed her. "You can start on the ratatouille."

Which meant lots of chopping and slicing, guaranteed to keep her busy rather than second guessing and fretting.

She walked out with him and watched as he wheeled the huge motorcycle out of the shed. They'd rearranged that space to make room for it, something she had suggested when the mistral had first kicked up. A simple yet thoughtful gesture that had unexpectedly tugged at his heart; not many women understood the relationship between a man and his mechanical beast.

The Ducati was a big, black badass of a machine with a touch-me-at-your-own-risk aura. Rather like its owner. The way he stroked it with the soft rag as he cleared away bits of dust and spiderwebs only reinforced how much he treasured the thing. It was not unlike the way he stroked her, sans cloth. That thought made her shiver.

He noticed, of course, and gave her a questioning look.

"She's a beauty," Lori said in all honesty.

"*Oui, elle est.*"

Satisfied his beauty was ready, he straddled it, turned the key, and pressed the starter. The motorcycle roared to life, and Laurent spend a few moments adjusting the choke, revving the engine, and making sure all her sundry parts were functioning. With a final grin—like a boy about to go galloping out on his favorite pony—he strapped his helmet onto his head, rocked the bike off its stand, and peeled out.

Though the breeze was still brisk, it held little of the chill from earlier in the week and the day had turned out to be a fine one. The design of Lori's house, aided by the surrounding trees and hedges, meant that the kitchen door could be propped open to the fresh air without the room being pummeled by the wind. As she worked in the kitchen, humming along to French jazz radio, she could hear the birds chittering outside and the occasional car going by on the road across the field. Engrossed in the simple pleasure of culinary pursuits, she didn't hear the footsteps on the gravel outside until it was too late.

"Well, well," came a rough voice from her doorway.

Lori nearly jumped out of her skin, whirling around with her knife in hand to face the door.

"Look who I found," the man continued. "Ms. Lorilee Sheridan, in the flesh." The broad south Philly vowels rendered his identity unmistakable. And belligerently leaning his large frame against the doorway like he had every right to be there, blocking her in, his body language screamed *bully*.

Fear spiked and adrenaline surged through her veins as *Oh, shit* blinked like a neon sign in her brain. For a brief instant, Lori considered jabbering at him in French but doubted that would get her anywhere. This *goon*—the only word that came to mind—obviously knew who she was. But that didn't mean she had to know anything.

"Who are you?" Score one for Lori—her voice came out stronger than a squeak.

Joe took a step through the door, and she lost whatever cool she'd been hoping to hang on to.

"Get out!" She held her ground but brandished the knife from the fifteen feet or so of distance between them. "Don't even think of coming inside. Who are you and what do you want?"

The outburst, or perhaps it was the enormous chef's knife, startled Joe enough that he retreated a half step, but that was as far as he went. He paused, listening carefully, but no other sounds came from within, confirming his assessment, as he'd watched the house and the woman inside, that she was alone.

Then the bastard smirked. "I think you know or you wouldn't be waiving that knife around. Country folk are supposed to be friendly, aren't they?"

Advancing a few feet, knife pointed at her trespasser, Lori did her best to muster up some courage. Gripping the handle of the knife like a lifeline, she took a couple of quick breaths. *Where is Laurent??* He'd been gone more than thirty minutes.

"Country folk don't come into people's homes uninvited. If you want to talk, you can do it from out there."

The smirk was replaced with a nasty glare, like the guy knew he held all the cards. "Okay, lady, fine. Have it your way. I'll make this real clear. You need to get your stubborn ass on a plane back to Philly, and you need to do it now."

It was Lori's turn to smirk. So far the goon hadn't threatened her with anything but his attitude; no guns or knives, thank God. But she did have a knife. Not that she knew how to use it on him even if she wanted to, but right now it felt good in her hand. "Or what?" *Where did that come from?* She really didn't want to provoke this asshole, did she?

The glare got even nastier. "Or I'll drag you back myself."

That sent a shiver down her spine. She didn't doubt for one minute that he would try. But unless the guy had a private plane waiting in the wings ... that improbability boosted her shaky bravado, and she held up her knife with a little more confidence. "And how were you planning on making that happen? Shoving me onto an international flight while I'm kicking and screaming? That might raise a few eyebrows, even among the French."

Joe seemed to consider that one like a B actor in a bad film, even scratching his whisker-covered chin and rolling his eyes skyward. "Hmm, well now, let me see. If you don't cut the crap and do what you're told, I imagine I'll just have to knock you out with a solid right hook, shove some drugs down your throat, and drag you onto the plane. As far as anyone would know, I'd be bringing home my poor, drug-addicted daughter who fell in with the wrong crowd in Marseille."

Lori blanched and had to give him points for that. She had no idea if immigration would look the other way, but she wasn't interested in finding out. The whole *solid right hook* and *shove some drugs down your throat* part did not appeal in the least. Before she could answer, the roar of a powerful engine cut through the air. Her body practically sagged in relief, the sound unmistakable.

Laurent spotted the gray Renault pulled over in a field as he rounded the last shallow curve on the tiny lane leading to Lori's property, and his brain fuzzed red.

"*Putain de merde!*" The curse was drowned out even to his own ears as he revved the engine and popped the clutch, accelerating through the break in the trees onto Lori's driveway.

Joe took a step away from the door and spat a curse of his own as the black blur of a motorcycle came speeding through the hedge. Amidst an unholy racket of overstretched RPMs and a cloud of dust, it raced around the vineyard without slowing. A spray of gravel peppered the yard and pinged against the red Renault as the Ducati rounded the last sharp corner and came to an abrupt stop in front of him.

So much for dealing with the woman quietly, Joe thought. But he still had something up his sleeve.

Pale-blue eyes blazed like cold fire from beneath the visor of Laurent's helmet. Lori, who had crossed the distance of the kitchen and now stood in the doorway, knife in hand, watched in fascination as he calmly kicked up the stand of the bike and dismounted with a graceful swing of one powerful leg. Calm as you please, he flipped the buckle beneath his chin and pulled off the helmet.

"You keep turning up like a bad *sou*," Laurent said without humor, not moving from his stance beside the Ducati. He looked relaxed, bored even, but that was fiction. Helmet in hand, he was primed and ready to attack, assessing the man who stood between them. Eyes not leaving their uninvited guest, he spoke to Lori.

"Are you okay, *chérie?*" He flicked a quick glance at her and his lips quirked up in a momentary flash of amusement at the knife she pointed at the man between them. "Holding your own, I see." He could also see that behind her bravado, she was terrified. "Why don't you step back inside and let me handle this?" The words were spoken calmly, but the ice in his eyes had not thawed.

Joe had been a bully most of his life and was used to people fearing him, thus he made the mistake of underestimating an opponent who still stood ten feet away. Taking advantage of that moment of Lori's indecision to move inside, thinking the man would be distracted by her, he lunged for her, grabbing her knife hand and yanking her against him. She squawked and dropped the knife as she tried to twist away. But Joe held on to her wrist in a bruising grip and started to reach inside his jacket with his free hand.

The instant Joe grabbed for Lori, Laurent threw his helmet—thrust it like a two-handed basketball pass. It hit Joe square in the face with an audible crunch at the exact moment Lori swung her knee straight into his groin.

Joe's weapon clattered to the ground as he howled and fell back, tripping on the low stone stoop and landing in a heap against the wall beside the door. One hand cupped his crotch, and the other flew up to cradle his face as blood gushed from his nose.

Laurent was on him in a flash, lifting him by the lapels of his jacket and slamming him facedown in the gravel. Joe yelped in pain but stopped struggling when Laurent pinned him with a knee to the back and wrenched both of his wrists around, holding them in a viselike grip. It was over in an instant, with Joe cursing and bleeding all over himself.

"Let's try this again," Laurent said, pressing Joe's revolver to the base of his skull. In French he told Lori to fetch him some clothesline. "Do you have a first-aid kit?" She nodded.

Her courage having finally deserted her, she was trembling so badly that it took her a moment to get moving. Once she'd snatched up her knife and disappeared into the house, Laurent asked the question that had been foremost in his mind.

"How did you expect this to work out for you?"

"Fuck you." The words were garbled, spoken through the blood and searing pain of a broken nose. And his breathing was labored, a combined result of his nose and his aching balls.

"Charming." Laurent rolled back and sprang up, hoisting the man up with him and frog-marching him to one of the chairs at the table. He shoved his captive ass-first into it and was rewarded with a nasty glare followed by a hawking spit of blood aimed at Laurent's feet. Laurent ignored both.

"You ain't making matters any better for her, and now you got this to answer for." Joe wobbled his head then winced, bringing a shaky hand up to his crooked nose. He hissed in a breath when his fingers came into contact with it. "Fucking bastard."

"You're lucky all I broke was your nose." Laurent ignored both the insult and the threat as he casually checked out the handgun. *Baby Glock with a ten-round magazine,* his brain cataloged. *Weapon of choice for private security because its diminutive size is easily concealed.* As he ejected the magazine and pocketed it, making sure the chamber was empty, he wondered how the bastard had managed to get it into the country.

But despite his laissez-faire attitude, he had a bad feeling about this. With mafia goons involved, there may not be an easy way out of this mess for Lori, no matter that she was completely innocent. And that, he just couldn't allow to happen. He'd spent his entire career helping innocents who, through no fault of their own, found themselves in the crossfire. He may be retired, but he wasn't out of the game.

Lori came out with an unopened package of clothesline, a bowl of water, towels, and a first-aid kit but stopped short when she saw them. Her gaze went to the gun as Laurent tucked it into the back of his jeans, then darted to his face. Blank and icy as she'd ever seen him, his look gave nothing away. Skirting around the table, she set the supplies down on the stone surface behind him and backed away a couple of steps.

Within minutes, Joe's hands were tied behind him, the sturdy line looping under the chair to secure his feet to its legs, and Laurent had the old man's chin in hand, prodding at that bloody nose.

"Fuck!" Joe cried, trying to twist away, but Laurent just gripped his chin tighter.

"Hold still, asshole, if you want me to reset it."

Whimpering like a baby, Joe stilled, then cried out again as Laurent yanked on his large beak and repositioned it.

Lori winced from her vantage point but handed over a wet towel, then exchanged the bloodied thing for gauze and tape when Laurent motioned for it. She watched in fascination at the swift expertise with which he dealt with the injury, but she couldn't find any emotion about the operation other than anger. Anger at Martin, anger at this arrogant old man, and perhaps a dose of anger at herself, too.

"Now what?" Lori voiced the question for Joe's benefit, knowing full well that the international police were expected any minute. As guests, but this fuckhead didn't need to know that. "We could turn him over to the *gendarmes,* but where does that leave me? I don't guess these people are going to back down just because the first person sent to find me gets arrested."

Laurent regarded the man thoughtfully. "No, probably not. But perhaps we can use him as a bargaining chip. I have a few friends that could help out." He winked at her, pleased to know they were on the same wavelength, then slanted a feral grin at Joe. "In a way that would avoid much of the red tape."

For the first time since they'd set eyes on Joe, his confidence appeared to falter.

Lori couldn't help but marvel at Laurent's ability to dissemble as he made a show of calling his *friends,* speaking in French so Joe had no idea what was being said. But she worried, too, about how deeply he was embedding himself into her stupid situation. He was supposed to be a sexy diversion, not a savior. She couldn't very well protest within earshot of their prisoner, however. As soon as Laurent finished his call, Joe's cell phone rang, pulling her from her downward spiraling thoughts.

"Let's see who's calling." Laurent snagged the phone from Joe's coat pocket and looked at the screen, then held it for her to see the caller ID.

Vinnie.

"Good to know he's paying attention," Laurent said as he let the phone ring through to voicemail.

Thirteen

If Uncle Joe's composure had slipped a fraction at the mention of Laurent's friends that could help without the red tape, it deserted him altogether when he got an eyeful of Matisse. Joe had been around toughs, had held his own with large, intimidating men his entire life, but he'd never seen anyone as scary looking as this one. He actually felt sorry for the SOB who'd given him that scar, because Joe was certain that man no longer drew breath. He'd assumed the one with the tattoo was military, but now he revised his thinking to *mercenary,* a far more problematic conclusion. And by the hard intelligence in the enormous man's piercing black eyes, not to mention the stunningly beautiful woman who accompanied him, *boss* was the most likely guess. *Well, hell.* Vinnie could not possibly have any idea who his lawyer's wife was connected to.

Matisse took one look at Joe and shook his head in disgust. He spoke in English to make sure the American thug understood his initial reaction. "He reminds me of Bernard. All puffed up arrogance at his perceived consequence. Untie him, Laurent. He is no threat." It was the worst of insults, no matter how accurate. "Does your employer know of your immediate circumstance?"

Joe could only stare at the man. He spoke English like an Oxford scholar, unlike any crime boss he'd ever known, but Joe knew less than nothing beyond the Italian family customs. "No, er, no, sir." Deciding that any show of disrespect would be a mistake, he glanced at Laurent. "He called but ... I couldn't take it."

"I see. Enlighten me as to your mission here, if you please. Is my understanding correct, that it was your intention to forcibly escort Ms. Sheridan back to America? How were you to do that, exactly, and to what purpose?"

The perfectly enunciated words and proper grammar from this giant brute—a man who could crush his larynx with his bare hands without breaking a sweat—was more intimidating to Uncle Joe than a collection of guns and knives. And the fact that the beautiful woman stood by his side so serenely, looking at Joe like he was lower than dog shit on her designer shoe, well, it was all beyond him. He ventured a glance at the man whose name he'd learned was Laurent and found him smirking, his thoughts clear. *A little over your head now, old man?*

With his choices narrowed down to one, Uncle Joe explained the problem, wheezing the words through his damaged nasal passages yet leaving out the precise contents of the flash drive. The oversight did not go unnoticed, but Matisse didn't press the issue. The contents were sensitive, of that there was no doubt, or else they wouldn't go to such lengths to find the thing, but the actual information contained on the device was less relevant to the immediate problem of ensuring Lori's safety than the location of the object itself.

"We have no intention of hurting the lady," Joe said, "but we need to search her storage unit."

That last comment had Matisse lifting one black eyebrow, his disbelief clear.

At the beginning of his little speech, Sabine and Lori had disappeared inside the house together, giving the further impression to Joe that Vinnie had badly underestimated this woman's connections. These weren't just friends of tattoo man; they were hers as well. *Shit.*

Doing more listening than talking, as was his habit, Matisse began to realize something. A glance at the former special ops colonel, who had remained silent since Matisse's arrival, told him that his friend may be thinking the same thing. Although if Matisse read him correctly, Laurent was angry, and getting angrier by the minute.

"A word," Matisse said to Laurent in English, moving a few steps away before switching to French. Their guest could hear but had no understanding of their conversation, increasing his anxiety. The effect was intentional.

"He thinks we're the French mafia," Matisse did his best to keep the humor from his voice. He'd walked into the situation with no intention of misrepresenting himself, but being a bit out of practice with barging in and flashing credentials—in truth he'd never been *in* practice—the unexpected consequence in this case could prove very interesting.

"I came to the same realization, *boss*." Neither laughed, but they shared a look of mirth. "I have no idea what constraints you work under in these circumstances, but I'm thinking if we can play this out, it may be the only way to extract Lori with her future intact."

Matisse eyed his friend thoughtfully. "You're worried about her."

"It's ripping a hole in my gut. Unless we come up with something very creative and very compelling, hers is a no-win situation—through absolutely no fault of her own but 100 percent because of her fuckwad of an ex. If I didn't think she'd hate me for taking away her own privilege, I'd tear out his entrails with my bare hands."

"What's your status?"

"Civilian, with a six-month window for recall in the event of a national emergency."

"Can you take other employment during that period of time? How long has it been?"

"Three months, and yes, I'm free to do whatever I want, subject to that proviso. What are you thinking?"

"I'm thinking that effective immediately, you will be granted temporary special agent status under my command. I can process your paperwork tonight. That is, if you are willing." Matisse speared him with a look that brooked no argument yet held a hint of amusement. "Take careful note of the *under my command* part of this before you answer."

A weaker man might have been intimidated, or worse, offended, but Laurent was neither. Just because he wanted to rip these American asshats a new one didn't mean he would do so without proper authorization. Military disciple was too ingrained in him.

"Do it" was the only logical response.

"How did you find this place?" Sabine admired Lori's spacious kitchen from her vantage point on a stool at the old butcher block. Country-style cupboards were painted periwinkle blue beneath a long L-shaped counter that took up most of two sides of the room, leaving the stone walls above the counters exposed but for a shelf that held the microwave and a framed poster of culinary herbs. An antique hutch filled with glasses and dishes stood against the opposite wall. The rough-hewn plank floor matched the wood beams in the ceiling and the thick timber lintels above the windows and doors, creating an airy, appealing room.

"It's great, isn't it?" Lori had fallen in love with the house the moment she'd laid eyes on it. "An old friend from London owns it. Nicholas used to take his holidays down here, but he was transferred to Hong Kong a few years ago and turned it into a vacation rental. When I mentioned to him that I was looking for a long-term lease in this area, he offered it to me at a price that was hard to ignore."

The kettle whistled. Lori flipped it off then set it on the block beside the tea things she'd already arranged. Over her steaming cup, she regarded her new friend. Sabine was twenty years younger, but Lori had liked her immediately when they'd met a week prior to the wedding. Now remorse pounded through her veins. "I'm really sorry to drag you into this mess."

Sabine waved off the concern with a graceful flick of her hand. "*Il n'y a pas de problème.* Etienne would have it no other way." She took a sip from her cup. "Is it true that your ex-husband is working for the Philadelphia mafia?"

"God, I can't believe it myself." Lori shook her head. "Wouldn't still, if the evidence wasn't bleeding outside my door. He's a corporate lawyer not a litigator. He does transactions, contracts, that sort of thing. In all honesty, I never paid much attention to who his clients were. We never, either of us, discussed specifics, unless we found ourselves working on opposite sides of the same situation." She shrugged. "In that case, one of us bowed out."

"And they think you have a file?"

A nod. "Which is stupid, and I'm going to kill Martin for making them think I do. He and I shared an office in our townhouse, but it was a large room with a double desk and separate file cabinets. We were always careful to keep our stuff separate because of confidentiality."

"How long have you been divorced?" At Lori's pained look, Sabine back-pedaled. "Oh, *merde*, forgive me. That is none of my business."

"No, don't worry about it. It'll be a year in June. He probably did us both a favor, and honestly, I should have seen it coming." She gave the short version of Martin's defection. "But for whatever reason, guilt probably, he was generous with the divorce settlement. We always kept our financial assets separate, so the only significant asset we owned together was the house and its contents. He basically handed it all over to me, and I wasn't too upset to refuse it." She made a show of brushing off her hands. "Clean, simple, done, and done."

"You think he left whatever this file is in the office and it got accidentally mixed up with yours?" Sabine frowned, the analyst in her not liking the odds. "That doesn't make sense, given what you said of the layout of that room."

"I know, right? That's just it. How could a flash drive from his file cabinets end up in one of my boxes? He packed his stuff up first."

"What happened to those cabinets?"

Philadelphia

Martin Malone strode the wide sidewalk between his downtown office and the coffee shop on the corner, to-go cup in hand. The pleasant morning temperature barely registered, his mind churning with the dozens of projects he had going. It was early for lunch, but the sidewalks bustled with pedestrians in suits and ties—professionals like himself, haring off to meetings or taking a late-morning break to grab a cup of joe. The sharp trill of his ringtone cut into his thoughts, and he absently pulled the phone from his pocket. When he saw who it was, he stopped in his tracks, oblivious to the near collision he caused when the person behind him had to jump to the side to avoid knocking into him.

"Lori!" he practically shouted. "For God's sake, where the fuck have you been?"

"Minding my own business on another continent, but you just can't seem to leave me alone, can you?"

Jesus Christ. The woman could drive him absolutely bat-shit crazy. "Listen, I've tried to reach you like a dozen times in the last few days—"

"I know. And now I know why. Your *friend* showed up at my house a little while ago."

"Oh, God. Listen—"

"No, *you* listen. That asshole tried to pull a gun on me, but *my* friends persuaded him to leave."

"Shit! Wait—he *tried* to pull a gun? What the hell happened?" *I'm gonna kill that son of a bitch.*

"Yeah, he tried. He got a kick in the balls and a broken nose for the effort."

"*What?*"

Lori's sigh came through loud and clear. "Look, it doesn't matter. I called to tell you that you win. I'll catch a flight back, go through my boxes, and prove that you're wrong. After you and your *client* apologize to me, you will never see me again."

"Lori—"

"Don't *Lori* me. I cannot fucking believe you put me in the middle of this. The only reason this asshole tried to accost me is because *you told them* I had that God damned thing, when you know damn good and well that I don't. There is nothing you can say to me that will make one fucking bit of difference. Give me your credit card number."

Martin was so stunned by all the four-letter words in that little speech—the Lori he knew rarely cursed—that it took him a moment to process that last comment. "My what?"

She laughed, but there was no humor in it. "Surely you didn't think I'd pay my own way to come back and do this for you? You'd better have plenty of room left on your limit because I'm not flying coach."

Ménerbes

Laurent's emotions waffled between pride in the way his lady shoved it up Malone's ass and fury that she was giving him what he wanted. Unfortunately, he couldn't see any other way to finish this. *If* her capitulation finished it, which, given who was ultimately pulling the strings, was not a foregone conclusion. Perhaps the illusion that Lori had mob protection of her own would be sufficient incentive for them to forget about her afterward. One thing was sure, that fuckwad would be paying for *two* round-trip first class tickets because there was no way in hell he was going to let her go alone.

Joe Carlucci had been dismissed, tossed to the curb like the trash he was. But not before Matisse had explained that Ms. Sheridan's safety was a point of personal concern—before, during, and *after* she was finished doing this favor for Salentino. He enunciated this directive in his freaky Oxford-perfect English then suggested Joe communicate directly with his own boss to avoid any misunderstanding. Satisfied the message would be conveyed, he nodded to Laurent, who escorted the man off the property to where the gray Renault rental had been left and told him, in far less polite words than Matisse had used, to get lost.

Once the bully's advantage had been taken away, he seemed more pathetic than dangerous. Whether he chose to hover in the neighborhood or return to wherever he'd been staying, they didn't care. Matisse was fairly certain he wouldn't go away permanently, but neither did he think the man would be stupid enough to attempt anything with Lori again. However, the fact that Lori and Laurent had both made an enemy this day was an undeniable truth they would be foolish to ignore.

The mood lightened considerably with the absence of the American thug. Etienne and Sabine joined in with dinner prep, finishing the slicing, searing, and arranging of the ratatouille ingredients. It was now sizzling away in a large casserole dish in the oven, filling the kitchen with the wonderful fragrance of roasted vegetables and herbs. Lori was a tiny bit intimidated by the mountain of a man in her house, but she found much about him that she liked. In addition to being a crack hand with a chef's knife, he was playful in a dry sort of way. He was also completely smitten with his beautiful wife.

Laurent watched over Lori's shoulder as she sat at the butcher block looking at flight options on her laptop. The most convenient airport for them was

Marseille, but the choices for direct flights from there to Philadelphia were limited.

"Crap," she said. "There's really no good option that doesn't either leave at the crack of dawn or route me all over the place."

"Make sure there are two seats available on whatever flights you pick."

Lori looked up at him in surprise. "Why?"

"Because you are not going alone."

"He's right," Sabine said, glancing at her husband then addressing Lori directly. "Now that it's a cross-border issue, we've opened an INTERPOL case file. We will use official resources to protect you and our quasi-diplomatic status to get in and out of the US without fuss."

Lori was stunned. "You can't be serious." She looked back and forth between the couple, so incongruous that she still wasn't used to seeing them together. *Beauty and the beast,* she'd thought the first time she'd met them, but she couldn't deny the deep bond that sparkled between them. Even now, casually leaning against her counter, their connection was obvious. "You want to go with me, too? Why?"

Matisse answered. "Two reasons. First, it's our job." He tilted his chin at Laurent. "The minute Laurent called, it became our case."

Before Lori could voice a protest, he continued.

"The second reason is that you are a friend *un ami de la famille.* Even if I wanted to let you fend for yourself, *which I do not,* Annie Macallister would never let me hear the end of it if I didn't do everything in my power to help."

As if mentioning the name had conjured the woman, a new car emerged between the hedgerows and rounded the track toward the house. Matisse smiled. "I have no doubt she will explain this to you herself."

A moment later the Macallisters stepped into the kitchen, Kaden toting an insulated wine bag. "Sorry we're late," he said, first kissing Lori in greeting, then Sabine. He nodded to Matisse and handed the bag to Laurent.

"You're not." Lori hugged her friend and whispered a heartfelt "Thank you for coming" into her ear.

"Wait till you hear," Annie said with a grin before she stepped back.

"Hear what?" But Annie was already greeting the others, who carried on as if this was just a social gathering and dealing with threats from mobsters was no big deal.

"This will do nicely," Laurent said, distracting Lori from Annie's cryptic comment as he pulled a chilled bottle of rosé from Kaden's bag and held it up with a grin. He set the bottle on the counter then peered back into the bag with the enthusiasm of a kid at Christmas.

"That's exactly what we need," Sabine said, snagging the bottle and reaching for the corkscrew. Lori couldn't agree more, and turned to fetch the glasses. She opened her mouth to ask her question again when her phone rang.

Philadelphia

"Your former wife has powerful friends." Vinnie Salentino turned from where he'd been staring out the window to look at the man entering his office. A man who looked every inch the successful corporate lawyer, down to the dark circles under his eyes. Quality tailoring covered a fit frame—his lawyer kept himself in shape—and all in all, he was nice looking for a man approaching his sixtieth year. And until very recently, someone Vinnie trusted. Wanted to trust, still.

Exhausted with worry, Martin looked at his client with undisguised confusion. He'd dreaded this audience, dreaded hearing what had happened when Uncle Joe confronted Lori, because she had somehow bested the asshole and that would make no one happy. Which was another problem in itself, but this ... he forced his brain to focus on the implied question. "She has friends in France, yeah. Good friends. I guess you could call Macallister powerful. He's a savvy investor, and rich as Croesus, but he's not involved in politics." He frowned. "At least not that I'm aware of, but—"

"Not those kinds of friends." Vinnie made a slashing motion with his hand. Forsaking the stiff suits of his father's generation unless absolutely necessary, Vinnie took a more casual approach to his attire. Most days, like today, he looked like he'd just stepped off the golf course. But his casual dress made him no less intimidating. He wore his bulk well, even without benefit of height, and no would dare call him fat. And if anyone ever mistook him for soft, it was a mistake that was not repeated.

But Martin had not achieved the sort of relationship he enjoyed with the Salentino heir without having a good measure of tenacity, if not outright toughness, himself. His strengths were not so much physical but intellectual. He had nothing whatsoever to do with Vinnie's dirty work, a condition he scrupulously held to and Vinnie respected. Rather, he handled the legal work for all the legitimate businesses.

Businesses that had flourished over the years since Roberto Salentino had been incarcerated and the empire had fallen to Vinnie.

With considerable skill and creativity, Martin had helped Vinnie reposition them, rework their contractual arrangements both internal and external, and generally reorganize their operations. He'd proved his value over and over, and he didn't have to pretend to look the other way with less-than-legitimate dealings because he knew nothing about them. Or at least, he had no firsthand knowledge of them.

Which was why Vinnie had entrusted him with the blasted flash drive in the first place.

"Then I don't follow you." Not having been invited to sit, Martin remained standing, fists resting on his hips. "Joe obviously fucked up, but she told me this morning that she'd come back anyway. So what happened?"

"Something out of the *French Connection* happened."

"What? What are you saying?"

"What I'm saying is that your ex-wife, in addition to having impressive self-defense moves of her own"—this was said with a glimmer of amusement—"is keeping company with some sort of badass soldier."

Vinnie leveled a glare at his lawyer. "And not too long after Joe was … *persuaded* to, ah, delay his mission, this guy apparently called in reinforcements, and the whole operation turned into a clusterfuck of epic proportions."

Not one bit of which made any sense at all, and Martin had to clamp his teeth together to keep from saying it. The self-defense moves he understood from Lori's earlier comment, but—*Soldier? What the fuck?* A spike of jealousy pierced his chest. He had no right to feel it, but that didn't stop the burning pain.

"I have no idea who these guys are. The only friends I know of there are the Macallisters." Certainly no badass soldier. "He's a wealthy investor and she's a former tax accountant, like Lori. But Lori lived in France for a couple of years, a long time ago, before I met her. And she continued working with people over there, too, after she came home."

Vinnie's glare didn't soften.

"For Christ's sake, she's a tax accountant, Vinnie. Squeaky clean. And the fact that she has friends that can stand by her when Uncle Joe tried to intimidate her? Well, good for her. But besides that, what you're telling me just doesn't make sense, so with all due respect, have you considered the possibility that Joe is mistaken?"

Martin was one of the very few people who had the nerve to argue with Vinnie Salentino, a fact that could be read plainly in the other man's irritated expression. But Martin's own stupidity had put Lori in danger, and it was time he manned up and defended her. Trying to diffuse this crazy situation seemed the best way to do that.

"Who her friends are is irrelevant as long as she gives us access to her locker. She didn't take the flash drive, Vinnie, she didn't even know it existed. I packed up my stuff, she packed up hers, and we went our separate ways. If it accidentally ended up in her stuff, we'll find it. If it didn't, it's not because of anything she did. And if her friends are really who you think they are, taking it any further than that serves no purpose."

He took a deep breath, knowing he was about to put himself in a very uncomfortable position. "Take it out on me for being careless if you must, but don't hold her responsible."

Philadelphia's reputed mob boss regarded his lawyer for long moments. The lawyer had balls—he'd give him that. It was one of the reasons why Vinnie liked him and trusted him, besides the fact that he was smart with the business end of things. Not so smart in his personal life, however. He thought of the Barbie doll that Marty had married a few months back. Interesting, that he'd take such a risk defending his former wife when he had that piece at home. Did the lingering affection go both ways?

After a lifetime reading people, Vinnie knew a lying face when he saw it. The man standing in front of him was worried, shocked even, but was telling the truth as he knew it.

"Then consider yourself collateral. You can tell her, for me, if she doesn't get back here *right fucking now* so we can search her storage locker, I'll slit your throat."

Stifling the urge to bring his hand to his throat, Martin managed to nod. "She's already agreed to come back." Meeting his client's gaze, he shook his head in disgust. "I'll call her again. *If* she takes my call, I'll make sure she understands how urgent it is. But you need to know, she's not what you'd call *happy* with me about now, and I doubt your threat will sway her much."

Fourteen

Vinnie watched his lawyer go pale at his pronouncement, but to his credit, Martin remained standing, parlayed even, to defend his wife. Ex-wife. After dismissing him, Vinnie turned back to the view out the window.

The City of Brotherly Love. The steel-and-glass buildings of its modern downtown sparkled in the sun. It may have been a collaborative society when the Founding Fathers first wrote down the principles by which they hoped the citizens of their new country would abide, but Vinnie knew better. Philadelphia had been a cesspool of graft and political corruption for many decades. And it was a situation that Vinnie abhorred with every cell in his body.

The fact that a man like Martin Malone feared him, after they'd worked side-by-side for more than five years now, was testament to how well he'd hidden his true nature. His father was a monster—there was no arguing with that fact—and if Vinnie could figure out a way to have him executed in his prison cell without fallout to himself, he'd do it in a heartbeat. And Roberto's son by his second wife carried the same monster genes as their sire. The idea of Claudio succeeding in his bid to take over Philly was so horrible to contemplate that Vinnie almost shivered at the idea.

That he, Vinnie, had been instrumental in putting the old man away was a dangerous fact that only one man still living was aware of. And that man had seriously erred in what should have been a simple assignment, possibly making enemies neither of them needed right now.

Ménerbes

Lori grimaced at the caller's name displayed on her phone.

"Hello, Martin." She accepted a wineglass from Sabine with a nod and took a sip as she listened to him relay Vinnie Salentino's ultimatum.

"You can't be serious," she all but snorted, plunking the glass down to fist her hand on her hip. "You must have left out a few details about our relationship if he thinks that's an effective threat."

Across the Atlantic, Martin chose to sidestep that comment. Whether she meant the surprise divorce or the thug on her doorstep wasn't clear and didn't matter.

"Lori, please. Work with me. Charter a fucking private jet, if that's what it takes. Can you please just get back here pronto? It'll take a day, two at most. Then you can go back to your soldier boy."

No response.

"Lori? Are you there?"

No, she wasn't. She'd disconnected the call.

On a long, suffering sigh, he redialed.

"Childish insults won't help your case, Martin. I told you I'd come back. I'm working on it now."

"Listen, I'm sorry. That was uncalled for. I just … Christ. I know this entire fucking mess is my fault, but I really need your help."

Lori glanced around at her friends after the second call ended. From the suppressed grins on their faces, they'd all heard both sides of the conversation. Okay, maybe hanging up on the jerk had been a tiny bit childish on *her* part, but whatever. It felt good, and she didn't regret it. She looked at Annie, who broke out laughing and came over to give her a hug.

"I've missed you so much." Then Annie glanced at her husband and grinned. "And I guess that clears up the whole private-jet issue."

Intellectually, Lori had always known that her friend's husband was wicked powerful, but what he managed to pull off for her was, in a word, impressive.

"In the spirit of adventure," he said, but typical of Kaden's style, he'd called in a favor from the CEO of one of his companies and secured the corporate jet for the jaunt to Philadelphia.

Now, around the long rustic table in the vaulted stone dining room of her farmhouse, amidst her closest old and new friends, enjoying the delicious meal they had all helped prepare, the practical reality of her situation sunk in.

"We can leave as early as tomorrow morning," Kaden said with a look to Matisse. "Does that give you enough time?"

"Tomorrow?" Lori struggled to process it all, at the same time trying to wrap her brain around what the cost of a transatlantic trip on a private aircraft would be and how she'd ever pay them back.

Then she remembered … "Martin will be footing the bill on this, and don't you dare let him off the hook."

"I wouldn't dream of it," Kaden said with a wink.

Then his previous words sunk in … "What a minute," Lori said. "We?"

"Yep," Annie said with a grin. "We're going with you, too."

"Oh, for God's sake, Annie. Don't be ridiculous." Although Lori welcomed the idea, it was ludicrous in the extreme.

"The more people with you, the less exposed you'll be. Don't even think about arguing this one—you know I'm right." She nodded at the hulking men attending to every word. "It was Kaden's idea, and Etienne agreed."

"But—"

"No buts. Look around you—we'll be a freakin' force of nature. You can talk all you want, and you can bang your thick skull against these stone walls till it's bloody, but that won't change anything."

Etienne didn't bother to confirm Annie's statement—there was no need, since it was nonnegotiable—but presented Lori with his opinion on the relevant question. "I propose we wait until Saturday. Alex and Louise get in late tomorrow night, and from a purely selfish standpoint, I would prefer that Ellie not have to spend a night without one of us."

All for giving herself a little breathing room, Lori nodded in agreement.

"That will also give us two advantages." He glanced at Laurent then back to Lori. "First, this small delay will give the impression that you are acquiescing to a *request,* not giving in to a demand."

Lori was really beginning to like this big guy. She skidded her eyes over to Laurent, who nodded his agreement but kept silent because Etienne wasn't finished.

"Second, it will give us some time to complete our dossier."

"Dossier?" Lori's question came out on a squeak.

"Standard procedure," Sabine said with a wave of her elegant hand. Like pulling up dirt on a powerful mob boss was an everyday occurrence. And maybe for her it was—what did Lori know about how the international police operated?

"We prefer to go into a situation with as much information as possible," Etienne clarified. "But we have another advantage as well, regardless of timing." His harsh visage didn't change but his eyes sparkled with amusement. "I believe that your *visitor* jumped to a conclusion about us, and I opted not to clarify."

"You mean you didn't tell him you're, um …"

Etienne gave her a slow shake of his head. "In truth, we arrived in no official capacity." His chin poked briefly toward Laurent. "Just friends coming over for dinner. What he chose to see was of his own making."

"I'm not sure I follow." Lori looked from Etienne to Laurent. Both wore boyish smirks, like they'd just put a toad in someone's bed with no one the wiser. "Who does he think you are, if not—"

"Don't worry," Sabine cut in, giving her husband a light smack on his beefy biceps with a roll of her beautiful sapphire eyes. "Etienne won't lie to them. In fact, as your escorts, we will notify our counterparts in Philadelphia of our pending arrival, and of our purpose on their turf. I wouldn't be surprised if your ex-husband's client has sources in immigration. Whether he thinks to use them or not …" Her shoulders lifted in a perfect Gallic who-the-fuck-cares shrug. "Our quasi-diplomatic status will simplify our group arrival in your country. But we have no obligation to identify ourselves beyond that."

Lori wondered what that meant—it wasn't difficult to pass through immigration in the US as long as one had a valid passport—but she held her question. This whole situation had taken on a life of its own. One minute Martin was whining about finding something in her file boxes; the next some mob thug was threatening her on her own doorstep. Now she was surrounded by French nationals chomping at the bit to protect her. It was all a little too much.

She and Annie cleared the table and cleaned up the kitchen while the others talked strategy, timing, resources, etc. Having learned that Etienne Matisse was not just an ordinary INTERPOL agent but an extraordinarily highly ranked one, his wife holding her own special status as well, Lori had given in. The truth was that she was frightened to be involved in this ridiculous situation and welcomed their help. She didn't know much about Vinnie Salentino, but what little she *did* know ... the thought of being on his radar made her break out into a cold sweat.

Laurent's self-imposed involvement was something else entirely. She hated that he was seeing her in such a vulnerable position. Her inner strength and independence were integral to her self-esteem, and both were being dealt a serious blow here. How could he possibly respect her after getting a glimpse at the idiot she'd been married to for twenty years? But it hadn't always been this way ... she squeezed her eyes shut then mentally shoved the encroaching regret back out of her brain. This was not her fault.

"Don't worry about this any more than you already have."

Lori jerked her head up and met Annie's concerned gaze. *Shit.* She looked at the mangled dishtowel in her hands. With a wobbly smile, she shook it out and draped it over the edge of the sink. "Kind of hard not to."

"Seriously, Lori. You'll get through this. Unless they come out with guns blazing—and that's just not going to happen—you've got two of the toughest, most seasoned guys on the planet at your back. Kaden and I are just along for the ride, true, but we'll have fun. Once you sift through your stuff under their eyeballs, there's nothing they can do to you. You can tell Martin to shove it, and we'll all go shopping."

At the earnest look on her friend's face, Lori took a deep breath and let it out with a small chuckle. "Okay." What else could she say?

Once plans had been discussed, evaluated, modified, and agreed upon to everyone's satisfaction, the party broke up.

Matisse, the most enigmatic man Lori had ever met, behaved as if his extraordinary pledge of support were just an ordinary thing. Rising from the table, he turned and offered a hand to his wife. Pulling her to her feet, he bussed her cheek, a gesture that was so sweet it made Lori want to weep.

"Get some sleep." There may have been a hint of a smile on Etienne's countenance with those words. "And don't worry. We'll have this well in hand by the time we board that plane."

Hugs and kisses from Annie and Kaden, then suddenly their guests were gone, leaving Lori alone in her house with a badass retired special ops colonel. Whose motives she still wasn't entirely sure of.

"Laurent, it's very sweet of you," she said after everyone left, "and I appreciate your concern, I really do, but I can't ask you to get involved in this mess."

"Sweet?" That was the second time she'd called him that, but despite her gross misread of his character, there was no way she was going back to Philadelphia without him. Rather than examine the visceral protectiveness that pulsed in his veins when it came to her, he pushed for logic.

"I'm the furthest thing from sweet there is, *chérie*, but I'm not stupid, either. And for the record, you aren't asking. I'm going, period."

That stubborn chin lifted, and he wanted to reach out and tilt it a bit more so he could kiss her frowning lips. "Do you trust me?"

She didn't hesitate, but her blond brows crossed in consternation. "You know I do."

"Thank you." Unable to resist, he leaned in and kissed her with a soft slide of his lips against hers. "Because you cannot trust anyone involved there, not your ex-husband and certainly not his *client*." The last word was spoken on a sneer.

"But, Laurent …" Her eyes pleaded with him to understand.

His left eyebrow arched, challenging her to keep arguing.

"It could be dangerous. If something goes wrong, if you got hurt, I couldn't forgive myself."

Mon Dieu, she's priceless. "I'm a soldier, sweetheart. I think I can handle dangerous."

"But that's my point exactly!" She all but stomped her foot. "You aren't— not anymore! After surviving a lifetime in war zones the last thing you should do is put yourself in the way of danger for some cowardly prick."

He reached for her, pulled her close, and wrapped his arms around her so she couldn't push away. "I'm not doing anything for some cowardly prick."

The gentleness in his voice made the meaning of his words clear. "I'm going, and that's final." He kissed her again. "Now are you going to stop arguing, or are you going to force me to make you stop." Another kiss, this one deeper.

Apt

Uncle Joe stood in front of the bathroom mirror and gingerly poked at the swath of gauze taped to his nose. It hurt like a son of a bitch, but the half bottle of Cognac he'd already downed was beginning to dull the pain. His trampled pride, however … the booze only intensified that particular hurt, coalescing into a simmering rage. *That fucking soldier will pay, so help me.* After another sloppy swig from the bottle, he wiped his mouth with the back of his cuff and turned away from his reflection.

His cell phone lay on the table in front of the television like a beacon. Beside it was a crumpled scrap of paper that held the license plate number of that black Ducati.

How much was revenge worth? The information he wanted would not come cheap, and there was no guarantee it would do him any good. He picked up the phone and flopped down on the bed, wincing when the motion jarred his nose. *Fuck!* Weaving the phone through his fingers like a playing card, he visualized making the call, but his hand-eye coordination was shot to hell and the thing squirted out of his hand. His intoxicated brain registered the thunk as it skidded off the bed and hit the floor while his other hand brought the bottle up to his lips.

"Fuck it," he said to the empty room and scooted his ass forward on the bed. Leaning over the edge he grabbed up the phone, listing to the side as blood rushed to his head. And that made his nose throb even more. Before he could talk himself out of it, he made the call.

Philadelphia

It wasn't until Friday morning that the call Martin had been waiting for came through.

"Tomorrow," Lori told him. "The plane will arrive sometime in the late afternoon."

"Flight number?" Martin reached for a notepad, but her words stayed his hand.

"There isn't one. It's a private jet. Which you are paying for, by the way. And before you ask, I have no idea how much. Kaden borrowed the plane from one of his companies, so you're probably getting a good deal."

Powerful friends, indeed. "Okay." There was an awkward pause while he waited for her to say more, but she didn't.

"I'll, um, I'll pick you up. We can go straight to your locker—"

"No."

"Lori, for Christ's sake, can you at least *try* to be reasonable? I'm sorry this is happening, but the sooner we can search there—"

"I meant, *no,* you do not need to pick us up, and for the record, I think I'm being extremely *reasonable,* given the circumstances. But we don't need a ride from you because there's already a car arranged."

Martin frowned. "Who's *we?*"

"You don't really think I would risk coming back into this mess of yours all by myself, do you? After having a gun waved in my face?" Not precisely the truth, but close enough, and even though she would have done exactly that—come back alone—if her friends hadn't insisted, Lori wasn't about to let Martin off the hook for any guilt he might be feeling.

"Who exactly is coming with you?" More unwelcome jealousy boiled up in his belly.

"You'll meet them. I'll text you from the air once I have a better idea of our arrival time."

"What about Joe?"

An unladylike snort came over the line. "What about him?"

"Is he coming with you?"

"Are you serious? I have no idea where that creep slunk off to. He can find his own way home. Or not. See you tomorrow."

Martin wanted to ask more questions, but she disconnected the call before he could voice any of them. *Shit.* At least she was coming and they'd get past this nightmare. He just hoped to holy God that flash drive was in one of her boxes.

Apt

It was Friday afternoon before Joe got the information he'd asked for, and not without a reminder of its price tag.

"I'll be in touch," his contact sneered. "You'll get your chance to pay up sooner rather than later if this thing I got in the works pans out."

Just fucking great, Joe thought on an inward groan, but said only, "I'm good for it." Whatever *it* is.

His 10:00 p.m. flight home was still eight hours away. GPS indicated the address he'd been given was an hour and a half away by car, and the airport was another hour-thirty from there. Not trusting the French, he planned to arrive at the airport a full two hours prior to his flight. Doing the math, and allowing for traffic, he figured he had at least a couple of hours' window to investigate his findings.

Already checked out, he'd been sitting on his backside at the local Starbucks waiting for that phone call. Now he pitched his empty cup into the trash and headed for his car.

Fifteen

Corporate jet, in Lori's mind, meant a sleek Learjet that filthy-rich celebrities like Tiger Woods and Roger Federer used. It never occurred to her that she'd be returning to Philadelphia on an enormous Airbus something or other, kitted out with lounge areas, conference rooms, dining rooms, and bedrooms on two levels! She doubted Air Force One could equal it in luxury. Too bad they couldn't just circumvent the globe for the next couple of days and enjoy it.

But despite the comfort, the upbeat attitude of everyone aboard, and the ease with which the whole operation appeared to come together, Lori suffered serious anxiety.

"Annie." Once they'd reached cruising altitude and the seat belt signs blinked off, Lori pulled her friend into a corner of the main lounge. "This is unreal," she said with a wave of her hand. "I don't even know how to thank you and Kaden for your help, but I'll be honest with you, even with all this manpower, I'm a little scared."

"Me too," Annie admitted. "I can't believe this is happening. I can't believe Martin is doing this to you."

"God, me neither. But I'm really glad you're here with me." After a pause, she said, "But, Annie, you can't be involved once we get there."

Her friend just shook her head. "There's no way I'm letting you do this by yourself."

"I won't be alone." As she said it, Lori's eyes drifted across the cabin, where Etienne, Sabine, and Laurent had their heads together, studying who knows what. As soon as they were airborne, files were pulled out and papers spread across the table. A laptop computer was open in front of them. Kaden leaned against the bar, relaxed as always, looking on.

For reasons she still didn't understand, Laurent had appointed himself her personal bodyguard throughout this entire episode. Matisse would be there, too, but given his official capacity, that made a little more sense. Though why they all jumped in with both feet to help out a virtual stranger was still beyond her.

Well, she and Laurent were no longer strangers, true. But why he didn't throw up his hands and step away was a mystery to her. He couldn't have been thrilled when his American fling turned into an international incident. To be fair, though, he'd never even hinted at wanting to back off. He'd been more supportive and determined to help than her jackass ex-husband had ever shown in *any* circumstance. It was almost as if he relished the opportunity to kick ass and take names.

And that was just too awesome to even believe.

Kaden looked her way and sent her a reassuring smile. The next thing she knew, he was beside them, budging up against his wife on the couch, his arm wrapping around Annie's shoulders and brushing his lips across her cheek.

"You don't need to worry, either of you. Matisse knows what he's doing." Spearing Lori with a knowing look, he said, "Dubois is just an added bonus."

Heat crept up Lori's neck and pinked her cheeks, causing Annie to laugh and Kaden to smirk. "He is that," she admitted. "Do you have any idea what they're planning?"

With the financial information Sabine had collected from her usual sources, along with what she had trolled from public internet sites—there was no lack of material about her subject—she now had a fairly complete dossier on Vincenzio Giancarlo Salentino. The sheer volume of information she'd amassed so quickly wasn't surprising, considering her access to private databases across the globe, but what she discovered was quite a surprise, indeed, given her initial profile assumptions for a known American gangster. The unavoidable time constraint precluded her from the thorough verifications and reconciliations she would normally perform—perfectionist stickler that she was, such lack forced her to rate the dossier at no more than 90 percent accuracy—but that didn't change the shocking truth that Vinnie Salentino was more than he appeared. Or less, depending on how one looked at it.

Not so the younger half brother, Claudio, a relationship she'd discovered during her research. That one was a menace and appeared to be, in every way that counted, different from the elder Salentino. He looked the part, too, and she shivered involuntarily as she studied a file photograph of him.

By the time their jet landed at half past four, Sabine had summarized what she'd learned for her husband and their newest contractor.

Lori was unsurprised to find Martin waiting for them outside immigration at the private terminal but relieved that he appeared to be alone. The look on his face when he spotted the tall man walking beside her was gratifying yet didn't dispel her simmering anger.

"You've got a nerve," she said by way of greeting, then turned to Laurent. "This is Martin Malone, my ex-husband and the reason we've all just flown three thousand miles." Turning to Martin, she flashed a false smile. "Martin, meet Colonel Laurent Dubois."

Badass soldier, indeed. The guy looked like he'd happily rip Martin's head off. *Where did Lori find him?* Whatever snide comment Martin was tempted to make along those lines died on his lips when he caught sight of the scariest looking man he'd ever seen following Lori and her soldier through immigration. The drop-dead gorgeous woman at his side made him blink like an idiot. All he could say was "Holy shit, Lori. Who *are* these people?"

"My friends." To Lori's delight, the couple offered only unsmiling nods rather than handshakes as she made the introductions. Juvenile? Sure, but she was entitled.

"They're INTERPOL agents, Martin, so keep your shit about you."

Martin jerked his wide-eyed gaze from Matisse back to Lori. "INTERPOL? But I thought they were—"

"I know what your *client* thinks," Lori hissed. Laurent had filled her in on what that douche bag Joe had presumed, which she had found highly amusing.

"If *you* actually believed that was true, then you're a bigger idiot than I thought." Lori leaned in close. "And if your brain hasn't been damaged from suffocation between those enormous boobs you married, you'll keep it to yourself. They didn't want me to tell you, but I don't believe in keeping honest people in the dark. Don't disappoint me in thinking you still fall into that category."

The colonel held himself back by sheer force of will. Martin Malone was an arrogant pussy, almost as big a fuckwad as the Uncle Joe character, and Laurent burned for the satisfaction of planting a hard fist into his smug face. The fact that Lori's acerbic words seemed to find their mark helped keep him in check. It also didn't hurt that the sight of Matisse clearly scared the piss out of the asshole. Laurent had been one of the advocates for keeping Matisse's true identity secret, but he'd respected Lori's wish—and Etienne's—to come clean. It was awkward enough operating in America without deliberately falsifying their identity. That it was a civilian who cautioned their contact about discretion was a convenient detail that could make their plan work.

Without a word, Matisse guided Sabine over to a row of chairs along the wall and pulled out his phone, leaving Martin standing awkwardly with his ex-wife and her ... lover? *Christ.* The Macallisters chose that moment to emerge from immigration, and their matching looks of hostility made Martin sigh inwardly.

"Gang's all here," he muttered to himself then nodded a greeting to the couple he had once considered his friends. "I didn't expect to see you, too, but thank you for arranging the plane."

Kaden regarded him for a moment, unsmiling, then shrugged. "I simply assured my CEO that you'd be reimbursing the company for flight expenses."

My CEO. Kaden Macallister was so low-key, Martin usually forgot what a big player he was. That he could *borrow* private transatlantic transport with two days' notice was a stark reminder of that fact.

Annie Macallister was not so nonchalant. "You've got a lot to answer for, Martin." Topping out under five and a half feet tall, Annie was nonetheless a force to be reckoned with. Fiercely loyal to those she considered her own, she stood now beside her oldest friend, arms crossed, shoulders back, and aimed a look of sheer malice at Martin.

"Annie, love, you're not helping." Kaden's tone sounded amused as he took a position behind her, rubbing a hand across her tense shoulder, but he didn't smile, nor did he take his eyes off of Martin.

"We've got our own transportation," he told Martin. "I imagine you'll want to follow along, but I suggest you stay in the background. Lori has agreed to do as you've asked, but that doesn't mean you're a welcome addition to the party."

"But I have to search the boxes—"

"No." Lori's stance mimicked Annie's, and Martin groaned.

"Lori—"

"Forget it, Martin. My files contain confidential information, and I'm not letting you or anyone else sniff through them."

"Vinnie's not going to be satisfied with that."

While Lori glared daggers at her ex, Laurent, who'd been silently taking in the exchange, muttered a curse in French behind her. She looked beyond Martin and saw what caused his reaction.

Uncle Joe, the old bastard, his bruised face sporting some sort of metal nose guard, was rambling toward them. And he wasn't alone.

His companion was younger, shorter, and wider, but the air of authority was unmistakable. Unfortunately, Lori recognized him, too. Not that she'd ever been face-to-face with him, but his picture had been in the newspapers enough over the years. The last time had been shortly before she and Martin split up. Something to do with cops being executed on the waterfront.

"This just gets better and better," she muttered.

The PHL terminal that served the private aviation traffic was not the teeming, surging sea of humanity that the main terminals were, but neither was it deserted. Well-heeled travelers were coming and going, and airport security was in evidence. Although no one seemed to be paying much attention to the tension radiating from their small group, only a fool would make a scene. Nonetheless, Laurent stepped out from behind Lori in a blatant show of protection. Martin took a quick step back and turned to see what had triggered that reaction.

And groaned again. This was *not* what he needed. Not what any of them needed.

"I'm gonna kill that fucking bastard." Uncle Joe fairly trembled with hatred when he caught sight of Laurent Dubois.

Vinnie Salentino abruptly halted in his march through the terminal, causing Joe to trip over his own feet to avoid running into his boss.

"If you so much as touch any of them, you're done. You will keep your fucking mouth shut and do what I say." Vinnie speared the taller man with a dangerous glare. "Am I clear? Is there anything about my words that you do not understand?" There was a reason Vinnie kept his agenda to himself; his ability to intimidate depended on a certain reputation.

"Yeah, boss. You're clear" came the grumbled reply. Unhappy with the dictate, Joe knew better than to argue. Or disobey.

Spinning around, Vinnie took one step then stopped again. "Jesus Christ."

In the span of that brief exchange, two others had joined the group around his lawyer. The giant with the dark, penetrating stare, currently trained on Vinnie, could only be one person. Vinnie hadn't actually believed Joe's description of the French mob boss, but now he realized that Joe had been generous.

Business. This is only business, Vinnie reminded himself, taking a deep breath. *No one is gonna pull out a Glock in the airport.* Then he cursed, realizing that the growing knot of people was beginning to draw attention. The last thing he needed was some sort of public altercation within sight or earshot of the authorities.

Ignoring everyone else, Vinnie went straight to Lori, hand outstretched. "Ms. Sheridan. Vincenzio Salentino."

Lori narrowed her eyes at him for a fraction of a moment before extending her own hand for a brief clasp.

"Thank you for coming so quickly. I wouldn't have asked it of you, but the, er, item that has been misplaced is of critical importance. The peace of this city depends upon it." His eyes slid to the soldier who was half-shielding her, then back to her. "You are in no danger."

"Forgive me if I find that difficult to believe." She glared at Joe, who had wisely stayed back a couple of yards. "And I don't recall being *asked* to do anything."

Flashing a scowl at Martin, who looked like he wanted to rebut the claim, Vinnie would have said more, but the giant, who had not taken his eyes off Vinnie, spoke first. His voice was quiet, more like a low rumble, but held unmistakable power. "Our transportation is here. We depart immediately."

"Good idea." Vinnie waved toward the door as if in invitation.

Annie scowled at both men then took Lori's arm. "Come on, let's get this done," she said and marched her friend forward.

Kaden and Sabine followed, leaving Matisse and Laurent to deal with the locals.

"I almost feel sorry for them," Lori said, glancing back over her shoulder, causing Sabine to chuckle in her wake.

"*Moi, aussie.* Etienne is like a grizzly with a thorn in his paw when he is irritated. And he is very irritated right now."

Built like a block of granite and equally expressive, Etienne Matisse was impossible to read, displaying none of the emotions that one would expect: anger, aggression, impatience, or even resigned cooperation. Prudence dictated that Vinnie behave cordially.

"It wasn't necessary for you to come, but you are welcome to enjoy my city all the same. I assure you, Ms. Sheridan is in no danger."

"How magnanimous of you." Etienne's features morphed into something that resembled amused indulgence but did nothing to diminish his aura of dangerous strength.

"And you are correct," he continued. "Ms. Sheridan is in no danger at all." He leaned a fraction closer. "I'm here to make sure of it. Excuse me."

Whatever Vinnie had expected, it wasn't a dismissal. But that's exactly what he got, left standing there without so much as a backward glance as Matisse and his companion—a man who appeared every bit as lethal—walked away. A surge of anger, followed closely by unease, welled up. *Fuck.*

"Let's go," he said, having no choice but to follow the French contingent out to the waiting vehicles.

"Why is Vinnie following us around?" Lori rode shotgun in the large SUV that Etienne had procured. "Doesn't he have minions for that?" She certainly hadn't expected to see the man himself, and the idea of being near him made her sweaty. As if she expected someone to jump out in front of them with a machine gun.

"Whatever is on the missing flash drive must be of the utmost importance."

"Do we have to let them in?"

They'd arrived at the storage facility, an acre or more of flat, single-story buildings surrounded by a no-nonsense iron fence with a coded entry gate. Lori recited the numbers for Matisse to punch in and turned to look out the back window at the mini-caravan behind them—Martin in his BMW coupe and the thugs in an obscenely large Mercedes sedan—while the gate slowly rolled open.

"No," Etienne said. "But you won't gain anything by pushing the issue."

"I'm not letting any of them into my unit."

The silence that greeted that statement was more persuasive than words would have been, and her shoulders slumped. "You think I have to."

A nod.

Lori looked to her old friend for help, but Annie shook her head. "I understand your concern, but if you don't let them in, and you don't find the flash drive, they're not going to believe you."

"But the stuff in those boxes is confidential!"

A large hand landed on her shoulder from behind, warm and sure. "They won't see much, a name or two but no details. We'll be watching; and it's not like they'll be taking pictures. But Annie's right, *chérie*. We're here now, and the last thing you want is to leave them with any doubt."

With a heavy sigh, she surrendered to the inevitable. The line of cars moved forward and she directed Matisse down the row to her unit. "Pull up parallel to the door," she said, pushing open her door and jumping from the high front seat the moment the car stopped.

By the time the others emerged, the locker door was rolled up and she was surveying the garage-sized room, hands on hips.

Annie smiled wide as she stood beside her friend. "Why does this not surprise me?"

No haphazardly stacked boxes or piles of junk here—Lori's obsessive neat-freak gene was on full display. A tidy row of cloth-draped furniture was arranged against the back wall. In one corner there was a collection of large, flat boxes, and the rest of the space was laid out in a neat grid of metal racking. Each rack, shelf, and box was labeled. There was even a folding table stowed against the front row, left there, no doubt, so that a box could be retrieved and sorted through without having to set it on the ground. Convenient.

"So I like to be organized. Sue me." Feeling defensive and oddly vulnerable, she reached for the table, but Laurent beat her to it.

"Just set it up there," she said with a weak smile, indicating the front edge of the space. "If you and Kaden can bring the boxes out one at a time, then everyone can watch while Annie and I go through them."

"For fuck's sake." Impatient with the entire operation and not understanding why Vinnie was letting this woman namby-pamby around, Uncle Joe pushed his way past Martin—who was toeing the line at the edge of the unit, looking like he wanted to step in but was afraid he'd get whacked with a ruler for misbehaving—and went straight for the rack marked *Office*.

Laurent was in the process of unfolding the table when he caught movement out of the corner of his eye. Slapping the leg he'd opened back in place, he used the table like a giant flyswatter and delivered a solid hit, connecting the flat surface of the table to the old man from thigh to sternum. Joe stumbled back, landing against the rented SUV.

"You will observe only," Laurent said as Joe struggled to stay standing.

"You fucking son of a bitch!" Joe raised a hand to cover his nose, at the same time readying himself to push off and launch himself at the soldier.

Laurent's "I wouldn't" was drowned out by Vinnie, who stepped forward and barked "Joe! Back off!" Finger pointed, like he was scolding a disobedient dog.

Joe hesitated, and for the first time ever, he considered ignoring a direct order from his boss.

"What the fuck is wrong with you? Get the fuck outta here. Now!" Vinnie was all up in Joe's face, and that was the last straw.

Joe stood tall, shook off the hand Vinnie had laid on his arm, and glared first at Laurent then at his boss. "I don't know who you are anymore."

Without taking his eyes off of his longtime, trusted man, Vinnie frowned. "I could say the same to you. Marty, take Joe back into town."

Vinnie won the brief standoff, but it rattled him. As Joe sauntered off with curses, it occurred to him that he might not be privy to all the details of what had transpired in France.

God damn it to fucking hell. His reputation, and the authority that went with it, depended on people like Joe, and everyone else on his payroll, obeying his orders without question. Never *thinking* to disagree, much less voicing it. It was tradition, the way of his father, and his father's father. Never mind that Vinnie sought to change things. Very few people knew of that agenda, and Joe was not one of them. But the fact that old Uncle Joe, a man who had been loyal to Vinnie's family for decades, a man who Vinnie trusted with *almost* everything, had just about gone rogue on him … well, that was something that he needed to think about long and hard.

But now was not the time.

Turning back to his immediate problem, he did what his mother had tried to pound into him: be polite, no matter what.

"I'm sorry about that, Ms. Sheridan." Vinnie glanced at Dubois then back to Lori. "Joe's had a bad week. I didn't mean for this to be any more unpleasant for you than it already is."

Lori glared at the man like she was preparing to launch a verbal grenade at him, but then she seemed to deflate. "Let's just get this done," she said with a shake of her head. "You can watch, search the boxes themselves, once I pull the files out, but my professional ethics prohibit me from allowing you to get close enough to see the words on the pages in these files. Can you respect that?"

Sixteen

Martin was pissed. At Joe, at Vinnie, and seriously fucking pissed off at his ex-wife. How dare she flaunt ... *Fuck*. He didn't know anything about her friends, other than Annie and Kaden. And the frigid reception he'd received from those two told him exactly what camp they stood in. Not that he could blame them, or had ever doubted it, if he was being honest with himself.

"That was a fucking stupid-ass move." Martin accelerated onto the on-ramp of I-95 South. "Where am I taking you?"

"Fuck off, Malone. Drop me at Big Al's on South 9th."

Suit yourself, asshole. Martin merged into unusually heavy traffic for a Saturday. An accident, knowing his current fuck-all luck. A handful of minutes passed, the slow trip and loud silence in the car almost enough to make him scream.

"How's it feel, Marty," Joe finally said, "knowing that soldier's doin' your wife?"

The car lurched to the right before Martin loosened his grip on the wheel and corrected. "Ex-wife, Joe. Who she's with is her own business." *God damn it.* He did not want to talk about this. Or even think it.

Martin could *hear* Joe smirking but kept his eyes on the crawling traffic ahead of him. "For your sake," Joe said, oblivious to the dynamite he was lighting, "I hope the sweet piece you got at home puts out. That bitch you call *ex* had to have frozen your nuts off."

"Argh!" Martin slammed on the brakes and swerved so fast that Joe almost banged his tender nose on the dash in front of him.

"What the fuck?"

"Get out."

Uncle Joe reached out like he intended to wrap his hand around Martin's throat, but the unmistakable metallic click of a bullet chambering stopped him short. Glancing down, he saw the business end of a big-ass handgun wavering six inches from his gut.

"Get out now."

If the old man noticed the barrel of Martin's .45 was trembling slightly, he didn't comment.

"You'll regret this, lawyer." Joe took his time undoing his seat belt and sliding out of the car. Traffic on the highway was moving slow enough that he was in no danger of being mowed over, but he had quite a walk ahead of him.

"I already do," Martin said after Joe's door slammed shut. "The whole sorry fucking episode." Hitting auto-lock, he tossed the gun onto the passenger seat and merged back into traffic.

Vinnie remained silent as the two women carefully sifted through each file, holding up the folders one by one and shaking them over the table before flipping through page by page, making sure nothing was stuck in between. Macallister and the soldier helped with the back-and-forth of the boxes, and there was low conversation, mostly between the ladies, but nothing that concerned him; it sounded like they were talking about whatever the files contained. Vinnie couldn't care less what the documents were about, only whether that flash drive had landed among them.

Why the hell was he here, anyway? He didn't have time for this; it was something Joe should have handled. And Vinnie would have left it to him, after what was supposed to be a quick welcome-to-my-turf goodwill gesture to the French boss at the airport. But Joe had fucked that up, and Vinnie hadn't trusted him not to do further damage. And he'd called that one right, damn it. So here he was.

On the other side of the table, with his back to the interior of the storage unit, Matisse stood as still and quiet as a statue, only his eyes moved as he focused on the search. Vinnie, on the other hand, was restless. His feet shuffled, he paced and fiddled with his phone, checking emails, sending texts—to his senior team about Joe, among others—and doing anything to keep his mind from dwelling on the fact that this was more than likely a useless exercise. Stealing more than a few glances at the leader of this group, Vinnie couldn't help but be impressed. The man hadn't moved a muscle, not even twitched a finger, for over thirty minutes, and Vinnie wondered how it was possible for a man to stand so still for so long. If it weren't for the keen focus in his eyes, which occasionally found their mark on Vinnie, Vinnie would have thought the guy might have fallen asleep standing up. If their roles were reversed, Vinnie would have been ranting and pacing and threatening, while Matisse was laser focused, his expression neutral, showing neither anger nor impatience. Showing nothing at all.

The man is a puzzle, Vinnie thought, glancing again toward the open door of the SUV. *The woman too.* The wife had settled herself in one of the back seats, plainly unconcerned, and was reading from files of her own. Not some fashion magazine she'd brought along to stave off the boredom … it looked like she was working on something. Interesting. These two did not behave like any heads of *la famiglia* that he'd ever met. They were too calm, too … thoughtful. And this short-notice trip had been very well organized. Almost like …

Vinnie narrowed his eyes at Matisse, seeing him in a new light. Joe had made an assumption that Vinnie had taken at face value. *Marty had questioned it,* Vinnie recalled. Seeing this man now, and the soldier, with his own eyes, watching their interaction with the people they were committed to protect, that idea just didn't fit.

At that moment Matisse shifted his gaze and caught him staring. Their eyes held for a moment, and Vinnie could swear the giant was reading his mind—a ghost of an expression that might have been a challenge crossed that frightening face. *What the fuck?* With a slight tilt of his head—a silent request that Matisse follow him—Vinnie turned and walked around to the far side of the vehicle.

For such a large man Matisse moved with both speed and grace, and it was no more than a heartbeat before they were standing face-to-face, his expression unchanged. Vinnie was used to people stepping and fetching around him, striving to make a good impression, and he had developed the habit of allowing others to speak up first. Apparently the Frenchman before him had nothing he felt compelled to get off his chest, because he remained maddeningly silent. Eventually Matisse raised an eyebrow in question.

Right. Vinnie had requested this "meet." He cleared his throat. "Who the fuck are you, exactly?"

Etienne Matisse had wondered when Mr. Philadelphia would clue in to the fact that his visitors were not who he assumed them to be, because evidently Malone had not tattled. He arranged a look of surprised innocence on his face—an unconvincing look on him—and glanced through the open window at his wife, who was listening and smiling.

"You didn't seem to be confused at the airport." He ignored Sabine's snort of laughter.

But Vinnie caught it, and it irritated him. He did not like being made a fool of. Scowling at the beautiful woman seated not two feet from him—he'd forgotten she was there until she laughed—he planted his hands on his hips and regarded Matisse. "Humor me."

Anything resembling humor fled from Etienne's visage. "Would you care to see my identification?"

"Would it help?"

In response Matisse fingered the lapel of his jacket and slowly opened it, then reached into his breast pocket and retrieved a slim leather case. Eyes not leaving Vinnie's, he flipped it open and handed it to the other man.

"Jesus H. Fucking Christ."

The INTERPOL ID card was the most high-tech Vinnie had ever seen. The glare-free material made it easy to read, although the badge pinned across from it glinted in the sun. He studied the 3-D photo image on the card, confirming the ugly mug was the same as the one standing in front of him. Not that he expected otherwise, but it gave him something to do while his mind searched for everything he knew about the international police.

Information coordination across global networks, with impressive access to data systems worldwide. Their broad scope would make them potentially less biased than local law enforcement, including the FBI. But didn't all these agencies work together?

"Things are not always as they appear," Matisse said, as if commenting on the weather.

Yet something in that simple sentence caught Vinnie's attention, and he shifted his gaze from the ID card to look into those perceptive eyes. "A true statement."

The two regarded each other for a long moment before Vinnie spoke again. "All of you are agents?"

"All but the Macallisters. They came along for a holiday."

Vinnie groaned and shook his head, but he appreciated the honesty. "Joe fucked this one up pretty bad."

"Understandable, given his frame of reference."

If there was an accusation in those words, Vinnie didn't appear to be offended. With a distracted nod, he flipped the leather closed and handed it back.

"So, what's your plan? Arrest me? Turn me into your American colleagues?"

Etienne returned the case to his pocket. "Should I?"

"For what?"

"Nothing that I can think of. As much as my friends would like to see your nuts pinned to the wall, it wasn't you who demonstrated bad manners in my country." And the American had acquitted himself far better than expected for a hotheaded mob boss. Matisse flicked his gaze to Sabine, and what he saw in her intelligent eyes coincided with his own assessment.

Martin pulled into his reserved space in the garage beneath his downtown office but didn't immediately get out of the car. *Where the fuck is that flash drive?* The question beat a tattoo against his brain, giving him a whopper of a headache. He leaned back and closed his eyes, letting his mind drift back, replaying the whole pack-up-and-move-out ordeal from almost a year ago. Lori had been shocked at his announcement that he was leaving, then hurt. Then angry.

She'd given him a week to get his stuff out of the townhouse, telling him flatly that anything left behind would be dumped in the garage for the trash collectors to haul away. His clothes and personal stuff had gone first, but most of that went into boxes in Teresa's garage until he could buy them a bigger place. The office stuff had gone next. And that was pretty much it—most of what they'd acquired together over the course of their marriage he thought of as *theirs,* not *his,* and he'd left it all with her. Not because he didn't like the stuff, but Teresa would not have let him bring any of it into their new home.

The office. Focus on the office. His head pounded, and he wished he had some water. The office. When he'd packed up his files, he filled about twenty-five boxes. The metal file cabinets were old and ugly but serviceable. Lori had wanted to replace them with something that looked a little nicer—something that matched hers—but they'd never gotten around to it, and then he started panting after his assistant, and then …

Well, then he'd managed to fuck up his entire life.

The office, he forced his brain to keep going. The file cabinets were the only furniture he'd moved from the house. They sat in the garage of the townhouse for a couple of days. Then a friend had come around with a truck and …

His eyes popped open and focused on the chain-link gate that was right in front of his bumper. The gate that led to the storage cages that office tenants could rent. *Are they still here?* Why hadn't he thought of this before? Fuck. Was it possible that flash drive could have fallen out of its file and be hiding in one of those file drawers? He'd gone through all the boxes, now stored on shelves in the basement of his current house. He'd meant to put them back into new cabinets, but he'd been busy and it hadn't been a priority.

He was about to jump out of the car when his phone chimed. Teresa. *Just what I fucking need right now.* "Yeah, baby, what's up?"

"You still at the office?" Teresa's gum snapped like a punctuation mark at the end of her sentence, and the picture of her in his mind's eye made him wince. *Christ, now what?*

"Yeah, I'm still here. Not sure how long—"

"Some kid came to the door looking for you. He wouldn't tell me nothing, but he was pretty upset. I told him you were at your office downtown, and he tore outta here." Another snap. "What's up with that?"

Uh-oh. "Was he a tall, skinny kid with short brown hair, riding a moped?"

"Yeah, that's him." Snap. "Who is he?"

Benjamin. Fuck. That could only mean one thing, but Martin still prayed he was wrong. "He, ah, the kid makes deliveries for one of my clients. You said he was upset? But he didn't say why?"

"Yeah, that's what I said." Snap. "What's up with him? How come I ain't never seen him before?"

"You *haven't ever* seen him because you haven't been at the office when he's come around." Enunciating the proper grammar was as far as Martin was willing to go to correct his wife's trashy speech unless he wanted a loud, trashy argument, and now was absolutely not the time.

The silence on the line meant that she got his not-so-subtle message.

"Listen, babe, thanks for the head's-up. I'll wait for him here. I've still got plenty to do." *Like find the friggin' key to the cage right in front of my face.* "Not sure how long I'll be, so don't wait on me for dinner." Which would be no hardship for her, since her cooking involved not much more than pulling a box out of the freezer and popping it into the microwave. Or ordering takeout.

Martin disconnected the call before his wife could make a snarky comment. Then he made another call.

———— ✦ ————

The shadows were lengthening by the time Lori slid the files back into the last box. Laurent settled the lid on top and returned it to its spot on the shelf. She hadn't realized how much she hoped to find the elusive flash drive until about halfway through her search.

Shoulders slumped with a combination of fatigue, irritation, and disappointment, she looked over at Vinnie for the first time since she'd started searching.

"I told you it wouldn't be here."

What else could she say? That she was sorry it didn't miraculously turn up in her stuff? She'd known it wouldn't, not unless Martin had purposely put it there. And she didn't believe—had never thought, even after his scumbag behavior—that he would stoop that low.

"It was a long shot, but I had to know." In the harsh light of the bare bulb fixed to the roof of the storage unit, weariness showed on Vinnie Salentino's face. She almost felt sorry for him. Almost.

"Well, ah ..." What was there to say to that? She looked to Laurent for help. *Now what?*

Vinnie's phone buzzed, rescuing them from the awkward moment. "Marty. They just finished. We got nothing."

He stared at Matisse while he listened to his lawyer. "*Jesus fucking Christ.* You're just remembering this now?" A pause. "Yeah, uh-huh, whatever. Jesus Christ, Marty. Yeah, okay. I'm on my way." Another pause. "I don't know, but I'll ask." Disconnecting the call, he looked at Lori, regret in his expression.

"Marty's just now realizing he never searched the original file cabinets. Says they're in a cage in the basement of his office building and he forgot about them. I'm heading there now." He looked at Matisse, conveying a silent invitation. If they found the flash drive ...

Lori's jaw dropped before she shook her head in disgust. "You cannot be serious. For Christ's sake, Sabine asked that question within two minutes of learning what was going on."

The look Lori speared him with made it clear to Vinnie what she thought of him, and he bristled. No one slung insults at him. No one. Not even unspoken ones. Not even if he deserved it. He opened his mouth to put her in her place—

"Is his office still in the same building?" Annie asked. "Isn't that close to our hotel? Let's go with him." She flashed irritated eyes at Vinnie.

Christ, her too? Vinnie suddenly felt like he was thirteen years old and had tripped his date at the cotillion.

"I'd like to clear this mess up and get us all back to France," Annie was saying, either not noticing or not caring about the impact of her tone.

"If our *host* doesn't mind," Etienne said, pulling Vinnie back to reality and smoothing past the explosive subtext he'd *not* missed, "I believe we should follow this through." His polite words belied the not-so-civilized promise in his dark eyes. "For Lori's sake."

Seventeen

Thanks to the lethargic, out-of-body stupor from the drug they'd shot her up with—heroine she guessed, from the purity of the high—Angelina Stripling managed not to gag on what the bastard ejaculated into her mouth. Her scalp ached from where he'd gripped her hair and the left side of her face throbbed, courteous of the backhand to her cheek when she'd tried to resist. But she knew, in the foggy recesses of her mind, those small hurts were the least of her problems. Her limbs weren't working properly, and she listed to the side where she'd been kneeling between his legs. One hand braced on the floor so she wouldn't topple over, she swiped the other across her mouth.

Smack! A fat hand knocked her head to the side, twisting her neck with the force and making her cry out.

"Aw, Angie, you wipin' your mouth like that makes me think you ain't glad to see me." Claudio pushed on her shoulders, and she scampered a few feet across the floor as he searched for the fly of his pants beneath the protruding mass of his belly.

"You're a little rusty, sweetheart." The raspy chuckle scraped across her nerves like broken glass. "But don't you worry—we'll whip you back into shape. You still got a hot little mouth on you."

The world started to tilt and go fuzzy, the words coming at her fading in and out. Angelina didn't even fight it, craving the softness of the gathering black mist over the nightmare she'd landed back into. As her elbow buckled under her weight and the grimy linoleum floor came up to meet her face, the last image in her head was of her precious boy crumpled against the back wall, blood trickling down from his innocent lip. *Bean!*

Uncle Joe waited at the back door of the restaurant while a burly man he recognized as one of Claudio's carried a woman out over his shoulder, her bony rear sticking up in the air. He glanced around as they passed. The woman was out cold. In the dim light, he could just make out her profile. Wait, wasn't that—

"Move it." He'd been searched for weapons, and the thug who did the job now gestured with Joe's own Glock for him to go in, following closely behind. When they reached the table, the man slapped the handgun down in front of Claudio.

"I didn't come to do you no harm," Joe said to the porcine man who made no move to rise from the table.

"Stopped by just to pay respects, did ya?" Claudio picked up the subcompact pistol and turned it over in his chubby hands. With a jerk he separated the magazine from the body of the weapon and emptied it of bullets. Next he pulled back the top slide and ejected the chambered round. Slapping it all back together, he scooped up the bullets and dropped them into an empty coffee mug beside an overflowing ashtray. Then he handed the gun back to its owner as if this was a regular routine.

Joe took the Glock and risked looking directly into Claudio's black eyes. The pillows of flesh surrounding them rendered that stare no less intimidating.

"You know I'm loyal to your family." Joe shuffled his feet and did his best to keep the man's intense gaze, gripping the weapon like a lifeline. He was one to follow orders, not give his opinion, and this visit was uncomfortable in the extreme, but necessary. Wasn't it? Doubt crept down his spine.

"My father's right hand for as long as I can remember," Claudio acknowledged. "And now you serve my brother. Puts us at odds, you and me."

"It doesn't have to be that way."

Claudio studied the man in front of him. When Claudio was a child, Joe had been a fixture in their house. It was Claudio who first called him Uncle Joe, for while there was no blood connection between them, Joe had treated him like there was, behaving like family in all the ways that counted, taking the time to give some attention to a lonely, overweight kid when his own parents couldn't be bothered.

But Joe had gone with Vinnie when their father was sent up. So why was he here now?

"The man is not stupid, and unless I am way off base, he wants our help." Etienne's assessment of Vinnie Salentino's behavior broke through the silence as he followed the man's vehicle through the streets of downtown Philadelphia. "Whatever is on that flash drive is a game changer. Something more than just a power play."

Laurent had taken the front passenger seat and was watching their surroundings like someone expecting an ambush. Annie and Kaden sat together in the third seat, leaving Sabine and Lori together in the middle. Light traffic made for a quick trip.

"His businesses are legitimate," Sabine added. "Not just fronts." She had enough experience to tell the difference from the financial reports and banking records she'd been able to access. "And they have grown significantly since he took over from his father. Expanded and become more profitable. Perhaps he's being blackmailed, or threatened in some other way."

Lori fairly snorted at that pronouncement. "Come on, you guys. He's mafia. His father was like a godfather or something. It was a huge media circus when the old man was convicted and sent to prison." She kept her gaze on the deserted sidewalks outside her window. "The saying *the apple doesn't fall far from the tree* was coined for a reason. If anyone is being blackmailed or threatened, *he* would be the one doing it."

"Drug trafficking has been reduced by more than 80 percent in Philadelphia since Roberto Salentino was sent upstate." Sabine looked up from the page she was reading from. "And the number of prostitution arrests has gone down by half."

"So he's smarter than his daddy and the girls don't get busted as often." Lori was born and raised in Philadelphia. Except for that stretch of years on the West Coast when she'd been at Cal with Annie, and then working at the firm in San Francisco, and the three years in Paris, she'd lived in this city her entire life. It was beyond her ability to believe that Vinnie was anything other than a modern-day version of his father.

"According to INTERPOL files, the drug-running and prostitution is connected to the younger half brother, Claudio, not Vinnie."

"Ugh. He's a disgusting pig, and scary." Lori shuddered. "But you can't think they aren't working together. These families are thick as thieves."

"Not necessarily." This from Etienne as he maneuvered a lane change to stay on Vinnie's bumper.

Before Lori could argue the point, they arrived at the entrance to the parking garage connected to the building that housed the Malone law firm. The man himself was waiting, and her stomach lurched. So much for not seeing him again. It wasn't like she was heartbroken—she'd moved well beyond that—but he was living proof that she'd been a fool. It was as if her association with him tainted her character. What idiot would stay married to a mob lawyer? The fact that she hadn't known made it even worse in her mind.

Martin waved a card in front of an electronic sensor and the metal arm lifted, allowing Vinnie's Mercedes to enter. Etienne watched it fall then waited as the card passed in front of the sensor again. The bar lifted once more, and the enormous SUV glided in.

The storage lockers were located on the first floor of the garage for easy access to the main elevators. Etienne pulled the SUV into a striped no-parking zone behind the Mercedes and cut the engine.

Laurent's silence during the drive had not gone unnoticed by Lori. In fact, he'd spoken few words since they'd arrived in Philadelphia. Even as he protected her from Joe's stupid move and helped jockey the boxes back and forth, he'd been quiet. From his position in the front seat, he'd not looked at her once, and she was beginning to believe he regretted his decision to get involved. Not that she could blame him; this whole trip across the Atlantic was turning out to be a colossal joke. It was embarrassing. Her ex-husband was embarrassing. How could someone like Laurent have any respect for her after seeing who she'd spent almost half her life with? And when did his opinion of her become so important?

Wrapped up in her lachrymose thoughts, she jumped when the door at her elbow opened. Glancing out, her gaze crashed into Laurent's. Whatever he saw in her face made his own hard expression soften a fraction as he reached for her hand.

"*Chérie,* are you okay?"

The tender words had her blinking back those tears that had been threatening. "I'm so sorry" was all she could muster.

"You have nothing to be sorry for. Come here." He gently tugged on her hand and helped her down to the ground. When she would have moved away, he blocked her path, and in a heartbeat she was leaning against his broad chest with his arms wrapped around her.

Stunned, she stiffened, but only momentarily. His warmth melted her surprise, and she sagged against him, letting his heat seep into her bones.

"This is not your fault, and whatever happens, it will be over soon." He whispered the words in her ear then brushed his lips against her temple.

The clanging of metal jerked her to attention, and she stood up straight but kept her arms around his waist where they'd ended up without her conscious thought. Pushing up on her toes, she kissed him then managed a smile. "Thank you."

He winked and let her go.

When she turned toward the open gate to the storage area, Martin was watching her with a wistful expression. For one instant she felt the urge to stick her tongue out at him—was sorely tempted—but settled for an honest smile instead.

Five beige metal file cabinets that had seen better days were crammed into a chain-link cage alongside cardboard boxes stacked floor to ceiling; decades' worth of long-forgotten legal documents moldering away until it was safe to destroy them. So tightly was the cage packed that they had to pull the cabinets out into the center aisle in order to open the drawers. It took less than fifteen minutes before they found what they were looking for. Lori wasn't sure who was more pissed off—Vinnie or herself.

The first three cabinets were empty but for a few paperclips and some unhappy spiders who clung to their position with a tenacity one could only admire. To be absolutely sure they weren't missing anything, the men yanked each drawer completely off its slides and shook it out. Laurent then lifted the empty shell of each cabinet and held it upside down before giving the girls an opportunity to search inside. The bottom drawer of the fourth cabinet snagged on something as Martin tried to pull it free. Taking out his frustration on the thing, he slamming it back into the frame before yanking it out again, but it caught once again. Matisse stopped him before he could do it again.

"Wait." With a wordless gesture to Laurent, the cabinet was upended. Etienne carefully drew out the stuck drawer until it caught. "A bit more," he said, and the cabinet was angled differently. That shift allowed Etienne to extend his long arm into the opening behind the drawer.

Fingers grazing carefully along the track upon which the drawer rolled, Etienne felt for the obstruction. There. He traced around it … *Yes. It can only be one thing.*

"Pull up," he said to Laurent. When his friend eased the weight of the drawer from its track, Etienne grasped what he could of the piece of plastic and yanked. Nothing. He wiggled it back and forth, twisting one way then the other before yanking it again, and finally the obstruction came loose.

He held it up. "Is this what you're looking for?"

"I don't believe this," Lori growled, ready to launch herself at Martin with the serious intention of strangling him. Her reaction, however, was overshadowed by a loud shout that had everyone, including herself, cringing.

"Fucking son of a bitch!" Vinnie might have popped a blood vessel if he wasn't so glad to see the stupid flash drive. He reached for it, but Etienne closed his fist around the thing.

"The international police need answers before I hand this over to you."

Eighteen

The two men stared at each other while everyone around them froze, the air crackling with tension. Etienne stood motionless, his expression as blank as an empty page, while Vinnie's face twisted into an ugly mask of rage. No one, *not anyone,* said no to Vinnie. For a moment it looked like he was going to explode.

"*Fuck!*" The curse came out on a sharp exhale as Vinnie broke the silence and spun away. He stomped, hands ripping through his hair, for three steps before spinning back. He glared and pointed at Matisse as if the big man was one of his lackeys. Unlike the members of that club, however, Matisse didn't flinch.

But then Etienne did something that surprised even his wife—he rolled his eyes and shook his head. Before Vinnie could launch another f-bomb, Etienne opened his hand to reveal the slightly mangled piece of plastic.

"Cease with the dramatics. If you did not want me to know what is on this, you would not have invited us to follow you."

That was the truth, but with the moment at hand, Vinnie's conscience engaged. Using these people to solve his problems with Claudio would free him from the situation and make the city a far safer place. And Claudio wouldn't know where the video evidence of the murder a year ago had surfaced from. Vinnie knew better than most that prison bars didn't stop orders to kill.

But Claudio was family—they were undeniably linked by blood, albeit the blood of a monster whom Vinnie abhorred. In that part of his brain that felt loyal to that connection, Vinnie had some notion that he could control his half brother with this evidence rather than bring him down. If the police got involved, Claudio would definitely go down. And unlike their father, who was sitting out three life sentences without possibility of parole, Claudio would be given the death penalty for killing two cops.

"Out of context," Vinnie said after a long pause, "the information on that thing could be dangerous."

"To you?"

"Yes." Claudio would be apoplectic once he learned of the recording, and if he ever found out that Vinnie had made it—ordered it made—he'd come after his older brother, blood or no. And he would know exactly how Vinnie had learned of the hit, and that person would be silenced.

But Vinnie suspected Claudio was planning to come after him anyway, based on the reports he'd been getting.

"Does it incriminate you?" Etienne's question was matter-of-fact, but he was no longer smiling.

With a glance around at the others, Vinnie took a deep breath. "No." A pause while the INTERPOL agent remained unmoving. "Listen, I'm prepared to discuss it with you, but no one else." He looked at Lori, who looked like she was ready to kill someone, then her ex-husband. "Not even Marty. He was keeping it safe for me—or was supposed to be. It's got nothing to do with him, he doesn't know what's on it."

Etienne appeared to consider the words for a moment before he nodded. "Fair enough." To Kaden he said, "Would you escort the ladies to dinner?" He indicated Annie and Lori. "My team will join you when we're finished here."

"Wait a minute." Lori was practically hyperventilating she was so pissed off. "Just like that"—she snapped her fingers, glaring at Matisse—"we're all good and going out to dinner?"

Laurent set a hand on her shoulder, but she twisted away. "No. Just … no." She glared at Martin, stabbing a stiff finger in his direction. "You arrogant ass. You drag me into this mess, send some psycho goon after me, and then suddenly—oops-a-daisy!—you remember that you have all these file cabinets here. After a God damned year?"

"Jesus, Lori. Calm down." Martin held his palms up as if to placate her.

Even Annie tried to reach a reassuring hand to her friend but Lori ignored her, too focused on Martin to care that she was on the verge of having a meltdown. "You are pathetic. You are disgusting. Do you have any idea what you've done to me? I hope you ..." Suddenly she deflated, mortification overcoming her anger.

"I need air." She turned to flee and crashed into the hard form of Laurent, who wrapped an arm around her waist. The hold kept her from bouncing back and falling on her butt. It also grounded her.

Lori's emotional outburst might have stunned her friends, but it didn't change the outcome. In fact, it may have solidified it. They were all, in a sense, victims of Marty's stupidity.

Vinnie included. And Matisse's unspoken opinion was clear, expressed with not just his piercing black eyes but his body language as well.

"Fine," Vinnie said. "Marty, let us into your office, but you can't stay. I don't want you involved."

What he meant, exactly, by *not involved,* Lori wasn't sure, but she was glad to distance herself from Martin. Reassured by the warm strength of Laurent's hand around hers as the group rode the garage elevator to the lobby, though not entirely recovered, she led her old friends out the front door of the building and into the evening while the others followed Martin to the main elevators.

This time of year, the sun set around eight o'clock, an hour that was fast approaching. The city sparkled in the magic light of that near-dusk glow as the last rays of sunlight reflected off the upper levels of high-rises in the financial district. Standing on the sidewalk in front of the tall glass doors of Martin's building, Lori did her best to shove aside the raw emotions and consider their options.

"The last time we were here," Annie said, "you took us to a nice wine bar. It was new then, but it's been awhile. Do you remember? Is it still here?"

"The Twisted Vine?"

"That was it. They have food, right? Even if we don't stay for dinner, I think we could all use a glass of wine and something to eat."

Lori smiled. *Amen to that.* "It's just around the corner. I haven't been there in a while." Because it was one of Martin's after-work hangouts, she'd avoided it after they split up.

She pivoted to head down the sidewalk, but before she could take more than one step, the revolving door of the office building spun in a squeaky whoosh and a boy in faded jeans and a hoodie came tearing out. Kaden was standing closest to the door, and instinct made him step into the kid's path. So focused on his trajectory, the boy missed the movement and slammed into him.

"Whoa." Kaden took him by the shoulders, holding the kid in place while he regained his balance.

"Sorry, mister!" The kid tried to twist away, but Kaden's grip tightened slightly.

"Hold up, son."

Kaden's tone—along with his grip—must have penetrated, because the young man ceased his struggling and tipped his face up. Kaden's heart almost shattered at what he saw. Tears streaked the boy's cheeks, and pure anguish poured from his eyes. Now that he'd stopped squirming, Kaden could feel his thin body trembling.

"*Please*, mister."

"Are you hurt?"

Vigorous shaking of his head. "Not me." A fresh gush of tears. "They took my ma. I've gotta find her before ..." He sucked in a deep breath, unable to finish the sentence.

Something about the boy resonated with Lori as she watched the interaction. He was tall but painfully thin, his mouse-brown hair cut short but sticking up in all directions like he'd been yanking on it, dressed in clothes that were faded and worn. His thin shoulders shook with emotion. Then it hit her.

"*Benjamin?* Ben, is that you?"

The kid jerked around, as if only just noticing that the stranger he'd plowed into wasn't alone. Hardly anyone called him Ben, much less Benjamin. Eyes wide as a spooked horse, it took him a second to register the face and the voice.

"Ms. Sheridan? Wh-what are you doing here?"

"Ben." Lori moved to the boy and leaned in to hug him. "Never mind that. What happened?" And that's when she noticed that his lip was swollen and bleeding.

Claudio happened. Or more precisely, his goons. As Lori dabbed at Ben's cut lip with a Kleenex from her purse, she coaxed the story out, and felt more rage building inside her.

"Angelina was clean." She looked at her friends. "I can't believe anyone would do this. She was making it. She had a job, and she was … God damn it! *Why?*" In reality the woman wasn't terribly strong, and Lori could only imagine the lure of the oblivion of drugs. She'd cleaned up and stayed that way for her son, but not without lots of counseling, encouragement, and legal threats.

Ben, better known as Bean to anyone in his neighborhood and at school, rocked on his feet. "They've been coming round, threatening her, saying stuff like … like didn't she miss her old life. She always said no, but … and tonight … tonight they came again and dragged her away. She screamed, and I yelled too, but they smacked me aside and shoved her in the car. Before I could get up, they drove off."

"What were you doing here?" Kaden nodded to the building. He had lowered himself to one knee so he could look the boy in the eyes, but Bean was tall enough that he looked down to meet Kaden's gaze.

"I came to find Mr. Malone. He's a lawyer and he … he looks out for us, but he's not here." Looking at the adult male who had asked the question, Bean missed Lori's surprised reaction to that statement. "I don't know who else to go to. I told him a couple of weeks ago about the men that came around. He said he'd take care of it, but he *didn't!*" That last word carried the pain of broken promises. "Now I don't know what to do. I don't know where Vinnie lives."

"Vinnie?" A common enough name, but Kaden didn't believe in coincidences. There could be only one Vinnie in the city who connected these people together, and Kaden wanted to see how much the kid would spill. Not to mention, he wanted to understand what the hell Vinnie Salentino had to do with this distraught kid. If that bastard was using this innocent as a runner, Kaden would kill the *mec* himself.

"Vinnie Salentino," Bean said, as if it was obvious. "He owns the block we live on, our apartment, the flower shop. He's the one who got her into that rehab program." He looked at his shoes. "Well, I guess it was Mr. Malone, really, but Vinnie paid for it. He's got some kinda foundation thing that gets people what they need."

"That's where I know Ben from," Lori said. "The Southside Women's Shelter. I was on the board. Angelina was treated there, and Ben stayed there, too, in one of the family rooms." An ideal arrangement for women with kids who would have otherwise been living on the streets, as long as the money didn't dry up. The Ninth Street Foundation funded the operation, along with whatever donations the directors could pull in. It was a halfway home, of sorts, for drug-addicted mothers. Lori had been treasurer when Angelina and Ben were there, and she'd been drawn to the serious kid who was always in the family area working on homework.

Wait. Rewind. *Some kinda foundation thing?* There was no fucking way that the Ninth Street Foundation had anything to do with Vinnie Salentino. Lori winced at her language even though it stayed in her head.

She was about to speak her thought out loud when the revolving door moved again and Martin stepped out into the street.

"Mr. Malone! You're here!" Ben practically levitated over to him then bounced on the balls of his feet like a pogo stick. "They took my ma! It was Jackal and … and another guy I never seen. Please! You gotta help me find her. They'll—they'll hurt her again." That last was barely audible on a whispered sob.

Martin set a quieting hand on the boy's shoulder and looked at his audience. Dense as a brick sometimes, and prone to being an unmitigated idiot, Martin was not stupid, and he quickly put two and two together. He trained his gaze on Lori. "You know him from Southside."

Bottled up hostility threatened to explode inside Lori's gut. She actually reached for Annie's hand. Her best friend from forever who was standing beside her like a sergeant at arms grasped on and squeezed.

"I do," she gritted out through clenched teeth. "What the hell do you and *Vinnie* have to do with Ninth Street Foundation?"

For the first time since Martin had announced his intention to divorce her, he looked at her with something other than contrition and regret on his face. His features hardened, though he still held a gentle hand to Ben's shoulder. "Later."

"Martin—"

"I said later. It's not important." He pulled his phone from his breast pocket and thumbed a contact.

"Martin, wait—"

"Yeah, Vinnie, we got a problem." Martin spoke into his phone but didn't take his eyes off of Lori. "Angelina got grabbed from the shop." Pause. "Yeah, Bean's here now—I'm out in front. We must've passed him in the elevator. Can't have been more than a couple hours ago." Another pause. "That's what I'm thinking. Uh-huh. Okay."

As he put the phone away, he shook his head to stop Lori from saying whatever it was she was about to say. "Things aren't always as they appear, Lori. With all due respect, you need to shut up, step off your high-and-mighty horse, and take a hard look around."

He glanced at the fierce scowl that Annie was sending him and included her in his next words. "Don't you dare go off half-cocked with what you *think* you know. Because you have no fucking idea what is really going on."

———— ▸ ◂ ————

"*Rien*. Nothing." Sabine shook her head then looked up from the laptop and pointed worried eyes at her husband. "The drive, it is not being recognized." This was the third computer they'd tried. It was clearly the thumb drive, not the computers. "It must have been damaged." The drive had been scraped up and slightly bent when it was eventually retrieved. Etienne had noticed it immediately, so the fact that it wasn't being read? No surprise.

While they jockeyed around with it, after the first attempt at accessing it had failed, Vinnie told them in a matter-of-fact recitation exactly what they would be seeing. If they could ever get the damn thing to work.

Laurent had been watching and listening, silent as always, revealing nothing of what he thought about keeping the video recording of a murder out of police hands, but now he stepped forward. Hand held out, he asked, "*Je peux?*"

Sabine extracted the stick from the USB port and handed it to him.

"I had an experience like this once in Africa." He fiddled with the thing, tugged a bit, but nothing happened. Reaching into a pocket of his military-style fatigues, he brought out a knife and snapped it open. Setting the stick on a pile of legal journals stacked on the corner of Martin's desk he stuck the tip of the knife into the edge of the casing and pried it up.

"Hey! Be careful with that thing," Vinnie barked just as the plastic casing snapped in two.

"Don't worry." Laurent grunted. "The data is on the memory card not the plastic casing." Holding the now-exposed circuit board up to the light, he squinted at the thing and cursed.

"Here, try these."

Laurent turned his head toward Vinnie, who held out a pair of readers. At Laurent's frown, Vinnie just shrugged. "Happens to the best of us. Don't be an ass—just take them."

With another grunt, Laurent took the glasses. He stuck them on the end of his nose and went back to studying the tiny device in his hand, ignoring Sabine's laughter.

"*Oui, juste ici.*" He held the thing out for Matisse to look at, twisted the front and back apart, and pointed with the tip of his knife. "This last pin is pulled off the pad. Can you see it? The solder is cracked."

"Fuck" was Vinnie's reaction to the discovery. "Does that mean the video is lost?"

"Not necessarily. But I'll need a small-scale solder gun to fix it." He looked around the posh office that was twice the size of his living quarters in Chaumont. "I don't suppose your lawyer has anything like that here?"

Vinnie's cell phone rang. He looked at the display then held it up before he answered. "No idea, but I can ask."

The question of a solder gun dropped in priority, however, as Vinnie listened to what Martin had to say.

"God *damn* that bastard." Vinnie wanted to kick something. "Bring the kid up here." He disconnected the call and looked at Matisse. "I don't expect you to understand why I kept that evidence to myself, but this time his victim is innocent."

Not waiting for a response, he looked back at his phone, called up a contact, and thumb-typed a text. By the time he'd watched it go and slid the thing back into his pocket, Martin returned with the sidewalk contingent.

Lori had her arm protectively around Bean's thin shoulders, but when the kid saw Vinnie, he stood up straighter and stepped away from her. Then ruined the effect by wiping his runny nose on his sleeve.

"We'll find her, son. It's not your fault. You did the right thing." Vinnie's voice was remarkably gentle.

"How are you involved with Angelina and Ben?" Lori's words were coated with hostility, and she took a step toward Vinnie, which may not have been very smart. Martin clearly didn't think so because he stopped her by gripping her arm.

"Lori, don't."

She yanked out of his hold. "Fuck off, Martin. I have a right to know." Turning back to Vinnie, she saw his frown.

"You know the kid?"

"Yes, and his mother. From Southside Women's Shelter."

Vinnie studied her for a moment, still frowning. Then something like understanding, or recognition, showed in his face as his eyebrows shot up. "You're *that* Lorilee Sheridan."

"What?" Hands fisted at her hips, she stared at him like he was nuts.

"You were treasurer there for, what, five years?"

And didn't that just stun her stupid. But before she could respond, he waved a hand in dismissal.

"Okay, fine, small world and all that. But we got a bigger problem than connecting the who's-who dots." He walked over to the boy. "Bean, can you tell me exactly what happened?"

Bean started talking, but Lori was still staring at Vinnie. Flummoxed, and no closer to understanding what the hell Vinnie had to do with Ben, she opened her mouth to protest, but a gentle hand on her shoulder stopped her. Jerking her head around, she found Laurent right beside her. When had he even moved?

"Let it go," he whispered to her in French and ran his hand down her arm in a soothing gesture, lifting her hand in his so he could kiss her fingertips. "I'll tell you later." He squeezed her hand. "Trust me."

And what could she say to that? She held his gaze for a moment then nodded. Refocusing back on Vinnie, who was listening intently as Ben finished his story, she saw something totally unexpected. The mob boss clearly cared about the boy and his mother. *Huh.*

Vinnie's phone buzzed, and he pulled it from a pocket and looked at the screen. "Got it." Holding the thing up, he said to Matisse, "This is where she is, at least for tonight. Can you help?"

Nineteen

It wasn't the waiting so much as the suspense of not knowing what was happening—*that* was the hardest part. Perhaps because Lori had no idea what to expect. How long did it take to bust into a, what … a whorehouse? And then rescue someone who'd been taken there against her will? How did they even go about doing that? Would there be guards? Armed guards? Did that even happen in America? *Of course it does, you idiot.* It was just so far out of her realm of experience that she had no idea about any of it.

But Sabine and Matisse were not rattled even a little bit. Without skipping a beat, they'd turned Martin's office into some sort of mission control post.

Lori watched the pair work from where she sat with the others in a conference room separated from the office proper by a glass partition. Etienne talked into his phone while his wife tapped away at her laptop and fed him information.

"I'll take three cards," Bean said in a serious voice, sliding his discards across the table.

"*Trois?*" Laurent affected a quizzical look, one eyebrow raised. "You are sure?" Lori knew he thickened his accent to sound more like the pirate he was pretending to be.

"Wee. Tu-wah." Bean's attempt at French was almost as comical. But bless her man, he was doing his best to keep the boy distracted.

Once Bean had understood this group of adults would find his mother and bring her back—there had been no hesitation in Vinnie's promise on that score, and Matisse had confirmed it—the tension in his thin body had loosened. Martin had been dispatched for take-out, as no one was going anywhere soon, and Lori had taken a small measure of perverse pleasure in watching

175

him being ordered about. It probably wasn't fair, but the emotion was honest. To his credit, he'd returned with a dozen fat, juicy hamburgers and a boxful of fries. When Bean yelled, "Yay! French fries!" both Kaden and Laurent shuddered in mock horror.

"*Pommes frites,*" they said in unison, enunciating each word carefully.

"Palm freet," Bean repeated. The high-five Laurent gave him had the kid grinning like Lori had never seen, and her heart squeezed. He'd had one hell of a life, and that he could even smile about anything was a wonder. Then he dived into his dinner, inhaling two burgers and about a pound of fries before he came up for air.

After the food was gone, Bean started to slide back into his fretting, but Kaden came to the rescue.

"Well, hullo, look what I found." The conference room had the obligatory polished wood table and a matching credenza, upon which perched an art deco coffee service. Affixed to the wall, a stylized shelving unit held a few token law books and some useless *objets d'art*. And a small acrylic trophy from some Atlantic City casino that encased a deck of playing cards.

With complete disregard for the sanctity of whatever the trophy meant to its owner, Kaden had cracked open the top, pulled out the cards, and proceeded, with Laurent as his willing accomplice, to thoroughly corrupt fourteen-year-old Benjamin. And they'd been at it now for over an hour.

While the latest initiate to the world of gambling was busy winning an impressive pile of coins from his new friends, Matisse did what only Matisse could do. After briefing his American colleagues at INTERPOL's DC headquarters, he received authorization to connect with the local jurisdiction. Although he was mildly surprised at how easily he'd gained the Yanks' approval to let him run things, it made sense. The abduction of Angelina Stripling was clearly linked to organized crime and, as such, related to his reason for being in-country. His unique status within the organization made him a low risk for going loose cannon on them, never mind that he was on hand with both the intel and a seasoned Lyon analyst. And most importantly, he was willing to take responsibility for it all on a Saturday night.

Normally the local law enforcement—in this case the PPD—would be the logical choice for a quick in-and-out. Just walk in, find Angelina, and take her away. Any other illicit activity that happened to be occurring on the premises at the time could be dealt with or not. However, there was no guarantee they wouldn't get a cop on the team who had his hand in Claudio Salentino's cookie jar.

The crime against Bean's mother arguably fell into both the kidnapping and human trafficking categories, and this gave Etienne options. The local police had jurisdiction, but because of the specific crime category, so did the FBI. Unlike France, the US has no single national police agency but overlapping layers of city, county, state, and federal enforcement jurisdictions. Matisse silently wondered how the hell anything ever got done.

The text message Vinnie had received gave the address of a motel in South Philly. Sabine found it on Google Earth, and from the Street View photos, it appeared to be a grubby building with bars on the windows. And it fit right in with the neighborhood, based on the one-eighty camera angles. Zooming in on a sign in one dirty window, she saw hourly rates posted for rooms. Disgusted, she accessed another database and learned that the building was owned by City Construction Company.

"City Construction," she said aloud, reaching for one of the files stacked beside her elbow. "I've seen this company before."

Vinnie looked up from his phone. "Claudio owns it." Then he narrowed his eyes and focused on her files. "But you knew that, didn't you."

Matisse caught him with a black gaze. "Down to yesterday's bank balance, knowing my wife."

"Jesus. And people think *I'm* scary."

Sabine directed a stunning smile at her husband that disappeared as quickly as it had arrived when she glanced back down at her computer.

There was no question that the local cops knew of the motel-slash-brothel, and the fact that it existed at all meant that someone, likely more than one someone, was getting paid to ignore it. That would change tonight … and the fallout could get messy. But in the meantime, the FBI's Philadelphia field office was just around the corner from their current location and seemed the safer choice.

While Matisse parleyed with one Nick Talenti, special agent in charge, Vinnie paced back and forth, talking on his phone, texting, and muttering to himself. Matisse finally told him to sit down or leave, and Lori silently applauded him. Vinnie chose to park it in one of the chairs that faced the desk, but when he learned the FBI team was headed to Martin's office, he stood.

"My involvement will only complicate things."

Matisse did not comment on that irrefutable statement.

"But I wouldn't mind borrowing your, er, associate to see about repairing this." Vinnie held up the bent flash drive.

Laurent looked up from the cards he'd been studying. "*D'accord.* Let me just finish this hand so I can recover some of my blunt."

Bean groaned. "Aw, man, I guess that means I gotta fold." He laid down the cards in his hand. "I got nothing but a pair of jacks this time."

"Then it's a good thing you folded." Laurent tossed his cards to the middle of the table. "You would have beat me. All I had was a pair of eights."

"Hey! No fair!" Bean looked around the room in indignation then pointed his finger at Laurent. "He cheated!"

Kaden, who'd already bowed out of the hand, chuckled and shook his head. "That's what is called a fake, son."

The girls had been watching, mostly because there was nothing else to do and both were trying not to bounce off the walls in impatience. Now Lori scowled while Annie laughed.

"That wasn't very nice," Lori said, but Laurent just shrugged as he scooped the change from the center of the table.

"All part of the lesson, *chérie.*" Then he grinned at the sulking Bean and winked. "Next time he won't be so quick to fold. Besides, he still has all of Macallister's coins and most of mine."

Bean looked stunned. "Do I get to keep it?" The neat stacks of pennies, nickels, dimes, and quarters in front of him easily totaled ten dollars' worth.

"*Absolument,* my friend. You won it fair and square." With that pronouncement Laurent stood. The coins had come from a jar in Martin's office, as neither Kaden nor Laurent had any American money on them, and Laurent wasn't about to make the kid give it up.

Martin was unaware that he'd made the contribution, having disappeared to somewhere else in the firm's office after delivering dinner. Lori doubted he'd ask for it back. It had been a pleasant surprise to witness her ex-husband's protectiveness toward Bean. One redeeming quality, she allowed.

It wasn't terribly late—only just past ten o'clock—but Lori was beginning to fade. Laurent noticed and consulted briefly with his INTERPOL superiors. Sauntering back into the conference room, he stood behind Lori and massaged her shoulders. "How about we drop you three off at the hotel? There's nothing any of you can do here, and you might as well try to get some sleep."

Lori wanted to protest, but she was too exhausted. It had been a very long day for all of them, since none of them had slept on the flight over. Besides which, what he said was true. Her bit part in this surrealistic drama was done. There was not one thing she could contribute other than getting in the way. She glanced at Annie who nodded in agreement, but ...

"What about Ben?"

The boy was shuffling and reshuffling the cards on the bare table, the coins that had been stacked in front of him having disappeared into his pockets the instant they were proclaimed his.

"He needs to stay with Matisse and talk to the FBI." Laurent looked at Bean, who appeared to be on the verge of losing his composure. "It will be okay, *mon ami*. My big friend over there won't let them touch you, but you need to tell them exactly what happened. Everything you remember."

Bean straightened his thin shoulders. "I will."

"All right, great," Vinnie boomed. "It's settled. Bean stays and the rest of us go." Anxious to get gone before the feds arrived, he ushered them out the door, but not before he put a hand on Bean's shoulder and spoke softly to him. "Don't you worry. We got this. Your ma will be back home before you know it."

In what condition, however ... Vinnie didn't dare make a promise that he had no control over keeping.

For such a large city, everything in the downtown area seemed close. After depositing Lori and her friends at their hotel, it was a few short blocks to a very upscale urban residential sector. Laurent masked his surprise when Vinnie hit a remote and a garage door opened. His personal residence?

"You have a solder gun here?"

"Among other useful tools." Vinnie's tone was dry, almost mocking, leaving Laurent to speculate on what the hell he might be witness to. What he found was the last thing he expected.

Vinnie didn't hesitate to lead the way down a steep stairway into a dark subterranean basement. Laurent's hand automatically reached for his weapon as his host flipped a few switches at the bottom. Bright florescent lights flicked on to reveal a space that was a hobbyist's dream workshop.

"*Pas mal*," Laurent muttered as he took in the far wall covered with pegboard that contained more small-scale tools than he'd ever seen, including three solder guns in various gauges hanging in a vertical row down the left side. Another wall was made up of artistically lit glass shelves showcasing scale models of vintage automobiles. Even from a distance, he could tell they were accurate to the smallest detail. Classic early and midcentury designs from Europe and America that he recognized. *Interesting hobby*. What did it say about a reputed mob boss—one who oversaw a veritable conglomerate of practical industries—who indulged in a hobby that was as solitary as it was tediously precise?

He moved to the center worktable where the current work in progress was spread out. It appeared to be an early twentieth-century fire truck. Fenders, doors, ladders, and other various parts were laid around the chassis on newspaper, having recently been painted, waiting to be attached. One thing was patently clear: the Philadelphia mob boss knew his fine work. And wasn't that just totally incongruous to his tough-guy image?

"Why do you need my help?"

Vinnie plucked the smallest of the solder guns off the wall. "Detail work I can do, but I don't know anything about electronics. And the contents of the flash drive are too important to risk screwing up." He handed the tool to Laurent. "Are you sure you know what you're doing?"

Laurent held out his hand for the memory stick. "Trust me with it or not, I don't give a damn one way or the other. There are no guarantees, but it's fairly straightforward."

After a moment's hesitation, the small device dropped into Laurent's outstretched hand. He held it up to the light, studying the damaged partition. "I need a clamp."

While Vinnie looked on, Laurent carefully fitted the tiny exposed circuit board into a small-scale workbench clamp and plugged in the gun. This time he accepted the loan of Vinnie's magnifiers without a second glance. Using a scrap of metal from the trash bin, he experimented with the tool until he felt he could control it.

The repair took only a second. A quick touch of the narrow tip left a precise little gob of molten metal, and the pin was reattached to the pad where the original solder had cracked.

"It needs to sit a moment." Laurent studied his handiwork as it cooled before handing back the glasses and unplugging the tool.

Outside Vinnie's Delancey Street townhouse, Joe Carlucci loitered in the shadows, unbelieving of what he'd just seen. Up until this moment, guilt had weighed heavily on his conflicted soul after his visit to Claudio. An ill-considered visit, the cognizance of which had come about ten steps too late. He'd been ready to betray his boss, his *family* for Christ's sake, all because of his own stupidity and wounded pride. But as he'd stood in front of Claudio's obese form a few hours earlier, the cold glint in those dark fleshy eyes had reminded Joe why he'd chosen the older brother.

Joe was not a nice man, had never tried or pretended to be one. He'd done things he wasn't proud of, but always his actions had been in support of, or for the protection of, the family. He had killed, but not indiscriminately. And never undeserved, at least not from the perspective of the world he inhabited. What he saw tonight in the eyes of the younger son of his mentor was ... black. Just like the old man had become. No conscience whatsoever. And then there was the woman.

What he'd originally come to confess—that Vinnie was making bad decisions, trusting the wrong people, and losing opportunities, and he, Joe, wanted to align with the brother who hadn't turned politician—dried up on his tongue. Instead, he'd made up something about respect and sharing and some other kumbaya bullshit, in the spirit of family and brotherhood and all that. Claudio had looked at him like he'd lost a screw. Which was quite possible.

"Uncle Joe, you know I love ya." Claudio had pressed a meaty fist to his chest. "And I get that you want to see Roberto's sons united. But the fact that Vinnie sent you instead of having the respect to come to me himself … well that's just fucked up, ya know? And it just proves that he's gone soft."

Joe had left the restaurant, the ammunition Claudio returned to him heavy in his pocket, and driven himself down to a park that overlooked the river. He needed to get his head twisted back on straight and think clearly without emotion. If he'd been in any other business, he'd have been long retired by now, dandling grandchildren or even great-grandchildren on his knee. But that wasn't his life—never had been. He'd joined the ranks of the Salentino organization back in the heyday of the fifties as a cocky teenager and had proved his loyalty to the family. When it became clear that Roberto, his friend and mentor, had let power and greed overtake common sense and had gone on a merciless killing spree, Joe had transferred his loyalty to the heir and helped put the monster behind bars. And he'd never once second-guessed that decision. Until now.

Now, all rational thoughts, including the realization that Joe should come clean with Vinnie about what he, Joe, had almost done flew out the window. That heavy guilt was pushed aside by a surge of anger and betrayal. Why the fuck had Vinnie brought that French bastard into his home?

First the pompous lawyer worms his way into family business and the boss is practically singing hallelujah at all the legit money he's making. Does he spend it on increasing the drug intake or branching into something even more lucrative? No, he dumps it into some neighborhood charity. A charity that benefited cousins and neighbors, but Joe conveniently forgot that salient point.

Then they go off all half-cocked over the flash drive. Whatever's on that thing is making Vinnie insane, and I'm a convenient target. Like it was my fault that the lawyer lost the thing? And the woman he thinks might have it has to be treated with respect. In the old days, it wouldn't have mattered who she was—she'd have been shaken down, slapped around, or whatever it took to get what they wanted.

The French mob lackey was the last straw to Joe's sanity. The fact that Vinnie actually put up with the assault at that storage locker was bad enough. That Joe's own behavior had triggered the man's reaction didn't even enter his mind. All he knew was that whatever was going on was big, Vinnie was trusting people he didn't even fucking know, and Joe was left out in the cold.

Inside the townhouse, Vinnie led the way back up the stairs to a home office straight out of *Architectural Digest,* carrying the repaired flash drive like it was a piece of antique Venetian glass.

"Do you have an external extension to plug it into?" Laurent asked. "There's still a risk the new solder won't hold."

"Yeah, well, I don't have anything like that, so I'm gonna have to take my chances."

They were silent as the laptop on the desk came to life. Vinnie carefully slid the business end of the memory stick into the USB port and held his breath. One heartbeat, two, three, four …

"Thank fuck." The flash drive's file menu popped up on the screen, and he ran his finger across the touchpad until the cursor pointed at the single file name. A double tap, and the little spinning hourglass did its thing. It seemed like it took forever, but suddenly the screen filled with the frozen first frame of the video.

Vinnie let the cursor hover over the START button and looked at Laurent. "Remember what I told your boss."

A curt nod of acknowledgment, and Vinnie tapped the pad.

The video played out, the sound muffled due to the distance between the camera and the action—except for the crack of glass when the second bullet penetrated the windshield—but words weren't necessary.

"The shooter is my younger brother, Claudio Salentino. And before you ask, *no,* I did not set this up. This is his idea of giving me the finger, among other things."

Laurent stared at the screen as the killer waddled back to his car and drove off. Then the video rebooted to the first frame, once again frozen on the screen. He had a dozen questions, but now was not the time. Forcing his voice to a normal tone, he said, "I suggest you save this to another drive while you have the chance; I can't vouch for the life of the damaged stick. Park it in the Cloud and password protect it."

The men regarded each other, and Vinnie seemed to make a decision. "How about if I email it to you?"

———————

The hostage recovery itself, after what seemed like hours of organization—or more precisely, hours of negotiation—took only minutes. Angelina was indeed at the ratty motel, alone in a room that hadn't had a Lysol experience in some time. Strung out and incoherent, they found her curled up in a fetal position on a filthy bed, her eye swollen and bruised with a cut on her cheekbone that was crusted with dried blood.

A search of all twelve rooms at the dump revealed three other women entertaining their *dates,* but the rest of the rooms were empty. As the feds observed no firsthand solicitation or money changing hands—sex between consenting adults was not illegal—and none of the women seemed anxious to be rescued, the team left with only Angelina. The rest of it could be dealt with later, or not, as determined by PPD.

After departing Vinnie's house, Dubois rejoined Matisse and Sabine, who were linked in by an audio com unit from their post in Martin's office. Once Angelina had been evaluated by the ER doc on duty at Philadelphia General and declared stable, they all breathed a sigh of relief. Poor Bean was practically climbing the walls, and Martin took charge of getting him to his mother's side. She would be monitored closely for a day or two as the drugs worked through her system, and the feds promised to post a guard in case her abductors tried anything stupid. There would be further inquiries and paperwork in the morning, but for now the crisis had been resolved.

Laurent let himself into the hotel room just past midnight, stifling a yawn as the door swung shut behind him. On missions in Africa, he'd often gone several days without sleep. He was trained for it, but he'd been out of that life just long enough that the twenty-four hours since they'd left Ménerbes were taking a toll. In truth he'd been awake only a couple of hours more than the civilians, and they'd held up pretty well. Riding the adrenaline, he supposed. Lori had only begun to fade in earnest after she'd downed her hefty American beef burger.

A glance over at the bed confirmed that she was asleep. Ambient light from the city high-rises infiltrated the gauzy curtains of their tenth-floor room, washing it in deep gray. Without turning on a light, he quietly brushed his teeth and undressed then slid between the sheets. They were soft but cool, and the warmth of Lori's slumbering form beckoned him. Not wanting to wake her but unable to stop himself, he carefully scooped her up and pulled her over to snuggle against his side. She sighed, mumbled something, and settled against him. Her satiny heat penetrated his skin, soothing the restlessness that coursed through his veins. *Mon Dieu, she feels good.* He resettled the duvet so she was covered to her neck, wrapped his arm around her waist, and closed his eyes.

Twenty

Lori woke to the sensation of being cocooned in warmth, a comforting weight against her back, and a smooth, hard source of heat beneath her. *Laurent.* Flat on his back, the thick arm that pinned her against his side had found its way beneath her nightie so his hand rested on the bare curve of her hip. The other was flung across the pillows on the other side of the bed. From where her head nestled just below his shoulder, she could see his broad chest rising and falling in a steady rhythm. Felt it, too. The banked strength of him was awesome. Impressive and fearsome and so incredibly beautiful, only enhanced by the sinuous dark swirls of his tattoo. If she wasn't very careful, she was going to fall in love with this man.

Torn between the sensual pleasure of simply watching him—*feeling* him—sleep, and the physical discomfort of needing to relieve herself, her options disintegrated when a loud pounding on the door shattered the peace.

"Police! Open up!"

The demand was followed by more pounding, and voices could be heard through the door.

Startled and alarmed, Lori grabbed the sheets to cover herself, but Laurent was instantly on his feet, pulling on his pants. "Get dressed. Quickly," he said in a low voice as he snagged his phone from the bedside table and tapped it. His call was answered immediately. "Police at the door. More than one," Laurent said then listened. "No idea." Pause. "*D'accord.*"

More banging on the door. "Open up!" Lori had her underwear on and was fumbling with her jeans, barely keeping herself upright as they tangled with her feet.

"Coming now," Laurent said loudly as he shoved the phone into a pocket and shrugged into his shirt not bothering to button it. Scooping up his SIG Sauer, he checked the clip in a fast, practiced motion. Then he glanced at Lori and inwardly cursed. She was white as a ghost. Her pants were up over her hips but not buttoned and her fingers shook as she fought to pull a sweater down over her naked torso. "Stay back, over there behind the bed." He wished he could reassure her, but there was no time. Whoever these people were, if he didn't open the door in the next minute, they would likely kick it in.

Weapon out of sight behind the door, he opened it as far as the security latch allowed.

"Police!" the belligerent uniformed man shouted again, shoving on the door. "Open this door now!" There were at least three other uniforms pushing in behind him.

"ID, if you please." Laurent's voice was calm, but his eyes flashed dangerously as he took a quick look-see over his shoulder. Lori was sitting on the bed now, tugging on her boots.

A badge was waved, visible for an instant in the crack of the door.

Laurent was unmoved. "Shiny enough, but it could be from a box of Cracker Jacks for all I know. I asked for identification. This is a familiar term, yes?"

"Show it to him," came a voice from the back of the pack. Laurent's superior height afforded him a view over the uniforms, and he saw a man in a suit behind them. It was the suit that had given the order.

On a muttered curse, the first man held up the badge again, this time turning the case over and angling it toward the opening in the door.

Laurent looked at the plastic card, studied the man holding it, looked at the card again, then nodded. Patrick Mulligan of the Philadelphia Police Department, in the flesh. *Bloody fucking hell,* he thought as he shut the door and jammed his handgun into his waistband. He glanced at Lori and gave her what he hoped was a reassuring nod before flipping the security latch and opening the door.

In a flash he was surrounded by aggressive cops, but rather than argue or try to fight, he let himself be shoved face-first against the wall and patted down. His handgun was confiscated along with his phone and wallet. The idiots didn't bother to check his boots, so he still had a knife. Not that he planned to use it.

"Hey!" Lori suddenly appeared in the narrow vestibule of the room, elbowing her way through the cops. "What the hell is going on?"

"Stay out of this, ma'am," one of the uniforms said, stepping in to block her access to Laurent as one of the others clamped handcuffs around his wrists.

"Like hell I will. You can't just barge in here and expect me to—"

"This man is under arrest for the murder of Vincenzio Salentino." It was the suit, in the same tone he might have used to comment on the weather, standing in the threshold with his hands in his pockets.

"*What?*" The words hit her like a pair of cymbals clashing around her head. "But ... but that's impossible! He was—"

"*Chérie.*" Laurent's voice cut through the ringing in her ears. She looked at him and caught the imperceptible shake of his head.

Huh? "But—"

"Matisse will handle it." Laurent spoke softly, but his eyes were blazing with fury.

But why? Lori wanted to scream. She also wanted to pound her fists on the PPD asshole who blocked her way as he handed over Laurent's wallet and phone to the man in the doorway. Another cop, behind her in the room now, wrapped a hand around her upper arm for an instant before she wrenched away.

"Get your hands off of me." The uniform scowled at her but didn't touch her again.

"Colonel Laurent Dubois," came a deep voice from just beyond the open door. The man in the suit jerked around, the wallet in his hand open to the military ID card that proclaimed that very name and rank, but he had to crane his neck up to look into the face of the person who'd spoken. What he saw had him taking a quick step back, straight into the doorjamb, and he would have toppled over if one of his officers hadn't righted him.

"His name is Laurent Dubois," Matisse repeated, closing the distance, his voice slightly louder this time and far more menacing. "Colonel. Recently retired from the French army and currently serving as special investigative agent for INTERPOL General Secretariat headquarters in Lyon. Arrived in the United States yesterday on diplomatic status, I might add, in connection with a cross-border investigation." Quasi-diplomatic status in reality, but in this case the result would be the same. "Do you mind telling me who you are and what's going on here?"

Suit struggled to recover his composure with an aggressive stance, but the effort failed when his voice squeaked, "Who are you?" an octave or two higher than before.

Matisse flipped open his own ID and handed it to the man. "Lieutenant Commander Etienne Matisse, INTERPOL, also here on diplomatic status. Ms. Sheridan." Turning away from the man in the suit as if he was irrelevant, Etienne held out a hand to Lori, and like Moses with the Red Sea, the uniforms stepped out of the path between them. *Allez avec Sabine.*

"Now hold on here just a minute." The suit, voice back to normal, stepped in to block Lori just as she reached the lifeline of Etienne's hand. "What the hell did you just say? You have no authority—"

"That is where you are mistaken, *monsieur.*" Another calm voice from the hallway, this one as sultry in her French accent as Matisse's was scary. "It is your authority in question here, not his. May I suggest you acquaint yourself with the interagency cooperative agreements of your own NCB?"

Suit leaned back into the hallway and looked both ways. When he caught sight of Sabine standing behind her husband in a pair of skinny jeans, calf-hugging boots and a black cashmere sweater that was at once demure and sexy as hell, he snapped to attention. "Well, hello, sweetheart. And who might you be?"

"Your worst nightmare," Matisse answered conversationally, "if you don't put your tongue back inside your head and resume thinking with the brain between your ears rather than the little one dangling between your legs. And I believe I asked that question first."

The poor guy turned a bit pale as he swallowed his wolf grin but didn't take his eyes off of Sabine. "Detective Richard Johnson, PPD."

"Thank you, Detective. Mrs. Robicheau is also a member of my team and will escort this civilian out of harm's way." Emphasis on the *Mrs.,* Matisse glared until the man shifted, allowing Etienne to guide Lori out of the room.

Concern and fear roiling in her gut, Lori was stunned speechless by the unruffled demeanor her friends displayed while she was nearly wetting her pants. She had only a brief moment to glance over her shoulder at Laurent before she was hustled away, but he was watching her and their eyes met.

And God love him, he winked. *Winked!* Like he wasn't handcuffed and accused of murder! For crying out loud, she was going to murder *him* when she saw him next.

Laurent watched Lori traverse the gauntlet of the imbecilic PPD dickheads, her shoulders high and her nose in the air. *Good girl,* he praised in silence. She was terrified, but she did not cower. He watched her disappear down the hall with Sabine then turned his attention back to his predicament.

Vinnie Salentino murdered? *Putain de merde.* It had to have happened shortly after he'd left the man's house last night. Vinnie had offered to drive him back, but Laurent had declined, wanting the opportunity to stretch his legs for the dozen or so short blocks back to Malone's building. Thinking back, he remembered feeling that tingle at the base of his neck, like someone was watching, as he'd stepped out onto the sidewalk. It had made him kick up into an easy jog rather than just walk—

"Excusez-moi, monsieur, but unless you have a search warrant, I will advise you to keep your hands out of closed bags." Laurent resisted the urge to bare his teeth at the cop poking into Lori's things. There was nothing incriminating in either of their satchels, but he wasn't going to sit by and have his rights trampled with improper procedure when this whole setup was a farce to begin with.

The cop turned and shot him a smirking just-you-try-and-make-me look, one he was probably well practiced at flaunting when he and his buddies outnumbered the perps. But that look disappeared as quickly as it had formed when Matisse stepped fully into the room.

"I suggest you take his advice. You wouldn't want to trigger an international incident, hmm?"

Perhaps it was the politely taunting way that Matisse spoke, but suddenly the cop reared up and settled his right hand on the holster at his hip. "Unless you want a slug in your chest for interfering with police business, I suggest you step back and let us do our job."

Oh, well, that was the wrong thing to say.

Etienne's smile was as friendly as a shark's, his even, white teeth gleaming in the morning light. One hand lifted slowly to show his phone. "I perhaps might have neglected to mention that I've been recording this entire tête-à-tête."

The officer took a half step back and swallowed nervously, stealing a glance at Detective Johnson.

"And I must say, so far I am rather unimpressed with local police procedures." Matisse spared a glance over his shoulder. Johnson was standing in the doorway tapping some text message out on his phone, the other uniformed officers appeared frozen in their tracks. Laurent stood calmly with his back to the wall.

"In addition to your misguided efforts in arresting an international law enforcement agent under false circumstances *and* having failed to advise him of his Miranda rights, you've now threatened the life of a senior diplomat for the serious infraction of reminding you of standard search protocol." Matisse shook his head as if scolding a recalcitrant child. "Not a wise career move, my friend."

Behind him, an incoming text pinged, but Matisse ignored it. The last thing he intended to do was turn his back to the pompous dick in front of him.

"Mr. Matisse," the detective finally said, his tone bordering on apologetic. "I have an eye-witness who took a photograph of Dubois here leaving Salentino's home last night. The time stamp on the picture matches the approximate time of death."

Without looking at Laurent, Matisse turned to face Johnson. "I don't deny that my agent was at his house; I sent him there myself. As it happens, Vinnie Salentino was assisting us with our investigation. Dubois left Mr. Salentino alive and well, and returned to the law offices where I was coordinating a hostage rescue with the FBI."

"What was he helping you with?"

"I'm afraid that's above your pay grade." Matisse didn't skip a beat with the insult. "How was he killed?"

Johnson hesitated before answering. "Gunshot to the forehead." His eyes darted from Matisse to Dubois, as if sizing up his capabilities. "Execution style."

"Who discovered the body?"

The temperature in the room had risen exponentially, and Detective Johnson belatedly realized he might be in over his head, resenting the hell out of the ugly brute who was making him look bad. It was an unfortunate truth that some cops cared more about their ego than finding the truth, and Johnson was one of those few. Not like he gave a shit.

"We're done here," he said with false bravado, expecting his authority to carry the day as it usually did. His finger swirled around in a let's-wrap-it-up gesture. The uniforms started to roll, one of them taking hold of Laurent's arm to march him out, but Matisse's voice cut through the room like a whip.

"Who. Discovered. The. Body."

Johnson stopped. Narrowed his eyes at the huge guy. Fuck. This was not what he needed right now. "One of his own guys. Joe something."

"That would be Joe Carlucci, recently estranged from his longtime employer over an incident of insubordination. An incident that caused further humiliation to himself in that I and my entire team witnessed the dressing-down."

His black eyes held the detective in place like the *Star Destroyer*'s tractor beam. "He was a very angry man when he last departed from Salentino. Dubois, where is your weapon?"

"Confiscated a few minutes ago, sir."

"Where is it?" The question was asked to the room, but Matisse never broke eye contact with the head guy.

"Er, I've got it." Officer Mulligan shuffled around. "Here it is."

Matisse looked over and saw the uniformed PPD officer pull Laurent's SIG Sauer from his own waistband and hold it out by its handgrip, nose down. With his bare hand. His fingerprints all over it.

His eyes tracked back to the detective, turning from irritation to disgust. "Perhaps I should have started off by asking for *your* identification, because

I am now finding it nearly impossible to believe that you aren't a bunch of imposters playing a dangerous game. If Dubois had actually fired that weapon last night, your team has compromised the evidence to such a degree that a first-year law school dropout would be able to spring him free."

Johnson blanched. "Now look here—"

"Detective." Etienne's voice was low and calm but cut across the room as ominously as the rumbling that preceded a great clap of thunder. "Before you do something so egregiously stupid that could cause you to lose your rank, I recommend that you call off your ..." He waved his hands at the men in uniform—boys in the brains department if this was a typical arrest scenario—who were looking more uncertain by the moment. "Your men, and contact your INTERPOL liaison. Immediately. Trust me, this will save you much headache."

Etienne looked down and fiddled with his phone, as if he was letting the words sink in. In fact, he was finding his camera, which he brought up and used to click a quick photo of the cop who still held Laurent's SIG Sauer in his hand like a rookie idiot. Then he took a picture of Laurent.

"If you insist on taking my man in, I have time-stamped photographic proof that he has no bruises or cuts on his face or torso at the time you picked him up. I also have proof that your team did not properly bag his weapon. Dubois, when's the last time you fired that thing?"

"Two weeks ago, sir, at Salon Air Base."

"Will you freely grant the detective and his men permission to search the room for another weapon?"

Dubois cast glacial eyes on the uniformed men around him. "On the condition that they are respectful of Ms. Sheridan's personal items, they have my permission to rip up the room to their juvenile delight."

There was no other weapon found, of course, and the room wasn't tossed asunder as Laurent had expected. But Detective Johnson did not acquiesce to Etienne's diplomatic pressure.

"And if he resists," the detective said sternly, "I can't protect him from rough handling." *Not that I would even try* was unspoken but clear in the man's expression.

Matisse was beginning to lose patience, and anger burned in his dark eyes. "Has he attempted to resist so far?"

"Well, he didn't open the door right away, and—"

"Asking for identification to ensure your tribe here wasn't of the same ilk that executed Vinnie Salentino is not resisting. Once your man produced the requested ID, Dubois opened the door." Matisse had been in the shadows of the hallway for that exchange, though the PPD had been so intent on their arrest, they'd stupidly missed him. It was his first clue that he was dealing with a bunch of sloppy amateurs. Or intentional sandbaggers.

The detective met that black stare as best he could, a challenge to both his fortitude and his physicality, Matisse being a good nine inches taller.

"Fair point," he allowed.

"Where are you taking him?" Matisse had every intention of following, and making some fast phone calls on the way.

If Detective Johnson thought he could win a staring contest with Etienne Matisse, he was mistaken. After a moment's hesitation, he seemed to realize this. "Third District headquarters on South 11th. But you won't—"

"Thank you, Detective. You will find Colonel Dubois to be the model detainee." A very temporary detainee, Matisse would make certain. "I'll see you shortly. Dubois." He nodded to Laurent then disappeared.

"They got Angie." Claudio's head hoodlum, Paulie, who preferred the anglicized version to his given name of Paolo, had waited for the boss to finish his phone call before stepping into the room to share the news.

"Yeah, well, someone got Vinnie, too, so I guess we're more than even." Although Claudio didn't sound overwhelmed with glee at that pronouncement.

Paulie hesitated for a moment. "What, you mean he got picked up?"

"Picked off." Claudio held up his doughy hand, thumb up and index finger pointed, held the tip of his finger to his forehead, and cocked his thumb.

"Damn. And you didn't … you weren't, er …" Paulie waved his hand in the air since he couldn't seem to get the question out.

That doughy hand turned into a fist and pounded on the table. "No, you stupid fuck. He's my brother. I didn't want him dead, just brought down a notch or two."

"Oh, okay, boss. Whatever you say." The guy hovered in the doorway, uncertain. "Well, then, I'm sorry to hear that. What are you gonna do now?"

"I dunno. Take over the businesses, I guess. Up the action on the street." *And figure out who killed my brother.*

Paulie was still there a few minutes later, watching his boss with a strange expression when Claudio looked up. "What? Get outta here." That pudgy hand waved in dismissal. "Put your ears to the street and get me something. Whoever killed Vinnie stepped over the line, and I want to know who it was." *So I can take out the motherfucker myself.*

Martin Malone looked down at the pale caricature of his client's face, the small red circle in the middle of his forehead crusted over with dried blood, and immediately heaved up his breakfast into the waste bin at the end of the table. No doubt placed there for just that purpose. It was the temperature of a meat locker inside the morgue, but Martin didn't notice; he was too numb. Ever since he'd gotten the phone call that morning, he'd been moving around in a state of shock.

"Sir?" The police officer's overloud voice jerked Martin out of his stupor. "Yeah, that's him."

The officer nodded at the attendant, who pulled a gray sheet back up over the body. *The body.* Jesus Christ Almighty. Who could have done this? And why?

An image of Lori's badass soldier—an apt description of the man—flitted through his mind, and he tried to reconcile the guy's behavior the night before with a cold-blooded killer. Vinnie's killer. There was no question Laurent Dubois had killed in the line of duty, but he didn't look or act the type to do so indiscriminately. And in any case, things just didn't add up. The soldier was an INTERPOL agent not some foreign vigilante. The whole lot of them had stepped in and marshaled resources to recover Angelina like they'd done that sort of thing a hundred times.

He felt a tap on his arm and looked up to see the morgue attendant holding out a paper towel.

"Thanks." He took it and wiped his mouth then wadded it up in his fist.

"Sir?" The police officer again, sounding like he was speaking through a wall of water. "If you're ready, sir, we're done here."

"Yeah." The word came out as a croak, and Martin cleared his throat. "Yeah, okay. Let's go." He turned and followed the man out of the meat locker, down an antiseptic yellowish corridor, and through some sort of hydraulic-powered sliding door. Oh, the elevator.

The trip up from the basement in the moving box sized for gurneys felt claustrophobic and seemed to take forever. Martin suddenly found his breath coming in shallower and shallower intervals, forcing him to compensate for the lack of air by breathing harder. His vision narrowed to a pinprick, making the door look like it was a mile away. He held his hand out as if to touch it when the floor jerked and the thing opened. The officer caught him before he crashed to the ground.

Twenty-One

"I can't believe this is happening." Lori slumped in her chair, staring morosely at the coffee getting cold in front of her. Her hair was pulled back into a loose braid, and she wore no makeup. Sabine had procured a small kit of toiletry essentials from the front desk, so she'd been able to brush her teeth. Beyond that, she didn't care what she looked like.

"You do not need to worry, although I understand it is hard not to." Sabine's beautiful voice was as warm and comforting as her steady gaze. Confident too. "Law enforcement loves its bureaucracy, no matter the jurisdiction. A process must be followed, but then he will be released. Etienne is making it happen as we speak."

In fact, Sabine had received a text to that effect from her husband just moments before. In the fifteen minutes it had taken for him to follow the police vehicles to the downtown substation, Etienne had been busy.

Their INTERPOL commander and close friend, Simon Purcell, lived for the challenge and drama of orchestrating complex international jurisdictional conflicts. He also enjoyed tweaking the noses of preening jackasses who were more interested in political posturing than the practical reality of guilt or innocence. Or sorting out the white hats from the black.

True to form, Simon had jumped in. Never mind that it was the middle of a Sunday afternoon in London. First he contacted the upper echelon at INTERPOL DC, most likely catching them at their breakfast tables, then moved on to the Philadelphia FBI, connecting with the very same special agent in charge who had aided them in the recovery of Angelina Stripling mere hours earlier.

Simon's status within the organization was complicated, and as a result, nobody fucked with him. He'd been around forever, was as senior as one could be without becoming completely removed from fieldwork, and embodied the spirit of international cooperation. He was also immune to political wrangling. Sabine knew of at least a half dozen times he'd tossed his resignation letter onto the SG's desk.

"She's right," Annie said, reaching out to cover one of Lori's hands with her own. "Etienne will get him out. It's a misunderstanding is all."

Lori gripped her friend's hand, grateful for the connection. Kaden sat on her other side at the table they'd taken in the hotel's restaurant, quietly sipping his coffee and reading some newsfeed on his tablet, a silent but steady presence. There was no place else to sit other than the lobby lounge, and the seating arrangements there were too spread apart for private conversation.

But despite the reassurances, the sinking feeling in her gut didn't lessen. "I didn't want him to come with me." A lie, though wrapped in truth; she'd been afraid she was dragging him into danger. And now look what happened. She shook her head, eyes focused somewhere in the middle of the table.

"I told him it could be dangerous, and he laughed at me. 'I'm a soldier,' he said, 'I think I can handle dangerous.' Those were the exact words he used, like I was being a dunce to worry."

Sabine's phone chirped with an incoming text, and she took a moment to read it. "They've deferred booking. Martin has arrived at the precinct."

"Martin? Whatever for?" Lori bristled at the idea that her lying bastard of an ex-husband would reinforce the farce of Laurent's involvement in Vinnie's murder. "If he thinks he can—"

"No." Sabine held up her hand to stop the tirade as another text popped up. "It's not like that." She typed a short message then watched the phone as she waited for a reply. When it chirped again she nodded, apparently satisfied.

"It's done."

Lori looked at her in shock. "Done? As in, he's being released?"

"*Oui, c'est ça.* Your, er, Martin provided irrefutable proof that Laurent could not have killed Vinnie Salentino."

Relief flooded through Lori's body at the same time that she frowned in confusion. "*Martin* got him off?"

"You have my thanks." Laurent held out his hand to his lover's former husband, not because he wanted to but because the man deserved it. The *mec* could have been the prick Lori believed him to be. He could have withheld the evidence, could have pretended he didn't realize its significance, but he'd not played those games. And to see the poor schmuck at the precinct, green around the gills and visibly clammy, Laurent figured Malone's morning had been worse than his own.

Detective Johnson proved to be a stubborn and ungracious impediment in spite of the new evidence brought forth. Probably because Matisse had not sugarcoated his recitation of the detective's failings during the morning's encounter. Or possibly because he'd been paid to make it difficult. After all, having a false suspect in custody took the limelight away from the real perp. *Something to pursue later,* Laurent told himself.

When Martin Malone arrived at the precinct and produced a message from Vinnie—the voice indisputably distinctive even as he identified himself—recorded ten minutes *after* Dubois was photographed leaving the house, Johnson refused to accept it. Until an irate chief of police called him personally and ordered him to drop the charges. When the top dog barks, the whelps fall in line.

That was undoubtedly Simon's doing, and Laurent made a mental note to thank him for it. It took another half an hour and a stack of forms signed in triplicate before his personal items were returned, including his SIG. Ironically, it was handed over in a sealed evidence bag. He'd exchanged glances with Matisse but said nothing.

Now, standing on the sidewalk under a gray sky that threatened rain, Laurent savored the clean air of freedom.

Martin took the offered hand despite the awkwardness of the moment. "You had no reason to kill him. I'm glad I could help, but I'm guessing your friends would have managed even without that recording."

"Nonetheless, I appreciate it," Laurent said. "How is the boy doing?" Angelina was still in the hospital, according to Etienne's FBI contact, and under Bureau protection, but Bean had disappeared.

"I don't know. He squirreled off somewhere, but he knows where to find me. And he will, eventually. Poor kid's seen more crap in fourteen years than most people find in a lifetime. Vinnie's death will be hard on him; Ben adored him."

"Why?"

"It's a long story." Martin studied the man in front of him, trying to gauge the tenor of the question. What he saw was not dismissive sarcasm but genuine interest, and perhaps a hint of compassion. For some odd reason, Martin felt compelled to reveal a small bit of truth that very, very few people knew.

"Suffice it to say, Vinnie Salentino the *mob boss*"—he sketched quotations in the air—"was a tough-guy front to a whole lot of good works on the south side of town. I hope I can continue to be as effective."

"How so?" This question came from Matisse, who'd been listening to the exchange.

"I'm the executive director of the Ninth Street Foundation. In addition to the women's shelter where Lori volunteered, we support a long list of neighborhood projects that make hard lives there a little easier." Martin cleared his throat, feeling a like a bug under the microscope of Matisse's intense focus. "We—Vinnie and I—formed it awhile ago, after the businesses started to turn profitable. Vinnie funds it—funded it—anonymously, although anyone who was intent on following the money could have figured it out. Fortunately, no one who mattered cared to look that closely."

"And now?"

"It continues." Martin shrugged. "Vinnie cared about the people in his old neighborhood, hated how his old man and his cronies had treated them. The foundation's charter is clear—I drafted it myself. But with Claudio in the picture, he couldn't do it openly. He had to make it look like he was using them somehow."

"The funding will continue? Who will take control of the companies?" Etienne had read the analysis that his clever wife had prepared, knew that the shares of all those companies were held by one umbrella company. The structure had puzzled him, but now it was beginning to make more sense. What he didn't know was who would inherit it all.

"Not Claudio," Martin said. "But it's complicated." He checked his watch. "None of this is your problem, or any of your business, really, and

I've got two shit storms coming at me. With Vinnie gone ..." He paused then sighed. "Listen, I appreciate your help getting Lori here safely and protecting her, and I'm really sorry that she got dragged into it. And now after all that, whatever was on that flash drive Vinnie was so hot about is irrelevant, but—"

"You mean you truly don't know?" Dubois hadn't believed it. How could Martin not have known what it was that he was supposed to be safeguarding? And what would he do with it now, if he knew?

"No. Only that it was incriminating to Claudio, and that's more than I wanted to know. Don't want to know more now, either. I've never had anything to do with that side of Vinnie's life, and now I've got too much other crap to worry about, like keeping Claudio away from everything honest and decent his brother built."

Etienne shot Laurent a look that said, *Now is not the time.* They shook hands with the lawyer again and climbed into their rented SUV just as the first splashes of rain began to hit the sidewalk.

Uncle Joe turned the Jack Daniel's bottle upside down and cursed when the last few drops hit his cheek. He'd been aiming for his mouth. Good thing it was empty. *Wait, that's not right—it's not good.* He wasn't through drinking because that red dot still danced on his retinas. That and the look on Vinnie's face. *Vinnie.*

Joe had opened the first bottle right after the cops let him go, but now he couldn't remember how long ago that was. Not that it mattered. They'd swallowed his story, hook, line, and sinker. He should be a fucking Hollywood movie star.

Of course it hadn't hurt that Dick Johnson was assigned to the case. But truly, taking a picture of that asshole had been brilliant, thank you very much, and by now the PPD would be crawling all over the Frenchie's ass. One mob family hitting another. Lots of drama, blah, blah. With luck they'd apply a little police brutality while they were at it.

On a wobbly heave, the bottle sailed across the room, but Joe frowned when the glass didn't shatter against the wall. Maybe he missed. He squinted at the shapes in the direction of his toss, but nothing came into focus. Holding a hand up to cover one eye, thinking that might help sharpen his vision, he found himself face-planted on the sofa cushion. Apparently that was the hand that had been keeping him upright. No longer sure why he cared, he closed his eyes and let the room spin out of control.

———————

"Laurent!" Lori's cry pierced the quiet of the hotel lobby, causing a few heads to turn toward the two tall men who'd just entered through the revolving glass doors.

"*Bonjour, ma belle.*" Dubois opened his arms as she launched herself at him.

"Oh, God, I was so scared, I still can't believe this happened, I'm so, so sorry. I told you not to come, I was so afraid something bad would happen, I just knew it—"

Laurent stopped the string of nonsense with a kiss that quickly changed the direction of her thoughts.

"Hoo-boy," someone said from behind her. Then snickered. *Annie.*

Lori felt her cheeks heating up as she unpeeled herself from her soldier, but she kept her hands on his hips because she didn't want to let go of him. Looking up into his amazing eyes, her own asked the question she couldn't bring herself to voice.

"I'm fine, *chérie.* No gratuitous hammering on my person by the feckless PPD." He stole another kiss. "Matisse had them too scared to even think about attempting it."

"Good." She turned to Etienne, who was giving his wife an equally enthusiastic greeting. And garnering some attention while he was at it, not that either of them noticed. Or cared.

"I don't guess they fed you in jail. As much as I'd like to get the hell out of here, I think we could all use a good breakfast first."

Breakfast wasn't in the cards until their flying palace leveled off at cruising altitude two hours later. Diplomatic status aside, with Vinnie dead—especially *because* he was dead—there were no guarantees of safety in Philadelphia, and Matisse made a strong case that they not linger.

In the first place, they'd made an enemy of Joe Carlucci, a wild card whose current whereabouts were unknown, and Matisse did not discount him as a threat. The photograph he gave to the PPD had been grainy—would not have stood up in court as positive identification—but it was definitely Laurent. That Joe had been the one to take it meant he'd been loitering outside Vinnie's house last night, watching or waiting. Or both; the why of it was anyone's guess. Whether or not he actually murdered his longtime boss—circumstantial evidence certainly suggested it—the old thug had already proved his ability to be dangerous.

The second unknown was the younger brother. Though Martin hadn't said it in so many words, Matisse surmised that Claudio Salentino would be quite surprised to learn of his deceased brother's instructions regarding control of the businesses. From everything Sabine had uncovered on Claudio, and what they'd gleaned from Vinnie and Martin's comments, the news would not go over well. The last thing they needed was to get caught in that crossfire.

And lastly—not that Matisse needed a third reason—the local police were not their friends. Even if one assumed the men in blue were free of Claudio's influence, the unavoidable resentment their team had fostered within the 3rd District was problematic. Despite orders from the top, Matisse did not put it past Detective Johnson to try something out of spite. He made a mental note to look closer at the detective's undisguised bias.

"I almost feel sorry for Martin." Annie made this pronouncement just before taking the first bite of her cinnamon-pecan waffle. "Hmm, oh, wow. This is delicious."

"Because he's left holding a legal morass of mafioso proportions, or because we're adding a three-star meal onto the price of the jet?" Lori blew on the small square of spinach frittata on the end of her fork giving off a waft of steam.

"Both," Annie said around a mouthful.

"It's a package deal," Kaden chimed in with a wink to his wife. "Chef and meals included." He took a bite of his sautéed potatoes before returning his attention to his iPad, as if having a gourmet breakfast on a private jet was a normal occurrence. Which for him, it was.

"Actually I was thinking about this Claudio person. He sounds like a serious creep."

"He is worse than that, from what I've learned." Sabine set down her teacup and dabbed her lips with a cloth napkin. "Nasty does not even begin to describe him, but the police can't seem to be able to pin anything on him. I worry for Angelina and Benjamin."

"My guess is that Angelina and the boy are safe for the time being," Etienne said, hoping it was true. "Vinnie suggested the abduction was a power play. With Vinnie out of the way, the harassment of those he sought to protect is a waste of effort." He carefully filled his fork with the last bite of his omelet, taking time to chew and swallow before continuing.

"Martin Malone, however, may not be safe, though the situation is of his own making. He's known all along that he could eventually face the very scenario confronting him now. He's prepared for it, such as it is. From what little he said, I get the impression the documentation is ironclad, but that doesn't mean he won't meet the same fate as Vinnie."

That thought made Lori shiver. She did not like Martin much right now, but she still cared about his well-being. He'd recently proven his capacity to be an obtuse moron, but prior to that they were together for a long time. She'd always respected his intelligence and his principles, and she knew him to be diligent and honest. It was why she'd been so shocked when she'd learned that Vinnie was a client. Was still shocked. From what she knew of Martin, it just didn't add up.

As if reading her mind, Sabine reached over and touched her hand. "Etienne will scold me for telling you this, but you should know that Martin did not serve as Vinnie Salentino's mob lawyer, in the sense that you think of it. He serves the manufactory and leasing businesses that Vinnie inherited from his father, and from what I've been able to discover, the two of them worked diligently to legitimize everything. Taxes are paid on time, union contracts are fair, banking practices are normal. Annual audits and so forth. Martin is a member of each board, and also serves as executive director for the Ninth Street Foundation, which is a charitable—"

"I know of it." Lori looked a little dazed. "I was treasurer of Southside Women's Shelter, the rehab center that treated Angelina Stripling. I served in that capacity until … until a month ago when I left Philadelphia." Had it only been a month?

"It was always a struggle financially, but such a needed service. There were always too many women in need and not enough space or money. Four years ago we received an unsolicited grant from the Ninth Street Foundation. It seemed to come out of thin air, but it was a godsend. I had no idea … Well, none of us on the board bothered to question it. The foundation committed to a million dollars over a five-year period, which they've made good on. It allowed us to …" Lori's eyebrows scrunched down. "Martin mentioned the foundation last night, after Ben ran into us. But I was too … he never said anything … never told me …"

Laurent had been listening to the conversation while steadily plowing through his own breakfast. The last person he wanted to defend to Lori was her ex-husband, but the man had done him a favor. A big one. The least he could do was set to rights a misunderstanding. Or, in this case, remind her of a decent man's character.

"The foundation was Vinnie's idea," he said quietly. "He wanted to help the people from his old neighborhood but couldn't do it directly without repercussions all around. Martin formed the charity and ran it, and Vinnie funded it anonymously through his companies."

Lori looked at him like he'd grown a second head.

"Vinnie Salentino was apparently a man with a heart and a conscience, disguised in the persona of the heir to a mob family." Laurent gave Lori a look that he hoped conveyed an apology. "Some things can only be accomplished if the world believes what they want rather than what is." That was a truth he'd learned in Africa.

"But he's … he was a crook." Lori couldn't wrap her brain around what she was hearing.

Sabine shook her head and took up the story. "*Non,* he was not. His father? *Oui, absolument.* His piggy little brother, for certain. But not Vinnie. Was he, as you say, squeaky clean? I think not. But from what I found in my research, corroborated by Martin, he was trying to make a difference. He was doing the best he could while trying to keep Claudio in check by playing the mobster."

"Huh." Lori sat back from her unfinished plate.

After a moment's pause, Annie asked the question that Lori was afraid to contemplate. "What do you think will happen to Angelina and Bean?"

Philadelphia, Monday morning

FBI Special Agent Ramon Alvarez parked his dark-gray Prius in the alley behind Angelina Stripling's flower shop. Before Bean could bounce out of the backseat, Alvarez turned to look at him.

"Your mama is still fragile, *mi pequeño hombre.* Will you help me get her inside?"

Bean settled immediately and sat up straight. "Yes, sir."

Angelina could have used another day or two resting in the hospital, but those without health insurance had little leverage when it came to advocating for their own care. As it was, she was pretty loopy on pain meds. After learning her history, Ramon had made sure they were non-narcotic. He took extra care extracting her from the car then nodded to Bean to precede them up the outside stairs. With one arm solidly around her waist and his free hand holding hers for balance, he walked her slowly up to the apartment.

Ramon was a solidly build man about ten years Angelina's senior, though between his Cuban genetics and the aftereffects of her drug-abused youth, he could have been mistaken for the younger of the two. Tasked with her first security detail at the hospital, he'd been undone with one look at the battered woman. She was far from beautiful, especially with a bruised and swollen cheek, but the love that shone in her tortured eyes when she beheld her son had given her a heavenly glow. Ramon had watched from his post at the door while Angelina held Ben in her thin arms and relaxed for the first time since they'd recovered her from that foul hellhole.

To Ramon, family was everything. His parents—may a merciful God give their souls peace—had perished in their bid for freedom in an overcrowded rowboat not ten miles from the coast of America. Ramon had been just five years old and the only soul in the craft to have the benefit of a life vest. He'd struggled mightily to hold on to his mother, and then his father, until they'd both succumbed to their watery graves. Picked up by a patrolling Coast Guard frigate, he'd howled and kicked and cried until he'd fallen into an exhausted sleep only to wake in a Miami detention center to a filthy letch fondling his privates. Sending a well-placed kick to the degenerate's teeth, Ramon had struggled free, swearing to his little boy self right then and there that he would never be vulnerable again. A vow that would eventually expand to include a personal commitment to champion those who lacked the strength to protect themselves.

That vow had carried him through the years spent in a church-run orphanage, middle and high school, college and eventually the police academy. The proudest day of his life was the day he'd been accepted to the intensive twenty-week program at Quantico. Over the years of his law-enforcement career, for each victim he helped, each family he reunited, Ramon felt that same surge of pride. Bone-deep satisfaction for being able to make a difference. But he'd never felt the emotional tug toward those previous victims like he felt around Angelina and Ben.

"Do you have the key, *mi amigo?*" Angelina probably had one in her purse, but Ramon didn't want to violate her privacy if there was an alternative.

"It's open. The Jackle broke the lock when he kicked it in." Bean pushed and the door swung wide, the shattered inside frame testament to the forced entry.

"I can fix this. But help me get your mama settled first."

Bean watched the stocky Hispanic gently shuffle his ma across the room like he was heading for the bedroom.

"She'll be fine here," he said, indicating the threadbare sofa. The cop seemed nice enough, but Bean trusted no one.

"She'd be better off in her bed." Ramon hesitated, torn between respecting the family's privacy and taking care of Angelina. Recognizing the wariness in her boy's expression, he went with the least invasive move and guided the woman to the sofa as her son requested.

Thin as she was, Angelina started to shiver as soon as he released her. "Can you fetch a blanket for her?"

Bean nodded, raced into another room, and returned with a quilt. It was tattered and faded but heavy enough to be warm. Ramon tucked it around Angelina, who had immediately sunk into the couch and fallen asleep, before he stood and looked around. The small apartment was clean and tidy, except for a table near the door that had been smashed and an overturned chair beside the wreckage. The residual from her abduction, he presumed. As if tracking his inspection, Bean went over and righted the chair. The table was toast, and his narrow shoulders slumped in defeat as he stared at it.

"Can you get your mama a glass of water?" Ramon would spare the kid the agony of reliving the scene in his mind if he could. "In case she's thirsty when she wakes up."

Again Bean did as he was bid, returning with a red Solo cup that would have fit right in at a keg party, but rather than hand it to Special Agent Alvarez, he plopped down beside the couch. "I'll just sit here with her."

"*Bueno.*" What else could he say? He had no authority here; his role was simply to keep them safe. And hope they listened to his ideas about how to do that. Ramon turned back to the door to survey the damage. The section of doorframe that had housed the strike plate was bent out at an odd angle, hanging askew by a few unbroken splinters. A fairly simple fix for a temporary job, requiring basic materials he could get at the hardware store down the street and tools he carried in his trunk.

For the longer term, however, the entire side of the doorframe should be replaced and serious deadbolts installed. The idea of having an excuse to come back and make himself useful was appealing in a way that he didn't examine too closely.

Twenty-Two

Martin Malone sincerely wished he could have jumped on that jet with Lori and her friends the day before, because what he now faced in Philadelphia was not appealing. Not in the least. And the man sitting at his kitchen table disrupting his first cup of coffee was only making it worse.

As it was, he'd been up half the night at the hospital with Angelina and Ben. Loyal, shy, scared Ben who refused to leave his mother's side. The FBI agent tasked to protect them—Alcatraz? Alvarez?—had finally persuaded him that he didn't need to stay. That they'd both be safe in his care. The man had seemed sincere, and Martin had been so exhausted he'd given in.

"Gino, it's been a very long weekend, and I have a shitload of work to do this morning." Like arrange a funeral, schedule a meeting at his office for a reading of the will, and figure out how to keep everything going. "Can you please just get to the point?"

"The point is Uncle Joe." Gino Giovanni, a cousin of Vinnie's two or three times removed—Martin couldn't remember—looked at him like it was obvious.

"What about him?" Martin hadn't seen Joe since he kicked him out of the car at gunpoint. A stupid move to be sure, but Joe had pushed too far.

"He came to see Claudio Saturday. It was right after they grabbed Angelina. He looked funny, and he sounded funny, too. Said stuff about Vinnie wanting to reconcile." Gino had ostensibly sided with Claudio after Roberto Salentino had been incarcerated. In truth, Gino was loyal—*had been* loyal—to Vinnie all along, serving as Vinnie's mole in his little brother's band of bullies. It was Gino who had tipped him off to the drug deal a year ago when the two cops were murdered, and it was Gino who had provided the intel of where Claudio had stashed Angelina. Thanks to Gino, Vinnie had been able to keep tabs on the other man's darker dealings.

But now Gino looked worried. Martin didn't blame him. Unchecked by his older brother, Claudio could quickly become a problem.

"What exactly did he say?" Something didn't make sense. Vinnie had not wanted to reconcile, not anymore. After Claudio's increasingly violent games, Vinnie wanted to put the fat bastard away for good. And he could have, with the contents of that flash drive. A flash drive that had gone missing *again*. Martin still hadn't seen the video, but the Frenchman briefed him on it. No wonder Vinnie had gone nuts over the damn thing.

"Well, I didn't hear it all. First he comes in all nervous, says stuff like he thinks Vinnie's acting strange, making mistakes and bad decisions. And then it's like he's having another conversation. Vinnie wants to work together; Vinnie wants to mend fences. I don't know how Claudio left it with him 'cause I had to go with Paulie and take Angelina to that motel." Gino looked at his hands. "I'm glad you got her outta there."

"Yeah, me too." That was the only thing that had gone right over the weekend. Well, that and his own part in getting Lori's soldier released, but the guy should never have been arrested in the first place. Martin pushed aside the threads of jealousy that threatened to twine around his heart. It had been something to watch that giant Matisse in action. What a surprise he'd turned out to be.

"—what you're gonna do."

"Huh?" Martin had zoned out and missed what Gino was saying.

"I said I don't know what you're gonna do. You know, about Claudio. He's already making noise about taking over."

"Yeah, well, he's got some surprises coming." Martin rubbed a hand over his face, fatigued already and the day hadn't even begun. "First, though, I've got an obituary to write and a funeral to arrange."

Gino looked worried. "Claudio ain't gonna like you taking charge of that—"

"Claudio can go fuck himself if he doesn't like it. I have a power of attorney and explicit instructions from Vinnie." Witnessed and notarized for just this reason. "I've already set things in motion with the coroner."

———————————◦◦———————————

It wasn't until after dark on Monday that Joe Carlucci crawled out of his alcoholic coma. Or tried to. The first sensation he recognized was a dampness beneath his cheek. Eyes closed, he brought a hand up to his face but, due to his lack of motor skills, managed only to shove a finger up his nose.

"Uhn." The grunt echoed between his ears and made him aware of a persistent pounding behind his eyeballs. Or was it at the back of his skull? The rhythm seemed familiar. Using the surface of his face as a guide, he directed his fingers to the damp spot that had caught his attention and realized the moisture was coming from his mouth. Drool. *Nice.* He wiped it from his chin with the back of his hand and tried to shift his cheek away from the wet.

"*Fuck!*" The pounding increased in both speed and intensity with that small effort, and it occurred to him it might be his own heartbeat. *One way to stop that,* he thought, but then couldn't remember what he'd done with the Glock.

Wait. Something about the Glock ... Joe tried to open his eyes, but his lids felt glued shut. Using the hand that was still resting next to his cheek, he dragged it over his face and knuckled out the crud, then blinked a few times. Nothing. He couldn't see anything. Was he blind now? *Just fucking great.* But then, no, he could make out some sort of shadows. He blinked again. Not blind then, just dark. Huh. He could have sworn it was morning when he ... Oh, right; now he remembered where he was. Facedown on his couch.

More or less awake, another uncomfortable problem made itself known, this one possibly more pressing than the hammer and chisel in his head, and probably what had woken him up. His bladder was painfully full. Which meant ... *Fuck.* It meant he had to find some way to get from horizontal to vertical. Or he could just piss in his pants. And that would be even worse than the drool on the couch. Wouldn't it?

He squinted into the dark room, trying to get his bearings. The shadows wavered and he closed one eye, trying to focus. There it was, just across the room. The door to the bathroom. On a deep breath, he levered up to one elbow and the room started spinning. Closing his eyes made it worse, and he ended up back where he'd started, but this time he was face up so that was a step in the right direction. Of course, now that he knew he had to pee, he had to go *right now*.

"*Fuckfuckfuckfuckfuck.*" The litany of profanity felt good but didn't help his situation. With single-minded focus Joe swung his feet off the couch and used the momentum to lift his rear end up off the cushion. He swayed then stumbled, kicking an empty bottle with his bare toe.

"*Mother fuck!*" He picked up his foot and bent over to rub the throbbing hurt and lost his balance. The low coffee table in front of the couch kept him from falling flat on his face, but the other empty Jack Daniel's bottle, the one lying sideways beside the remote controls, dug into his gut like a punch as he crashed down onto it. And that was game over for his full bladder.

At least the table held, he thought remotely, sighing as wet warmth spread across his groin and thighs. And the relief from the pressure was just … a relief. No reason to try to stand now. He slid forward into a slow-motion drunken somersault and landed in a crumpled heap on the other side of the table. Wondering if this was what incontinence felt like, he closed his eyes and drifted off.

Two hours later he came to again, this time with his face pressed into the carpet. He managed to roll over but didn't try to get up right away. His head hurt like a son of a bitch and his mouth tasted like roadkill swathed in cotton, but the room was no longer spinning, though it smelled like urine. He pushed to his elbows and felt wetness press against his skin. *What the …?*

Oh, God. Disgust at the realization of what he'd done spurred him on, and he crawled to his knees then used the coffee table to push himself to his feet. He swayed but managed to stay standing. Hands out in front of him for balance, and to grab on to something if he started to go down, he shuffled his way to the bathroom.

A raging thirst took precedence over the pounding of his head, and he turned on the faucet then stuck his hands underneath the water, trying to scoop handfuls of it up to his mouth. When that didn't work, he leaned down and, directing the spray at an angle with one hand, drank straight from the flow as best he could. He ended up with water all over his face, but it was cool and wet and felt better than anything he could remember. Hanging on to the counter with one hand, he rubbed a wet hand over his face. Then he risked flipping on the light. Blinding at first, but after a few blinks, he was able to squint at himself in the mirror.

Bad move. He yanked open the medicine cabinet so he wasn't staring at the mirror, found his toothbrush and used it, and followed that with a handful of aspirin. Next he stripped off his clothes and stood under the shower's icy spray until it warmed up. By the time he'd soaped up and rinsed a few times, the agonizing pain in his head was starting to fade, allowing the memories of why he'd tried to kill himself with Jack Daniel's to resurface.

Ménerbes

Lori felt adrift.

With the time change, they'd arrived back in Marseille in the wee hours of Monday morning. A hired car waited at the airport for the Macallisters, so there was not much more she could do than hug her old friends, thank them, and watch them drive away. She and Laurent rode back to Ménerbes with Etienne and Sabine, both of whom seemed unaffected by either the intensity of the weekend or the lack of sleep.

Another round of hugs, thank-yous that seemed wholly inadequate for what they'd done, and a heartfelt *à bientôt,* and she watched them drive off, too. Then she fell into bed with Laurent and slept until noon.

He'd been watching her when she finally opened her eyes. With a tenderness that almost broke her heart, they'd made slow, delicious love. Afterward, he'd pulled her into the shower and seduced her all over again.

And then he'd left, needing to check in on his sister and Sebastien. Lori understood, she really did, and frankly, it was a relief to be alone. Even in all the years of her marriage, she couldn't recall spending so much close time with Martin.

Tuesday dawned into a lovely, warm morning in Provence, the pure, cloudless blue sky promising heat. But at the stone table beneath the wide plane tree where Lori sat with her laptop, the air was cool and refreshing. She searched the newsfeeds on the internet for anything about Vinnie Salentino's murder. Other than a brief mention of what she already knew—that the man had been found dead in his home by a longtime employee—there was nothing. At least there was that; it was tempting to believe the whole surreal weekend had been nothing but a weird twist of her imagination.

The familiar rumble of a distant tractor blended with the chattering birds in the hedgerows. A car sped past on the road across the field. She looked out over the vineyard and watched a pair of birds flitting and diving after bugs. Everything seemed so … normal. Had it really been less than a week ago that her peace was shattered by that creepy old man? She shivered, thankful once more that Laurent had been there.

Prior to that episode, she'd been comfortable with the isolation of her house—delighted with it, in fact—trusting in the safety of the neighborhood and the locks on her doors. Theft was a common nuisance in rural France, and rental properties that stood vacant for weeks at a time were tempting targets. It was why all the homes had stout shutters that were as functional as they were charming. But violent crime was rare, the breaking and entering occurring—for the most part—when the properties were unoccupied.

Now … now she didn't know what to think. Logic told her nothing had changed. Joe Carlucci was haunting the streets of Philadelphia and was no longer a danger to her. She'd given him what he wanted, or more accurately, she'd done what he came to France to fetch her for. She needed to simply forget about him and enjoy Provence as she'd originally intended. Enjoy her retirement while reacquainting herself with French culture and spending quality time with her friends. And if part of that enjoyment meant an occasional evening with a sexy soldier, then that was okay.

But putting it all behind her was easier said than done. Part of her wanted to call Martin and find out what was going on. Her rational side tossed that idea into the trash bin. Whatever was going on in Philly was no longer her concern. She took a sip of her coffee and thought about Angelina. And Ben. *Crap.* She reached for her phone.

Uzès

At the same time Lori was enjoying the morning beneath her tree, Laurent sat at a patio table just outside the door of Le Jardin. With his back to the wall, his position on the high side of the square gave him a clear view of everything and everyone. To a casual observer, he was relaxed, simply enjoying an espresso like everyone else, but if anyone watched him for long, they might have noticed that he barely moved a muscle except to bring his demitasse to his lips. The stillness was a habit and had served him well in the military. Because the truth was, he was not relaxed.

Julia hustled past and shot him a half smile, as ignorant of his agitation as everyone else in the vicinity. She was in her element, tray full of empty cups and plates with a fresh round of orders recorded on her pad. This was her life, and it suited her. A trace of sadness could still be seen in her pretty eyes, but she was more animated than when he'd left a week ago, like she had made a decision to move forward rather than linger in a past that was gone forever. It lightened his heart to think she was finally on the mend.

Uzès was relatively quiet on a Tuesday, and it was a testament to the café's popularity with the locals that his sister had a full complement of customers this morning. Saturday the town turned into a zoo with its famous flower market, and Wednesday's culinary-focused market brought in almost as many people. Laurent was glad, grateful even, for Julia's success and refused to feel guilt for the relief that brought him. He loved his sister and nephew but was weary of being their crutch.

Merde, that was cruel, not to mention untrue. Julia and Sebastien would always be important to him, and he welcomed their reliance on him, to a point. He intended to keep his promise about staying close, but living with them was not what he wanted. A once- or twice-weekly visit was more like it, sharing holidays, birthdays, and the other special days he'd missed with his sister her entire life. A month ago he wouldn't have imagined having these thoughts. But that was before he'd met a beautiful woman who was as independent and self-reliant as he was. As lonely too.

From that first moment in the gallery, she'd gotten to him, and it had started him thinking. In the army he'd rarely been by himself for long, but physical aloneness was not the prerequisite for lonely. Something he'd begun to recognize only recently, because the military quashed one's emotions as effectively as it put one's life at risk.

However, the true source of Laurent's unease was not the unsettled situation with his sister, his budding self-awareness, or the siren-like allure of his American lover but the contents of the envelope that Julia had handed him that morning. An envelope that had been left in her mailbox the day before he'd boarded that private jet to America.

I know where your family lives. No one fucks with me and gets away with it.

A week ago Laurent would have attributed the threat to some old military opponent, someone who held a grudge. No question there were one or two of those from his past. But this note, written in sloppy English on a piece of paper torn from a spiral-bound notebook, could only be from one person. And the fact that it had been left for him at his sister's house meant that Joe Carlucci had resources.

What he didn't know was whether it was an empty threat, some sort of parting shot to rattle him, or a promise. One thing was certain: he wasn't going to risk the only family he had left on a guess. He had resources, too, and he would use them.

Philadelphia

Vincenzio Giancarlo Salentino was laid to rest beneath overcast skies in the plot beside his mother, as per instructions he'd left with his lawyer. His directive to keep the memorial service small and private was more difficult to oblige because Vinnie had been genuinely respected by the many people who called him boss. Martin didn't think it was right to deny them a chance to say their final goodbye. And then there was family. Although he had no wife or children of his own, Vinnie's father had been the youngest of eight and there were dozens of cousins across generations that still lived in the area. Some had been closer than others, a few even worked for him. Martin was pretty sure they were all at the cemetery that morning. The uncharitable side of him supposed they'd shown up for the thrill of it rather than out of any real affection, because among the attendees was none other than convicted felon Roberto Salentino.

Martin had submitted the request to the federal penitentiary, not because he thought there was a snowball's chance of the man being allowed out but because it was what Vinnie had asked him to do. He'd been shocked when the answer had come back in the affirmative. Of course, the feds weren't taking any chances. The senior Salentino was garbed in an orange prison jumpsuit, shackled ankles to wrists, and surrounded by no fewer than six armed guards. Other than eye contact, they were allowing no interaction between their prisoner and his family. The caged van he'd arrived in was parked at the curb with the engine running; there would be no attending the wake for Roberto.

Martin glanced at the news van parked just beyond the police barricade and the cameras and personnel swarming around it. The speculation about Vinnie's killer, and Roberto's presence at the service, had motivated the chief of police to provide some extra resources. As Martin turned back around to listen to the final words of Father Francis, he caught sight of Uncle Joe.

The old man stood with a group of cousins in the general vicinity of Claudio's entourage. Martin recognized Gino and a few others, but there were many he didn't know. He recalled Gino's words, spoken in concerned confidence just two mornings earlier. Gino had been suspicious of Joe's visit to Claudio the night of Angelina's abduction. The night Vinnie was murdered.

The investigation was ongoing, but Martin had no details beyond his own interview and the circumstances surrounding the false accusation of the Frenchman, Dubois. Once the FBI vouched for Martin's whereabouts that night—it was ironic that Claudio had unwittingly caused that scenario—the police lost interest in him altogether. Which was just as well because he had his hands full.

As Vinnie had instructed, the reading of the will would occur at the law office tomorrow morning. Those present would be Claudio, the other five members of the board of directors that governed Vinnie's parent company, and PPD's chief. It would be Vinnie's coming-out party, in a sense, though regrettably his work would be honored posthumously.

Lost in thought, Martin realized the service was over and the pallbearers were being summoned to lower the casket into the earth. He took his place and numbly followed the cues. When it was done, and Roberto had been allowed to drop the first handful of dirt into the hole before being escorted back to the waiting van, Martin felt a prickling sensation at the back of his neck. Looking over his shoulder, he caught Joe Carlucci's snake-like black gaze.

He suppressed a shiver as he turned to walk back to his own car. No, pulling a gun on that man had not been his wisest move.

Twenty-Three

Salon-de-Provence Air Base, France

Laurent Dubois sighted down the barrel of his SIG Sauer and with a practiced touch, squeezed the trigger. And again, followed by four more rounds in succession. He held his stance—hip forward, extended right hand wrapped around the SIG, the left one loose at his side, and his eyes on the target twenty meters away—until the reverberation of his shots grew silent. With a curt nod of satisfaction, he popped out the clip and set it and the gun on the counter before pressing the lever for the pulley to bring the target forward.

"Not bad." An understatement, delivered in Matisse's familiar dry tone. From his position a few paces behind Laurent, the six holes that formed a neat circle around the center of the target were clearly visible.

"Care to give it a go?" Laurent pulled off his protective earmuffs, reloaded the clip, and snapped it into place then handed both the ear protection and the weapon to Matisse.

"*Bien sûr, porquoi pas?*" Matisse smirked. He donned the headgear and weighted the SIG in his hand while Laurent attached a fresh target sheet to the fastener and ran the pulley out to the end of the range.

Though not as elegant as Laurent's perfect circle, Etienne nonetheless hit the target, decimating the center with five out of his six rounds. The one outlier was just a few centimeters to the left.

"Not bad yourself," Laurent conceded. "I'm relieved to know you could cover my ass if ever needed."

Matisse smiled a rare smile. "That might have been luck. I'm just an analyst, after all."

"Of course you are."

They stayed at the range for another hour, taking turns with the handgun until Laurent was satisfied with his consistency. With nearly three months left in his mandatory recall period, he could not afford to let his skills slip. Not now. Maybe not ever.

"You don't really expect me to believe you came all the way down here to evaluate my marksmanship?" Laurent asked the question casually as he disassembled his firearm at one of the tables in the back of the gallery and commenced to clean it with meticulous care.

"*Non,* but it's good to know that you haven't lost your touch."

"I'm relieved you think so. What's on your mind?"

"Martin Malone tells me that the reading of Vinnie's will is scheduled for tomorrow morning."

Laurent didn't bother to hide his surprise as he looked up from his task. "You are in communication with him?"

"Among others in Philadelphia, thanks to you."

"*Moi?* What did I do?"

"The general mailbox at headquarters received an email from Vinnie Salentino, marked to my attention, with a zip drive attached. A very large file—it apparently backed up the server, to the aggravation of everyone. Sent just before his death as far as I can tell."

"Ah. The video. I had almost forgotten about it." Not really, but he'd put it out of his mind as best he could. With Vinnie dead and Lori safely out of Philadelphia, it hadn't seemed important. And the police would have found the flash drive on Vinnie's person in any case. "It can't be relevant anymore if they've got the original."

"That's just it. They don't."

"*Vraiment?*" That was news. "Are the American police so dense? I watched him slide it into his pocket after he saved the video to his laptop. If you received it, he must have sent it just after I left."

"Yet there was no flash drive found on his person and no laptop in his office."

"*Merde.* I used that thing myself. And my fingerprints ..." Laurent thought about that as he ran the soft cloth one final time over the exposed parts of his SIG then clicked them all together with practiced ease. He slid the weapon into his shoulder holster and stood.

"It's already established that you were with him in his office, and you've been cleared. The fact that we didn't mention the flash drive won't change that. I myself chose to withhold that piece of information."

"So then it seems logical to assume that whoever killed him knew of the flash drive."

"Logical, yes."

"Martin didn't kill him, so that leaves only one other person. But what does that have to do with me?"

Matisse nodded to the exit, and Laurent led the way out. They walked in silence to where the Ducati sat beside Etienne's black SUV. "Proving Joe pulled the trigger won't be easy unless they find the murder weapon and can tie it to him. At any rate, it's not my case and not my problem, though if I learn anything I'll pass it along. And we cannot say with certainty that no one else knew of the video. But the first problem is the video itself, and making sure the evidentiary rules are followed in the event they do go after Claudio for those shootings. For that, your testimony is required."

"Why? Doesn't the thing speak for itself?" Laurent secured the weapon in one of his locking saddlebags and turned to face his friend. "I'll do whatever is needed, of course, but it seems a bit redundant."

"It does, but these matters are never simple. For one thing, we have no idea who actually filmed the thing. Vinnie never said, at least not to me."

"Nor to me," Laurent said at Etienne's questioning look.

"INTERPOL is nothing if not cooperative with our member countries' police forces." There might have been a slight smirk in that statement. "The FBI wants a detailed report of how we came to learn of the thing and how it came to be in our possession, for all of the brief time that it actually was. And I intend to give it to them. I'm trying to keep Lori out of it, but you may want to warn her, in the event they want her testimony, too."

"Jesus Christ." Laurent unlatched his helmet and shoved it down onto his head. "There is no way in hell she's going back to Philadelphia to dance to their tune."

"On that we are agreed. And although our involvement originated with her, she had nothing to do with any of it. Martin will attest to the fact that she had no knowledge of the thing until he suggested it might have inadvertently become mixed up with her files." Matisse opened his door. "Worst case, it means a trip to headquarters in Lyon."

Laurent nodded. "Good to know." He latched his chin strap. "Any word on that other matter?" Meaning Joe Carlucci's vague threat.

"We've initiated a watch on his passport. Unfortunately, that's all we can do until he makes a move. So far he's staying put, but if he shows up here, we'll know about it." And on that last word, Matisse climbed into his SUV and drove off.

Twenty-Four

Philadelphia, Thursday morning

"What's he doing here?" Claudio's large body jiggled as he paced the expanse of Martin's office, waving his pudgy hand at the conference table behind the glass where Police Chief William Forrester sat stirring sugar into his coffee. "This is private. Family business."

"Your brother's instructions," Martin answered without looking up from his computer screen.

"What'd he do, leave his charity to the PPD?" The word *charity* came out on a sneer as unbecoming as the fat man himself.

"No." This time Martin met Claudio's porcine gaze. "No, he did not." He glanced at his watch and cursed the idiot directors who didn't have the courtesy to arrive on time. He wasn't sure how long he could contain the brewing Molotov cocktail of Claudio Salentino and Chief Forrester in the same room. "And I'll ask that you show some respect for your late brother, as he would have done for you."

"Watch your attitude, lawyer. Your time with Salentino family business is limited." The words were accentuated with a fat finger pointing at Martin. "Don't make me cut it even shorter."

A single knock on the door alleviated the need for a reply, and Martin looked over as his wife, for once dressed the part of a legal assistant rather than a tart, let five men into the room. *Safety in numbers,* Martin thought but could hardly blame them.

"Gentlemen." Rising from behind his desk, he shook hands then directed them to his private conference room. Shooting a glance at Claudio, he motioned with his head for him to follow the other men in. "Let's get started, shall we?"

Claudio waddled forward and sank into the chair at the head of the table.

Cocky bastard, Martin thought. If he wasn't so exhausted, he would almost be pleased at what was about to go down.

"Thank you all for coming," Martin said, addressing the room from the other end of the table. "Vincenzio Salentino—Vinnie to those of us who were close to him—was a friend as well as a client, and I'm honored and humbled to be standing here today on his behalf."

Claudio shifted his bulk and farted.

Rather than pretend to ignore it, Martin looked directly at Claudio. "Do you need a moment?" He gestured to the others in the room. "We'll wait."

Any other response might have fed Claudio's game, but pity only pissed him off. "Fuck you, Malone. Get on with it."

The directors all studied their fingernails, but Chief Forrester directed a look of disgust at Claudio. His own presence here wasn't strictly necessary, but he thought he knew why Vinnie had requested it. As distasteful as it was, it was the least he could do for the man who'd done remarkable things under difficult circumstances.

"As you wish." Martin launched into the usual preamble, explaining unnecessarily that the purpose of this gathering was to read the last will and testament of Vincenzio Giancarlo Salentino. After reciting a page of mumbo-jumbo legalese, he rattled off a list of individuals and the various small bequests they had been granted—family members and employees for the most part. Then he got to the meat of the estate.

"For the rest of it, Vinnie wanted to explain it to you in person."

"Too bad he's fucking dead," Claudio said on a snort.

Martin ignored the vulgar remark and held up a thick sheaf of paper. "It's all here in writing, of course—properly executed, witnessed, and notarized—but as I said, Vinnie wanted you to hear it in his own voice." Swiveling his chair around, he picked up a remote control and aimed it at the flat screen behind him. A still shot of Vinnie Salentino appeared on the screen.

"What the fuck is this?"

"Vinnie was rather fond of creating audiovisual messages; don't be surprised if others pop up in the near future." Martin speared Claudio with a contemptuous look. "This one was made about six months ago. With the escalation of violence in the city and your blatant disrespect for his authority as head of the family, he took precautions. Personally, I thought he was overreacting." His gaze shot to the chief before landing back on Vinnie's half brother. "Obviously I was wrong."

Claudio pushed to his feet faster than seemed possible for someone of his girth and pounded his fist on the table. "Now you wait just a fucking minute—"

Chief Forrester stood, too. He was a big man and imposing even without the sidearm holstered at his hip. "Shut up and sit down. He's not making an accusation"—the chief glared at Martin—"just stating a fact that every citizen of this city understands."

If looks could kill, the chief of police would have been smote dead. Those mean black eyes squinted dangerously, and one meaty finger pointed at him menacingly while Martin silently congratulated himself that he'd had the presence of mind to activate the metal detector in the lobby. Claudio had been relieved of a handgun that might have possibly come into use about now if he still had it on his person.

"This proceeding is nothing more than a reading of a will," Martin said, his calm voice belying the strain he felt. "As Vinnie's representative, I'm asking that you sit down and listen to what he has to say. You'll get a copy of the document to take with you for further study."

After a tense minute as Claudio and Martin and Chief Forrester stared each other down, Claudio held up his pudgy hands. "Fine, whatever." *Whadevah.* He planted himself back into the chair and waved like an indulgent sovereign for the proceedings to continue.

On a deep breath, Martin nodded and started the video.

"My name is Vincenzio Giancarlo Salentino, and if you are watching this, then I am dead."

The blunt speech made Martin flinch even though he'd been there when it was recorded.

"My attorney, Martin Malone, is following my explicit instructions by playing this recording in front of my half brother Claudio Salentino, the directors of Southside Industries, and whoever holds the current position of chief of police for the PPD. Thank you for being here and indulging me in this exercise. My intention is not to be melodramatic at the reading of a fairly straightforward will but rather to ensure that this is heard in the proper context. Be assured that the details set forth in my legal documents reflect my absolute intention and conviction."

The only sound in the room was of chairs creaking as the occupants settled or shifted nervously.

"My father was a criminal and the worst kind of bastard, and I am proud to have been instrumental in putting him away for good." Vinnie's eyes gleamed, and he stared straight at the camera as he made this shocking pronouncement.

A profane howl of protest erupted across the room, and Vinnie's image smiled, expressing more sadness than joy. "I can hear you shouting from my grave, Claudio—a place you may have had a hand in sending me—but I ask that you sit down and hear me out." Vinnie paused and looked intently at the camera and oddly, his words worked.

"I didn't do it, Vinnie. I never wanted you dead." The confession was whispered to the image on the screen as Claudio sat back.

"Running drugs, women, and guns leaves nothing but fear, grief, and death in our wake. I saw it with my father and vowed to change things. Do we get rich as fast? Well that's an interesting question, and I want you to listen carefully. It's like playing poker with a stacked deck—works well until someone notices that you're cheating. Whether it's the cops or your business partners ... all the money in the world don't mean a thing if you're dead. Which, by the way, is a place we all end up. Some sooner than later, my humble self a case in point. But who knows, maybe it was a heart attack?

"I won't bore you with the final straw or how I went about it, but all of you know about the changes I've made to the *legacy* my father left me." He gave the word the same emphasis one might give a pile of dog shit one just stepped in.

"With the dedication our dear old dad once gave to breaking innocent girls to a life of prostitution, the men around this table helped me take money-laundering operations and turn them into respectable businesses. It took balls and a hell of a lot of risk—not the kind that would get us killed but the kind that would bankrupt us—but because of intelligence and tenacity and a God damned boatload of hard work, we have a thriving empire of legitimate businesses."

Martin had rolled his chair away from the table to a position immediately behind the chief, where he could watch reactions from most of the men in the room. Claudio sat with eyes narrowed and pudgy hands resting on the edge of the table, like he'd explode any moment. The directors stole occasional glances at him and looked … wary. *Huh. Interesting.*

The voice of the elder Salentino brother turned regretful as he continued. "I tried to steer you to my way of thinking, Claudio, you know I did. But you were too fucking stubborn. I slowed you down whenever I could, I messed with your plans, but I couldn't stop you. Killing those cops last year was the final straw."

"What the fuck?" Claudio's eyes went wide above the rolls of his fat cheeks and darted around the room. "That's a fucking lie! I had nothing to do with that!"

"It's not a lie, little brother, and I have proof." It was freaky, how well Vinnie knew his younger brother. Too bad that familiarity was not reciprocated. "I had intended to keep it in the family, so to speak, an incentive for you to change your ways. Regrettably for both of us, if you are only learning of this now, it means you've effectively killed us both." Those words were followed by a sad shake of his head. "Irrefutable evidence will be delivered to the right people at the right time."

Chief Forrester had not taken his eyes off the younger brother since his last outburst and so noticed the moment dark stains of sweat began to show beneath the arms of the man's button-down shirt. *What evidence did Vinnie have? Is that why I'm here?*

Meanwhile Vinnie continued in a businesslike tone as if he had not just dropped a bomb into the well-appointed conference room.

227

"The rest of my will goes like this. Eighty percent of my shares in Southside Industries, Inc., are to be donated to the Ninth Street Foundation. The remaining 20 percent I bequeath equally to the existing directors"—he named the five men around the table—"possession of which will commence one year and a day from the date of my death, provided each individual remains active in his current position. That, plus your existing holdings, will give the directors a total of 30 percent ownership."

As a group the directors did a poor job of suppressing their pleased shock at that pronouncement.

"I imagine this is more than you expected," Vinnie said, "but we all know that we couldn't have reached our current position without your collective efforts, and it's only fair that you benefit from your unwavering dedication. Selfishly I am hoping that my generosity here will ensure your continued dedication, for only through the success of the businesses will my long-term goals for the foundation be realized. Martin will assume my position as chair of the Southside Industries board, by the way, because he will continue on as head of the foundation. Any personal funds and investments that remain after the specific individual bequests and the settlement of my personal outstanding debts will also go to foundation.

"The Delancey Street house and its entire contents, with the exception of my personal laptop computer and the items belonging to my father, which Marty has a list of, will be sold. Those specific items will be stored properly until such time as he is directed by their rightful owner as to their disposition. The laptop goes to Chief Forrester, or whoever holds that position at the time of my—"

"This is bullshit!" Claudio shouted, leaning forward like he wanted to dive across the table. "You can't do this!"

"—death, along with all current passwords. It is my intention that the chief have full access to all files found thereon."

Martin and Chief Forrester exchanged glances.

"The proceeds from the house," Vinnie continued, "will be held in trust for you, Claudio, to be used for your legal defense. Anything that remains after the courts are finished with you will revert to the foundation."

"Wait just a fucking minute—"

"If any of the beneficiaries attempts to contest my will, his bequest will be withdrawn. That means your legal fund, Claudio, so think before you act. Any questions, Marty can answer them." Then Vinnie smiled. "See you on the other side."

The video ended with that smile frozen on the screen, and the room pulsed with tension in the sudden quiet. Martin gathered his documents together in a neat stack, the shuffling of paper loud in the still air. Removing his reading glasses, he looked around the table. "That's everything, gentlemen. Like Vinnie said, if you have any questions—"

The heavy mahogany conference table shook with the force of Claudio's balled-up fist slamming down onto its surface.

"I got questions, lawyer." The man's face was almost purple with rage. "What about all the rest of it?"

"The rest of it? I don't follow—"

"The companies. The real estate. The warehouses. Vinnie owned a hell of a lot more than what you covered. I got shares in those companies, too. I know they exist."

"Ah." Martin remained calm, though a quick glance around the table showed that his fellow directors were ready to bolt from the room. The chief wore an inscrutable expression, likely wondering what would be found on the laptop. "*The rest of it,* to use your terminology, is owned by Southside Industries, Inc., a holding company that Vinnie created about five years ago to consolidate all of his holdings."

"But those are my companies, too! You can't just give 'em to some fucking charity!"

"You own a minority interest in each one, shares that were given to you by your father, and that doesn't change. Thanks to the efforts of these fine men," he nodded to the others, "and barring an economic downturn, your shares will continue to increase in value and pay out dividends."

"*Fuck that,* lawyer. Those companies were supposed to be mine." The menace and anger in Claudio's voice made Martin glad that Chief Forrester was wearing a sidearm.

"With all due respect, you are mistaken. The transfer of shares to the holding company was valid, and you have no ownership or claim to that company or its assets. Your brother was very clear about that and went to some lengths to ensure his wealth was beyond your reach."

"I don't believe you. That will is bullshit no matter what you or that fucking video says. I'm his brother. His property is supposed to be mine."

"Claudio, perhaps we can excuse—" But the words were a waste of breath because with a shift and a shove, Vinnie's half brother lifted his bulk out of the chair and stormed out of the room.

Across town, Joe Carlucci twisted the cap off his third beer. He chugged half of it while glaring at the laptop, resisting the growing temptation to throw it across the room. The God damned piece of shit was password protected, and nothing he tried could get him beyond the first screen.

He wasn't even sure what had compelled him to take the thing. Rage, jealously, betrayal, or some equally useless emotion—same as whatever had finally caused him to snap, raise his gun, and pull the trigger. But when the cops asked him if he'd seen it, he knew his instincts had been right. About that, at least. And that flash drive. It sat on the table beside the computer, silently mocking him. That fucking thing had started this whole clusterfuck.

Vinnie had waved it in his face that night before returning it to his pocket. "Marty had it the whole time," he'd grumbled. "Fucker just tonight remembered where he'd stashed the file cabinets from his house, and wouldn't ya know it, it had fallen out of a file and got stuck in one of the wheel tracks."

Rather than relief, Joe had felt a surge of fury. "So that whole fucking trip to France was a waste of time."

His boss had only shrugged. "Yeah, well, shit happens. We're good now, though. I finally got what I needed." Vinnie had been sitting in his chair, diddling with the laptop. "And it wasn't a total waste. Your fuckup in France managed to connect me with some very powerful people."

It wasn't the insult; it was the smirk that accompanied it. It was the lack of respect, lack of consideration, the lingering sting of having been dressed down in front of those *powerful people* earlier in the day. It was years of being a faithful dog and never getting the biggest bone. It was the hatred for that fucking soldier that had gained his boss's respect from the beginning. All of it churned together in his gut to create a perfect storm of rage.

"Fuck you, Vinnie."

"Watch it, Joe." Vinnie had been concentrating on the laptop. He hit a few keys then nodded in satisfaction before he looked up. Straight into the barrel of Joe's Glock.

"Too late, Vinnie. One fucking insult too late."

Regret was a merciless bitch. Joe finished his beer and tossed the bottle in the trash on his way to the fridge for another. He knew a guy who could probably hack the computer, but he didn't trust an outsider. Not with what might be on it, and definitely not with the knowledge of who it belonged to. The fourth beer was opened, downed, and tossed. Belching loudly, he grabbed another and walked back to the couch. The flash drive was the key. Joe didn't know exactly what was on it, and the fucking thing wasn't giving up its secrets, but he knew it had something to do with Claudio—something that was big enough to cause serious trouble for the younger Salentino brother if it fell into the wrong hands.

Joe was a follower, not a leader. He'd been part of the Salentino family for too long, so it was too ingrained in him and he wanted—needed—the sense of belonging. He'd pulled a trigger to prove his loyalty in the past, and he would do it again. His mentor was in prison and the heir was dead, but the spare—the new heir—was alive and well. Joe had no doubt that Claudio would reign terror like his father had. Vinnie had tried for civility, and look where it got him. No, it was time to shift camps. There was really no other choice.

The remaining men looked at each other, but none made any attempt to move.

"That went about as I expected. Better, actually," Martin said with a strained smile. "I'm still alive."

"For now," Trey Keller said without humor. Like each of the directors present, Keller served as CEO for one of the five companies that made up the Salentino conglomerate. His was the one that operated from the riverside warehouse that had seen the worst of Claudio's shenanigans. Thus his comment was based on more than idle speculation.

"I assume you've prepared for fallout." This from Chief Forrester.

Trey nodded. "We've implemented increased on-site security as well as a systematic change of access codes for all physical locations and the computer systems." The other CEOs echoed the declaration.

"What about personal security?" The chief's sharp eyes made contact with each man around the table. "Your biggest vulnerability is at your own homes."

While that realization sunk in around the table, Forrester stood and paced to the frozen image of Vinnie that still hung on the screen. "Why did he want me to have the laptop?"

"I can give you some information on that, but with all due respect"—Martin shifted his gaze from the chief to his fellow directors—"the less these gentlemen hear about that side of things, the better." He didn't have to say it twice. As a group, the directors stood.

"I'd venture to guess that you are in the crosshairs more than we are," Trey, the self-appointed spokesman for the group of directors, said to Martin. "But we'll alert the security company to increase patrols around all of our families, including yours."

After handshakes and a promise from Martin to call a special meeting soon to take care of the myriad of details that would be required to implement Vinnie's final wishes, all but the chief of police filed out of his office.

Once they were gone, Martin didn't hesitate. "Vinnie kept tabs on his brother and collected what evidence he could of his dealings. He struggled with the right and wrong of handing it over to you, hoping to resolve it within the family, but recently ... well, let's suffice it to say, he was on the brink of pulling the plug on Claudio when he ended up dead. There was a flash drive with an incriminating video—"

"Did that have something to do with why your ex-wife and her INTERPOL friends were here?" Forrester's Sunday morning had been rudely interrupted by a senior member of INTERPOL's DC branch with the news of the arrest of a French national who had the quasi-diplomatic status of an INTERPOL agent. Along with the aggravating details of his own department's sluggish response to the required protocol. The man who'd been arrested was connected to Martin Malone's ex-wife. Forrester had gone ballistic when his own balls were threatened by the international police, so he was naturally a tad sensitive to this entire strange connection.

"Christ." Martin pinched the bridge of his nose and tried to massage away the pressure that was building there between his eyes. "A year ago, Vinnie entrusted me with a flash drive that was too important to be left where it might be found by his brother. I knew it was sensitive, but I didn't know what was on it. I … when I moved out of my old house, the thing went missing." In as vague of terms as possible, Martin relayed the facts of the situation, down to the eventual discovery of the thing and Dubois's part in recovering its contents.

"Dubois managed to fix the drive by resoldering the pins or something, and he claims they recovered the video. He apparently told Vinnie to save it somewhere in the Cloud because he couldn't vouch for how long his temporary repair would last. The next thing he knows, he's being hauled out of his hotel room and arrested for Vinnie's murder.

"But I can tell you—he didn't do it. Someone arrived at Vinnie's townhouse after Dubois left, killed him, and took the laptop and the flash drive." Martin gave the chief a pointed look. "As far as I know, excluding my ex-wife and her friends from France—all of whom have alibis, not to mention no reason to commit murder—there was only one other person who knew that flash drive existed, and he was the one to call in the murder. Your people arrived and processed the scene, but when I asked about the laptop and the flash drive, no one had any idea what I was talking about."

Twenty-Five

Ménerbes

The familiar sound of a motorcycle engine downshifting as it slowed had Lori doing one last check in the full-length mirror before she closed her wardrobe and hurried downstairs.

It had been only three days since she'd kissed him goodbye, but she couldn't suppress the excitement coursing through her veins in anticipation. Perhaps it was because she'd almost managed to talk herself into doubting his continued interest in her. In their short acquaintance, she'd brought him nothing but baggage and grief. He'd been arrested, for Christ's sake. In America! Their time apart would have given him a chance to think about that, realize what a bad bet she was. Although, he'd taken it all in stride at the time, waving off her concern.

"It was Joe's way of giving me the finger," he'd said with a shrug. "I've spent longer stints in the African desert waiting for an extraction. Cooling my heels for an hour in an interrogation room will have no lasting impact on my psyche."

Still, she'd worried. But here he was, helmet in one hand, duffle in the other, and her doubts fled when he smiled at her.

"*Tu es belle ce soir.*" In fact, she was more than beautiful. She looked good enough to eat with her long hair hanging free, a softly draped dress skimming her slender torso before it flared out below her hips in folds that fell to her ankles. His first thought was how easy it would be to slide it up over her head, but he quickly leashed the inner animal. There would be time for that later.

And he loved that she came out of the house to greet him, like she was happy to see him. She always did that, he realized.

"*Merci.* You look pretty good yourself." She leaned up and kissed him, tracing the dark swirl visible above his collar with a fingertip. Then she tugged the helmet out of his hand and carried it inside. He followed, enjoying the subtle sway of her hips beneath the fabric of her dress.

The helmet went on a coat hook beside the door, and when she turned around, he was there, capturing her with his free arm around her waist. "*Bonsoir, chérie.*" He dropped the duffel to the floor and anchored his other hand in her hair as he kissed her properly, passionately, as if it had been weeks not days since they'd last been together.

Precisely eight kilometers to the east, Etienne Matisse was enjoying a similar moment with his wife. Not to make up for days of absence but a good hour, at least. The time it took for him to complete the shopping with Ellie in tow, a ritual he and the little girl had enjoyed together since she was an infant. But more importantly, it was a kiss to remind Sabine that he was her slave in all things.

A kiss that was interrupted by that same little girl who raced into the room. "S'bine!" Little arms stretched up in a practiced plea.

Unable to resist even when she recognized the manipulation, Sabine stooped down and picked her up. There was a time not so long ago when Ellie had acted out with anger and jealousy around Sabine. That time had passed, and now they shared shameless affection.

"Hello, sweetie. Did you have a good trip?" The adults in the house made sure to speak both English and French to Ellie. English during the day and French at night. At just past five o'clock it was technically still daytime, so the question was asked in English.

Ellie answered in French, not yet grasping the rule. "*Oui! Il y avait chansons au marché.*"

"Songs at the market?" Sabine looked at Etienne, not quite sure of Ellie's vocabulary.

"Musicians singing and playing an interesting array of instruments. Some sort of medieval band, I think. It was quite entertaining, and they were particularly taken by Ellie's enthusiasm."

"Ah." She turned back to the imp in her arms. "And did you dance?"

"*Oui!* Papa Et-een take the songs."

Sabine arched an eyebrow at her husband, who held up a CD, a sparkle in his black eyes.

"They really were quite good." Etienne kissed both of his ladies, their cheeks being at the same level, then turned to the grocery bags on the counter.

"So what did Simon have to say?" Etienne handed his wife a glass of wine as he asked the question. He'd waited until the groceries were stowed and Ellie was occupied at her little table in the family room with a coloring book and the new music playing through the speakers.

"The Americans are concerned about evidentiary integrity. Claudio is slippery as an eel, and to their credit they don't want to screw this up."

"Christ. Their damn lawyers can be worse than their criminals. Sorry," he added when Sabine scowled and glanced toward Ellie in the other room.

"What is it with the military and cussing? Your speech has spiraled into the gutter since you've been spending time with Laurent Dubois."

Etienne laughed and agreed as he poured himself a glass of wine. "Too much time away from the ladies."

This time Sabine smiled. "It is surprising, no? How smitten he is with Lori Sheridan?" Then she frowned. "I truly hope he doesn't turn out to be an ass and hurt her. I like her."

"I like her, too. And as for Dubois, I'm pretty sure he likes her more than he's willing to admit. Perhaps more than he is comfortable with."

"What is that supposed to mean?"

Matisse took his time unwrapping the roast that would become dinner, wadding up the paper and tossing it into the trash. He had vowed to withhold nothing from his wife, not when she asked directly. But he did consider his words carefully.

"I told you he was my commanding officer for the two-year stint of my military service." He paused to wash his hands and then studied the spice rack, selecting several jars and setting them on the counter.

Sabine sipped her wine and waited. She had learned a long time ago, many years before Etienne had finally professed his love for her, that her husband did things, said things, only in his own time. Patience was a necessity in dealing with him, then and now.

"Laurent Dubois has always been a loner. He was an only child. To make matters worse, his father was a fighter pilot and moved the family around from base to base, a lifestyle that all but ensured his son made no lasting friendships. I got the impression the old man wasn't around much. His mother died of an illness when he was still in secondary school, and his father remarried right away."

"And had another child. Laurent's half sister, Julia."

"*Oui, c'est ça.* As soon as he was of age, Laurent joined the army. And thrived."

"It was a family, something he had perhaps not fully experienced. For once side-by-side with men and women who could be trusted to stick around."

Sabine's insight had Etienne looking over his shoulder and nodding. "I believe you are correct in that, but I think the key point is men. Women are not uncommon in the French army as you know, but in the elite unit that Dubois was attached to, there were none." He sliced lemons and crushed a handful of garlic cloves with the flat of his knife. "The only women were the camp followers, so to speak. The waitresses at the bars, those who worked in the small businesses in the town near his base, and others." Meaning the loose women who hung around the base hoping to snag a soldier.

"Are you saying he does not respect women?"

"*Non.* Not that. Just … Christ, he would slit my throat if he knew I was telling you any of this."

"Etienne!" Sabine hissed out his name, glancing over at Ellie. The child was oblivious, lost in the fantasy of her coloring book.

"*Désolé, minette.* I only mean to say that the Laurent Dubois I knew back then would have avoided anything close to an entanglement with a woman.

He was no monk—he took what was offered when it suited him—nor was he a cad. Just … emotionally unavailable."

A quantity of fresh herbs went under his knife next. "Don't forget he's spent his entire adult life as a soldier—a trained killer, to be blunt. He's been everything from peacekeeper to diplomat to spy, where the wrong step could end in disaster, not to mention the times he's toed the front line of military aggression. Loyalty and trust among his men was not just important—it was paramount to his unit's survival. He's never had the luxury of letting down his guard or trusting anyone outside of that tight group." The herbs went into the bowl with the garlic, and Etienne reached for the can of olive oil.

"From what I gathered, his only emotional tether outside the army was his sister. He had no time or use for women beyond the obvious, and I doubt very much that he has ever met a woman like Lori. Self-sufficient and strong with original opinions and thoughts of the world."

"You make him sound like a Neanderthal."

"Lack of experience." Matisse speared her with a look. "Not unlike my humble self—not that you need reminding of my shortcomings—but with slightly different facts."

Sabine thought about that. "Perhaps."

"And I would not have invited him to the wedding, would not have revealed Lori's whereabouts to him, if I thought he was beyond redemption." Setting aside the onion he had begun to chop, he came over to where she sat at the table. Kneeling down, he smoothed a lock of hair from her forehead, taking a moment to rub the soft strands between his fingers. "If I can be saved, I will never begrudge anyone else the opportunity. Have I told you lately how much I adore you?"

She leaned over and kissed him, running two fingers down his scar in a rather possessive stroke before cupping the side of his face in her hand. "Just this morning, in fact. If you think Laurent is sincere, then I will stay out of it."

Etienne tilted his cheek into her palm for a moment, took her hand in his, and kissed her fingers, then stood. "What else did Simon say?"

And thus it was when two members of the international police married. Conversation went from case details to intimate confidences and back again faster than an onion could be chopped.

"The FBI wants video depositions from both of them. The sooner the better. A written statement won't be enough."

———————————

Laurent's phone vibrated in his pocket, but he didn't check it immediately. He was having too much fun in the wine cellar of the Coustellet *boucherie*-slash-restaurant watching Lori ponder the evening's wine selection.

"There's a Côtes du Rhône Villages from Cairanne, which is only a few kilometers from Rasteau," she said over her shoulder. "How different can it be? Or should we splurge on Châteauneuf du Pape? The Cairanne is a lot less expensive."

"Well, I guess it depends on what you're having."

"I'm having the duck and you said you wanted the lamb, so either would work. Maybe we should look at Bordeaux. But geez, I hate to drink wine from another region—that's the whole fun of France."

"*Chérie,* I'm sure anything you pick will be fine, but if it matters, I vote for the Châteauneuf. And don't forget we need a white, too, for the asparagus." It was the height of a very short season for the coveted local white asparagus, and the chef had prepared a delicious-sounding trio as an appetizer.

"Hmm, good point. I'd normally go with a Grüner Veltliner but there's nothing close to that from this area. Maybe Rolle? It's citrusy and herbal, and typically unoaked. Oh! Here's one from a pretty famous producer down by the coast. Their vineyards are supposed to be practically on the sand. Yikes, though, it's kind of pricey. What do you think?"

He plucked the bottle from her hand. "I think it will be perfect." Retracing their steps back to the first red she'd looked at, a 1998 Châteauneuf du Pape, he lifted one of the dusty bottles from the bin. The producer was unknown to him, but the vintage was one Kaden talked about, and it was far less than what they would have paid at Bruno's restaurant below the ruins. "We're done. Let's go back upstairs."

She laughed and followed him up the narrow steps to the restaurant. The young lady waiting at the top took the bottles from him, and Lori rolled her eyes when the girl gushed at his selections. But then he guided her back to their table with one warm hand against her lower back, and she immediately forgot her annoyance. Dating a gorgeous man came with these sort of moments, she realized. And she could hardly blame *him* for it; it wasn't like he did anything to encourage the women who all but swooned over him. They just came on to him naturally. *Gads.* Was this what she had to look forward to if they continued to see each other?

The white was opened, tasted, and set in an ice bucket to chill while their server brought the *amuse bouche.* It was a delectable little crostini slathered with puréed *petit pois,* topped with slivers of house-cured salmon and a dab of crème fraîche. Laurent downed his in one bite and felt his phone vibrate again.

"*Désolé,*" he said as he fished it out of his pocket then looked at the screen. *Well, that settles that,* he thought on a resigned sigh.

"Is everything okay?"

"Yes, there is no problem. I was hoping it wouldn't go this far, but I'm afraid the FBI is insisting on deposing you."

"What? Why?" Alarm sparked in the pit of her stomach. "Wait, why is this information coming to you and not to me?"

He reached over the table and wrapped his hand around the one gripping her wineglass. "Because I'm now an active INTERPOL agent." He gently squeezed. "And Matisse knows that I am with you tonight. He mentioned this was a possibility, but I didn't want it to worry you if it didn't come to pass."

"But … they can't expect me to go back to Philadelphia! Not again—I won't do it." She pulled her glass away and took a gulp of wine.

"*Non,* you will not. Matisse will arrange for you to do it at the Lyon head-quarters by videoconference. Sabine will go with you, too, as will I."

Her head cocked to the side, and she frowned. "You too? But why?"

Laurent regarded her, wondering about her reaction. "Would you prefer that I not accompany you?"

Something in his tone got her attention, and this time she reached over to him. "I would prefer that this whole mess never happened. This is not me. I am never helpless or out of control. It's mortifying to think you … this is *not* how I want you to see me."

They were interrupted by the delivery of their first course. Long rectangular pieces of slate served as the plates, each holding a demitasse of white asparagus soup, white asparagus tips dressed in some sort of caper vinaigrette, and what looked like char-grilled white and green asparagus pieces tossed with *lardons*. The server poured the wine, shot a totally inappropriate smile at Laurent, who wasn't even looking at her, then flounced off.

"I see a strong and beautiful woman," he said when they were alone again, holding Lori's amazing blue eyes with his own. "One who is dealing with a distasteful situation not of her making and doing so with courage, grace, and good humor." He picked up his wineglass and tilted it at her, leaning in. "I have never thought of you as anything but that. Not a victim, not someone who needs to be saved." Although he would protect her with his life it if came to it. "I've been around that type of woman and, *chérie*, I can say with complete certainty that you are not that woman."

She studied him for a moment, then her eyes softened. "Thank you."

"*De rien.* I just call it like I see it." He nodded at her plate then took a sip of his wine. "Now I want you to forget about all that and enjoy our dinner."

She did. It was a deadly combination: excellent food and wine coupled with a large dose of gorgeous, charming soldier. Like their first night, they talked and teased, building the sensual tension throughout the meal, oblivious to the knowing glances from nearby tables.

The night was clear but cold when they finally left the restaurant, and Lori's quaint but drafty farmhouse kept little of the chill at bay. Dumping her purse on the table by the door, she eyed the stack of firewood in the alcove beneath the stairs.

"Soldiers know how to build a fire, don't they?"

"Only if they want to survive."

The fireplace in the main lounge was large and set in a raised hearth. Laurent carried up an armful of split logs, some smaller kindling, and an old newspaper that had been stashed with the wood. Within minutes a cheerful fire was crackling away. They moved chairs aside and pulled cushions from the couch, arranging them in front of the hearth. With a pile of extra blankets and pillows, it was cozy and warm and very, very private.

Twenty-Six

Philadelphia

Claudio looked at the thin notebook computer in front of him. He'd never seen the thing before but didn't doubt it was what Joe proclaimed it to be: Vinnie's laptop. The one that was supposed to be handed over to the PPD chief. The blinking login screen taunted him. If things had gone as they should have, he, Claudio, would have been given the passwords to access the data locked behind that annoying blink. Now he couldn't decide which emotion was stronger, rage or suspicion. With an uncharacteristic reserve of patience, he tamped down both.

"And you ended up with this, how?"

"I told you. When I found Vinnie dead, I took precautions before calling 911." Joe had practiced the lie in front of his mirror so he could say it with a straight face. "You know, I coulda just left the thing. But I thought it might be important—I thought it might be important to *you*. Who knows what's on it? Maybe something you can use. There's no way to prove that he, er, that his killer didn't take it. Why leave it? I stashed it outside before I called the cops. Then I went back for it after."

"The killer left it." It was a statement, not a question. Claudio ran the pads of his fingers across the keyboard, more for the sensory feel of connecting with something that had belonged to Vinnie than for any effort to crack into the thing. "You say you saw that Frenchie running away from the house. I heard he was picked up, but he was released almost immediately. You must have been mistaken."

"It was him, I swear it. Somehow that fucking lawyer got him off."

A lawyer that both men were beginning to really hate, although for different reasons.

"Joe, I gotta tell ya, I don't get it." Claudio continued to pet the keys. "I don't get how you just happened to see the soldier leaving Vinnie's then found him dead. Especially 'cause there is solid evidence that he was still alive at least ten minutes after that soldier left." Claudio lifted his hand away from the laptop and stared at Joe through mean, dark eyes. "It would be a real shame if I learned you had anything to do with my brother's murder. Because you know, as much as I love you, Vinnie was my brother. My own flesh and blood. I never wanted to hurt him. Show him up, make him nervous, bring him down a notch, sure. But hurt him? Never."

So much for being heralded the hero for handing the younger Salentino his opportunity to take over the dark side of the city. The cold suspicion in Claudio's voice had Joe suppressing a shiver. Thank fuck he'd hedged.

But Claudio wasn't finished. "Just because we didn't understand each other completely," he said, "don't mean I wanted him planted six feet under."

Joe might have been dense, but he wasn't entirely stupid. His right hand toyed with the flash drive in one pocket while his left fisted in the other. Too late, Joe realized his mistakes were not just with Vinnie.

Doubts and regrets swirled in a miasma in Joe's chest, giving him the worst heartburn he could ever remember suffering. An hour after leaving Claudio's lair without the laptop, Joe found himself on the broad spectator steps along the east bank of the Schuylkill Rowing Basin watching the late-afternoon scullers ply their narrow crafts through the flat current of the river.

How long would it be before Claudio confirmed his suspicions? Joe's hope for any sort of refuge in that camp had evaporated with Claudio's cold words. It was only a matter of time. Whether or not the cops connected the dots and came after him, Vinnie's little brother didn't need proof to believe what he would. Was possibly organizing the hit at that very moment. Joe had never done much retirement planning—he'd always assumed he'd die on the job. A viable possibility still.

Before his self-castigation could draw him even deeper down into the morass, his cell phone rang. He took one glance at it and cursed. Payback time.

"Joe here."

"It's your lucky day, Carlucci. I'm calling in my marker."

Just fucking great. Holding back the oath that threatened to surface, Joe did his best to keep his voice level. "What do you need?" *Whadeyah need?*

A raspy chuckle came through the connection, as if the man picked up on Joe's tension. "You're getting off easy. I gotta guy coming in from Europe through Canada, and I need you to drive up to Toronto and meet him, give him your passport, then drive down through another entry point. He'll come through Niagara Falls. You can return through a different port of entry. Buffalo's fine, it's closest. You just need to give him enough time to get through and disappear. You'll probably be able to get back in with your driver's license, but you might get delayed. Eventually they'll let you back in. Like I said—easy."

Joe frowned. *Give him my passport?* "Who is this guy?"

"An important colleague. He might be a little hot, but he'll be through the border before you, so even if they get suspicious, he'll be long gone. Think of yourself as a distraction. Just some dumb old guy who lost his passport."

Hot? Joe ignored the insult and asked, "How hot?"

"TMI, my friend. You just need to make sure he has your passport. Turns out, you and he look a lot alike."

"Jail time wasn't part of the deal."

"Nah, no jail time. Well, maybe a couple hours in the border patrol office, if it even comes to that, but they'll figure out pretty quickly that you were duped. Just play dumb and it won't be a big deal. You owe me, so you don't really have a choice." The voice turned hard. "I coulda had you play mule. Count yourself lucky."

Fuck. The asshole had a point. The marker he'd given was essentially unconditional. Unless he wanted to end up with Vinnie sooner rather than later, there was really no choice.

"Yeah, I'll do it, you know I will." Then he had an idea. "The guy's coming from Europe, eh?"

"Don't matter to you none, but yeah."

"Then I have a condition." Joe held his breath through the momentary silence on the other end of the connection, knowing he was crossing a line.

"Conditions aren't part of the deal, my friend." The tone was dangerous, but Joe had little to lose at this point.

"A suggestion then. Just hear me out. If this guy looks enough like me to get by with my passport …" He laid out his plan.

"Yeah, all right, I can live with that. It'll make things more solid. But this is happening fast, so be ready."

INTERPOL Headquarters, Lyon, France, Friday afternoon

Lori followed her friends through the ultramodern security gate on the ground floor of INTERPOL headquarters, trying not to gape like a country bumpkin at the impressive technology. As a general rule, all urban skyscrapers and other high-profile buildings around the globe have some level of security, and throughout her career she'd experienced an array of measures designed to keep everyone within these sensitive structures safe in the face of growing threats. But the security gauntlet at INTERPOL headquarters was beyond anything she'd ever seen. It rivaled the White House.

In addition to the staffed checkpoints in both the lobby and the basement they'd descended to, high-tech scanners for both her person and her purse put TSA equipment to shame. They whirred and clicked as she, Laurent, and their escorts passed through.

"Welcome to the Vault," Sabine said with a grin directed at her husband. Then she leaned over and whispered in Lori's ear. "Don't let it intimidate you. I promise it's easier to get out than it is to get in, so if you feel the urge to run, you probably won't be stopped."

The absurdity of the sentiment made Lori laugh, which was Sabine's purpose, she realized. "Good to know."

Etienne directed them to a glassed-in conference room on the far edge of the massive sprawl of workstations. A technician was waiting for them, the large flat-panel screen on the wall lit up and ready for the conference.

Once the connection between the FBI and INTERPOL headquarters was established, Ramon Alvarez introduced himself over the video screen as the liaison responsible for the depositions, then introduced his chief, Nick Talenti—known to Matisse from the Philly experience—who would be sitting in. Matisse introduced the small party gathered in Lyon.

Then Alvarez surprised them all. "Ms. Stripling and Bean—er, Benjamin—extend their greetings to you and their thanks for your efforts on their behalf." The shocked silence following that pronouncement had Ramon adding, "I told them I would be speaking with you today. They don't know the reason."

Lori relaxed and leaned forward. "They are well? Angelina is … she's doing okay?"

Alvarez didn't smile, but his eyes conveyed warmth, causing Lori to sit up straighter. "Remarkably well. She had very little aftereffects from the drugs, and her bruises are healing. Bean's an amazing kid." This time he did allow a hint of a smile, one that revealed a pride. "He won't let her slip."

"Do they have—are you—um …" Lori cut an uncertain glance toward Sabine, who was sitting next to her. "Are they safe?"

Ramon's eyes hardened. "Yes, they are. Thank you for your concern. I'll let them know you remembered them. For my part, I've promised to keep them safe."

Lori couldn't discount the sincerity in the man's demeanor and wondered if Angelina had finally, quite serendipitously, found an honorable man. She hoped so.

The depositions were standard, though lengthy. Lori went first, followed by Laurent. Lori suppressed her surprise at some of the details Laurent revealed; she hadn't realized the depth of his involvement. No wonder the PPD had believed the accusation against him! When it was done, both Alvarez and Talenti were satisfied.

"Thank you for this," Talenti said to Matisse once the interviews had concluded. "It's our plan to move quickly, but I'm sure you appreciate our challenges."

"Yes." Matisse looked at his wife. "Sabine, would you escort our guests up to the lobby? I have just a few more details to cover with these men."

"*Bien sûr.*" Sabine bestowed on her husband a smile that was as lovely as it was professional, then bade the FBI contingent *au revoir* with no hint that she was offended by her dismissal. The simple truth was that she was not offended in the least because her trust in Etienne was unshakable. If he needed to speak with someone privately, she would ensure he had the opportunity. There were no secrets between them. If she hadn't already guessed what he was up to, he would tell her later.

"Well, that was fun." Lori shook out her hands to dispel some of the built-up tension. She'd spent an hour answering questions about a situation she should never have been involved in, then another hour listening to Laurent do the same. Was police work always so tedious?

"I think we've earned our dinner." Laurent ran a warm palm down her spine, letting it rest with his thumb hooked casually into the back of her jeans. Leaning in for a kiss, he whispered, "But I would be amenable to taking you back to the hotel to *freshen up*. Our reservation is not for another hour."

That earned him a laugh, which was his aim, and Lori's shoulders relaxed a fraction.

Back in the conference room, Etienne faced the screen and directed his signature black stare at Talenti. "Carlucci's passport popped up on the grid today. He boarded a flight to Toronto. According to the ticket he booked, he's planning to return to Philadelphia today." Matisse glanced at his watch. "In fact, he should be boarding a flight back shortly. Can you find out what's going on, verify that it is him?"

"Why?" The resigned sigh in the agent's voice only fueled Etienne's irritation.

"Because he is your number one suspect for the Salentino murder and this could be his attempt to escape your jurisdiction." The soft tone of voice was almost more powerful than if he had shouted the words.

"I realize there is no hard evidence—yet—but I would stake my reputation on his guilt. With all due respect, you Americans need to get your heads out of your arses and look at what is in front of you. Nothing else makes sense, and no one else had the opportunity. Not to mention, no one else knew about that flash drive. As far as I am concerned, he sealed his fate when he took the photo of Dubois leaving the townhouse."

"So you say, and believe me, I don't necessarily disagree—"

"What is the point of the very public information-sharing agreement executed not six months ago between INTERPOL's secretary general and the FBI director if not for this sort of thing? Just because Carlucci is not classified as a terrorist doesn't mean our intelligence on such matters should be dismissed."

Toronto, Canada

Joe Carlucci could not dispute his resemblance to the man whose Irish passport proclaimed him to be Joseph Blackstone, though he suspected the other man was younger than his appearance suggested. And his eyes ... Uncle Joe might have passed himself off as a doting relative while Blackstone had the look of someone who might possibly enjoy blowing up the Easter bunny. But no matter—the ruse should work provided no one paid too close attention, and his debt would be paid. It was better not to ask too many questions.

Whatever misgivings Joe might have had about this situation were overshadowed by the prospect of revenge. It was a perfectly teed-up opportunity to fuck with the bastard who had fucked with him. Poetic justice, etc., etc. Joe chose to ignore the challenge of getting out of France once his mission was accomplished, but he had copies of his real passport buried in his bag. The American embassies in Europe were there to help stranded American citizens, after all. And it wasn't like the French mafia would have a bead on his whereabouts. Nope. He'd walk in, wreak havoc, and walk away with no one but the bastard soldier knowing what had happened.

Lyon

The vibrant energy of the city's nightlife buzzed around them. Strolling past the Olympic pool–sized fountain that sprayed graceful arcs of water through colored lights, Etienne Matisse savored the fresh air on his face and his wife's warm hand in his own. The nagging loose ends of their recent American adventure took a backseat for once, and he let himself enjoy the pleasure of an evening out with friends.

He had missed Lyon. Although never with more than a very small handful of friends, he'd always enjoyed good food, and the city was truly the gastronomic heart of France. The two couples had dined at one of the newer restaurants, a smallish establishment tucked into the warren of small streets that surrounded the wide plaza they now strolled.

Their peaceful promenade back to their hotel was interrupted by the ping of an incoming text. Matisse pulled out his phone and read the message, then stopped in his tracks.

Here's your man, safely back in Philly.

The message was accompanied by a still frame of a tall man with a bad gray comb-over exiting a jetway, the angle of the photo suggesting it had been taken from one of the ceiling-mounted security cameras. The only problem was, it wasn't Joe Carlucci.

"*Merde.*" He tilted the phone for Sabine to see it.

"*Qui est-ce?*" She cast a confused look at her husband.

Lori and Laurent caught up to them then, and one look at their faces told Lori that the mellow atmosphere of their evening had just been shattered. "What happened?"

Matisse ran a palm across his jaw and considered the possibilities. It could just be a mistake, but if it wasn't, he couldn't very well discuss it in front of a civilian, no matter her recent involvement.

"I'm not sure yet." His answer sounded a bit uncertain, but then his dark gaze shifted to Lori. "I apologize, but I cannot discuss this in front of you."

"Oh." *Well, duh, international police business.* "Of course."

"It's possible that I will continue to require your assistance," he said, this time to Dubois. "For now, would you mind escorting Lori back to the hotel? I need to make a few phone calls, but we'll catch up to you there."

Laurent looked like he wanted to ask questions, but Etienne cut him off with a quick shake of his head. "Nothing of an emergency nature. In fact, I cannot be certain if there is anything to this." He waved the phone. "Tomorrow morning will be soon enough for us to do whatever may be required, but I'll fill you in on what I learn tonight."

"*D'accord.*" Laurent nodded then turned to Lori. "*Allons y.*"

"What do you supposed that was all about?" Lori asked after they'd put a dozen paces between them and their friends.

Matisse wasted no time in placing the call once the other couple was out of earshot.

"Alvarez."

"It's not him." Matisse got right to the point. "Are you sure this is the person carrying Joe Carlucci's passport?"

"No. The passengers on that flight went through passport control in Toronto, which is not uncommon for flights coming into the US from Canada. We do know his passport was scanned, and the airline confirmed that he boarded the flight. I watched the entire stretch of footage at the arrival gate, and this is the only guy who looks like his passport photo, as much as anyone does."

"How long ago?"

"Two hours."

Matisse cursed. Not exactly real time, but then the FBI didn't have the resources of INTERPOL. Which was the whole point of their information-sharing agreement. By now the man, whoever he was, would be long gone.

"Okay. Send me the flight details. I'll pull up surveillance tapes from both airports, and we'll start combing through them in the morning." *Looking for a needle in a fucking haystack.* "Meanwhile, you might want to send someone around to Carlucci's address. I'll feel a lot better about this if he's snug in his bed." Not that that would answer the question of why someone else was using his passport—if that was, indeed, the case. Matisse made a mental note to run facial recognition software on the photo he'd been texted.

Sabine waited, and when he ended the call, he filled her in on the other side of the conversation.

"It looks like we'll be staying in town for at least one more day," he said. "We'll need Dubois's help with this, too, and I doubt very much he'll want to send Lori back to Provence on her own. Do you still have your museum passes? She might enjoy a day of culture while those of us who can't manage to stay retired get some work done."

Twenty-Seven

"There." Dubois tapped his keyboard, and the image on the screen froze. Joe Carlucci blended in well with the dozens of travelers striding through a wide corridor at Toronto Pearson Airport, but his height had caught Laurent's attention.

The others leaned over his shoulder. "That's him; good eye. Which camera?"

Laurent handed Matisse the control sheet he'd been working from. "First one in the second group."

"Terminal 3," Matisse said after a moment. "Located at Gate A13." He spent another minute cross-referencing the location to a map of the terminal layout. "Here."

"Okay." Laurent leaned over to look. "What does that mean?"

Sabine studied the map and tapped a slim finger on it. "The flight from Philadelphia arrived at this gate over here. What's the time stamp on that image?"

The mouse moved with a flick of his wrist. "9:41."

"His flight arrived at nine fifteen. Allow fifteen minutes to deplane and another few to use the toilets, it would take, what, five minutes at the most to walk from here"—she pointed to the arrival gate then slid her finger along the concourse to the location of the captured image—"to here."

"That would be about right," Matisse said. "What time did the return flight depart?"

"Not until 1400. The flights suggest he had something to do up there that would take a few hours. If that was the case, why is he heading deeper into the terminal instead of exiting the airport?"

"Whatever he was doing—or whoever he was meeting—might have been at the airport." Laurent shrugged. "It's not uncommon … don't most airport lounges have meeting rooms that can be reserved?"

"There are plenty of restaurants and coffee shops, too. And look at this." Sabine indicated a point on the map just beyond where the camera would be aimed. "There's a lower level. May I?"

Laurent stood and offered his chair, then watched over her shoulder as she leaned in to get a better look at the image still frozen on the screen.

"Hmm, I think …" Sabine tapped the keyboard, and the image sprang to life. Just before Joe moved out of the camera's eye, she froze it again. "I think he's heading toward the escalator that leads to the lower level. Etienne, is there another camera that gives us a view of it?"

Triangulating the location of the cameras with the terminal map took a few minutes. There was no clear shot of the escalator itself, but they found one that faced the opposite direction of the camera that had captured that first image of Joe. It was a wide shot, like a fish-eye, encompassing the entire width of the concourse, but the very top of the escalator could be seen in the upper left corner.

Sabine's hunch had been correct. The footage from the new angle, taken in the interval before they'd found Joe, showed another man who could have been Joe walking to the escalator and disappearing down to the lower level. But they knew it wasn't Joe because he appeared a few moments later coming from a different direction.

"That is no coincidence," Etienne said.

"Are there any cameras in the lower level?"

Etienne studied the control sheet before shaking his head. "No."

Sabine rolled the chair back, stood, and stretched. They'd been at it since early in the morning, and it was now closing in on noon. This was the first bit of progress since they'd started their search, but it was significant.

"Let's review what we can prove so far." She commandeered a white board and picked up a marking pen. Etienne and Laurent both leaned against the desk in identical stances, ankles and arms crossed. They said nothing, just watched. Laurent was beginning to realize what Etienne had always known: Sabine was very good at this.

"First, we know Joe took that flight to Toronto." She drew two dots on the board, one marked *P* and the other *T,* with an arrow between them. Above the arrow she wrote, *Joe.* "Immigration has the scanned record of his passport, and we just got a visual of him that proves he was there. And we know it was him, not the double.

"Second, the double—identity presently unknown—is at the same terminal at the same time, heading toward what is, in all probability, an encounter with Joe." Below the first diagram she wrote, *Joe meets double.*

She glanced up at her husband, a thought suddenly occurring to her. "Do you think it's possible that Joe didn't know about this guy? Maybe he was set up and his identity stolen."

They considered that for a minute, but then Laurent pointed out that Joe hadn't been found dead or unconscious anywhere, and he hadn't reported his documents stolen.

"Good point," Sabine said. "Though inconclusive, and begs the next question." She turned back to the board and wrote, *Where is Joe?* "But let's continue with what we actually know.

"Regardless of whether Joe expected the encounter or not, we know there was, in fact, some sort of encounter because the double was seen exiting the flight Joe was supposed to be on. Joe's ticket and passport were used, but no Joe." She drew another diagram of an arrow between two points, this time from *T* to *P,* and above the arrow she wrote, *Double.*

"Alvarez confirmed that he's not at his apartment in Philadelphia," Matisse added. "But that doesn't mean he didn't find another way back, or is finding his way back as we speak. I'm not familiar with current border-crossing protocols for American citizens returning from Canada, but it's conceivable they would let him in with a valid driver's license. One thing I am positive of, however, and that is he would not be able to fly out of Canada to the US or any other country without his passport."

"You think he could drive across the border?" Laurent asked. He knew next to nothing about non-EU border issues.

"It's possible. I know that used to be the case, but the border is tighter now than it was pre-9-11. I'll see if I can find credit card records. Perhaps he rented a car."

"Etienne, something about this doesn't feel good." Sabine stood with her back to the men, staring at her diagrams. "Joe left the US with his own passport, and someone that looks like him used it to get into the country. Joe hasn't popped up anywhere reporting it missing. In fact, he hasn't popped up anywhere at all. Perhaps that's because he's now using this other man's documents?" She swung around and looked at him. "How much longer on the facial recognition software?"

Matisse grimaced. "It could take through the night. There are tens of thousands of images in the database. But you raise an excellent point, *minette.*" He turned to Laurent. "We'll continue watching the security footage. They should both eventually come back up the way they went down because there's no other public exit. Now that we have somewhere to focus we can narrow our scope."

By late afternoon they'd collectively watched hours of security tapes from cameras located all around Pearson's Terminal 3 but had learned very little they hadn't already presumed. True to expectation, both men returned to the main section of the terminal, spaced about ten minutes apart. The double headed toward the departure gate for the flight they knew he had boarded, and Joe headed the other direction. Laurent caught his image from a camera near one of the exits just before he slipped through a revolving door that led to ground transportation. As he watched the footage of his nemesis disappear beyond the glass, Sabine's earlier words echoed in his brain. *Something about this doesn't feel good.*

If Joe had switched passports—and plane tickets—he could be anywhere. Credit card tracking was one thing, but only if they knew who they were chasing. At this point they might as well be looking for a ghost. It was pretty clear the two men were working together in some capacity. The question was, who was helping whom? Was the point of their deception to get the double into the country undetected, or to get Joe out without being tracked? The latter possibility made Laurent very nervous.

According to Matisse, the FBI was nervous about it, too. Alvarez and Talenti were as impatient for the results of the facial recognition software as

Laurent was. As soon as they knew who they were dealing with, they'd be able to track another name through the system.

The last record of Joe Carlucci was around 10:30 a.m. yesterday when he'd left the airport. Or more correctly, exited Terminal 3. There was no evidence he'd actually left the airport, and no credit card charges to suggest a rental car. Could he have been heading for the international terminal?

Alarm for his sister suddenly gripped Laurent. What if Joe was using this other *mec*'s identity to slip back into France? *Christ, the bastard could be here by now.* But that was pretty far-fetched, wasn't it? As far as they knew, Joe still thought they were mafia. He wouldn't know the French contingent could track by his passport or credit cards. Still … he had a good reason for the Americans to lose track of him, too.

"Matisse," he said.

Etienne tapped his keyboard to stop the footage he was watching and looked up.

"Do we have access to airline databases?"

"To discover what, exactly?"

Not a *no*. "If Carlucci booked a round-trip ticket in and out of Philadelphia for the purpose of switching with someone, it is possible that the double did the same. Joe left a clear message that he intended to return and do harm to my family. Can we search the database and isolate round trips booked from here with short stays in Toronto?"

"Yes," Matisse answered, his eyes narrowing in thought. "But unless we narrow down the departure city, the algorithm could take several days."

They whittled it down logically—by sheer volume of passengers, and thus, flights. Heathrow, Charles de Gaulle, Frankfurt, and Amsterdam were the only European airports in the top fifteen of the world's busiest. A check of flights showed multiple daily direct-flight options in and out of Toronto from Paris and London, but not the other two. In the interest of expediency, they went with just those two.

Matisse had the search program fine-tuned and ready to launch when Laurent's phone buzzed with an incoming text. The lovely Ms. Sheridan, back from her day of roaming museums, was wondering when they might be finishing up.

Torn between wanting to keep plowing through security tapes or relax with his lady, Laurent was relieved when Sabine spoke up. With a woman's sixth sense—or perhaps because of the look on his face—she knew exactly who his text was from.

"*Alors,* I think there is nothing more we can do tonight. Without a name for our double, or a hint as to what flight he may have arrived on, we are hacking at straws."

"Hacking at straws?" Etienne suppressed a smile. "*Minette,* I can speak like a native in seven languages but I cannot credit that expression to any of them."

His good-natured laugh at her scowl was so endearing that Laurent felt a sharp stab of envy. He'd never envisioned wanting that sort of relationship for himself, had never had the experience of witnessing one like it before now. But to see Etienne Matisse with such a remarkable woman ... well, it made him realize that his long-held beliefs had been misguided in the extreme. And it made him want to ditch the surveillance tapes for the night and get back to his sexy American.

"Don't be a donkey," Sabine said, but Laurent could tell she was suppressing her own laughter. "You know what I mean ..." She reached out her hand and clutched the air to demonstrate her intended word.

"Ah," Etienne said with a grin. "*Grasping* at straws. I understand you now." He glanced at Laurent with a mirthful expression that Laurent would have sworn the man was incapable of. "And you are quite right, *mon amour.* I, for one, am ready for an aperitif." He punctuated his words with an affectionate kiss to the tip of her nose.

———— ✦ ————

Philadelphia

Angelina Stripling applied a final brushstroke to her eyelids and regarded herself critically in the mirror. Maybelline could not erase years of hard living, but it did add a touch of softness around the edges. Not to mention cover the last of her fading bruises. Satisfied that she'd done everything she could, she gathered her small collection of cosmetics into its plastic pouch and stored it in the medicine cabinet. The little kit was new—had been a tiny splurge, in truth, though she'd purchased it at the Dollar Store. Whatever she'd owned before had been discarded along with her old life, and until recently, she'd had no desire to wear makeup of any sort.

But tonight was special. Tonight she had a real date. Whatever it was that Ramon Alvarez saw in her, she couldn't have guessed, but she was smart enough not to question it. He'd watched over her in the hospital and helped her after she was released, fixing her front door. Since then he'd stopped by the shop at least once a day to check up on her. Always polite, his voice gentle when he spoke, like she might spook if he wasn't careful. And he listened. Listened to Bean, too, giving her boy more considerate attention than anyone she could ever remember. Even Mr. Malone.

"Ma?"

Angelina turned to see her son staring at her with an odd expression on his face. "What?" She glanced down at her dress, wondering if it was ripped or if the lining was hanging below her hem. "Is something wrong?"

"You look different." He was as tall as she was, and now he looked her up and down, but his eyes kept coming back to her face. "Pretty."

She blushed. *My son thinks I'm pretty?* "Thank you, honey. Ramon is taking me out to dinner tonight."

Bean frowned. "You like him." A statement—almost an accusation.

Uh-oh. "I do. Are you okay with that?"

The boy looked at her for a moment then shrugged. "Sure." He turned toward the kitchen, but Angelina stuck out her hand to stop him.

"Bean? Be honest with me. I haven't been on a date—I haven't been with *any* man since …" She couldn't finish the sentence, nor could she stop the blush that crept up her cheeks. To have this conversation with her fourteen-year-old son was … disconcerting. Angelina hadn't been with a man in over a year, not since she'd committed herself to rehab and gotten herself cleaned up. She hadn't wanted to. And a date? A real date that didn't end up with cash left on the dresser? Not since Bean's father. But now, now she was ready. And she really liked Ramon Alvarez.

Bean studied his mother and realized this was important to her. Not just the date, but his approval of it. And really, what was there to disapprove of? Alvarez was a cop, sure, but he was a decent guy. Far more than any of the PPD dickheads that Bean had ever encountered. Maybe the FBI had more integrity than city cops.

The woman standing before him had been through hell and back, but she'd cleaned herself up when given the chance and was doing her best to stay that way. If there was a sketchy line between who was taking care of whom in their little household, that was less important than the fact that it *was* a household. It wasn't her fault what had happened a week ago. And the fact that she'd pulled through it stronger than ever was an indisputable fact. Perhaps the FBI agent had had some influence in that regard.

"Nah, I'm good with it, Ma. He's been good to you. Good to us," he admitted. But then he frowned. "But if he ever turns mean, you get away from him."

"I don't think we need to worry about that, but I won't ever be stupid like that again, Bean. I promise you."

The squeak and rattle of the outside stairs signaled someone was coming up. Mother and son shared a look of wariness until a sharp rap, followed by "Angelina, it's me, Ramon," had them both breathing out in relief. No one from Claudio's crew had come around since Vinnie's murder, but neither of them were ready to let down their guard. She smiled, gave Bean a quick hug, then went to let the man in.

"Hi," Angelina said as she opened the door. Any other words she might have spoken froze in her throat when she saw what he held in his hand. It was a bouquet of roses. Not the hothouse kind like she might have sold him, but the uneven, multicolored variety that came from someone's garden.

"Hi, yourself." Ramon caught her look as she noticed the flowers and held them out to her. "I didn't buy them from anyone else, Angelina. I wouldn't have done that. But, well ..." He smiled shyly. "It wouldn't have been a surprise then. They came from the rose garden at my parish church. The pastor's wife, she let me cut them."

"They're beautiful." And they were. Some almost fully open, others just buds. An array of cream, yellow, and variegated pink. Then she realized he was still standing outside. Reaching for the roses, she stepped aside. "Come in."

"Hey, Bean," Alvarez said as he came through the door, shutting it behind him. "How you been?"

"Good. You?"

Alvarez shrugged. "Been better. Rough at the office right now, if you know what I mean. Frustrating."

Though careful not to leak any confidential information, Ramon kept them in the loop regarding Claudio's gang. They'd wasted no time in causing trouble since Vinnie's funeral, and as Angelina and Bean were considered at risk, the FBI allowed some leeway with information in order to keep them out of the line of fire.

"Yeah? How come?"

Angelina took the bouquet into the kitchen to fuss with it. They might not have glasses to drink from, but they had vases for flowers. She let her boys chat—if whatever was between her and Ramon was going to work, her son had to trust the man like she did—but she listened in all the same.

"We've got clean evidence that Claudio Salentino did those two cops last year, and everyone's ready to jump on him, but the DA is being a dick about it. Sorry, Angelina, but it's true."

Bean went perfectly still. "Why?"

Ramon was watching Angelina fuss with the roses in the kitchen. Something about her was different. Softer. Maybe it was that he'd never seen her in a dress. Or with her hair fixed up.

"Huh?" He refocused on Bean, who was bouncing on his toes. At Quantico he'd been trained to recognize agitation in both witnesses and perps, and as sure as his name was Ramon, Bean was hiding something. Something that had to do with Claudio?

"Bean, my man. You wanna ask me something?"

No hesitation. "What evidence?"

The man and the boy shared a look. There was a reason that Ramon had been recommended for elite training, a reason he'd made it through. Instinct.

Instinct and awareness. And those qualities told him Bean knew something. Against protocol, against regulations, Ramon decided to trust this quiet kid.

"There's a video recording of Claudio killing those cops." He spoke quietly, glancing at Angelina to make sure she couldn't hear. "Vinnie had it but lost it. Those French guys who were here found it—they found it for Vinnie right before he was killed. It's possible Vinnie was killed because of it. The only problem is, no one knows who recorded the thing. The DA won't let us move on Claudio without knowing who made it."

Ramon shook his head in disgust. This was one of the things he hated about being a cop. They had clear evidence of a murder, but the bureaucrats stifled evidence on a technicality. No one could have faked that video. The FBI techno-weenies had been over the thing with a fine-toothed comb and all the high-tech shit known to mankind, and every single one of them had determined it was original. No doctoring. Yet, the DA refused to let it stand as evidence without knowing who shot the thing.

"The fucking bastard is tearing a strip through this city, we have solid evidence he did the crime, but we can't bring him in."

Bean had gone pale, his hands fisted in the pockets of his too-loose jeans. Ramon noticed—he was trained to notice—but said nothing. To give the kid some space, he wandered toward the kitchen where Angelina was arranging the flowers into a pretty vase. In his peripheral vision, Ramon could see Bean shifting around, clenching his jaw tight. Squirming. Like the truth was trying to jump out of his throat if only he'd open his mouth to let it escape.

"You about ready, Angelina?" Ramon turned his focus to his date, a woman who had captured his interest even when she'd been beaten and broken. For the first time, she'd put on a nice dress and a little makeup. Not that she needed it in his opinion, but he understood and appreciated it. And it was not a wasted effort. Angelina Stripling was a pretty woman, and the look in her eyes when she glanced his way made her even prettier in his opinion. She was not a blushing virgin, but neither was she a brainless idiot. Angelina was a survivor, just like him. She had backbone and courage. And the look in her eye told him she was ready to give this aspect of her life another go.

"Almost. These roses are so beautiful, Ramon. So much nicer than anything you could have bought. Thank you."

The smile she sent his way practically sent him to his knees. Okay, more than pretty. Beautiful, at least in his eyes. He watched as she took the vase into the main living area, appreciating the view of her cute little backside in the modest dress. Caught up in the anticipation of a night out with a woman he could easily fall in love with, Ramon didn't notice Bean approaching until he tapped his arm.

Startled, Ramon spun around.

"It was me," Bean whispered. "Vinnie promised he'd send Ma to rehab if I did it for him." The kid was practically in tears. "Please don't send me to jail. I could make it, but Ma would never get through it."

Twenty-Eight

Lyon

Laurent was comfortable to his toes in the big, soft hotel bed. Quite like the feeling he'd become used to in the one at Lori's farmhouse. After so many years of sleeping in narrow cots and bivouac bags, he couldn't imagine ever taking this luxury for granted. Lori was curled into his side, the fluffy duvet pulled up to her chin, her cheek resting on a dark swirl of ink below his shoulder. The whisper of her warm breath against his skin as she slept was soothing. Her trust in him, overwhelming.

Outside, clouds had obscured the moon, but the street lamps below kept the room from complete darkness. The red digits on the bed table clock read 4:08. He took a deep breath and let his cells settle, the nerve endings in his skin registering a thousand sensations, all pleasant. Thinking back to that fateful night in Nîmes, he tried to remember what had spooked him so badly. Nothing she had done, that was certain. On the contrary, she had been refreshingly intelligent and worldly with an adorable dose of innocent vulnerability, and so shamelessly honest in her desire for him. Or rather—he smiled in the dark at the memory—for his tattoo, but that was a turn-on he couldn't deny. No, it wasn't *her* that had him hightailing it back to Uzès without a backward glance. It was his own insecurities. His own long-held belief that any sort of deep attraction for a woman would be a chain rather than an anchor.

As a soldier he was trained to act decisively. He rarely regretted his decisions, but that cowardly move made the short list. The fact that it had taken him two weeks instead of two hours to realize his mistake was testament to how screwed up he'd been. Actually it hadn't taken even two hours for the realization to hit, but he'd been too much of an idiot to do anything about it. Since fate had smiled on him at Alex and Lou's wedding, he'd conveniently ignored what an ass he'd been in Nîmes. Lori said she understood, but she hadn't been able to hide the hurt in her eyes when she'd told him not to leave again without saying goodbye. *Merde.* Then her good-natured spirit had resurfaced, and he'd forgotten the hurt.

Since then, they'd spent only a few nights apart. Sure it had been just two weeks since he'd found her again, but before he met her, more than two nights with a woman made his skin itch. No matter the pleasure shared between the sheets, his previous hookups had generally lost their appeal in the broad light of day. It was like he could see the hopes of wedding bells and baby carriages glittering in their eyes. Those starry eyes and needy looks sent him away as fast as his Ducati could go.

With Lori, he wanted to burrow in and hibernate. She was a safe haven, not a prison. He liked the idea of coffee in the morning beneath her big tree, searching for the most perfect tomatoes at the *marché,* tasting wine with her friends. Now his friends, too. And to his surprise, he liked the image of his ring on her finger. At the gallery he'd told her to move her diamond to the other hand. When he'd seen her again at the wedding, he noticed she'd done it. And then she'd taken the thing off at some point before they flew to America and hadn't put it back on since. The possessive side of him liked the unspoken meaning of that gesture. *Is this,* he asked himself as the fuzzy edges of slumber crept over him, *what it feels like to fall in love?*

Morning intruded far too early, courtesy of an incoming text message. The digital clock read 6:15. *Christ.* Laurent reached for his phone, feeling the loss of Lori's heat when she rolled out of bed on the other side.

We have matches. Be ready to leave in 10.

All vestiges of sleep were gone in an instant as he jumped out of bed. He tapped out his reply while the sound of running water beyond the partially closed bathroom door told him Lori had beat him to the shower. *Might as well save a little water.* He smiled when she squealed to find his chest pressed up against her back beneath the hot spray. Despite his urge to linger, he behaved himself, soaping up quickly and letting her know of his imminent departure for the Vault.

"I'm sorry you can't join us, *chérie.* I didn't expect this to happen, but I'm concerned for my sister." Since the threat to Laurent's family could be construed to extend to Lori as well, Matisse had agreed to let her in on what was going on, trusting her to keep it confidential. Which was not a hardship because other than Annie, who would only worry if she knew, there was no one else to tell.

"I know." Lori shut off the water and accepted the towel he handed her. "I can keep myself amused here—Lyon is a beautiful city and there's a lot to explore."

She watched him rub his own towel quickly over his hair before swiping it across his wet skin with practiced efficiency. He was already finished shaving by the time she stepped from the glass-enclosed shower, but he took a moment to lean in and rub his smooth cheek against hers and plant a quick kiss on her lips before relinquishing the sink to her.

When she emerged a moment later wearing the cushy hotel bathrobe and a towel tied turban-style around her head, he was dressed and ready to go.

"Have a nice day at the office, dear," she said with a smile, batting her eyelashes.

He laughed and wrapped his arms around her, giving her a lingering, sensuous kiss. "I'd rather go with you," he confessed and kissed her again before he said something stupid. Like *I love you.* "Stay out of trouble."

Lori watched the door swing shut behind him and sighed. Not exactly how she'd envisioned this little getaway, but she was relieved they were making such an effort to find that dirtbag Joe Carlucci. She didn't trust the bastard, and just the thought of him coming back to haunt them gave her the willies.

"Putain de merde." The curse was akin to a growl, Etienne's harsh visage blacker than usual. With good reason.

The trolling programs he'd set in motion the preceding day had yielded answers, but not the kind that made anyone feel happy. From the British Airways database, they'd learned that a Joseph Blackstone had arrived in the UK yesterday morning on the return end of a round-trip ticket between Heathrow and Toronto. His stay in the Canadian city had been less than eight hours. The bad news? The Irish passport photo bore a close resemblance to Joe Carlucci. It didn't take long to access the security camera feed at Heathrow for the flight's arrival gate—the Brits really did have cameras everywhere—to get a visual on their old friend.

Worse yet, the facial recognition software produced another match: one Blaine O'Brien, a Red Notice Irish national with IRA connections who'd been on INTERPOL's Wanted List for several decades. Whatever the bloody hell he was doing slipping into the US now couldn't be good. Ditto with Joe Carlucci's presence in the EU, who had a good twenty-four-hour head start on them.

"Dubois, call your sister."

───────◦◦───────

Uzès

It had been remarkably easy to get this far, thanks to the helpful little lady at the information desk at Heathrow. Rather than question Joe's lack of planning, she'd happily booked train tickets, rental car, and hotel for his impromptu "Avignon holiday." She'd even wished him a cheery *bon voyage!*

The hotel turned out to be one that catered to budget-conscious British travelers, and she probably got a commission for the booking, but that was fine with him because the staff all spoke English. And it was close to the train station. The fact that it was located in the industrial outskirts rather than in the charming old city center did not bother Joe in the least. His purpose had nothing to do with sightseeing. He'd arrived in time for dinner the night before and polished off a bottle of wine with his steak but then fallen asleep before inspiration hit.

Thus here he was, almost to his destination, still unclear of how to accomplish his goal. Or even what, precisely, his goal was.

Not entirely true. He wanted to hurt that bastard Dubois. Make him bleed, literally or figuratively. Bring him to his knees in pain, anguish, and misery. If the woman who lived at the address he'd discovered a few weeks ago meant something to him, then hurting her would do the trick more effectively than a bullet to the bastard's chest. Soldiers needed to protect their own—would die trying. And live with the unbearable pain if they failed.

Joe intended to make sure the bastard failed.

Resolve surged through his veins as he drove slowly through the middle-class neighborhood, trying to get a feel for what the Sunday-morning routine was here. Along with a dose of resignation. For this, possibly his final act, he had no plan. Only a big knife and a bottle of whisky to fuel his simmering rage. Laurent Dubois had fucked up Joe's life, turning Vinnie against him. And now the whole family was lost to him. He didn't kid himself that there would be a convenient out for him, even if he succeeded today. People in his line of business retired only when they stopped breathing.

When the opportunity to take revenge had dropped into his lap, Joe knew better than to miss it. *Thank you, Joseph Blackstone, whoever the hell you really are.* If he was going down, he'd take pleasure in causing as much pain as possible.

Ironic that the marker he'd been forced to give up for getting this address a few weeks ago would be the reason he was back. He didn't know who lived here but was pretty sure it was family. Could be a wife, but Joe didn't think so. He'd caught a glimpse of the woman a couple of weeks ago, wheeling a bicycle out of the gate and heading off toward the center of town. She was pretty enough to keep a man's interest, and Joe doubted the soldier would stray with an older woman if he was married to the younger one. A daughter, possibly, or a sister. And there was a kid, too. Joe hadn't seen him—or her, but there were toys in the front yard and the lady's bike had a child seat on the back.

He rounded a corner and then circled back, driving past the house. A powder-blue Fiat 500 was parked in the driveway, same as before. No motorcycle but that didn't mean it wasn't parked in the garage. The thing was probably worth more than the midget car. The streets in this neighborhood were narrow and offered no real place to park, but there were a few parked cars straddling the low curb, mostly out of the street. Halfway down the block from the address he was looking for, he pulled over the same way.

With a fedora pulled low on his head and dark sunglasses hiding his eyes, he climbed out of the rental. It was fairly early for a Sunday morning, only nine thirty. With any luck, he'd catch them at home, but first he needed to make sure the soldier wasn't here.

In a casual stroll with his hands in his pockets, he worked his way down the street, listening to the sounds of normal life. A television blared incomprehensible jabber through the open window of one house, American rock and roll came from another. The clackity-clack of a manual lawnmower could be heard from the backyard of the next one. Birds flitted and chittered among the numerous mature trees, and a dog barked from somewhere nearby. All in all, a pleasant neighborhood. But for the fact that every house stood behind fence, hedge, wall, or gate, he could have been anywhere in America.

When he reached the target house, he paused and looked around, relieved to see he was alone on the street. Channeling nonchalance and alert for any sound from within, he lifted the latch on the gate and walked up the short path to the front door. Another glance around confirmed he was still alone before leaning his ear against the door. Nothing. No television, no voices, no running water to suggest anyone was home. Stepping back off the front-door stoop he was about to walk around to the back of the house when a woman appeared on the street. She looked at him and frowned.

"Elle n'est pas à la maison."

Oh, shit. Not knowing what else to do, Joe smiled and waved, then stepped back up and knocked on the door.

"Je l'ai dit, elle n'est pas à la maison."

Joe bit back a curse and turned to her. She stood her ground, hand on one shapely hip, frowning at him. "Sorry, lady, but I don't speak French." He hoped that would make her go away. A nosy neighbor was a complication he didn't need.

"Ah, you are American."

That startled Joe enough that he answered truthfully. "Yeah."

The woman eyed him for a moment before the awkward moment was shattered by a string of high-pitched yaps.

"Pépé, shh." She leaned down and picked up the noisemaker, a miniature beast that resembled a shaved rat. The thing yapped again then wiggled furiously and licked her chin.

Seeming to remember she'd been in the middle of a conversation, the woman looked at Joe again. "I said, she is not at home. Julia works at the café on Sunday mornings."

Things were suddenly looking up. A nosy neighbor might just come in handy after all. "Oh, ah, I didn't know." Then he took a risk. "And Laurent? Do you know if he's here?"

Her interest in him sharpened. "You know Laurent?"

The drive from Lyon city center to Uzès normally took about two and a half hours, but Lori was pretty sure this trip would clock in under the two-hour mark. Sunday-morning traffic on the A-7 was characteristically light, and Laurent drove Etienne's SUV like the back end was on fire. Not that she blamed him. It would have been comical if it wasn't so frightening, and it didn't help that she was second-guessing her decision to come with him. But damn it, she was responsible for this mess, and she was just as determined to protect Laurent's sister as he was. She gripped the handhold on the door tighter and kept quiet.

Thanks to their early wake-up call, the team had arrived at the Vault just after six thirty. It hadn't taken long to confirm that Joe had landed at

Heathrow and entered the UK using the Joseph Blackstone passport. Not waiting to confirm where he'd gone from there, they all assumed the worst. Matisse tossed Laurent the keys to his vehicle, and while Laurent raced back to their hotel, Sabine called Lori, catching her in the breakfast room.

"Pack up—you're heading back to Provence. Don't waste time asking questions; just be out in front of the hotel in eight minutes or Laurent will likely leave without you. The only reason he's going back to the hotel is because he left his handgun in his duffle. Don't take it personally, but I don't think he's considering you at the moment. And don't you dare take no for an answer when you tell him you're going with him. Just get in the car. We'll settle up with the hotel. Now get moving."

It was a lot of *don't*s, but Lori got the message. Thanks to Sabine's warning, she was just stepping out of the hotel's door with both of their bags at the precise time he screeched to a halt in front of it.

Laurent called his sister's cell phone as he drove down the deserted Quai Charles de Gaulle toward the hotel, but received no answer. Cursing, he called Le Jardin, but of course, no one would answer at seven fifteen on a Sunday morning. The café opened at eight, and he knew everyone would be busy in the kitchen right up until the time the doors opened. That is, if she hadn't already been abducted by Carlucci. He shut his mind to that possibility.

When he saw Lori standing on the sidewalk with his bag and hers, his mind screamed, *No!* But before he could open his mouth, she was buckled into the front seat.

"Just drive."

Wisely, he did so without argument.

Lori hadn't known about the threatening note. When she ventured to ask why he was so sure Joe would be heading for Uzès—between updates from Matisse and Laurent's every-other-minute attempts to reach Julia—he explained. That he hadn't told her about the note until now punched a hole in her heart, even though the logical part of her understood why. In the interest of teamwork and focusing on what was important, she shelved her own feelings to focus on ensuring Julia and Sebastien were safe.

Finally, *finally* someone answered the phone at Le Jardin, and Lori had to reach over to pinch his forearm—hard—when Laurent started shouting for them to put Julia on the line. "For God's sake, soldier. Find your center."

The terse command accompanying a stinging pinch knocked him out of his panic. He closed his eyes briefly—thank the Lord it was brief because he was going over ninety miles an hour—and took a deep breath. "*Désolé*," he muttered under his breath to her, then repeated the word louder to the person on the other end of the line.

"This is her brother, and there is an emergency. Please, can you get her to the phone immediately?"

A moment later her worried voice came on the line. "Laurent?"

"Julia, *Dieu merci*. Where is Sebastien?"

"He's here with me. Laurent, what's going on? Mathieu said you were screaming at him."

"I'm sorry, sweetheart. We have a situation and, well, I need you to be careful. It's possible that someone is coming after you to get to me. Don't let Sebastien out of your sight. Keep him inside. I'm an hour away."

"What? Laurent, you can't be—"

"*Chére, s'il te plait*. Don't argue with me—just do what I say. I'll be there before you know it. Do not let yourself get separated from your employees. Work inside if you can, at least until I get there."

There was a pause on the other end of the line, and Laurent literally held his breath. "What does he look like?"

Good girl. "Tall, late sixties or older with a bad gray comb-over. American. He might try to come on as a sweet old man, but don't be fooled by his charm. He's already tried to—just be careful, sweetheart. I'm on my way."

"He's already tried to what?"

"Julia, please just be careful. Tell your people to be on the lookout, and for God's sake, keep Sebastien inside."

Laurent ended the call before banging his fist on the steering wheel in frustration.

True to Lori's unvoiced prediction, they reached Uzès just inside of two hours from when she'd bulldozed her way into the front seat. Laurent parked near the top of town, as close as he could get to Le Jardin. He took only a moment to fish the SIG out of his duffle and fill the empty clip. Sliding it into the back of his jeans, he nodded to Lori.

Matisse had not been idle during their race south. A team of *gendarmes* was waiting for them just around the corner from the café. Dubois went directly to them.

"*Je suis Colonel Laurent Dubois. Ma sœur est—*"

"*Oui, nous savons,*" the senior *gendarme* interrupted. "Lieutenant Commander Matisse has already briefed us." The officer held up his cell phone. "We have a photo of the suspect."

"Have you seen him yet?"

"*Non.*"

"Have you been to her house?" Lori asked.

The looks of bewilderment on the *gendarmes'* faces was answer enough, and Laurent cursed.

"*Désolé,* we were told to watch her at the café."

"Never mind," Laurent cut off whatever response Lori was about to make. He didn't notice her eyes narrowing at his presumption. "I want to catch this bastard. I assume your other men are not obvious?"

"No more than normal this time of year." This being the beginning of tourist season, a time that brought out pickpockets and other thieves.

"Laurent." Lori spoke firmly enough to get his attention. When he turned to her, she stood rigid with her hands on her hips. "I can go in without being noticed by any of your sister's employees. Call her, describe me to her, and tell her to ignore me. I'll introduce myself to Sebastien and sit with him. I can watch from the interior while you all"—she included the police in her sweeping gaze—"watch the exterior."

"Lori, I would prefer—"

"I know, but we don't have that luxury." Before he could answer, she walked away, ignoring the stab of pain that he'd called her Lori, instead of Lee. Lee was his lover. Lori was the woman who had caused him so much trouble.

Laurent swore under his breath as he made the call.

Lori had never been to Le Jardin, or Uzès for that matter, but Annie's description of the place stuck in her mind, and she had no trouble recognizing the cute café around the corner from where they'd found the *gendarmes*. The brick patio was, indeed, surrounded by planters of riotous flowers and a small, dark-haired woman who resembled Laurent bobbed among the tables. Lori watched as the woman stopped in her tracks and pulled a phone from her back pocket. When her eyes swept the perimeter, they passed right by Lori then skidded back, recognition clear. Satisfied that Julia knew her purpose, Lori gave her a barely perceptible nod before walking across the patio and stepping inside the restaurant.

Typical for a sunny morning in France, the patio was bustling, but the interior tables were empty. In the back corner, at a table near the kitchen, an adorable dark-haired little boy sat absorbed with crayons. Wearing the heather-gray tee shirt with an image of Ben Franklin flying a kite Laurent had bought for him at the airport. It was too big, swamping his slight frame, but he obviously had wanted to wear it. She suppressed a smile.

"*Bonjour*," Lori said to him with a smile, taking a seat at the adjacent table.

Sebastien looked sideways at her then back at his page. "*Bonjour*." The word was spoken so softly, she barely heard it.

Before she could say anything else, Julia appeared in front of her, exuding equal parts hostility and fear. "*Avez-vous choisi?*"

"*Oui, café au lait, s'il vous plaît.*" Before Julia could walk away, she added, "*Me présenter à ton fils, s'il vous plaît.*" *Introduce me to your son.*

Julia hesitated, her motherly instincts not liking the situation or this blond woman whom Laurent was thrusting at her, and certainly not wanting to let her cozy up to Sebastien. But she trusted her brother and knew he would not do something like this if it wasn't absolutely necessary.

"Sebastien."

The little boy, who had been carefully attending to his drawing, looked up at his mother.

"This lady is a friend of Uncle Laurent. Her name is Lori. Can you say hello?"

"I already did, *Maman*. Is Uncle coming to see us today?"

The yearning in the innocent question ripped at Lori's heart. She answered without thinking. *"Oui, il sera."*

If Lori's command of French surprised Julia, she didn't show it. "Do what she says, sweetie." The words practically choked in her throat, but Sebastien regarded Lori with new interest.

"You know my uncle?"

"I do. And I promise you, he will be here soon. What are you drawing?"

Satisfied that Lori was situated where she could watch over Sebastien, Laurent took up a post just inside the tourist office window next door. He wasn't exactly out of sight, but he was counting on Joe's arrogance in thinking he could take his sister by surprise. Despite Laurent's desire to seize the bastard as soon as he showed his face, the *gendarmes* cautioned against that.

"The Americans could very well push back if we nab him before he shows his hand, Colonel." The logic of the statement, coupled with the deferential tone in which it was imparted, forced Laurent to see reason. Matisse had thought of everything, including making sure these locals understood his rank. The *gendarmerie* was, after all, a branch of the French military. And strategically, the *capitaine* was right; Laurent had seen it all too often in other countries.

It was not unusual for the *gendarmerie* to patrol the city streets of their jurisdiction and make their presence known, much like the municipal police they stood in for, but the team with Dubois remained in the shadows in order to avoid spooking the target. Fortunately, they did not have long to wait, though Laurent could barely contain his shock when he saw who walked beside the man threatening his family.

"The café is just there," Adele said, guiding her new friend along a narrow street and pointing to a restaurant across the main road through the upper village. "I know Julia will be happy to meet a friend of Laurent's. She's very fond of her brother."

Pépé the Chihuahua trotted double time at her heels as his mistress and her companion made their way along the cobblestones, until some scent caught his nose. Then he would pause, yelping each time his collar got yanked when he fell behind. After half a dozen such events, Adele stopped to scold.

"Really, Pépé, you are making your *maman* very angry." She jerked on the lead for good measure. "You do not need to sniff at every post." The dog yelped again before falling back in line.

Joe found Adele amusingly transparent. Her infatuation with the bastard soldier was obvious, despite her flirtatious behavior toward himself, a happy circumstance he had no qualms exploiting. Pushing the late end of her thirties, if not early forties, there was a somewhat desperate quality about her. But even so, to Joe's mind the voluptuous slightly over-the-hill Adele was far more alluring than that stiff Sheridan bitch. Joe could easily see Dubois taking what had obviously been offered, and if Adele's hints were to be believed, he had done. Another point to exploit, if necessary.

In the short time since he'd made her acquaintance, she had given him a good amount of information. In truth she'd barely stopped talking, but her jabbering had been worth listening to. Dubois was devoted to both his widowed sister and his nephew. Dubois had recently retired from a senior military position in the French army. Dubois had been living with his sister until recently. No, she didn't know where he was, but she intimated that he would be back soon to enjoy more of their *friendship*.

Adele scooped up the pooch to cross the road, making sure Joe got an eyeful of her cleavage, then set him down on the bricks on the other side. Just beyond the sidewalk was an array of tables delineated from the otherwise open square by a border of planters. Joe looked around. The place was busy. Still unsure of his plan, he decided a crowd served his purpose. No one wanted to make a scene. He'd use Adele's connection to snatch the kid if possible. The sister was his second choice, but not out of the question.

And speak of the devil, there she was. Moving efficiently through the maze of tables, smiling at customers, clearing plates and cups, scribbling on her pad, taking money, and giving change. She glanced up at them, then took a double-take when she saw Adele. Even from a distance of twenty or so feet, he could see her eyes glance from Adele to him and back. Then she looked directly at him and frowned. Nodding at an empty table on the perimeter, she strode back inside the restaurant.

"Come on," Adele said, scooping up the dog again and sashaying through the throng to the empty table Julia had indicated.

"He is here." The words were hissed low as Julia bent over to retrieve Lori's empty cup. "He is with my neighbor, one who sometimes helps me with child care. Please …" Julia's eyes implored her with the unspoken plea. Lori suddenly wished she could make all three of them disappear but managed what she hoped was a reassuring nod.

"Sebastien," Lori said when his mother had passed into the kitchen. "Do not get up from the table, no matter who you see. Okay? This is very important. It is not a game."

The little boy frowned but nodded. Lori wished she had a leash.

From his vantage point, partially hidden by a rack of brochures, Laurent watched Adele saunter across the street with Joe. *What the fuck is she doing here with him?* And with that stupid dog, too. Tapping his phone, he connected immediately with the *capitaine*. "He's here, with a woman—a neighbor of my sister's. I can't say if she knows what he's up to, but don't trust her. She's a vindictive bitch."

If the captain was surprised by the assessment, he kept it to himself. "What's her name?"

"Adele. I don't know her surname."

"Does she know the boy?"

"She was his babysitter for a couple of months."

"I see."

Suddenly the dog let out an earsplitting barrage of yaps then took a flying leap out of Adele's arms, trailing his leash behind him. The squirrel he'd spotted raced up the nearest tree in an equal riot of noise. At the same time, Joe veered away from the table and headed straight for the restaurant entrance.

"*God damn it,* there he goes. Alert your men at the rear." Laurent sprinted to intercept him, but the commotion caused by the dog had people shifting for a better look, hindering him. Elbowing his way through the crowd, he just caught the profile of Joe's face again as he crossed the threshold.

"Pépé!" Sebastien jumped up from the bench and started for the door but wasn't quick enough. Lori reached out and latched on to the back of his tee shirt, halting the boy's progress.

"Sebastien, no!"

"But it's Pépé!" The little boy struggled, and for a moment Lori thought he might wriggle out of the oversized garment and race for the door.

"Sebastien, remember what your *maman* said. You must stay here and mind me."

"But I want to see Pépé." His lower lip started to tremble.

Oh, crap. Lori guessed Pépé must be the dog making all the racket outside, but from where she was sitting, she couldn't see what was happening. "Don't worry, sweetie. We'll just wait for your *maman* to say it's okay."

She stood and took the boy's hand, venturing a step toward the door, looking for Julia. *Oops.* Big mistake. Joe appeared in the doorway, blocking out the light. *Crap, crap, crap.* She backed up, towing the kid with her.

"Come on, Sebastien. Let's go into the back and find her." She kept walking backward, dragging the squirming and now whining kid with her, all the while keeping her eyes locked on Joe.

Who grinned, the bastard, but it was with a sort of grotesque sadistic glee rather than good humor. "Cute kid. Sounds like he knows the little shit squirter."

Her foot tangled with a chair, but she kicked it aside and pushed Sebastien behind her, ignoring his cries. "If you don't want another knee to your balls, I suggest you back off now. Sebastien!" Her voice was louder than she intended but the kid quit struggling. "Calm down and stay behind me."

Joe smirked. "That trick only works once, lady." He narrowed his gaze and reached inside his jacket, taking a step forward at the same time. "And this time, it's me with the knife."

Oh, shit. The blade that suddenly appeared in his hand was something out of a jungle movie. A door swung open behind her, followed quickly by a gasp and the sound of dishes crashing to the floor. Lori jumped but didn't dare risk a look around.

"*Maman!*" Sebastien wailed and resumed his struggling, but Lori gripped his little hand like a vise.

"It's okay, I've got him." Julia. *Thank God, I think.*

"Are you sure?"

"*Oui.* Let go. It's over." Julia's voice was closer now, just behind her, probably on the other side of the table she'd run into.

"Over?" The question came out like a squeak. "How do you figure?"

"Because my brother will kill him."

That matter-of-fact statement was punctuated by a distinctive metallic click of a gun being cocked, and Lori realized that Laurent was there, right behind Joe. She'd been too terrified to take her eyes from the Rambo knife to notice him.

But then Joe whirled, whipping the knife around in a slashing arc aimed straight for Laurent's neck.

It was over before the echo of Lori's scream died down. Laurent blocked the swing with his right elbow then brought his left fist across for a brutal uppercut. Joe's head snapped back with an audible crack. The knife clattered to the floor, followed a moment later by the crash of the man who had wielded it.

Twenty-Nine

Parc national des Cévennes, one week later

Taking down the old man had been the easy part. Copping to the cold fear that had almost crippled him? Not so much. Unfamiliar feelings churning in a growing emotional quagmire of doubt-filled muck, Laurent sought the solace he'd always relied on to clear his head. Speed.

He pushed his Ducati beyond its safe limits. And the big black beast, built for speed and crazy recklessness, responded. Laurent drove his baby like it was the last time they'd ever be together. Accelerating when he should have pulled back, leaning forward when he should have let up. The heady speed fed the need for more. Tearing up the mountain road, pressing the beast to the pavement through curve after hair-raising curve, leaning so far over that if he hadn't been wearing his thick leather chaps, his knees would have been bloody hours ago. As it was, the leather was shredded where it had touched the asphalt more than once around the most severe curves.

And then he almost did succeed in killing himself. Hugging the middle line through an exhilaratingly tight curve, he came within kissing distance of a Ferrari doing the same thing—from the other direction. *Talk about a wake-up call.* Thinking about ending it was one thing. Facing the inevitable was quite another. At least the adrenaline rush proved he wasn't dead yet.

After that close call, Laurent finally slowed, coming to a stop on a narrow turnout at the edge of the rugged gorge. He was too much of a coward to kill himself so deliberately, and the near-death brush made him realize he didn't want to put his sister through that nightmare. Or anyone else—if she still cared.

Now, holding his glove-encased hand at eye level, he acknowledged the tremors were still visible. *Fuck.* Looking past the glove to the rugged landscape of the gorge beyond, he almost chuckled. He stood on a precipice surrounded by a vast, empty landscape. What an appropriate metaphor for his life.

A week had passed since Joe Carlucci had been carted off in the custody of the Uzès *gendarmerie,* but all Laurent could see when he closed his eyes was that wicked hunting knife poised above Lori's honey-blond head. So he tried not to close his eyes.

His own part in the drama had ended four days ago. Kicking into full military mode after the incident, locking emotions back into the box where he'd always kept them, it had been satisfying in the extreme to interrogate the worthless thug regarding the fictitious Joseph Blackstone. Matisse was still involved with the case, coordinating with his American counterparts. Hopefully the information Laurent was able to extract would lead to finding the old terrorist who had slipped into the US on his purloined passport.

The news of Claudio's arrest for the murder of those two cops meant his and Lori's depositions hadn't been a waste of time. Actually Laurent didn't care one way or another about the Philadelphia situation, but he was grateful they'd been in Lyon when word had come about Joe. There was no telling what would have happened if they hadn't had real-time access to the Vault's resources.

But now, without the distraction of work, he had way too much time to think. And was oddly unable to maintain the military lockdown on his emotions. The pain in his heart and the shame of his own cowardice could not be suppressed.

Nothing seemed to center him. Not long sessions at the shooting range, grueling taekwondo workouts, or even playtime with his nephew. Sebastien had come through the ordeal unaware that there had actually been an ordeal, and other than his natural curiosity as to why his uncle had decked a customer, he'd forgotten it all. He hadn't really understood what was happening other than that ridiculous dog had caused a racket. Lori had kept him shielded until Julia could take hold of him. Another contribution she'd made to saving his family from a monster.

Racing through the remote mountains of the Languedoc wasn't helping either. No matter how fast he went, he couldn't outrun the truth of his current reality. Never in his life, even in the darkest parts of Africa, had he felt so lost.

As he stood there on the edge, more alone than ever, he felt the phone in his pocket vibrate.

L'Isle-sur-la-Sorgue, Luberon Valley

Lori was doing her best to go through the motions of *normal.* Like her world hadn't been upended and her heart wasn't breaking apart in her chest. It had been seven days—not that she was counting. She'd agreed to meet Annie at the big Sunday market, and so here she sat. But her head was stuck in replay, uncaring of either the espresso in front of her or the teeming, pulsing humanity around her.

She had rather hoped the crushing blow Laurent delivered would shove a bone up into Joe's brain and finish him for good, but they weren't that lucky. Probably just as well, because even as angry as he was, she suspected the last thing Laurent needed was another death on his conscience. Regardless of how well deserved it would have been.

After the confrontation, he'd been distant. That cold ice she'd seen in his eyes when they'd first met had returned, not fading as he methodically followed along with the procedural stuff. Giving his statement, getting hers, coordinating with Matisse and the local *gendarmerie,* and whatever else was needed.

Lori had stayed out of the way in the café, sitting with Sebastien until Laurent convinced his sister to let her employees handle the business for the day and take the boy home. The poor kid had had a traumatic experience, though it could have been much worse if they'd ignored the signs. Etienne, Sabine, and Laurent had done an impressive job at puzzling out Joe's plan and by doing so had prevented a disaster.

That crazed look in Joe's eyes had been unmistakable; Lori was absolutely positive he would have used the knife on her and the boy if he'd had the chance. The fact that they'd prevented it from happening should make her feel proud. Ecstatic even. Yet somehow, the victory seemed hollow.

The only satisfying moment in the aftermath had been Laurent's reaction to the woman who'd led Joe to the café. The one with the stupid dog. She'd come gushing up to Laurent like some long-lost lover and wrapped her arms around him. That contact had lasted only as long as it took for him to shove her aside. Then he'd had her arrested for aiding and abetting the assault on his family. The look on her face when she was handcuffed and dragged off was priceless. Unfortunately, stupidity wasn't a crime and Lori doubted the arrest would stick, but she hoped the lady would stay away from Laurent for good.

Although why she cared at this point, she didn't know. She hadn't seen or talked to him since that day.

"Earth to Lori." Annie Macallister bumped shoulders with her, knocking her out of her musings.

"Sorry." Lori smiled but knew her friend wasn't fooled.

"Okay, spill."

Lori's pained smile lightened a bit. They were seated elbow to elbow at a café table alongside the river, enjoying a respite from the crush of market goers. The Sunday-morning market was in full swing, and the quaint town of L'Isle-sur-la-Sorgue was packed with locals and tourists. They jammed the narrow streets, streets made even more narrow by the rows of vendors that lined both sides and filled the town's squares. It was a noisy, colorful, happy crowd, and precisely the reason Lori had chosen to live in this part of the world, but today it wasn't filling her with joy.

"All right, Miss Nosy, the truth is that he hasn't called me in a week, and I miss him." There. She'd said it. Admitting that her heart was crushed by his abandonment was the first step in getting over him, right?

"And?"

"And what? It was great while it lasted. I even fell a little bit in love with him." A lot in love with him, actually. In the head-over-heels category. "And it was wonderful. But his family comes first, and frankly, after all the shit that knowing me brought to him—to *them*—I can't blame him for washing his hands of me." She shrugged, trying to convince herself it didn't matter. "And there's that little fact that I'm almost ten years older than him. Christ, Annie. He has women half his age drooling after him. Why would he possibly want me?"

"Oh, for God's sake." Annie shook her head in disgust. "Girlfriend, the man was crazy for you. First of all, you're awesomely fit, gorgeous, and frankly way more pulled together than any thirtysomething that might think to poach on him. Those women are nothing compared to you, and don't you forget it. But most importantly, I cannot imagine that he blames you for any of this. Knowing what little I know about him, I'm guessing he probably blames himself."

Lori scrunched her eyebrows down, but the motion didn't hide the blush that crept up her cheeks at Annie's blatant compliment. Doing her best to ignore it, she pushed the point that was foremost in her mind. "How do you figure that? If Martin hadn't been such an idiot, none of this would have ever happened."

"Yeah, and if Laurent hadn't broken that Joe guy's nose, he wouldn't have been so hell-bent on revenge."

She had a point. But really, what did it matter?

"Have you tried calling him?"

"What? No." Lori shook her head emphatically. "No. He's got his own stuff to deal with, and I don't want to interfere." Or appear needy. It was like she told him before. She wanted him to see her as the strong, independent woman she had always been.

"Don't you think he might be afraid to call you?"

"Huh? Why? He knows how I feel."

"Perhaps he's ashamed of his own behavior. You said he shut you out from the moment you began that race from Lyon. Then he panicked, and you had to practically slap him to snap him out of it."

Well, yes, there had been that … it was a pinch not a slap, if one was splitting hairs. But that couldn't possibly be—

"Men are dense, Lori. And they can have a very warped sense of pride. Especially the strong ones. You just don't know this because you never had any sort of deep emotional tie with Martin, and his idiotic tendencies didn't hit you where it hurts."

"Hey—"

Annie made a slashing motion in the air. "It's true, and you know it. But this isn't about Martin. Has it occurred to you that Laurent needs you, and misses you, as much as you do him?"

No, that hadn't occurred to her at all.

"He had the shit scared out of him. The big, bad soldier who doesn't think twice about going into a killing zone with a smile and a knife between his teeth—with only his *own* life at stake—had a *teeny-weeny* emotional hiccup when his only living family was threatened while he was racing against the clock to reach them."

"And you happened to witness that little emotional blip." Annie let that sink in while she took a sip of her coffee. "He probably thinks you've lost respect for him."

"What? But that's ridiculous. The way he—"

"Save it for the one who counts, sister. I already know." Annie's smile was gentle. "The tough guys get all twisted up with their emotions just like everyone else, but because they're so tough they don't let anyone see it. The trick is to help him untwist himself while letting him maintain his dignity."

Parc national des Cévennes

I miss you.

Talk about being pulled from the precipice. Thank God and the French utilities for cell service in the middle of nowhere.

Laurent stared at the text message like the lifeline it was, willing it to say more, wanting—*needing*—the subtext. He missed her too. So much it hurt to breathe. Like that time he'd cracked a few ribs when his jeep had been blasted off the road in Mali. Only this was worse. Because physical pain he could handle—it's what he'd been trained to do. The bruising pain to his heart ... not so much.

She hadn't been far from his mind since last Sunday. That was a lie—his thoughts were consumed by her. Visions of her expressive eyes taunted him.

The sound of her sultry laughter was on auto-replay in his brain like a song he couldn't stop humming. Not that he wanted the memory to go away. Quite the contrary. He wanted to wrap his arms around her and bury his face in the sweet fragrance of her hair, run his fingertips down the soft skin of her cheek. See those beautiful eyes look at him with love. But he'd been such an ass, such a coward, he was afraid of what he'd see in those eyes now.

I miss you. Meaning what? Just that, or more? Did that mean she wanted to see him again? God, he hoped so, but he was so pathetically inexperienced with relationships that he was terrified that he'd already blown it. Perhaps that was the point of her message. Nothing more than an honest expression of her feelings. Perhaps she understood he was a moron with women and was reaching out to him in the only way her own pride would allow. Letting him know … what? That she wouldn't judge him? She wouldn't have sent a message if she didn't want a response, right?

And he really, *really* wanted to respond. But … shit. He'd been such a fucking coward. Just the thought of it made him cringe. The calm, rational, ultra-trained warrior had degenerated into a screaming maniac. She'd had to give him a verbal slap to refocus. *For God's sake, soldier. Find your center.* And bless her, it had worked, but he'd been so mortified that it had been necessary, he could barely meet her eyes.

Then she'd walked into the thick of it to protect Sebastien, a boy she didn't even know. And she'd done it with unwavering heart and courage. She stood up to that bastard Carlucci, stood her ground even when he'd pulled a knife. She was terrified but so fucking brave, and what had he done? Rather than wrap his arms around her and never let go, he'd let the ice crust over his emotions. It was the only way he could keep from losing his shit in front of his sister, his nephew, and the squad of *gendarmes.*

When she offered to drive Matisse's SUV back to Lacoste so Laurent could stay with his family, he'd simply handed her the keys. She'd given him a small smile, kissed his cheek, and walked away. Letting him have the space she knew he needed even before he realized it himself.

I miss you. Three simple words that gave him hope as sure as they tore a hole in his heart. God knew she deserved far better than him. He had nothing to offer her but the love in his heart—love she had put there. With her, it felt awesome. Without her, it hurt like hell.

How poetic. But would it be enough? Even all that sweet emotion came heavily encumbered by his damaged psyche. He didn't even have a home to call his own, no safe sanctuary he could give her. Did that make him a selfish bastard for wanting her anyway? Before he could overthink it, before he could fall back on the excuses that had worked for him in the past, he sucked in a deep breath and reached for what he wanted.

Ménerbes

I miss you too. Have dinner with me?
Lori blinked when his reply text came through. Was it really that easy? A shiver of pure happiness tickled her skin, and she laughed. She reread his words but could find no hidden meaning. Like her message to him, it was honest and direct.

Score a point for Annie. *Men are clods,* she'd said. *Don't judge him because he can't read your mind. Judge him for how he responds when you tell him in plain language what you want.* Apparently Kaden had similar issues, and Annie had had a couple of decades to learn how to deal with them.

Christ, Lori realized, she'd been an idiot. But then, so had Laurent. She shook her head. Time to stop acting like teenagers.

Will you come here? I have a beautiful Bresse chicken to roast.
His reply was immediate: *I'll bring the wine.*

Uzés

"You're leaving again?" Julia looked up from her pastry dough when Laurent appeared in the doorway. With her hair pinned up in a haphazard twist and a smear of flour on her cheek, she looked much younger than her thirty years. She also looked happy. When was the last time he'd seen her eyes so clear of pain?

"For a couple of days. Maybe more." Setting his duffle on a chair beside the door, he walked into the kitchen and surveyed her work. "This looks serious. What am I going to miss?"

She smiled. "I'm trying out ideas for a new summer menu. With the *fête de la musique* coming up, I thought it might encourage more people to come for a late dinner. There will be a band on the corner by the fountain, and my patio will be prime seating."

"Ah. Good idea." He lifted the lid from a pot on the stove and sniffed. Just before he stuck his finger into the dark *confiture,* she swatted his butt with her rolling pin.

"Use a spoon, not your finger," she huffed. "I swear you are worse than Sebastien."

He grinned. "Probably."

She resumed rolling the fat wooden dowel across the dough. "Where are you going? Another job?"

Laurent cleared his throat. He hadn't told his sister about Lori—who she really was to him. It had felt too personal. And awkward. It still did, but Lori deserved better. "Remember the woman who protected Sebastien last week?"

The pin stopped. "The one who put herself between my son and your crazy American?"

"Not *my* crazy American, *chére,* but yes, that's her." Laurent lifted another lid to avoid looking at her eyes, not wanting to see her disapproval. Although why she would disapprove, or had any right to … *Christ, get a grip, soldier.* He dropped the lid and turned to face her.

Julia leaned against the table, arms crossed. "I never even got a chance to thank her. Have you worked with her before? Don't tell me you're hitting on her. Isn't there some policy against that?"

Laurent almost choked. "What?"

"You know, fraternizing with colleagues." After the episode with Joe, Laurent had confirmed that he'd taken an assignment with the international police in order to apprehend the man but had given her no further details.

"You thought she was—of course you did." He dragged a palm down his face in an agitated gesture. "*Merde,* I've been such an idiot."

"Laurent, you're not making any sense."

He pinched the bridge of his nose, feeling a headache coming on. "Lori is not a colleague, she's … she was … Christ. I think I'm in love with her. No, scratch that, I know I'm in love with her."

Julia's eyes widened to saucers. "How long have you known her? Is *she* the reason you've been gone recently?"

Not liking the tone of that question, Laurent stood straight and crossed his arms in a mirror image of her stance. "I met her in Nîmes, the night of—"

"The night of Jacques's exhibit." Julia regarded her brother then nodded. "That's right, you left early." She pursed her lips thoughtfully. "And why have you not told me about her until now?"

"I'm not a teenager, Julia." Although he was fidgeting like one. "You don't get to interrogate me over a woman." This was becoming ridiculous. He just wanted to get out of there and go see the lady.

And then to his surprise, her eyes softened. "Oh, Laurent. Does she know how you feel?"

They stared at each other for a few moments, the compassion in her eyes finding the rare vulnerability in his. He blinked first and looked down at his feet.

"Probably not. I've not had the courage to tell her, and after last week, I can't be sure she isn't completely disgusted with me."

"What do you mean?" Her compassion evaporated, and she narrowed her eyes at him. "Do you mean to say you haven't spoken to her since then? What sort of an idiot are you?"

That made him laugh, though it was hardly humorous. "The worst kind, I'm afraid. Listen, thanks for your vote of confidence, but I need to go. For some reason, she's offered to cook me dinner tonight, and I'm planning to do my best groveling."

His beautiful sister stepped up to him then and gave him a hug. "I didn't think you would ever meet a woman who could match your strength, but I think you finally have."

He returned the embrace and kissed her forehead. "I think you're right. Wish me luck."

"Good luck, you blockhead. I love you."

"I love you too, *chére*. Perhaps if I'm lucky, she'll agree to be my date for the *fête*. She has friends here in Provence who I think you would like very much."

"That sounds wonderful, but don't get ahead of yourself."

He laughed, picked up his duffle, and headed out into the perfumed air of early evening. Julia watched from the window as he roared off on his motorcycle. When he was gone, she found herself smiling. It was a good feeling.

Ménerbes

Immersed in the luxury of a rare bath, Lori realized Annie was right about something else, too, as much as it pained her to admit it. Her marriage to Martin had been a comfortable convenience, nothing more. She and Martin had been friends, professional equals, and compatible at home. They'd enjoyed each other's company, had a pleasant enough sex life in their early time together, and shared similar values. There had been no insecurities, no passionate outbursts, and certainly no fits of jealous rage. No wonder Martin had been lured away; there'd been no strong emotions binding him. The tears she'd shed over the divorce had been tears of humiliation, not heartbreak. Because in truth, her heart had been no more engaged than his.

Not so with her soldier. He'd captured her heart that very first night. Had he never reappeared, he would still own a small piece of it. That night he'd shown her a side of herself she scarcely knew existed. But since then, the tenuous threads of his possession had strengthened. Had she had a similar effect on him?

The days were getting longer in the south of France as the calendar marched toward the summer solstice. The sun didn't set until nine o'clock now, and tucked into the valley floor where the heat of the day pooled, Lori's little slice of paradise was ideally suited for al fresco dining. She draped a pretty Provençal runner across one end of the outdoor table and laid place settings on each side. She was in the process of arranging a bouquet of early sunflowers for the center when the roar of an engine announced Laurent's arrival.

Flower bowl in hand, she watched him come through the hedgerows and toward her down the track. Even hidden by the helmet and black leather jacket, he was a beautiful man. The Ducati only emphasized his power. The bike came to a halt a few yards from where she stood, and she was grateful for the flowers. She needed a shield—he was just too potent.

Laurent didn't hesitate to kick out the stand and dismount. He popped off the helmet and crossed the distance between them, his pale-blue eyes lit with a yearning that seared her. He stopped with less than a foot between them, only because the flower bowl prevented him from getting any closer. Then he pulled off a glove and brought his bare fingers up to caress her cheek.

"*Bonsoir, chérie.*"

She had to clear her throat to answer. "*Bonsoir.*"

"Thank you," he said, his eyes burning into hers.

Her brow arched. "For?"

"For sending me a lifeline." He leaned over the flowers and pressed his lips briefly, gently to hers. "I love you."

"You do?"

"I do." He kissed her again. "I'm sorry for not making it more clear."

Lori was still back at *I love you*. "But why—"

"*Chérie*, let me take this before you dump it down my pants." He eased the bowl away from his body and tilted it back upright.

"Oh!" She laughed and it broke the tension, but she felt her cheeks turning pink. "Sorry. That wouldn't have been very comfortable."

Flowers safely on the table and no longer in his way, he snaked an arm around her waist and brought her in close. Burying his face in her hair as he'd yearned to do for the past week, he groaned at the sublime feel of her pressed against him. "I've missed you so much. All I could think about was how magnificent you were, how brave and beautiful. I wanted to come over here and bury myself inside you, but I didn't think you could stand to see me."

Lori was doing a little groaning of her own. Her soldier was back, and she didn't ever want to let him go. But she eased back and looked into his eyes. "Why would you possibly think that?"

He swallowed, that rare vulnerability making another appearance in his clear-blue eyes. "Because I lost control. If you hadn't snapped me out of it, I don't know what I would have done. I behaved like a cowardly ass and then … *merde,* then when it was over, I was too ashamed to face you."

The look of incredulous surprise on her face had something inside him shifting.

"Laurent, you didn't *lose* control, you *took* control." She reached up and cupped his face in her hands. "Don't you see? You had no control of that situation at all, yet you wrestled it into your grasp. That gave me the courage to follow your lead."

"You didn't need any courage from me, sweetheart. You would have kept Joe away from Sebastian until you had no breath left in your body. You scared ten years off my life, but when I saw you there, holding Sebastien back … you were magnificent, like a Valkyrie, and I … I could only … Christ, I don't know what happened." He closed his eyes to the pain of his shame.

"What the hell are you talking about? I was scared out of my wits, not to mention backed into a corner. Joe would have slashed that knife at me if you hadn't been there, and then he would have gone after the boy." She threaded her fingers through the hair at his nape.

"And then when he spun around … God, I thought he was going to kill you. But he didn't stand a chance. If anyone was magnificent, it was you. You kept us all safe, just like I knew you would. Do you honestly think I could have gone in there otherwise? What happened was exactly what needed to happen, and because of you, everyone is okay."

He looked into her eyes, so clear, so sincere, so fierce, and knew she spoke the truth. Her truth, at any rate. And he found that counted for more than he could have imagined. He'd have to give the whole episode more thought. Later. For now, there was something else he needed to know.

"*Chérie.*" His hands rested on her hips, and he let them slide up to her waist. "Can you forgive me for being an ass?"

She opened her mouth to reply, but he gently pressed two fingers to her lips. "It probably won't be the last time. I have no experience being with a woman—"

Her eyes twinkled with laughter.

He tweaked her nose. "Being in a *relationship,* I meant to say. I'll screw it up regularly, no matter how hard I try. But I want to try, if you'll have me. I want to laugh with you and cry with you. I want to make love, explore new places, and learn new things with you." He leaned in and kissed her. "I want to make you love me as much as I love you."

Lori felt the tears building behind her eyes and blinked them away. "You won't have to work very hard on that one."

He frowned, not understanding. The uncertainty in his eyes just about slayed her.

"I already love you, more than I've ever known love. I didn't mean for it to happen, but ..." She shrugged. "And I want those things, too."

His frown turned to a beautiful smile, and he leaned in, ready to seal the deal with a hot kiss, but she stopped him with a hand on his chest.

"But, Laurent, promise me that when you need space, you'll tell me. I won't judge you or begrudge your need. Trust me, I get it—I need it too, and I'll be honest when I need to be alone. We've both been independent for too long to be able to give up that freedom. No more disappearing, no more guessing. Knowing how you feel, and you knowing how I feel ... that means a lot. God knows I'm no clingy female, but I deserve respect, just as you do."

"You do, and you have mine." He kissed her then. A heartfelt, honest, loving kiss that she returned in kind. And with that kiss, he finally understood what the poets had always known. There were no chains with the real deal, only a sturdy anchor in a safe harbor.

A few hours ago he'd been ready to pull a Thelma and Louise with the Ducati, but it was the leap of faith he took with his heart that would be his salvation.

Thirty

Rasteau, one week later

"That's the last one." Annie Macallister fit the insulated bag into the back of the old truck alongside a large cooler and several other boxes and bags. On a grunt, she hefted up the gate, pushing until it clicked into place.

"You've got the wine?" Lori was leaning over the open bed, poking through bags.

Annie laughed. "I'd never hear the end of it if I forgot that."

"Corkscrew?"

"Check."

"Glasses, plates, napkins, and cutlery?"

"Yep."

"Serving utensils?"

A pause. "Crap, no. Give me a sec." Annie ran back into the house, returning a moment later with a handful of tongs and tossing them into one of the bags. "Okay, let's go. As long as we have the food, wine, and water, all else will be forgiven."

They climbed into the front seat of the dusty truck, laughing as Zorro, the Macallisters' enormous Siamese cat who'd been napping in the sun on the worn cushions, made a disgruntled snort and jumped from the truck.

"Sorry, buddy," Annie called as the cat sauntered over to the back porch. The truck started up with a rattle and a cough.

"I can't believe this thing still runs." Lori buckled her seat belt and grabbed the handle above the door as Annie backed up. Loaded down with supplies, the old truck rambled up the steep track that would take them up and around the vineyard to where the crew would meet them for lunch.

"No joke. We don't usually take it farther than town, but it's good for this sort of thing."

The truck bucked and bounced along. Whether the neck-twisting ride was due to its wonky suspension or Annie's driving as she managed to hit every pothole on the road was anyone's guess. Possibly both, based on the grin she was sporting.

"Look, there they are."

As the road leveled out and they began the traverse across the upper edge of the property, they had a clear view of the vineyard that sloped away toward the valley. The sun was high in the sky, so bright it seemed to reflect off of everything. About halfway down they could just make out a staggered string of men steadily working their way toward the western edge of the vineyard.

Judging their progress, Annie nodded. "We should be able to get everything unpacked and set up before they finish their rows."

It was a tradition at Domaine de la Terre des Roches to provide a midday meal for the vineyard workers. Many years ago the task fell to their neighbor Sophia, who also served as housekeeper to what had been a bachelor abode for many years. Annie never quite understood the relationship between Kaden's widowed uncle and his neighbor—she only knew that it was one of deep affection and trust.

When Annie had first arrived and was hell-bent on pulling her weight in the vineyards, she'd been grateful for the respite in the shade, the hearty meal, and the refreshing rosé. In the years after Annie joined the household as Kaden's wife, Sophia continued to serve up her delicious yet simple Provencal cuisine in the vineyard. Annie had many wonderful memories of those meals. When Sophia passed away, followed shortly by their beloved uncle Henri, it felt as if the fabric of their existence was torn apart.

At that time the role of mistress of the property weighed heavily on Annie's shoulders, but out of respect for her wonderful role model—a woman who had become a very good friend—she'd taken her responsibility for overseeing the domain's hospitality seriously. And though she rarely admitted it, the older she got, the more she preferred providing the meal rather than working in the vineyards.

Now, after more than a decade of doing just that, Annie didn't hesitate. With a maneuver perfected over years of practice, she cajoled the old truck into a neat U-turn that had the dust blowing away from the tables but the back end of the truck conveniently close for unloading. Standing on the running board to look out into the vineyard before jumping down, she smiled.

"We've got about ten minutes before the first one gets here. Let's move."

Like a drill sergeant at a parade ground, Annie rattled off instructions to her troop—her best friend—and between the two of them, they had tables dusted off; cloths laid; plates, glasses, napkins, and cutlery set in neat stacks; and covered dishes arranged down the length of the tables. Cold water and wine was opened and waiting in a cooler by the time the first man emerged from the rows of vines.

"Hullo, love." Sweat dripping from beneath the brim of a battered baseball cap, his damp tee shirt clinging to taut muscles, Kaden stopped at the cooler. Grabbing an ice-cold bottle of water, he unscrewed the cap, and guzzled half of it.

Uncaring of her husband's sweaty, stinky state, Annie walked over, wrapped her arms around his shoulders, and kissed him soundly. "Hi. Would you like a hot towel?"

"A what?"

"Hot towel." She grinned. "It's my latest addition to the vineyard lunch." She opened a small plastic tub. Amid a waft of steam, she extracted a white towel with a pair of sugar tongs and held it out to him.

"Wow. This is better than first class on Virgin Atlantic." He took the proffered towel and ran it across his face, then folded it over and ran it across the back of his neck. By the time he'd wiped his hands thoroughly on the now-cool towel, the others had begun to emerge from the vines.

"So is the food," Lori said with a smile. The hot towels had been her idea, but she wasn't going to steal her friend's pleasure by taking credit for it.

"And the wine." Annie looked at her friend and winked. She'd actually balked at the idea of serving up hot towels in the vineyard, but seeing how much her husband enjoyed it, she mentally added it to the mandatory midday repertoire.

"I don't doubt that." Kaden dropped his dirty towel into the bag Annie held up, then leaned in and kissed her. "Thanks, love. That was much appreciated."

"What's that?" Henri asked, just as sweaty but not dragging nearly as much as his papa. Youth had much to recommend when it came to back-breaking work under the Mediterranean sun.

"Hot towels to clean up with before lunch."

"No fucking way."

"Henri!" Annie looked like she was about to smack her son, but Lori interceded.

"Way," she said with a smirk, handing him a steaming towel.

"Really? Awesome. Why haven't we ever had these before?"

"New technology," Lori said, deadpan. Then ruined the effect by laughing at the look on Henri's face.

"Henri, please try to keep your tongue out of the gutter," his mother admonished, although she knew better than most that foul language was part and parcel of a long day among the vines.

"Sorry, Mom. Cursing in English is usually safer than French." His handsome grin was anything but repentant. Annie rolled her eyes and collected his dirty towel.

Laurent was the next to stagger out of the vineyard, followed closely by the other men that Kaden employed on a part-time basis during the summer. Each accepted the hot towels with equal parts surprise and appreciation.

Lori hung back, letting her man jockey around among the guys, chug water, fill his plate with food, compare notes on the morning's labor. She smiled at him when she caught him watching her, and he winked back. A moment later he was by her side. He was just as dirty and sweaty as the others, but in her mind, on him, it was sexy.

"Enjoying yourself?" She stole an olive from his plate and popped it in her mouth.

"Very much. More than I could have imagined." He reciprocated her theft with one of his own, purloining her wineglass for a sip of rosé. "I have much to learn, but there is something … something very satisfying about digging into the soil of my homeland."

The words were spoken softly, but Lori felt the passion in them. Laurent had been little more than a transient his entire life—his only permanent billet a bunk in the barracks at Chaumont when he wasn't off in some foreign country. Now, for the first time, he was feeling a visceral connection to the land. Lori recognized it because it was exactly the same tone of voice Annie had used all those years ago when she'd tried to explain why she had to leave San Francisco, chuck her high-powered career into the bay, and come to France to live off the land.

"I know." She leaned over and kissed his cheek. "I know."

Dinner was early that night, and simple. The men were exhausted, and frankly so were the ladies, having served as caterers and clean-up crew for all three meals that day, not to mention nursing the invariable blisters and cuts acquired on the first day of serious vineyard work. Over an aged bottle of *vin doux naturel* and a plate of cookies, Kaden finally asked the question that had been torturing Lori all day long.

"*Alors, mon ami.* How did you find the day's work?"

Laurent made a show of stretching out his neck and grinned. "Quite satisfying. How many days did you say this first pass will take?"

"Ha-ha! Just you wait. That euphoria your tired muscles feel now will turn to fatigue before tomorrow night, I promise. But since you asked, I'd say that at the pace we set today, we should be finished with our own vineyards by the end of the week."

"Then it is a good thing we are enjoying your hospitality, because after another day of this, I doubt I could stay awake for the drive home. Much less the return trip before dawn." He reached under the table to lace his fingers with Lori's.

Kaden smiled. "Our hospitality is at your disposal regardless of how well you acquit yourself in my vineyards; I trust you realize that. But in all sincerity, we appreciate your help." He glanced at Henri, who nodded his agreement. "You are quite the natural. Are you sure you've never worked in a vineyard before?"

"Never a vineyard, though I did help with the cocoa harvest in Ivory Coast once." He shook his head and grimaced at the unpleasant memory. "We were stationed near the Guinea border during their last civil war, and the regular migrant workers couldn't reach the plantations. It was hot, humid, miserable work. The cocoa trees grow in what amounts to a rainforest, full of insects the size of my fist. My men and I spent days wielding machetes and hoping we weren't destroying the trees in the process. Working with your vines was much more agreeable."

Lori studied him over the rim of her wineglass, trying to picture him stripped to the waist but for a machine gun strapped to his back, hacking his way through a rainforest with a machete. Even for her sexy soldier, that seemed extreme. Because she was watching him so closely, she noticed the shadow that passed across his expression then cleared.

"You said we'd be finished with your own vineyards by the end of the week," Laurent said to Kaden. "Are there others that you are responsible for?"

Father and son exchanged glances before Kaden answered. "Yes. Our neighbor directly to the east. We manage his vineyards in exchange for the right to purchase the fruit."

"The crew will move over there once we're done here?"

Kaden nodded. "The holding is much smaller, no more than five hectares. The vines are old but productive. Since we buy the fruit, it's in our best interest to take good care of them." He took a considered sip of his wine. "It's two days' work, no more."

"Isn't that Sophia's old property?" Lori asked the question as she rose to take the water pitcher back to the kitchen for a refill. She'd spent enough time in Rasteau over the years to gain a basic understanding of the lay of the land.

"It is," Annie answered to her friend's back. "Her daughter sold it after Sophia passed away."

"Thank God for that, because she would have found a way to destroy it." Kaden muttered to Laurent. Kaden had plenty of reason to dislike Sophia's conniving daughter, Monique. Their history was unpleasant, to say the least, though Kaden had never held the daughter's disgraceful behavior against her mother. It was fortunate for all of them that Monique had long ago cashed out her parents' legacy and left the area.

"Isn't the property up for sale again?"

Annie's softly spoken question triggered a chain of events beyond what she could have ever anticipated. Or maybe that was her intent.

The next morning the household roused itself before dawn to down strong coffee and croissants the *boulanger* had delivered at oh-dark-thirty from the village. Fortified for the chilly morning, the men headed out into the vineyards, but Kaden and Laurent set out in a different direction from Henri and the rest of the crew.

They walked up the dirt track behind the cellar, through a stand of pine trees that marked the ridge, and emerged above a southeast-facing slope of gnarly old vines. The sun had not yet crested the eastern horizon—a horizon formed by the recognizable shapes of Mont Ventoux and the Dentelles—but there was enough light for Laurent to clearly see the contours of the land, the weedy rows of old plants, and a snug stone farmhouse set in the dip between the hills beyond.

"An Englishman owns it," Kaden said. "He bought it for next to nothing when Monique was keen to sell. Back then, Rasteau was mostly known for its VdN cooperative. The dry reds were still labeled as Côtes du Rhône. He doesn't live here full time, but he and his wife come down several times a year to ride. They're cycling enthusiasts and have recently taken to bringing paying groups with them, but the house isn't large enough to accommodate more than four guests. He's got his eye on a larger property on the other side of town but needs to sell this one first."

"Are all the vines this old?"

"This field is the oldest. Henri found records to indicate it was planted in 1932."

Laurent whistled. "What about the quality of the fruit?"

"Exceptional, to be honest. It's been farmed organically from the outset, and the vines are quite healthy. I'd venture to guess this vineyard will continue to go strong for at least another twenty years. There are three other parcels, there"—he pointed to the slope above the house—"and there, on the other side. Those are maybe forty years old. Henri helped to plant them, when Sophia's husband was still alive."

That slope was still in the shadows, but Laurent could see the vines were smaller.

"And you would continue to buy all the fruit?"

Kaden nodded. "It's an informal arrangement that dates back to before I arrived. Sophia's husband passed around the same time as my aunt Hélène, and Henri and Sophia learned to rely on each other. She took care of him, and he took care of her vines."

"And the Englishman has let it continue. Smart. Gives him some cash flow from the property without having to lease out the house."

"He's a decent chap. We give him a few cases of each vintage for bragging rights, and we keep an eye on the place when he's not here. In exchange he gives us a fair price for the fruit, in addition to paying us for vineyard management. The property hasn't been listed yet, but that won't last long."

"Any idea of the asking price?"

Kaden named a figure, watching the other man's reaction. If the number was higher than Laurent had anticipated, it wasn't obvious, but Kaden added, "You may be able to negotiate that down a bit if you come in with a noncontingent offer. I get the sense he's anxious to move, now that he's identified the other property. Whoever he sells to, he'll make a fat profit—with the village having its *cru* status now, we're getting a lot more attention. Property values within the AOC have gone up across the board. This property is small but primely situated."

"What's the house like?"

"Three bedrooms. It's in decent condition, though a bit dated. Let's go take a look."

Laurent hadn't taken his eyes from the vineyard as they conversed, mesmerized as the first rays of sun kissed the tips of the vines. He looked over at his companion and smiled in response to a grinning Macallister, who held up a key.

Thirty-One

By week's end Laurent was exhausted and his back ached, but he would not have traded the feeling for anything. It was different from the bone-deep exhaustion of months in a war zone, though a deep-tissue massage would not have been unappreciated. Satisfaction permeated the very fiber of his being. From that first morning in the chill of predawn, he'd known. One touch of his fingers to the fragile new life sprouting forth from Macallister's vines, and his future was set. One way or another, he *would* own a vineyard of his own. He didn't care so much about making his own wine, but he wanted that connection to the land. That he'd apparently been transparent in his desire didn't really bother him; it was his inability to dissemble on that score that brought him the opportunity now to cash in. Cash in a good portion of his life savings, that is, along with a healthy chunk of his monthly pension.

"You are sure?" Kaden's enthusiasm of a few days earlier had morphed into an irritating caution as documents went back and forth with the seller, *notaire,* and bank.

Laurent slanted him a look. "Are you trying to talk me out of it? Having second thoughts about not buying it yourself?" Even as the words left his mouth, Laurent knew the accusation was unfounded. If Kaden had wanted to buy the hectares, he would have done so without ever mentioning them to anyone. The fact that he *had* mentioned them, to Laurent, was telling. For one thing, it meant that he wouldn't mind having Laurent as his neighbor. For another … well, maybe that was the only reason. If Kaden had wanted the land, he would have it.

"Not at all. I just want to make sure you understand that the life of a farmer is far from easy or guaranteed."

"*Merci, je comprende.* My aching back is proof of my understanding on this point. But I want this, more than I could have thought."

They were driving back from the old vineyard at the top of the village, the last parcel of estate vines to be worked on, and also the smallest. They'd finished it before noon even without benefit of the hired workers. Henri rode with the tools in the truck bed, giving the two men privacy in the cab.

There was an easy camaraderie between them that had grown over the long week of manual labor. Kaden usually made it a point to stay out of other people's business, especially their relationships, but Lori was his wife's best friend. Practically family. Her happiness was important to both of them, so he figured his nosiness was justified. "Have you mentioned it to Lori yet?"

Dubois kept his eyes on the road, though he wasn't driving. "Not yet. I wanted to make sure my offer was accepted first." That bit of paperwork had arrived in his email yesterday, news that he'd shared with Kaden only. As he labored in the vineyard that morning, he pondered how he wanted to share it with the person who counted the most. "I have preliminary loan approval, but of course it's contingent on the appraisal."

"That won't be a problem." And if it was, Kaden would simply make the loan himself. The idea of having Dubois as a neighbor was very appealing. On many levels. First and foremost, the man had integrity—that had been obvious with the whole Philadelphia mess—but in the past week, Kaden's respect for him had grown. He'd proven himself to be a good companion; he listened, worked hard, and maintained a sense of humor. And he was strong as an ox, a quality that was never unappreciated when it came to manual labor. Kaden looked forward to spending more time with him. And if Lori's feelings for the soldier were anywhere close to what the man clearly felt for her, Kaden suspected he would get to know the man quite well, indeed.

"I might need your help—yours and Annie's. Not with the purchase, I mean with how I tell her. I'd like to do it in some sort of …" He was about to say *romantic way,* but that was too schmaltzy for man talk.

Kaden smiled. "I get it." He drove through the stone pillars that marked the entrance to his property and parked the truck in front of the cellar. "I'll figure out some way to distract her while you talk to Annie." He smirked. "I'm sure she'll have some ideas."

"She knows?" Laurent looked a bit alarmed.

"Don't worry, she hasn't said anything. Nor will she." Kaden climbed from the truck while Henri jumped from the back. "A word of advice, though," he said before Laurent followed the younger Macallister into the house. "You won't stay married for very long if you keep secrets from your wife."

Dubois actually laughed. "Noted."

Your wife. Words that once would have sent him backpedaling in denial had an altogether different effect on him today. The bewilderment of finding himself in love with a woman for the first time in his life at the age of forty-eight had been replaced by a sense of rightness. They'd spent the week much as he imagined they would spend the rest of their lives—if she fell in with his plans. The intense vineyard work was not a year-round proposition, thank God, but came in maybe a half dozen or so spurts of a week or more each year. The rest of the time would be spent more leisurely, tinkering in the vineyards more than actually working in them, puttering in a kitchen garden, repairing things around the house, doing whatever a homeowner and landowner did. Kibitzing with the neighbors. Attending markets, fairs, and whatever passed for cultural events in the rural Rhône Valley.

"Hey, soldier."

"Hey, yourself." Laurent took Lori's outstretched hand and reeled her in for a kiss. "What's for lunch?"

She affected a heavy sigh. "I get it. You only love me for my food."

"Not *only* for your food." He draped an arm around her shoulder. "But I confess the Macallister mess hall turns out a far finer cuisine than the one in Chaumont." He kissed her temple. "No wonder their contractors have stayed with them so long."

"Are you saying your military career was not chosen for the food?"

"Minx." The others were already seated around the kitchen table, or he would have hauled her up into his arms and kissed her properly. Instead, he settled for another kiss to her temple, knowing full well that Annie was watching. He winked at his hostess before holding Lori's chair for her then taking his own.

"I'm serious about the food, though. I have a hard time believing everyone in the valley eats as well as we have been."

"Mom's cooking always gets better when Aunt Lori's around." Henri offered this zinger as he forked a generous serving of salad onto his plate.

Annie snorted. "At least you've got food to eat." She turned to Laurent. "It's an old family joke—not that I think it's funny—that I couldn't boil water when I met Kaden. And Sophia was a pretty darn hard act to follow."

"I tried, honestly I did," Lori chimed in. "We were roommates in college, and neither of us could afford to eat out all the time."

"Right, and we had a microwave and a freakin' hot plate." Annie rolled her eyes and passed a steaming plate of quiche to Laurent. "And a tiny little refrigerator that barely held a head of lettuce. Very conducive to learning how to cook."

"Hey, I made plenty of great meals on that hot plate."

"While I couldn't even get a hot dog right." She turned to Laurent. "I actually exploded a couple in the microwave before she explained to me that I had to poke them with a fork first." Everyone laughed at that. "But I've had lots of *instruction*"—she shot a narrow-eyed glance at her husband—"since then. Uncle Henri helped a lot. I think he took pity on me."

"I love it when you cook, *chérie*." Kaden smiled into the quiche that Laurent passed over. It was one of his own recipes, but to her credit, his wife truly *had* learned to cook in their twenty-five years of marriage, and working together in the kitchen was a favorite pastime.

"Thank you, sweetie." She toasted him with the bite of salad on the end of her fork. "But I confess, it's been wonderful to have Lori here to help. She's got more culinary genius in her left pinky than I'll ever have in my entire being."

Lori blushed then glanced at Laurent. "I've always loved to cook. When I lived in Paris all those years ago, I was actually tempted to give up accounting and go be an apprentice in a restaurant somewhere."

"The only thing that stopped her was that no one would take on a woman in the kitchen." Kaden winked to soften the insult to the female gender. It would have been true, had she ever really attempted it. "Unfortunately, things haven't changed that much."

The conversation around the lunch table continued in that vein, food and cooking being the primary topic, until the serving platters were empty and everyone's plate was clean. Hard work definitely primed one's appetite.

Henri was the first to push back from the table. "No rest for the weary," he said with a wicked grin. "Or the aged."

Kaden and Laurent both sent him dirty looks. "Careful, *garçon*," Laurent teased. "You're still outnumbered and outweighed."

As it turned out, Kaden didn't have to distract Lori because his son did it for him. Something about a label design he was working on, that she had made some suggestion about earlier in the week, and they were off to look at his computer while the others finished cleaning up the dishes. And plotted a romantic surprise.

"Jesus, Lori. You're going to ruin me. I can't possibly match this." Annie stared at the colorful antipasto platter, complete with roasted tomatoes and bell peppers, char-grilled asparagus, and marinated artichoke hearts, all artfully arranged around the *saucisson, jambon cru,* and cured olives. Fresh spring onions, peeled so their green parts curled, fluffed out on one end of the platter; plump spicy radishes graced the other side. Even the bread looked amazing, cut at a dramatic angle, rubbed with garlic and olive oil and toasted to perfection. They'd been working on it all afternoon, along with the fennel-roasted chicken thighs and creamy potato salad that made up the bulk of their evening picnic.

"Don't be a spoilsport. I may never have an opportunity to do this again. Something about the agrarian nature of this life just brings out my creative juices."

"Agrarian?"

"Would you prefer I said *peasant?*" Lori laughed at Annie's expression. "Hardly a fitting term to describe the Macallisters."

"Actually I was thinking that you're going overboard trying to impress a certain sexy colonel. I gotta say, though, I just about swooned when he walked out of the vineyard yesterday without his shirt."

Lori laughed. "Not that I blame you, but don't let Kaden hear you say that."

"I'm happily married, not dead. Your man is seriously hot."

"Don't I know it. I still can't believe he's mine."

Annie regarded her friend thoughtfully, a little shadow of a smile gracing her features that she couldn't quite hide. "He is that, isn't he." A statement, not a question.

Lori met her friend's gaze and shrugged, not feeling nearly as nonchalant as she wanted to. And for once, she missed the significance of her friend's smile.

"So he says." Then her shoulders slumped. "I'm toast either way. He seems sincere, and I know him well enough to know that he wouldn't lie about this for my sake. And I know that this … this having-a-girlfriend thing, it's new to him. He's incredibly sweet, and endearingly worried about doing the wrong thing."

She looked down at the masterpiece of culinary art she'd created with him in mind then looked at her friend, all the vulnerability she'd been trying to hide evident in her eyes. "I'm completely in love with him, Annie. I have been since we first met. What am I ever going to do when he decides to move on?"

Kaden started the crew at the bottom of the most easterly parcels first, putting the men in full sun as they worked their way up the slope. The day was warm but not hot, and a refreshing breeze blew in from the west. With just the three of them working—Henri had declared Laurent alone was worth two of his hired hands and dismissed the others at the end of the day yesterday—it was past seven before they finished the two parcels on that side of the estate. Either Annie had a sixth sense or Kaden had texted her with their progress, because just as they reached the top rows, the old truck came rambling across the rise.

There was a picnic table situated at the top of the hill directly above the farmhouse, with an outstanding southwest-facing view of the valley and the sunset. Laurent had scouted it out earlier, mentally rehearsed the words he wanted to say and where he wanted to say them. There was an escarpment not too far away, the high vineyard being shaped somewhat like a slice of pie, the narrow end at the top and the wide edge following the contours at the bottom. A rough bench made from a fallen tree graced the eastern edge of the ridge, and the view was just as good. Better yet, it afforded a clear view of the entire property, border to border. He hadn't had time to buy a ring, but when he thought of that huge diamond she used to wear, and her lack of sentiment about it, he hoped the offer of a home would make a better impression.

The men finished their rows at the same time, emerging as a tall, dark, and broad-shouldered trio from the vineyard. With the sun behind them casting long shadows ahead and obscuring their features, they might have been aliens emerging from a spaceship, so surreal was the scene as they walked up the last bit of hill to where the girls had set up supper.

"Holy crap, Annie." Lori was stunned by the quantity of testosterone heading their way.

"Tell me about it. Welcome to my world. Now snap out of it, girlfriend, it's our turn to work."

Annie passed out hot towels—she hadn't been kidding when she vowed to make them a vineyard ritual—while Lori opened the wine. As the sun sunk lower toward the western horizon, they devoured the antipasto platter; talked about the day; postulated about the growing season, the price of grapes, the AOC laws, and all things wine related; and opened more wine. It was a lovely evening in a lovely spot.

Lori soaked it all in. In the far recesses of her mind, she had envied Annie this incredible lifestyle, and now she had a small toehold in it herself. What an incredible thing it would be, to live here permanently and look forward to evenings like this in every season. Her *carte de séjour*, the French equivalent of a resident visa, allowed her to stay indefinitely, but she still felt like a visitor. Would that ever change?

"Walk with me, love."

She tore her eyes from the tantalizing horizon and smiled, taking Laurent's outstretched hand. "Okay."

He refilled their wineglasses before guiding her along the track that paralleled the ridgeline.

It was a short distance to the tree-trunk bench, and he guided her to it then sat down beside her. They were within sight, but out of hearing, of the others. Still, he was nervous.

"*C'est très joli, non?*"

"*Plus qu'un simple jolie. C'est beau.*" *More than just pretty. It's beautiful.*

"I love hearing you speak French." He lifted the hand he still held in his and kissed her knuckles.

She smiled. "Likewise."

"Your friends have an enviable lifestyle. I find I've enjoyed myself here far more than I anticipated ... and I had very much looked forward to it."

"They do," she agreed. "I've always envied Annie for all of this, but I could never quite picture myself here."

"Never?" A fission of alarm whispered up his spine.

"Well, not until recently. I couldn't, you see, because I wouldn't have been able to do my job. My life, by choice and necessity, was elsewhere. Now, however ... now it's different. Now I can't imagine being anywhere else."

He let out the breath he hadn't realized he was holding then took an undignified gulp of his wine.

They watched the sun morph into a huge orange ball as it began its inevitable descent behind the distant horizon. It had the effect of washing the vineyards below them in a hazy, magical golden light that practically shimmered from the heat coming off the rocky soil.

"If this was yours," he nodded to the vineyards that sloped away down the hill, to the stone house that lay on the flat area between the contours. "Do you think you could you be happy?"

She laughed, letting her eyes dance across the beauty spread out below them. "In my wildest dreams. This is so beautiful, and right next door to my best friend. I don't think anything could be more perfect." She took a sip of her wine and sighed. "Wouldn't it be wonderful if the owners decided to sell? I'd be first in line."

"I'm sorry to tell you, you're too late."

"What?" She looked at him with serious consternation. "Don't tell me it was for sale and Annie didn't mention it. I'll kill her."

His smile turned into a broad grin as he stood, reached into his pocket and pulled out a single key. Dangling it from a plain key ring, he shook his head. "It was, and she did know, remember? She mentioned it a week ago. But I was listening and you were not—or perhaps you had just stepped out of the room." His eyes twinkled as he said that last bit, knowing full well it was the truth. "And now it's mine. Or it will be, if the bank agrees. Ours, if you agree, too."

Lori stared up into the pale-blue eyes of the man she loved more than anything. "Agree to what?"

Like a *chevalier* from another era, Laurent lowered himself to one knee. He didn't have a ring, but he held the key out to her in the palm of his hand. "I'm nothing but a tired old soldier. I don't have much to offer you; not even this slice of heaven is secured yet, but I hope it will be soon. I love you, and I want to spend whatever is left of my life with you. Will you marry me? Will you be a humble farmer's wife and live season to season with me? I'll probably be a jerk more than once, screw it up, and make you cry, and we will never be rich like your friends, but if you say yes, we'll be rich in love, rich in life, and you will never, ever be alone, even when we're apart, because I will reside in your heart, and you will reside in mine."

The sun glinted off the key in his hand and seemed to fracture into a thousand pieces of light. He was handing her the key—literally—to her most cherished dreams.

"Oh."

His brow arched. "Oh?" He'd laid his heart out in front of her feet, and all she could say was *Oh?*

She smoothed two fingers across his eyebrows. "Oh, as in *oh, cripes,* I never thought I'd ever, in a million years, be so in love with a sexy soldier that my panties would melt when he offered me my dream."

Laurent tried to smile, but it was wavy. "Your panties are melting? That sounds pretty enticing, but, *chérie,* I'm dying here. Does that mean yes?"

"You really want to marry me? After everything I dragged you through?"

He smiled. "Does this mean we're going to argue about everything?"

She smiled too. "Maybe. Probably. Yes."

His smile turned to a frown. "Yes, you'll marry me, or yes, we'll argue about everything?"

"Both." She leaned forward to hug him, but he lost his balance—or pretended to—and they ended up on the ground, with her sprawled on top of him. Things would have spiraled out of control from there had they not been in full view of their friends, who at that moment began whooping and hollering at them.

Lori waved then flipped them off. Laughter filtered across the distance, and she realized something.

"They knew."

"Yeah, they did. They gave me no end of grief. They love you, you know."

"I know. I love them, too."

"We'll be neighbors."

"That is so awesome." Lori shifted so she was straddling him instead of sprawled out on top of him. "But the best part is that we can kiss them good-bye and walk across the field to our own house. Actually, they'll be doing the walking because I'm the better cook."

"So modest. I love you."

"In fact, I am. Modest, that is. And I love you, too." She leaned over him from her straddled position and gave him a scorching kiss. The peanut gallery egged them on, ensuring that Laurent was incapable of joining the group immediately when Lori finally climbed off of him.

Epilogue

Domaine de la Terre des Roches, Rasteau

"Quit fussing." Annie slapped Lori's hand away before she could mess with the baby's breath Annie had painstakingly fixed into her friend's coiffure. "It's perfect. Leave it alone."

"I was just wanting to admire it a little. Geez, you're a drill sergeant today."

And there was much to admire. Lori looked beautiful, the pale rose of her dress showing off her creamy skin, blond hair, and blue eyes to perfection.

Before Annie could reply, her twenty-year-old daughter, Marie, bounced into the room. "Are you guys ready yet? The car's here. Oh, *wow*. Aunt Lori, you look awesome! *Très chic. Magnifique.*"

"*Merci, ma chére.*" Lori fluttered her eyelashes at the niece of her heart like she'd been doing since Marie was a child.

Louise crowded into the room next, followed by Sabine. "*Ooh la la!*" Sabine crooned. "*Tu est très, très belle.*"

Lori snorted at that. "Get real. I'm pushing the speed limit here."

"Only in America, like twenty years ago," Annie said. "Here it's at least eighty."

"Ha-ha-ha." Lori made one more attempt at shifting the little flowers in her hair, but bossy Annie was having none of it, intercepting her hand as it snaked up to the coif. "Okay, fine, just tuck that top one in a little, will you? It looks like I'm sprouting flowers out of my head."

"That's because you are. Which is the point." But she tucked it down a little anyway.

"All right, ladies. Time to go." Kaden rapped sharply on the door but was smart enough not to enter. "Matisse is parked out back."

Annie and Lori shared a look—then Lori stood and hugged her dearest friend. "I love you."

"I love you, too," Annie said before pressing an ancient, butter-soft linen hankie into her friend's hand. "Something borrowed, something old. This belonged to Hélène. I never knew her, but from Uncle Henri's stories, she would have loved this."

Etienne was indeed waiting just outside with the doors of his gleaming, enormous SUV open for the ladies. Marie and Louise scuttled into the far backseat, Annie and Sabine took the middle, leaving the front seat for the bride.

"You look lovely, *chérie.*" The compliment from Etienne Matisse, a guy scary enough to make grown men piss their pants, accompanied by a quick buss to her cheek, was a confidence-boosting experience.

"Thanks." She gave him a once-over as he assisted her into the high front seat of the vehicle. "You look pretty good yourself."

Sabine's tinkling laugh filtered over from the backseat. "He is delicious in a tuxedo, no?"

"*Minette,*" Matisse scolded, but Lori caught the smile he was trying to hide.

"To the *mairie!*" Annie shouted. And they were off.

It was mid-August, exactly forty-one days after Laurent had taken ownership of, and moved into, his Rasteau property—forty days being the minimum residency requirement to be married at the local city hall. And fortunately for the handful of attendees, including the bride and groom, a couple of weeks before the start of harvest.

Ceremonies at the Mairie were public. Because the Macallisters were well-known and loved in the little village, the archaic requirement of posting of the banns meant that most of the citizenry were aware that a wedding would be taking place. Thus it was no surprise that a crowd had gathered around the gorgeous men who waited for the female entourage. Kaden, his son Henri, and his cousin Alex Bouvier—who resembled Kaden enough to be his thirty-plus-years-younger twin—stood with the handsome groom on the steps of City Hall, along with their friend and neighbor the *mairie,* or mayor, who would officiate the ceremony.

Julia stood in the crowd with Sebastien, who was dressed in a smart little suit that matched his uncle's. She struggled to keep a serene smile on her face and her emotions in check, because she knew that any sign of tears would distract her brother from his own well-deserved happiness. The truth was that she was thrilled for him and for the lovely lady that he'd found and fallen for so quickly, and she was very much enjoying the process of getting to know her new sister-in-law. But at this particular moment, she couldn't stem the sadness that came from her own lonely heart, knowing full well she'd never again have that sort of love. The arrival of a big black SUV distracted her, and she squeezed Sebastien's hand, laughing as he reacted to the cheers of welcome.

When the ladies poured out of Etienne's SUV, the crowd took a collective gasp. A more captivating entourage could not have been imagined. Young Marie Macallister led the way up the steps, her beauty making Kaden simultaneously preen and curse the saints, followed by the lovely Louise, then Sabine, then Annie—Kaden winked at his wife as he held out his hand to her—and finally Lori, on the steady arm of Etienne Matisse.

The civil ceremony held none of the pomp and circumstance that a church wedding entailed, but that didn't mean the moment couldn't be enjoyed. Etienne took his role seriously, delivering the bride to the anxious groom at the top of the old stone steps, giving his best evil eye that said, *Take care of her or else.* Even Laurent smiled at that.

In a trice it was done, and they all exited the government building to an applauding crowd. They waved and spent a few minutes greeting their neighbors and taking photographs before jumping into the waiting vehicles and returning to Domaine de la Terre des Roches for the real celebration. Most of those same neighbors and friends, plus a few more, would be joining them to welcome the newlyweds properly to the neighborhood.

It wasn't until late in the evening that the bride and groom were able to steal away from their own party.

"Laurent! I can't walk this fast in my heels."

His answer was to lift her up and swing her onto his back. "Hike your skirts up, love." She did and would probably have been mortified to know that her tinkling laugh was heard by her best friends, who had stepped outside to watch the newlyweds sneak away over the hill.

"He's really in love with her."

"She's really in love with him."

They'd spoken at the same time, then looked at each other and laughed.

"Who would have ever guessed?" Annie said, looping her arm through her husband's and snuggling into his side.

Kaden turned to his beloved wife and cupped her jaw in his hand before leaning down for a sweet kiss. "Life is full of surprises, isn't it? And you are by far the best one that ever happened to me." He tapped his index finger on the tip of her nose. "They remind me of us, only he was smarter than me, not waiting so long. I will only ever wish them joy."

The velvet warmth of the night embraced them, the celebration continuing inside the house as if the presence of the hosts and guests of honor was neither here nor there.

"Me too." Annie sighed, budging closer. "It's kind of fitting, don't you think?"

"That they found each other?"

"That it happened here. Where we can all grow old together. After all these years, Lori and I have finally come full circle. I've missed her so much, but now the time we spent apart feels like barely a blink."

A moment passed, then another, but Kaden remained silent. Eventually, Annie peered up at him.

"What are you thinking?"

His lips found hers for another gentle kiss. "Simply appreciating all that I have."

She wrapped him in a tight embrace and whispered against his chest. "Something I try to do every day."

He might have responded, but at that moment the back screen door slammed shut as two people moved down the path that led from the house to the barn. Hidden in the shadows uphill from the path, Annie and Kaden watched in mutual horror as their son escorted—more like half-carried—a giggling young woman away from the party.

"Oh, God," Annie moaned. "Perhaps we spoke too soon."

Author's Note

I hope you enjoyed reading about the fictional adventures of Lori and Laurent as much as I enjoyed writing them—it was super fun to bring these two characters back to life in this final installment of my Foreign Affair series. Although perhaps a little less excitement is what we all have in mind for our own retirement! The idea for this book came to me at the very café in Uzès that I used for Julia's Le Jardin (though it goes by a different name) when I saw Laurent sitting at that table by the door, complete with military haircut, square jaw, and sexy tattoo. I knew right then and there that I needed to use him in my next book. Too bad I didn't take a picture, but frankly I was too stunned just watching him.

I'd like to take this opportunity to remind you that fiction, by definition, is something feigned, invented, or imagined. While many of the places in this story are real, and organized crime is still an unfortunate reality in both America and Europe, none of the law enforcement–related events described in the story are real. INTERPOL does exist, of course, and its worldwide headquarters are, in fact, located in Lyon, France. INTERPOL's mission is "preventing and fighting crime through enhanced cooperation and innovation on police and security matters" on a global scale, with priorities that include corruption, crimes against children, cybercrime, human trafficking, counterfeit, terrorism, and more, but the fieldwork described herein, and the integrity and talents of the Philadelphia police force and the FBI, are purely plays of my imagination, created to bring life to my characters. If I've offended anyone by the portrayal of any of the agencies, I apologize. My intent was to tell an entertaining story, not create a documentary on international or domestic policing policies.

About the Author

Nancy Milby lives in Laguna Beach, California, with her husband, Steve, and their lovable cats Beckham and Boo. After finding her own way out of the corporate world, Nancy founded the local cooking school, Laguna Culinary Arts, which, for twelve years was synonymous with great fun, great food and wine, and great culinary adventures to destinations around the world. Currently, Nancy runs the breakaway division, LCA Wine, a boutique wine shop and wine education center, where she shares her passion by teaching wine classes and leading small groups of food and wine enthusiasts on overseas adventures.

To check out the fun, go to www.lcawine.com or www.nancymilby.com.

A Word with You Press
Publishers and Purveyors of Fine Stories

In addition to being a full-service publishing house founded in 2009, *A Word with You Press* is a playful, passionate, and prolific consortium of writers connected by our collective love of the written word. We are, as well, devoted readers drawn to the notion that there is nothing more beautiful or powerful than a well-told story.

We realize that great writers and artists don't just happen. They are created by nurturing, mentoring, and by inspiration. We provide this literary triad through our interactive website, www.awordwithyoupress.com.

Visit us here to enter our writing contests and to become part of a broad but highly personal writing community. Improve your skills with what has become a significant, *de facto* writers' workshop, and approach us with your own publishing dreams and ambitions. We are always looking for new talent. Visit our store to buy from a distinguished list of our books, which include the work of a Pulitzer Prize winner, an award-winning poet, winners of USA awards and the Isabelle Allende Miraposa and first-rate literary fiction. Attend our seminars and retreats, and consider joining our growing list of published authors.

A writer is among the lucky few who discovers that art is not a diversion or distraction from everyday life; rather, art is an essential expression of the human spirit.

If you are such a writer, join us on our website, **www.awordwithyou-press.com**. If you have a project to discuss, we will assess the first thirty pages you send us *pro-bono*. Send your inquiries to the Editor-in-Chief, Thornton Sully, at **thorn@awordwithyoupress.com**. Be sure to indicate in the subject line *"pro-bono assessment"* and send your submission as a word doc attachment.

Available or coming soon from

A Word with You Press

Falling for France
by Nancy Milby
The first in *A Foreign Affair* series finds Annie Shaw having to choose between a successful career and real romance with a French aristocrat, and wanting both.

French Twist
by Nancy Milby
The saga continues as American archeologist Louise Marcel becomes entangled in nasty business on French soil, as she conceals her own hidden agenda.

Finding France
by Nancy Milby
The third in *A Foreign Affair* series finds Gabrielle Walker lamenting a life unraveling when a letter informs her she is the inheritor of a large estate in France. Then it gets complicated!

Finding Home
by Nancy Milby
Etienne, the recurring enigma in the series *A Foreign Affair*, is brutal to his enemies but a gentle giant to those he loves. Can the secret woman in his past enter his life again? Perhaps, but not with complications—some predictable, but some…

Almost Avalon
by Thornton Sully
A young couple struggles with love and life on the island
frontier just twenty-six miles west of Los Angeles.

The Mason Key: Volume One
A John Mason Adventure
by David Folz
A street urchin in England about the time the Colonies declare independence cheats the hangman to begin this historical adventure series. He discovers that his father's death may not have been an accident at all, but part
of a broader conspiracy.

The Mason Key II: Aloft and Alow
A John Mason Adventure
by David Folz
The historical saga continues as young Mason becomes
a mid-shipman on the very ship on which he was as
stow-away at the conclusion of *The Mason Key, Volume One.*

The Mason Key III: The Return
A John Mason Adventure
by David Folz
Mason and Marie fend off pirates en route to her father's plantation. John
struggles with the Third Principle, Honor, and the Cruelty of Slavery while
making his way back home.

The Gift of an Imaginary Girl:
Coco and Other Stories
By Kristy Webster
The first in our *Magical Realism Collection* by an award winning author blends rich imagery with a little magic to help bind us to our greater, unrealized selves in this collection of fables.

The Coffee Shop Chronicles, Vol. I,
Oh, the Places I Have Bean!
An anthology of award-winning stories inspired by events that occurred over a cup of coffee.

The Courtesans of God
by Thornton Sully
A novel based on the real life of a temple priestess in the palace of the King of Malaysia.

Left Unlatched
in the hopes that you'll come in...
A Book of Poetry by R.T. Sedgwick
Winner of the 2012 San Diego Book Awards—Poetry.

The Sky is Not the Limit
and other select poems
A Book of Poetry by R.T. Sedgwick
As every caterpillar knows, the sky is the limit; as every butterfly knows, that's a lie. Robert Sedgwick's newest volume of poetry defies gravity, and colors the air with the flutter of wings.

The Boy with a Torn Hat
by Thornton Sully
Debut novel was a finalist in the 2010 USA
Book Awards for Literary Fiction
"Henry Miller meets Bob Dylan in this coming of age romp played out in the twisted alleyways and smoky beer halls of Heidelberg. Sully is a cunning wordsmith and master of bringing music to art and art to language. Excessive, expressive, lusty, and once in a blue metaphor—profound."
—Jonathan Freedman, Pulitzer Prize winner

Raw Man
by Fred Rivera
This lightly-novelized Vietnam memoir, winner of the 2015 Isabelle Allende Miraposa Award for Best New Fiction, derives its title from the author's epiphany: "Twenty-seven years after I got on the flight home, I saw that Nam war was just *raw man* spelled backwards. I'm pretty raw today."

How to Live with Yourself and Enjoy It
by Don Hanley
What makes *How to Live with Yourself and Enjoy It* unique and so welcomed is that it is not a grandiose tutorial from a lectern, but a fireside chat guided by a highly credentialed man with no other agenda than to alleviate suffering of his fellow creatures. Dr. Don Hanley is both warm and insightful, accepting of his own flaws and is a refreshing example of humility.

How to Live with Your Partner and Enjoy It
by Don Hanley
This small book contains a vast amount of wisdom and insight that will be helpful to all couples and individuals who wish to enhance their lives in relationship.

Visit our on-line store at *www.awordwithyoupress.com*. Most books are available as print editions and ebooks. We have also a growing selection of gifts for writers, and please check out our latest contests! We'd love a word *from* you!

A Word with You Press
Editors and Advocates of Fine Stories in the Digital Age
310 East A Street
Suite B
Moscow, Idaho 83843